SHALLOW GROUND

ALSO BY ANDY MASLEN

DI Stella Cole:

Hit and Run
Hit Back Harder
Hit and Done
Let the Bones Be Charred

Gabriel Wolfe Thrillers:

Trigger Point
Reversal of Fortune
Blind Impact
Condor
First Casualty
Fury
Rattlesnake
Minefield
No Further
Torpedo
Three Kingdoms
Ivory Nation

Blood Loss – A Vampire Story

SHALLOW GROUND

A DETECTIVE FORD THRILLER

ANDY MASLEN

THOMAS & MERCER

Text copyright © 2020 by Andy Maslen
All rights reserved.

Published by Thomas & Mercer, Seattle

www.apub.com

Amazon, the Amazon logo, and Thomas & Mercer are trademarks of Amazon.com, Inc., or its affiliates.

ISBN-13: 9781542021098
ISBN-10: 154202109X

Cover design by Dominic Forbes

Printed in the United States of America

To Jo, with love, as always.

'The animal's heart is the basis of its life.'

William Harvey, 1578–1657

SUMMER | PEMBROKESHIRE COAST, WALES

Ford leans out from the limestone rock face halfway up Pen-y-holt sea stack, shaking his forearms to keep the blood flowing. He and Lou have climbed the established routes before. Today, they're attempting a new line he spotted. She was reluctant at first, but she's also competitive and he really wanted to do the climb.

'I'm not sure. It looks too difficult,' she'd said when he suggested it.

'Don't tell me you've lost your bottle?' he said with a grin.

'No, but . . .'

'Well, then. Let's go. Unless you'd rather climb one of the easy ones again?'

She frowned. 'No. Let's do it.'

They scrambled down a gully, hopping across boulders from the cliff to a shallow ledge just above sea level at the bottom of the route. She stands there now, patiently holding his ropes while he climbs. But the going's much harder than he expected. He's wasted a lot of time attempting to navigate a tricky bulge. Below him, Lou plays out rope through a belay device.

He squints against the bright sunshine as a light wind buffets him. Herring gulls wheel around the stack, calling in alarm at this brightly coloured interloper assaulting their territory.

He looks down at Lou and smiles. Her eyes are a piercing blue. He remembers the first time he saw her. He was captivated by those eyes, drawn in, powerless, like an old wooden sailing ship spiralling down into a whirlpool. He paid her a clumsy compliment, which she accepted with more grace than he'd managed.

Lou smiles back up at him now. Even after seven years of marriage, his heart thrills that she should bestow such a radiant expression on him.

Rested, he starts climbing again, trying a different approach to the overhang. He reaches up and to his right for a block. It seems solid enough, but his weight pulls it straight off.

He falls outwards, away from the flat plane of lichen-scabbed limestone, and jerks to a stop at the end of his rope. The force turns him into a human pendulum. He swings inwards, slamming face-first against the rock and gashing his chin. Then out again to dangle above Lou on the ledge.

Ford tries to stay calm as he slowly rotates. His straining fingertips brush the rock face then arc into empty air.

Then he sees two things that frighten him more than the fall.

The rock he dislodged, as large as a microwave, has smashed down on to Lou. She's sitting awkwardly, white-faced, and he can see blood on her leggings. Those sapphire-blue eyes are wide with pain.

And waves are now lapping at the ledge. The tide is on its way in, not out. Somehow, he misread the tide table, or he took too long getting up the first part of the climb. He damns himself for his slowness.

'I can lower you down,' she screams up at him. 'But my leg, I think it's broken.'

She gets him down safely and he kisses her fiercely before crouching by her right leg to assess the damage. There's a sharp lump distending the bloody Lycra, and he knows what it is. Bone.

'It's bad, Lou. I think it's a compound fracture. But if you can stand on your good leg, we can get back the way we came.'

'I can't!' she cries, pain contorting her face. 'Call the coastguard.'

He pulls out his phone, but there's no mobile service down here. 'Shit! There's no signal.'

'You'll have to go for help.'

'I can't leave you, darling.'

A wave crashes over the ledge and douses them both.

Her eyes widen. 'You have to! The tide's coming in.'

He knows she's right. And it's all his fault. He pulled the block off the crag.

'Lou, I—'

She grabs his hand and squeezes so hard it hurts. 'You *have* to.'

Another wave hits. His mouth fills with seawater. He swallows half of it and retches. He looks back the way they came. The boulders they hopped along are awash. There's no way Lou can make it.

He's crying now. He can't do it.

Then she presses the only button she has left. 'If you stay here, we'll *both* die. Then who'll look after Sam?'

Sam is eight and a half. Born two years before they married. He's being entertained by Louisa's parents while they're at Pen-y-holt. Ford knows she's right. He can't leave Sam an orphan. They were meant to be together for all time. But now, time has run out.

'Go!' she screams. 'Before it's too late.'

So he leaves her, checking the gear first so he's sure she can't be swept away. He falls into an eerie calm as he swims across to the cliff and solos out.

At the clifftop, rock gives way to scrubby grass. He pulls out his phone. Four bars. He calls the coastguard, giving them a concise description of the accident, the location and Lou's injury. Then he slumps. The calmness that saved his life has vanished. He is hyperventilating, heaving in great breaths that won't bring enough oxygen to his brain, and sighing them out again.

A wave of nausea rushes through him and sweat flashes out across his skin. The wind chills it, making him shudder with the sudden cold. He lurches to his right and spews out a thin stream of bile on to the grass.

Then his stomach convulses and his breakfast rushes up and out, spattering the sleeve of his jacket. He retches out another splash of stinking yellow liquid and then dry-heaves until, cramping, his guts settle. His view is blurred through a film of tears.

He falls back and lies there for ten more minutes, looking up into the cloudless sky. Odd how realistic this dream is. He could almost believe he just left his wife to drown.

He sobs, a cracked sound that the wind tears away from his lips and disperses into the air. And the dream blackens and reality is here, and it's ugly and painful and true.

He hears a helicopter. Sees its red-and-white form hovering over Pen-y-holt.

Time ceases to have any meaning as he watches the rescue. How long has passed, he doesn't know.

Now a man in a bright orange flying suit is standing in front of him explaining that his wife, Sam's mother, has drowned.

Later, there are questions from the local police. They treat him with compassion, especially as he's Job, like them.

The coroner rules death by misadventure.

But Ford knows the truth.

He killed her. *He* pushed her into trying the climb. *He* dislodged the block that smashed her leg. And *he* left her to drown while he saved his own skin.

SIX YEARS LATER
| SUMMER |
SALISBURY

DAY ONE, 5.00 P.M.

Angie Halpern trudged up the five gritty stone steps to the front door. The shift on the cancer ward had been a long one. Ten hours. It had ended with a patient vomiting on the back of her head. She'd washed it out at work, crying at the thought that it would make her lifeless brown hair flatter still.

Free from the hospital's clutches, she'd collected Kai from Donna, the childminder, and then gone straight to the food bank – again. Bone-tired, her mood hadn't been improved when an elderly woman on the bus told her she looked like she needed to eat more: 'A pretty girl like you shouldn't be that thin.'

And now, here she was, knackered, hungry and with a three-year-old whining and grizzling and dragging on her free hand. Again.

'Kai!' she snapped. 'Let go, or Mummy can't get her keys out.'

The little boy stopped crying just long enough to cast a shocked look up into his mother's eyes before resuming, at double the volume.

Fearing what she might do if she didn't get inside, Angie half-turned so he couldn't cling back on to her hand, and dug out her keys. She fumbled one of the bags of groceries, but in a dexterous act of juggling righted it before it spilled the tins, packets and jars all over the steps.

She slotted the brass Yale key home and twisted it in the lock. Elbowing the door open, she nudged Kai with her right knee, encouraging him to precede her into the hallway. Their flat occupied the top floor of the converted Victorian townhouse. Ahead, the stairs, with their patched and stained carpet, beckoned.

'Come on, Kai, in we go,' she said, striving to inject into her voice the tone her own mother called 'jollying along'.

'No!' the little boy said, stamping his booted foot and sticking his pudgy hands on his hips. 'I hate Donna. I hate the foobang. And I. Hate. YOU!'

Feeling tears pricking at the back of her eyes, Angie put the bags down and picked her son up under his arms. She squeezed him, burying her nose in the sweet-smelling angle between his neck and shoulder. How was it possible to love somebody so much and also to wish for them just to shut the hell up? Just for one little minute.

She knew she wasn't the only one with problems. Talking to the other nurses, or chatting late at night online, confirmed it. Everyone reckoned the happily married ones with enough money to last from one month to the next were the exception, not the rule.

'Mummy, you're hurting me!'

'Oh, Jesus! Sorry, darling. Look, come on. Let's just get the shopping upstairs and you can watch a *Thomas* video.'

'I hate *Thomas*.'

'*Thunderbirds*, then.'

'I hate them even more.'

Angie closed her eyes, sighing out a breath like the online mindfulness gurus suggested. 'Then you'll just have to stare out of the bloody window, like I used to. Now, come on!'

He sucked in a huge breath. Angie flinched, but the scream never came. Instead, Kai's scrunched-up eyes opened wide and swivelled sideways. She followed his gaze and found herself facing a good-looking man wearing a smart jacket and trousers. He had a kind smile.

'I'm sorry,' the man said in a quiet voice. 'I couldn't help seeing your little boy's . . . he's tired, I suppose. You left the door open and as I was coming to this address anyway . . .' He tailed off, looking embarrassed, eyes downcast.

'You were coming *here?*' she asked.

He looked up at her again. 'Yes,' he said, smiling. 'I was looking for Angela Halpern.'

'That's me.' She paused, frowning, as she tried to place him. 'Do I know you?'

'Mummee!' Kai hissed from her waist, where he was clutching her.

'Quiet, darling, please.'

The man smiled. 'Would you like a hand with your bags? I see you have your hands full with the little fellow there.' Then he squatted down, so that his face was at the same level as Kai's. 'Hello. My name's Harvey. What's yours?'

'Kai. Are you a policeman?'

Harvey laughed, a warm, soft-edged sound. 'No. I'm not a policeman.'

'Mummy's a nurse. At the hospital. Do you work there?'

'Me? Funnily enough, I do.'

'Are you a nurse?'

'No. But I do help people. Which I think is a bit of a coincidence. Do you know that word?'

The little boy shook his head.

'It's just a word grown-ups use when two things happen that are the same. Kai,' he said, dropping his voice to a conspiratorial whisper, 'do you want to know a secret?'

Kai nodded, smiling and wiping his nose on his sleeve.

'There's a big hospital in London called Bart's. And I think it rhymes with' – he paused and looked left and right – 'farts.'

Kai squawked with laughter.

Harvey stood, knees popping. 'I hope that was OK. The naughty word. It usually seems to make them laugh.'

Angie smiled. She felt relief that this helpful stranger hadn't seen fit to judge her. To tut, roll his eyes or give any of the dozens of subtle signals the free-and-easy brigade found to diminish her. 'It's fine, really. You said you'd come to see me?'

'Oh, yes, of course, sorry. I'm from the food bank. The Purcell Foundation?' he said. 'They've asked me to visit a few of our customers, to find out what they think about the quality of the service. I was hoping you'd have ten minutes for a chat. If it's not a good time, I can come back.'

Angie sighed. Then she shook her head. 'No, it's fine . . . Harvey, did you say your name was?'

He nodded.

'Give me a hand with the bags and I'll put the kettle on. I picked up some teabags this afternoon, so we can christen the packet.'

'Let me take those,' he said, bending down and snaking his fingers through the loops in the carrier-bag handles. 'Where to, madam?' he added in a jokey tone.

'We're on the third floor, I'm afraid.'

Harvey smiled. 'Not to worry, I'm in good shape.'

Reaching the top of the stairs, Angie elbowed the light switch and then unlocked the door, while Harvey kept up a string of tall tales for Kai.

'And then the chief doctor said' – he adopted a deep voice – '"No, no, that's never going to work. You need to use a hosepipe!"'

Kai's laughter echoed off the bare, painted walls of the stairwell.

'Here we are,' Angie said, pushing the door open. 'The kitchen's at the end of the hall.'

She stood aside, watching Harvey negotiate the cluttered hallway and deposit the shopping bags on her pine kitchen table. She followed him, noticing the scuff marks on the walls, the sticky fat spatters behind the hob, and feeling a lump in her throat.

'Kai, why don't you go and watch telly?' she asked her son, steering him out of the kitchen and towards the sitting room.

'A film?' he asked.

She glanced up at the clock. Five to six. 'It's almost teatime.'

'Pleeease?'

She smiled. 'OK. But you come when I call you for tea. Pasta and red sauce, your favourite.'

'Yummy.'

She turned back to Harvey, who was unloading the groceries on to the table. A sob swelled in her throat. She choked it back.

He frowned. 'Is everything all right, Angela?'

The noise from the TV was loud, even from the other room. She turned away so this stranger wouldn't see her crying. It didn't matter that he was a colleague, of sorts. He could see what she'd been reduced to, and that was enough.

'Yes, yes, sorry. It's just, you know, the food bank. I never thought my life would turn out like this. Then I lost my husband and things just got on top of me.'

'Mmm,' he said. 'That was careless of you.'

'What?' She turned round, uncertain of what she'd heard.

He was lifting a tin of baked beans out of the bag. 'I said, it was careless of you. To lose your husband.'

She frowned. Trying to make sense of his remark. The cruel tone. The staring, suddenly dead eyes.

'Look, I don't know what you—'

The tin swung round in a half-circle and crashed against her left temple.

'Oh,' she moaned, grabbing the side of her head and staggering backwards.

Her palm was wet. Her blood was hot. She was half-blind with the pain. Her back met the cooker and she slumped to the ground. He was there in front of her, crouching down, just like he'd done with Kai. Only he wasn't telling jokes any more. And he wasn't smiling.

'Please keep quiet,' he murmured, 'or I'll have to kill Kai as well. Are you expecting anyone?'

'N-nobody,' she whispered, shaking. She could feel the blood running inside the collar of her shirt. And the pain, oh, the pain. It felt as though her brain was pushing her eyes out of their sockets.

He nodded. 'Good.'

Then he encircled her neck with his hands, looked into her eyes and squeezed.

I'm so sorry, Kai. I hope Auntie Cherry looks after you properly when I'm gone. I hope . . .

◆ ◆ ◆

Casting a quick glance towards the kitchen door and the hallway beyond, and reassured by the blaring noise from the TV, Harvey crouched by Angie's inert body and increased the pressure.

Her eyes bulged, and her tongue, darkening already from that natural rosy pink to the colour of raw liver, protruded from between her teeth.

From his jacket he withdrew an empty blood bag. He connected the outlet tube and inserted a razor-tipped trocar into the other end. He placed them to one side and dragged her jeans over her hips, tugging them down past her knees. With the joints free to move, he pushed his hands between her thighs and shoved them apart.

He inserted the needle into her thigh so that it met and travelled a few centimetres up into the right femoral artery. Then he laid the blood bag on the floor and watched as the scarlet blood shot into the clear plastic tube and surged along it.

With a precious litre of blood distending the bag, he capped it off and removed the tube and the trocar. With Angie's heart pumping her remaining blood on to the kitchen floor tiles, he stood and placed the bag inside his jacket. He could feel it through his shirt, warm against his skin. He took her purse out of her bag, found the card he wanted and removed it.

He wandered down the hall and poked his head round the door frame of the sitting room. The boy was sitting cross-legged, two feet from the TV, engrossed in the adventures of a blue cartoon dog.

'Tea's ready, Kai,' he said, in a sing-song tone.

Protesting, but clambering to his feet, the little boy extended a pudgy hand holding the remote and froze the action, then dropped the control to the carpet.

Harvey held out his hand and the boy took it, absently, still staring at the screen.

DAY TWO, 8.15 A.M.

Arriving at Bourne Hill Police Station, Detective Inspector Ford sighed, fingering the scar on his chin. What better way to start the sixth anniversary of your wife's death than with a shouting match over breakfast with your fifteen-year-old son?

The row had ended in an explosive exchange that was fast, raw and brutal:

'I hate you! I wish you'd died instead of Mum.'

'Yeah? Guess what? So do I!'

All the time they'd been arguing, he'd seen Lou's face, battered by submerged rocks in the sea off the Pembrokeshire coast.

Pushing the memory of the argument aside, he ran a hand over the top of his head, trying to flatten down the spikes of dark, grey-flecked hair.

He pushed through the double glass doors. Straight into the middle of a ruckus.

A scrawny man in faded black denim and a raggy T-shirt was swearing at a young woman in a dark suit. Eyes wide, she had backed against an orange wall. He could see a Wiltshire police ID on a lanyard round her neck, but he didn't recognise her.

The two female civilian staff behind the desk were on their feet, one with a phone clamped to her ear.

The architects who'd designed the interior of the new station at Bourne Hill had persuaded senior management that the traditional thick glass screen wasn't 'welcoming'. Now any arsehole could decide to lean across the three feet of white-surfaced MDF and abuse, spit on or otherwise ruin the day of the hardworking receptionists. He saw the other woman reach under the desk for the panic button.

'Why are you ignoring me, eh? I just asked where the toilets are, you bitch!' the man yelled at the woman backed against the wall.

Ford registered the can of strong lager in the man's left hand and strode over. The woman was pale, and her mouth had tightened to a lipless line.

'I asked you a question. What's wrong with you?' the drunk shouted.

Ford shot out his right hand and grabbed him by the back of his T-shirt. He yanked him backwards, sticking out a booted foot and rolling him over his knee to send him flailing to the floor.

Ford followed him down and drove a knee in between his shoulder blades. The man gasped out a loud 'Oof!' as his lungs emptied. Ford gripped his wrist and jerked his arm up in a tight angle, then turned round and called over his shoulder, 'Could someone get some cuffs, please? This . . . gentleman . . . will be cooling off in a cell.'

A pink-cheeked uniform raced over and snapped a pair of rigid Quik-Cuffs on to the man's wrists.

'Thanks, Mark,' Ford said, getting to his feet. 'Get him over to Custody.'

'Charge, sir?'

'Drunk and disorderly? Common assault? Being a jerk in a built-up area? Just get him booked in.'

The PC hustled the drunk to his feet, reciting the formal arrest and caution script while walking him off in an armlock to see the custody sergeant.

Ford turned to the woman who'd been the focus of his newest collar's unwelcome attentions. 'I'm sorry about that. Are you OK?'

She answered as if she were analysing an incident she'd witnessed on CCTV. 'I think so. He didn't hit me, and swearing doesn't cause physical harm. Although I am feeling quite anxious as a result.'

'I'm not surprised.' Ford gestured at her ID. 'Are you here to meet someone? I haven't seen you round here before.'

She nodded. 'I'm starting work here today. And my new boss is . . . hold on . . .' She fished a sheet of paper from a brown canvas messenger bag slung over her left shoulder. 'Alec Reid.'

Now Ford understood. She was the new senior crime scene investigator. Her predecessor had transferred up to Thames Valley Police to move with her husband's new job. Alec managed the small forensics team at Salisbury and had been crowing about his new hire for weeks now.

'My new deputy has a PhD, Ford,' he'd said over a pint in the Wyndham Arms one evening. 'We're going up in the world.'

Ford stuck his hand out. 'DI Ford.'

'Pleased to meet you,' she said, taking his hand and pumping it up and down three times before releasing it. 'My name is Dr Hannah Fellowes. I was about to get my ID sorted when that man started shouting at me.'

'I doubt it was anything about you in particular. Just wrong place, wrong time.'

She nodded, frowning up at him. 'Although, technically, this *is* the right place. As I'm going to be working here.' She checked her watch, a multifunction Casio with more dials and buttons than the dash of Ford's ageing Land Rover Discovery. 'It's also 8.15, so it's the right time as well.'

Ford smiled. 'Let's get your ID sorted, then I'll take you up to Alec. He arrives early most days.'

He led her over to the long, low reception desk.

'This is—'

'Dr Hannah Fellowes,' she said to the receptionist. 'I'm pleased to meet you.'

She thrust her right hand out across the counter. The receptionist took it and received the same three stiff shakes as Ford.

The receptionist smiled up at her new colleague, but Ford could see the concern in her eyes. 'I'm Paula. Nice to meet you, too, Hannah. Are you all right? I'm so sorry you had to deal with that on your first day.'

'It was a shock. But it won't last. I don't let things like that get to me.'

Paula smiled. 'Good for you!'

While Paula converted a blank rectangle of plastic into a functioning station ID, Hannah turned to Ford.

'Should I ask her to call me Dr Fellowes, or is it usual here to use first names?' she whispered.

'We mainly use Christian names, but if you'd like to be known as Dr Fellowes, now would be the time.'

Hannah nodded and turned back to Paula, who handed her the swipe card in a clear case.

'There you go, Hannah. Welcome aboard.'

'Thank you.' A beat. 'Paula.'

'Do you know where you're going?'

'I'll take her,' Ford said.

At the lift, he showed her how to swipe her card before pressing the floor button.

'If you don't do that, you just stand in the lift not going anywhere. It's mainly the PTBs who do it.'

'PTBs?' she repeated, as the lift door closed in front of them.

'Powers That Be. Management?'

'Oh. Yes. That's funny. PTBs. Powers That Be.'

She didn't laugh, though, and Ford had the odd sensation that he was talking to a foreigner, despite her southern English accent. She stared straight ahead as the lift ascended. Ford took a moment to assess her appearance. She was shorter than him by a good half-foot, no more than five-five or six. Slim, but not skinny. Blonde hair woven into plaits, a style Ford had always associated with children.

He'd noticed her eyes downstairs; it was hard not to, they'd been so wide when the drunk had had her backed against the wall. But even relaxed, they were large, and coloured the blue of old china.

The lift pinged and a computerised female voice announced, 'Third floor.'

'You're down here,' Ford said, turning right and leading Hannah along the edge of an open-plan office. He gestured left. 'General CID. I'm Major Crimes on the fourth floor.'

She took a couple of rapid, skipping steps to catch up with him. 'Is Forensics open plan as well? I was told it was a quiet office.'

'I think it's safe to say it's quiet. Come on. Let's get you a tea first. Or coffee. Which do you like best?'

'That's a hard question. I haven't really tried enough types to know.' She shook her head, like a dog trying to dislodge a flea from its ear. 'No. What I meant to say was, I'd like to have a tea, please. Thank you.'

There it was again. The foreigner-in-England vibe he'd picked up downstairs.

While he boiled a kettle and fussed around with a teabag and the jar of instant coffee, he glanced at Hannah. She was staring at him, but smiled when he caught her eye. The expression popped dimples into her cheeks.

'Something puzzling you?' he asked.

'You didn't tell me your name,' she said.

'I think I did. It's Ford.'

'No. I meant your first name. You said, "We mainly use Christian names" when the receptionist, Paula, was doing my building ID. And you called me Hannah. But you didn't tell me yours.'

Ford pressed the teabag against the side of the mug before scooping it out and dropping it into a swing-topped bin. He handed the mug to Hannah. 'Careful, it's hot.'

'Thank you. But your name?'

'Ford's fine. Really. Or DI Ford, if we're being formal.'

'OK.' She smiled. Deeper dimples this time, like little curved cuts. 'You're Ford. I'm Hannah. If we're being formal, maybe you *should* call me Dr Fellowes.'

Ford couldn't tell if she was joking. He took a swig of his coffee. 'Let's go and find Alec. He's talked of little else since you accepted his job offer.'

'It's probably because I'm extremely well qualified. After earning my doctorate, which I started at Oxford and finished at Harvard, I worked in America for a while. I consulted to city, state and federal law enforcement agencies. I also lectured at Quantico for the FBI.'

Ford blinked, struggling to process this hyper-concentrated CV. It sounded like that of someone ten or twenty years older than the slender young woman sipping tea from a Spire FM promotional mug.

'That's pretty impressive. Sorry, you're how old?'

'Don't be sorry. We only met twenty minutes ago. I'm thirty-three.'

Ford reflected that at her age he had just been completing his sergeant's exams. His promotion to inspector had come through a month ago and he was still feeling, if not out of his depth, then at least under the microscope. Now, he was in conversation with some sort of crime-fighting wunderkind.

'So, how come you're working as a CSI in Salisbury? No offence, but isn't it a bit of a step down from teaching at the FBI?'

She looked away. He watched as she fidgeted with a ring on her right middle finger, twisting it round and round.

'I don't want to share that with you,' she said, finally.

In that moment he saw it. Behind her eyes. An assault? A bad one. Not sexual, but violent. Who did the FBI go after? The really bad ones. The ones who didn't confine their evildoing to a single state. It was her secret. Ford knew all about keeping secrets. He felt for her.

'OK, sorry. Look, we're just glad to have you. Come on. Let's find Alec.'

He took Hannah round the rest of CID and out through a set of grey-painted double doors with a well-kicked steel plate at the foot. The corridor to Forensics was papered with health and safety posters and noticeboards advertising sports clubs, social events and training courses.

Inside, the chatter and buzz of coppers at full pelt was replaced by a sepulchral quiet. Five people were hard at work, staring at computer monitors or into microscopes. Much of the 'hard science' end of forensics had been outsourced to private labs in 2012. But Wiltshire Police had, in Ford's mind, made the sensible decision to preserve as much of an in-house scientific capacity as it could afford.

He pointed to a glassed-in office in the far corner of the room. 'That's Alec's den. He doesn't appear to be in yet.'

'*Au contraire*, Henry!'

The owner of the deep, amused-sounding voice tapped Ford on the shoulder. He turned to greet the forensic team manager, a short, round man wearing wire-framed glasses.

'Morning, Alec.'

Alec clocked the new CSI, but then leaned closer to Ford. 'You OK, Henry?' he murmured, his brows knitted together. 'What with the date, and everything.'

'I'm fine. Let's leave it.'

Alec shrugged. Then his gaze moved to Hannah. 'Dr Fellowes, you're here at last! Welcome, welcome.'

'Thank you, Alec. It's been quite an interesting start to the day.'

Ford said, 'Some idiot was making a nuisance of himself in reception as Hannah was arriving. He's cooling off in one of Ian's capsule hotel rooms in the basement.'

The joviality vanished, replaced by an expression of real concern. 'Oh, my dear young woman. I am so sorry. And on your first day with us, too,' Alec said. 'Why don't you come with me? I'll introduce you to the team and we'll get you set up with a nice quiet desk in the corner. Thanks, Henry. I'll take it from here.'

Ford nodded, eager to get back to his own office and see what the day held. He prayed someone might have been up to no good overnight. Anything to save him from the mountains of forms and reports that he had to either read, write or edit.

'DI Ford? Before you go,' Hannah said.

'Yes?'

'You said I should call you Ford. But Alec just called you Henry.'

'It's a nickname. I got it on my first day here.'

'A nickname. What does it mean?'

'You know. Henry. As in Henry Ford?'

She looked at him, eyebrows raised.

He tried again. 'The car? Model T?'

21

She smiled at last. A wide grin that showed her teeth, though it didn't reach her eyes. The effect was disconcerting. 'Ha! Yes. That's funny.'

'Right. I have to go. I'm sure we'll bump into each other again.'

'I'm sure, too. I hope there won't be a drunk trying to hit me.'

She smiled, and after a split second he realised it was supposed to be a joke. As he left, he could hear her telling Alec, 'Call me Hannah.'

DAY TWO, 8.59 A.M.

The 999 call had come in just ten minutes earlier: a Cat A G28 – suspected homicide. Having told the whole of Response and Patrol B shift to 'blat' over to the address, Sergeant Natalie Hewitt arrived first at 75 Wyvern Road.

She jumped from her car and spoke into her Airwave radio. 'Sierra Bravo Three-Five, Control.'

'Go ahead, Sierra Bravo Three-Five.'

'Is the ambulance towards?'

'Be about three minutes.'

She ran up the stairs and approached the young couple standing guard at the door to Flat 3.

'Mr and Mrs Gregory, you should go back to your own flat now,' she said, panting. 'I'll have more of my colleagues joining me shortly. Please don't leave the house. We'll be wanting to take your statements.'

'But I've got aerobics at nine thirty,' the woman protested.

Natalie sighed. The public were fantastic at calling in crimes, and occasionally made half-decent witnesses. But it never failed to amaze her how they could also be such *innocents* when it came to the aftermath. This one didn't even seem concerned that her upstairs neighbour and young son had been murdered. Maybe she was in shock. Maybe the husband had kept her out of the flat. Wise bloke.

'I'm afraid you may have to cancel it, just this once,' she said. *You look like you could afford to. Maybe go and get a fry-up, too, when we're done with you. Put some flesh on your bones.*

The woman retreated to the staircase. Her husband delayed leaving, just for a few seconds.

'We're just shocked,' he said. 'The blood came through our ceiling. That's why I went upstairs to investigate.'

Natalie nodded, eager now to enter the death room and deal with the latest chapter in the Big Book of Bad Things People Do to Each Other.

She swatted at the flies that buzzed towards her. They all came from the room at the end of the dark, narrow hallway. Keeping her eyes on the threadbare red-and-cream runner, alert to anything Forensics might be able to use, she made her way to the kitchen. She supported herself against the opposite wall with her left hand so she could walk, one foot in line with the other, along the right-hand edge of the hall.

The buzzing intensified. And then she caught it: the aroma of death. Sweet-sour top notes overlaying a deeper, darker, rotting-meat stink as body tissues broke down and emitted their gases.

And blood. Or 'claret', in the parlance of the job. She reckoned she'd smelled more of it than a wine expert. This was present in quantity. The husband – what was his name? Rob, that was it. He'd said on the phone it was bad. 'A slaughterhouse' – his exact words.

'Let's find out, then, shall we?' she murmured as she reached the door and entered the kitchen.

As the scene imprinted itself on her retinas, she didn't swear, or invoke the deity, or his son. She used to, in the early days of her career. There'd been enough blasphemy and bad language to have had her churchgoing mum rolling her eyes and pleading with her to 'Watch your language, please, Nat. There's no need.'

She'd become hardened to it over the previous fifteen years. She hoped she still felt a normal human's reaction when she encountered murder scenes, or the remains of those who'd reached the end of their tether and done themselves in. But she left the amateur dramatics to the new kids. She was a sergeant, a rank she'd worked bloody hard for, and she felt a certain restraint went with the territory. So, no swearing.

She did, however, shake her head and swallow hard as she took in the scene in front of her. She'd been a keen photographer in her twenties and found it helpful to see crime scenes as if through a lens: her way of putting some distance between her and whatever horrors the job required her to confront.

In wide-shot, an obscene parody of a Madonna and child. A woman – early thirties, to judge by her face, which was waxy-pale – and a little boy cradled in her lap.

They'd been posed at the edge of a wall-to-wall blood pool, dried and darkened to a deep plum red.

She'd clearly bled out. He wasn't as pale as his mum, but the pink in his smooth little cheeks was gone, replaced by a greenish tinge.

The puddle of blood had spread right across the kitchen floor and under the table, on which half-emptied bags of shopping sagged. The dead woman was slumped with her back against the cooker, legs canted open yet held together at the ankle by her pulled-down jeans.

And the little boy.

Looking for all the world as though he had climbed on to his mother's lap for a cuddle, eyes closed, hands together at his throat as if in prayer. Fair hair. Long and wavy, down to his shoulders, in a girlish style Natalie had noticed some of her friends choose for their sons.

Even in midwinter, flies would find a corpse within the hour. In the middle of a scorching summer like the one southern England was enjoying now, they'd arrived in minutes, laid their eggs and begun feasting in quantity. Maggots crawled and wriggled all over the pair.

As she got closer, Natalie revised her opinion about the cause of death; now, she could see bruises around the throat that screamed strangulation.

There were protocols to be followed. And the first of these was the preservation of life. She was sure the little boy was dead. The skin discolouration and maggots told her that. But there was no way she was going to go down as the sergeant who left a still-living toddler to die in the centre of a murder scene.

Reaching him meant stepping into that lake of congealed blood. Never mind the sneers from CID about the 'woodentops' walking through crime scenes in their size twelves; this was about checking if a little boy had a chance of life.

She pulled out her phone and took half a dozen shots of the bodies. Then she took two long strides towards them, wincing as her boot soles crackled and slid in the coagulated blood.

She crouched and extended her right index and middle fingers, pressing under the little boy's jaw into the soft flesh where the carotid artery ran. She closed her eyes and prayed for a pulse, trying to ignore the smell, and the noise of the writhing maggots and their soft, squishy little bodies as they roiled together in the mess.

After staying there long enough for the muscles in her legs to start complaining, and for her to be certain the little lad was dead, she straightened and reversed out of the blood. She took care to place her feet back in the first set of footprints.

She turned away, looking for some kitchen roll to wipe the blood off her soles, and stared in horror at the wall facing the cooker.

'Oh, shit.'

DAY TWO, 9.05 A.M.

In metre-tall dark red digits, smeared and dripping, someone had daubed a number.

666

Feeling her heart thumping in her chest, and not enjoying the sensation, Natalie spoke into her Airwave.

'Control from Sierra Bravo Three-Five. That G28 in Wyvern Road? Looks like a double homicide. Two deceased. Adult female and young child, a male. A boy, I mean. Christ! A little boy!'

'Sierra Bravo Three-Five from Control. You OK, Nat?'

'Yeah, yeah, I'm fine,' she said. 'Send the grown-ups.'

'Which ones?'

She glanced at the bloody number again. 'All of them.'

'OK, Nat. On it.'

She saw a roll of kitchen towel on a pine spindle. Pulled off a half-dozen sheets. Cleaned her boot soles as best as she was able. Scrunched the bloody wad into a tight ball and stuck it in the bin. She'd have to tell the CSIs to take impressions of her soles for elimination purposes, even though she hadn't seen any other footprints on her way in.

Downstairs, she knocked on the front door of Flat 2. The wife opened the door, still in her gym clothes. Maybe she thought she could still make the class. *Not. Going. To. Happen.*

'Mrs Gregory, can I come in?'

'Yes, of course.'

She stood aside and Natalie entered the cleaner, brighter, not-smelling-like-a-butcher's-shop version of the flat upstairs.

'I need to take statements from you and your husband. Is he around, please?'

The woman nodded and offered a tight smile. 'Rob!' she yelled. 'The policewoman's back. She wants to talk to us. Sorry,' she said, turning back to Nat, 'he's a freelance designer. He listens to music while he's working. It's the only way I can get through to him. Do you need a tea or a coffee or something? I have herbal. Peppermint, chamomile, chai, ginger, or even some builder's somewhere.'

Nat didn't answer at once. *My God, you're a cool one, aren't you? Are you used to living underneath murder scenes? Did you have something to do with this one?* She pushed the thought down. *Above my pay grade.*

'Builder's would be fine, thank you.'

◆ ◆ ◆

Ford was writing a report when his force-issued mobile rang. Grateful for the interruption, he answered without looking at the screen. 'Ford.'

'It's Alan in Control, sir. Nat Hewitt's at a crime scene. Says it's a double homicide. You're the duty DI.'

'Address?'

'Flat 3, 75 Wyvern Road. CSIs are already there. Plus, I called the coroner and the pathologist.'

'OK, thanks. I'm on my way.'

He shrugged on his suit jacket, patting the pockets for wallet, car keys, notebook and his own mobile. He grabbed a black nylon hold-all from beside his desk. His murder bag contained everything he might need for a scene, from Tyvek 'Noddy suit' with matching bootees to a set of lock picks and a selection of screwdrivers. He unplugged a slim black power pack from the wall and dropped it in. Most important of all, his policy book: an A4 notebook in which he recorded every decision on every case, including justification and possible consequences.

Moving through the Major Crimes command, he called out to a young DC, Julie Harper.

'Jools! You're with me.'

'Guv?'

'Double homicide. Wyvern Road.'

On the short drive over, Jools spoke without taking her eyes off the road. 'You OK, guv?'

The concern in her voice made him want to lash out. He felt a flash of anger, then forced his jaws to unclench. 'You're the second person to ask me that today.'

'Sorry. It's just, today's . . .'

'Yes, Jools! I know. The anniversary of my wife's death. Why is it that once a year everybody treats me like I'm made of porcelain?'

'Because they care about you?'

'I'm fine without, thanks. We're here. Find a spot and let's get on with it.'

A long, tree-lined street of mainly Victorian terrace houses, Wyvern Road stretched in a gentle incline from Castle Street in the west to the ring road carrying two lanes of traffic between the Southampton and London roads.

Two marked cars blocked off the street between Piccadilly Road and Chayne's Close, sun flaring off the yellow squares in their Battenberg livery. Blue-and-white police tape fluttered in the summer breeze as they drew closer to the principal crime scene.

Ford and Jools nodded at the uniformed loggist stationed on the north-side pavement, who was sweating in the heat. She took their collar numbers then lifted the tape for them to duck under.

Outside 75, a white CSI van had been parked on a double-yellow line. Uniforms were already knocking on doors, talking to neighbours.

Another cordon to cross, this one yellow-and-black crime scene tape. Before they entered, Ford and Jools climbed into their Tyvek suits. He ignored the glances she kept shooting him.

A woman's voice called out. 'Sir?'

Ford turned to see Nat Hewitt hurrying across the road.

'I wanted you to hear it from me before anybody else told you,' she said as she arrived.

'What? You look like you're going to throw up. Bad one, is it?' he asked, jerking his chin in the direction of the house.

'Yes, but that's not it, sir. I had to walk right into it. The blood. I had to check the little boy wasn't dead.'

'And was he?'

'Poor little mite.'

'You did the right thing. Just see the CSIs get your boot prints for elimination.'

She nodded, and hurried away to the far end of the cordon. Ford tracked her as she approached a group of onlookers, phones held aloft. Why did they feel this compulsion to film horror and then upload it to their social media accounts? He hated it.

'Bloody ghouls,' he grunted to Jools, who stood behind him, rustling in her Noddy suit. 'Come on. Let's get inside.'

Ford paused at the door. Looked up. The three-storey house must once have been a spacious family home. Since its conversion into separate flats, it had slid a few rungs down the social ladder.

The downstairs hallway retained its turquoise, rust and cream encaustic tiles with their intricate geometric pattern. But the surface was dulled through neglect and several were chipped, the missing corners filled in with dirty cement. A grubby radiator cover was piled high with takeaway menus.

The hallway was wide enough for them to stand side by side, but the stairs were narrower. Ford led them up to the first floor, where the forensic pathologist was pulling a hood back from a sleek bob of silver hair.

Dr Georgina Eustace was in her mid-fifties. Her base was Salisbury District Hospital, but she liked to come out to the more 'exotic' crime scenes, as she called them. In Ford's opinion, she took the concept of gallows humour to a whole new level. But she was a damn good pathologist, which, he felt, allowed her some leeway.

'What've we got?' he asked, not reluctant to venture up to the main crime scene, just keen to get her initial impressions while they were still fresh.

'I'll go on up,' Jools said. 'Make a start.'

Ford nodded, then turned back to the pathologist. 'Cause of death?'

'From the bruises around her throat and the amount of blood, I'd say strangling and exsanguination will have played their part in the young woman's death,' she said. 'Although it's always possible the killer may have found some other method of doing her in.'

'The boy?'

She shook her head. 'No obvious sign of trauma. I emphasise the word "obvious". He's not bled, or not from the side you can see, so I'll have to wait till I get back to SDH,' she said. 'They're both at the very early stages of bloating so, making allowances for the extremely hot weather we've been having, they've been dead no more than a day or two.'

Ford appreciated the way Eustace would give him more than the usual litany of exasperated headshakes and tutting whenever he, a lowly plod, dared to ask a pathologist for ideas *before* the post-mortem.

He nodded. He was thinking that fresh corpses meant recent murders. And recent murders were easier to clear up. The clock had started ticking. 'Thanks,' he muttered. 'I'll see you later.'

'I've signed the ROLE form on both victims, by the way,' Eustace said.

Recognition of Life Extinct. It was one of the first steps in the sad, bureaucratic process through which a once-living human being, a person, became transformed into a thing. A body. A case. A PM report. The property of the coroner. A deceased and sadly missed. A body smashed by a falling rock. Then washed off a ledge and dumped on a Welsh beach. *Oh, Lou! I wish you were still with me.*

Stuffing the memory back down, he took a small, flat rectangular tin from his pocket, and extracted two filters for rolling cigarettes and a small bottle of oil of menthol. Knowing his 'stink-busters' wouldn't help, but needing the ritual, he squirted a couple of drops of the strong-smelling mint oil on to each of the filters, then stuck them into his nostrils. A smear of oil of camphor on his top lip and he was ready.

He tugged his hood up, settled his face mask over his nose and climbed the final flight of stairs to Flat 3. He didn't dread seeing corpses any more. Carrying one around with him at all times had dulled the shock to a constant, low-level ache.

If the first-floor landing was tight, the third-floor landing was like a crowded train compartment.

DAY TWO, 9.31 A.M.

White-suited CSIs bearing bagged samples moved in and out along a common-approach path of bright-yellow plastic tread plates. Jools was talking to a uniformed sergeant.

Kneeling beside them, the photographer worked at a laptop propped on a tall stool.

'Backing up,' he said, without turning away from the screen.

Ford stepped across the threshold, losing his balance as one of the tread plates shifted beneath his foot. He swore, causing those inside the flat to turn. The common-approach path led along the hall to the kitchen, tight to the left-hand edge of the corridor.

He picked out a set of bloody footprints leading away from the kitchen. *Nat's.* He frowned with irritation. And then he thought of her instinct to try to save the little boy. And of his own wife's desperate entreaty to him: *You* have *to. If you stay here, we'll both die. Then who'll look after Sam?*

He felt his throat clutch: he pushed on, steeling himself. And then he entered the crime scene.

It happened here. Obviously. You don't murder somebody outside then bring the body back to dump it in their own kitchen.

Rather than barging into the centre of the working CSIs, firing off questions and asserting his authority, he observed from the edge of the room.

And he didn't stare, either, or focus in so tightly on the heinous scene before his eyes – the intertwined bodies and the lake of blood – that he got tunnel vision and failed to see the bigger picture. Because that's what he was there for: to see the scene as a whole. The CSIs and the snapper could pick up far more details than he ever could, or wanted to. One thing preoccupied Ford: the killer. Because Ford knew all about what it was like to kill.

He felt it on the back of his neck first. Fresh sweat chilling his skin. His stomach lurched. He slid a black plastic bag from his inside pocket. As the scene impressed itself upon him, and the wave of nausea rolled through him, he opened the bag and threw up, as quietly as he could manage, then knotted it and placed it a corner.

He noticed Jools watching him. Only her eyes were visible, but he'd seen that look before. The look that said, 'I understand.' *No, Jools, you don't. Not at all.* He turned away from her and began to look. The nausea subsided to a background tremor. He knew where it was about to take him, was ready for the journey.

Three chairs hemmed the table. Groceries had spilled from one of the bags, but nothing had rolled or fallen to the floor.

Multicoloured paintings covered the fridge door, enthusiasm more in evidence than skill. They reminded Ford of Sam's earliest artistic endeavours: plenty of finger paintings, a couple of stars that said 'potato print' to Ford, and a drawing of two figures. One a wobbly orange oval with two lines straggling down to the bottom edge of the paper, the other a smaller version, their 'arms' – more single spidery lines – linked. Dots and crooked curves that might have been faces were set within squashed circles balanced atop the bodies.

Underneath, in coloured crayons, someone had printed 'Kai and Mummy'. *No Daddy, then? Was your mum bringing you up on her own, Kai? Bearing all the weight on her own? Did your daddy come back? Lose his temper?*

Coloured magnetic plastic letters held the artworks in place. None had been torn, swiped off-centre or knocked free. It meant 'no struggle' to Ford.

He viewed each of the four walls in turn – registering the grotesque graffiti – then moved on to the ceiling, and finally the floor. He let his gaze soften, blurring sharp edges, rounding corners.

He inhaled and, as he breathed out, pushed a little at that part of him that allowed him to inhabit the mind of a murderer. He felt the killer's presence. *Became* the killer.

Now he did look at the bodies. The dead woman and the dead child.

You trusted me. Even at the point when I attacked, you didn't think it was going to happen. You didn't fight back. I didn't give you time to. I didn't give you a reason *to.*

I'm taking a final look around at my handiwork before I leave you. I wasn't angry, or not at you, at any rate. That's why I didn't mutilate you. I could have, if I'd wanted to. Cut. Stabbed. Bitten. Worse. I could have played around and had some fun, especially with the boy. So small. So defenceless.

But I like blood. I love the stuff, the more the better. Look at it! I've left it everywhere for the cops to find. Because I know they'll find you. And I don't care. What will they make of my mural? I wonder. Idiots! Nothing.

They won't catch me. They can't. I'm too smart for them. They're not good enough.

Someone spoke to him. The voice sounded blurry, as if underwater.

'DI Ford?'

He snapped into the present, shuddered, felt a runnel of sweat crawling down his ribcage from his armpit.

One of the CSIs was standing in front of him. China-blue eyes.

'Sorry, Hannah, what is it?'

'I asked if you wanted to get a closer look at the bodies. We've finished taking samples.'

He squatted down, one foot on each of two yellow tread plates placed square on to the bodies. He concentrated on the bruises around the woman's throat, the way they extended around her neck. A textbook pattern.

Among the reddened swellings at her throat, two dark oval bruises stood out, one each side of her windpipe. *My thumbs did those.* More bruising at the sides of the neck, including well-defined round bruises in a cluster. *My fingers. I throttled you from the front. I looked into your eyes. I watched you die.*

He looked down at the boy. Her son. *'Kai and Mummy'.* He looked peaceful, curled up into a comma shape. Enclosed by the woman's splayed legs. No visible wounds. Why did they have to hurt kids? Poor little lad hadn't lived long enough to cause anyone any pain. Growing up without his dad would've been hard enough.

He let the killer speak again.

I've got nothing against kids. He was just in the wrong place at the wrong time. She's the one I wanted.

'So why did you pull her trousers down?' he murmured.

He looked around the side of her hips and lifted the tail of her shirt up with the end of his pen. Her underwear was in place. *Not sex, then.*

The posing of the bodies felt wrong. Almost tender – if you ignored the hideous fact that some stranger had burst into this family's life and snuffed out two of its members. Which prompted him to think. *Where's the dad?* Jools was a good copper. She'd be on it already.

Ford peered at the side of the woman's head. Her hair, mid-brown and worn loose, was matted with blood on the left side. *Yeah, it's matted. Because I smacked her one, didn't I? That's how I subdued her.*

36

He moved to the wall with the blood-daubed numbers. He knew the photographer would have taken plenty of shots. Different angles to capture the light falling across the surface of the marks, the better to determine what the killer had used to make them. He pulled out his phone and took a picture himself, anyway.

You bastard. You heartless, soulless, evil bastard. You did this, and you enjoyed yourself, didn't you? And this is your idea of a joke, isn't it? To taunt me. Well, it's working. Because I'm going to find you. And I'm going to send you away for a very long time.

Ford left the kitchen. He walked the length of the hall, the clicks from the photographer's high-end digital camera whirring behind him, adding its buzz to that of the flies. He swatted one away from his face as it zigzagged along the narrow space. He found Jools flicking through a photo album in the sitting room, a little blue railway engine on its side by her right toe.

'She was married,' she said, pointing at the mantelpiece.

Silver-framed wedding photos clustered together in the centre. Ford's gaze travelled right, to a large photo on the wall, mounted in a pale wood frame.

A man, a woman and a toddler were laughing and looking at the camera. They wore white, and the photographer had chosen lighting, or some sort of Photoshop effect, to blur their edges, as if they were fading into the white background.

The woman, he recognised from the kitchen. The toddler was blond and bore enough of a resemblance to the boy for him to be sure on that count, too.

'Find the husband. That's our number-one priority. If he's at work, we need to get to him before some idiot leaks this or posts a video online,' he said with a scowl. 'I don't want him finding out his family's been murdered from Facebook.' *Assuming he doesn't already know.*

Jools shook her head. 'Too late for that, guv. He's dead.'

'What? Where's the body?'

'Not here. I found the death certificate in her bedroom. In the dressing-table drawer with her underwear.'

A widow, then, and a single mum. Ford's heart lurched. *You were doing your best for Kai. But in the end it wasn't enough. You couldn't protect him, and you couldn't save him.*

'Next of kin, then. Brothers, sisters, parents. Find them, inform them.'

'Me, guv? I did the last death knock. Can't one of the others do it?' Ford stared her down. 'OK, fine, I'll do it. I'll sort out a family liaison officer as well.'

Ford sat on the sofa, registering the sagging springs beneath his thighs as it took his weight. *Old. Second-hand?*

'What do you think?' he asked Jools.

She got to her feet and pulled an armchair round to face him. She clasped her hands between her knees. Fixed those brilliant green eyes on his. 'If it's a domestic, an angry boyfriend or whatever, I'll buy everyone in the team a curry and unlimited beers.'

'Too weird?'

'Too weird.'

'So, what then?'

'It didn't look frenzied, did it? He took his time. And I haven't found any evidence of robbery as a motive. I spoke to Nat. There was a handbag on the kitchen table and her phone and purse were still inside,' she said. 'Not a lot of cash, mind, but a fiver and some change. She still had her wedding and engagement rings on, too. The bedroom's untouched.'

'No perv stuff?'

Jools shook her head.

Ford rubbed the stubble on his chin. 'He left her knickers on, so sex is out as a motive,' he said. 'What do you make of the numbers on the wall?'

'My Lord High Satanic Majesty Beelzebub made me do it!' she growled in a passable imitation of a movie Satanist.

'Or it's a jealous ex and he's trying to throw us off.'

'Could be, but it's a hell of a bit of set-dressing.'

'Maybe we *are* dealing with a nutter,' Ford said. 'But when we catch him, I'm going to do my damnedest to see him locked up, not sent to a hospital where some shrink'll try to *understand* him.'

'Agreed.'

'At this stage the number's just another piece of information,' Ford said. 'Let's clear the ground under our feet. It was probably someone she knew.'

'I'll start with the neighbours downstairs. They called it in.'

With Jools gone, Ford returned to the kitchen. Keeping his gloves on, he retrieved the dead woman's bag and took it back to the sitting room. He sat on the sofa, leaned forward and emptied it on to the coffee table.

A plastic ID on a royal-blue NHS lanyard skittered across the polished surface, face down. He turned it over. And met the dead woman.

'Angela Halpern. Staff nurse. Salisbury NHS Foundation Trust,' he intoned.

So he had a name and an occupation and a place of work: Salisbury District Hospital, which made Angie's co-workers his first line of enquiry. He made a note in his policy book.

DAY TWO, 10.00 A.M.

On the other side of the city, the staff on Bodenham Ward were feeling the full force of their master's displeasure. Charles Abbott, consultant haematologist, was not happy.

'My God, woman, this blood is contaminated!' Abbott employed a level tone he knew frightened even the most experienced of his colleagues. 'A week's research down the tubes because you didn't check the seal. What did you keep it in back in India? Milk bottles?'

The junior doctor had arrived at SDH from a hospital in Mumbai a week earlier to take up a coveted research post.

'I'm—' She coughed and started again. 'I'm sorry, Mr Abbott.'

Abbott observed the young woman's trembling lower lip with interest. He thrust the open bag at her. 'Take it. And get it out of my sight.'

She reached out a hand and took it from him, but it slipped from her shaking fingers. Abbott jumped back. She stood, rooted to the spot, as the bag burst, spattering her shoes, ankles and calves. Not one drop hit Abbott's dark pinstripe suit.

He registered the shocked faces of his staff as the junior doctor ran from the room, stifling a sob. Was it wrong to feel a tiny rush of pleasure at the ease with which he could control their emotions?

He dismissed the question. They'd be just the same when – if – they became consultants.

He spotted a man in short-sleeved navy scrubs pushing in through the swing doors, bearing a tray of sterilised instruments.

'You! Porter!' he barked.

The porter frowned. 'It's Matty, Mr Abbott.'

'I don't care what your name is, man. Get this mess cleaned up. And quick about it,' he added. 'The CEO's due on one of his interminable inspection tours in half an hour. Then get down to the blood bank and fetch another unit of whole blood, O positive, yes?'

The porter nodded and offered a small smile. 'Yes, Mr Abbott.'

◆ ◆ ◆

As the ward returned to normal, Matty knelt at the edge of the blood pool and began soaking up the worst of it with paper torn from a roll. He brought the dripping wad to his nose and sniffed, then shoved it into the gaping mouth of a yellow clinical waste sack.

He kept up a low monologue as he mopped and wiped, combining Abbott's name with an inventive mixture of obscenities. He flexed the muscles in his right arm and imagined grinding Abbott's face into the gore. He smiled.

He looked up to see if anyone was watching him. Everyone was too busy with their own tasks. He stretched out a finger and poked two small dots in the smeary residue. He added a downturned mouth and enclosed them all in a circle.

'Fuck you, Abbott,' he muttered, jabbing his index finger down to make a nose. 'I wish this was yours. Then you'd care what my name was.'

'What on earth are you doing, Matty?'

He looked up, heart racing. Sister McLaughlin was standing over him, hands on her hips. Peering down at him over that sharp beak of hers, through those stupid old-lady glasses. Nosy bitch.

He gave her his best 'Who, me?' smile. 'Nothing. I—'

'That is a serious health and safety risk. And why aren't you wearing gloves?' She tutted. 'Get it cleaned up, please. Then go and wash your hands. Thoroughly,' she added, before spinning on her heel and stalking off.

He watched her swaying rump for a little while. Imagined caning it. Hard. Drawing blood. The fantasy faded, and he bent to his task again, still seeing Abbott's face before him and feeling the stirrings of an erection.

◆ ◆ ◆

On the drive to the hospital, Ford's phone rang. He glanced at the screen and punched the 'Answer Call' button on the steering wheel.

'What have you got, Jools?'

'A neighbour said she thought Angie might have a sister. No obvious troublemakers hanging round the victim. The little boy's her son, Kai. Three years old. Usually with a childminder. Donna Reid.'

'Good work. I'm nearly at the hospital. Going to talk to HR. See what I can get from them.'

A few minutes later, he was facing the hospital's HR director across her paper-strewn desk.

'I'm afraid one of your nurses has been killed,' he said. 'Angela Halpern?'

All colour left her face.

'Oh, my God! That's terrible.'

'Did you know her?'

She shook her head. 'We have five thousand people working here. Half of them don't know anyone outside their own ward. Who'd want to kill a nurse? They're the kindest, the nicest—'

'They are. And right now what I'm trying to do is identify her next of kin. They need to be notified.'

She nodded, rapid bobs that set her hair swinging. She tapped her keyboard, speaking as she typed.

'OK. Halpern, A.' Her red-painted fingernail clicked on a key. 'Staff nurse. Men's surgical ward.' Another plasticky click from the keyboard. 'Personal details. Contact details. Next of kin. She's listed her sister. Cherry Andrews.'

'Like the fruit?'

'Yes. C-H-E-R-R-Y. Do you want her contact details?'

'Yes, please.'

Ford noted down landline, mobile and work numbers, plus work and personal email addresses.

Outside again, he walked away from the main entrance towards the A&E department. At the top of the ambulance ramp, he leaned on a rail and looked out over the farmland to the south of the hospital's sprawling complex of buildings and car parks.

The sun illuminated the landscape with summer intensity, causing the ripening wheat fields to shimmer like gold. In the distance, silvery threads spread out against the green where the River Nadder meandered through a water meadow.

Alec and Jools had been right to ask him how he was feeling. Because he felt shit. Not the background level of shittiness he carried around all the time. Not the sadness that caused him to seek solace in work and to keep Sam at a distance when he knew he should be pulling him close.

This was the special grade reserved for this one day in the year. The anniversary. He divided his life into two, sharp-edged pieces. Before he killed Lou. And afterwards.

He turned away from the landscape and called Cherry Andrews.

'My name is Ford. I'm a detective inspector with Wiltshire Police. In Salisbury. Are you at work?'

'I am, but you've got me worried now. What's this about?'

'What's your work address, please?'

'I'm on Churchfields, the industrial estate? Brady Engineering. Harpenden Road. Just ask for me at reception.'

On the way, Ford rang Jools. 'You're in luck. I've found the next of kin. A sister. I'm on my way now.'

'Thanks, guv. I owe you one.'

'Yes, you do. In a pint glass.'

'Be gentle, guv.'

'Aren't I always?' He knew what she meant. His heart used to sink when he had to deliver bad news. He'd sweat, feel embarrassed and anxious at the same time. But not any more. Not after his wife's death.

'Just . . .' Jools hesitated. 'Be kind, OK? It's a massive shock. Try not to sound like you're reciting a script.'

'Noted.'

◆ ◆ ◆

Moving stiffly, Cherry Andrews showed Ford into a meeting room off the main reception area. The walls were dotted with grease marks from peeled-off Blu Tack. A pedestal-mounted fan moved the warm, humid air around the room.

'Please have a seat,' she said, gesturing at one of the hard, plastic-backed chairs around the table. Her face was pale. 'What's happened? Why are you here?'

Her forehead was grooved with concern. Ford looked her straight in the eye. He may not have felt any nerves or dread, but that didn't mean he enjoyed the moment when you planted a bomb in the centre of a family and detonated it. Whatever Jools said, he knew their pain better than anyone. He just couldn't bring himself to admit how much. Or why.

'There's no easy way to tell you this, so I'll be straight with you. I'm afraid your sister has been killed. Her son, too. We're treating their deaths as suspicious. I'm sorry for your loss. Truly, I am.'

Then he waited. You had to. You had to wait to see how the family member whose emotions you'd just blown to pieces was going to react. Some went into shock, not moving, not talking, barely breathing. Others hit you, beating their fists against your chest until they collapsed, sobbing. Others got angry, the men especially, railing at you, yelling, swearing. Others denied it. Even after you cuddled them and told them how sorry you were, Sam, but it's true. Mummy's dead. She's not coming back. It was an accident.

'How?' she asked, after ten seconds of silence.

'We're not sure. But I have to tell you, it looks as though they were murdered.'

'Looks?' she said, louder this time, her eyes glistening. 'What do you mean, "looks"? Were they or weren't they?'

He nodded. 'Yes. They were.'

This wasn't protocol. He was supposed to wait until the results of the post-mortem. But hell, it wasn't as if Angie Halpern had accidentally killed her son, throttled herself and then bled herself to death.

The tears overflowed Cherry's lower lids, spilling down her cheeks and splashing on to the tabletop. A sob broke free, a gluey croak that hung in the air between them. She pulled a tissue from a pocket and wiped her nose.

'Did she . . . I mean, were they . . . ?' she asked in a voice clotted with sudden grief.

He knew what she meant. What she wanted to know. Relieved that at least he could offer her this small crumb of comfort, he told

45

her what she wanted to hear. 'It looks as though they died quickly.' *They didn't. I'm sure of it.* 'We need to wait for the pathologist to conduct her tests' – *not 'perform an autopsy'; nobody wants to picture knives and saws at a moment like this* – 'and there were no signs of any sexual assault.'

The language was brutal. But so was violent death. He'd never found that relatives responded well to euphemisms. It was as if, in this moment of extreme emotion, only the truth would do. The plainer and more unvarnished, the better.

She looked at him with eyes streaked black as her mascara ran. 'What do you need from me?'

'I need to find out as much as I can about Angela. Who she—'

'Call her Angie. Please. She hated being called Angela. Said it reminded her of Mum.'

'Sorry. I need to build up a picture of Angie as a person. The people she knew. Who she worked with, socialised with. Who she confided in. Did she have any enemies? People who might have wished her harm?'

Cherry dragged the tissue across her eyes, reducing it to a soggy, frayed scrap. He offered a fresh one from a packet in his jacket pocket.

'I need to think. Oh, God, what do I do about the funerals? There's so much I don't know.'

Like, how do you tell your relatives? How do you stop yourself weeping through her funeral? Beating your fists against your father-in-law's black-suited chest and sobbing uncontrollably as he pats your heaving back? There'll a grief counsellor. But you can't tell her why you're so fucked up. You'd go to prison. Sam would grow up an orphan. Work's good, though. Work's always there for you. You can forget about your grief if you keep working.

'I'm going to assign a family liaison officer to you,' he said quietly. 'She'll help you get through this, Cherry, I promise. But I need you to know that we won't be able to release the bodies until all our tests are done and we have all the evidence we can find from' – *from their bodies, from their* dead *bodies, don't say it* – 'a careful examination.'

She'd passed from the heightened emotion he'd seen so many times before into a passive state. She looked at him, but her eyes barely focused. She twisted and picked at the second tissue until it was a pile of damp shreds on the table in front of her.

She nodded. 'Thank you.'

'I have to go. I'm sorry.'

He handed her his card and repeated the mantra about getting in touch with information, however insignificant it might seem.

Back at Bourne Hill, Ford passed his own office and headed for its neighbour, bigger by a factor of two and with much better furniture. Time to inform the big boss: Detective Superintendent Sandra Monroe. He knocked and entered.

DAY TWO, NOON

The woman behind the desk looked up from a phone. She pushed her ash-blonde hair out of her eyes. 'Henry! What news from the frontline?'

'Double homicide. Bad.'

'And when you say "bad". . . ?'

'Mother and child. Posed together in a lake of her blood. The number 666 daubed on the wall in blood. No robbery. No sexual violence. No witnesses.'

Sandy said nothing at first. Ford waited. He knew what she was doing. Running through the scenarios that could affect the progress of the case, from investigative to legal to public relations. The higher up the ladder you went, the more politics you had to worry about.

'We'll issue a basic press release. No conference yet,' she said. 'If you can catch him inside a week, we won't have a media circus on our hands.'

'Agreed.'

'Anything you need?'

He shook his head. 'I'm good.'

'That's my boy. Because my budget's enough to pay your wages and toner for the printers, and that's about it.'

Ford gathered his team together in a conference room. And now, surrounded by cops rather than dead bodies and blood-gorged flies, on his home turf, he felt the nerves kick in good and proper. His guts squirmed.

He surveyed the officers and police staff sitting round the U-shaped table. His 'inner circle' in particular.

To his left sat Jan Derwent, a steady detective sergeant with fifteen years in. Her moans about her big-hipped figure and her habit of bringing in home-baked cakes were, Ford felt, somewhat at odds with each other. Jan was the team's POLSA – police search adviser. She'd earned the team's admiration when she'd uncovered a Yorkie bar missing from another officer's lunchbox in Mick Tanner's desk.

Mick was his second DS, by his own admission 'an old-school copper'. He'd joined the police straight from school. At thirty-eight, Mick had built up an impressive network among the city's criminals, along with a physique honed by many hours in the gym. During a recent red-faced rant on the topic of compulsory diversity-awareness training, Jools had quipped that Mick's black goatee and shaved head made him look like 'a bald Satan'.

His two detective constables were on the way to making a decent team, if they could channel their professional rivalry into policework and not undermining each other. Julie 'Jools' Harper had, after boarding school in Salisbury, followed her father and grandfather into the army and spent her last three years as an MP in the Criminal Investigation Branch. With her slight but muscular runner's build, pixie-cut red hair and flashing emerald-green eyes, she resembled a feisty elf; the kind who would follow the evidence, build a case, interview suspects and make arrests with a single-minded determination born of a lifetime's adherence to rules.

Completing the quartet was Olly Cable, a fast-track boy with a degree in criminology. At twenty-four, he was five years Jools's junior. He still had to learn the difference between knowing something and letting everyone else know he knew it. Olly had rowed at university and carried his six-foot frame well, clothing it in designer suits, and wore his dark hair in a fashionable forties look. Ford had noticed him bestowing longing glances on Jools when he thought he was unobserved.

Until recently, Ford would have been sitting among them, a DS like Jan and Mick. Then he'd got the coveted DI's post after the previous holder left for the Met. Overnight, those comfortable, banter-filled relationships changed. Not least with Mick, who'd made no secret of the fact he'd felt the job was his by right.

'Mine for the asking, Henry,' he'd crowed, just before Sandy had made the formal announcement a month earlier. Sandy had already given Ford the good news the previous evening, shaking his hand then enveloping him in a tight hug.

Some who'd been on the receiving end of a 'Monroe Special' alleged they were the reason for her nickname: the Python. Frowned upon by HR, no doubt, but a sign she'd accepted you. Others swore blind it was her habit, when a front-line copper, of squeezing the truth out of suspects in muscular coils of evidence, forensic questioning and, when all else failed, a good old-fashioned dose of intimidation.

Was she in tune with the times? Nobody would accuse her of that. Was she a gold medallist in bringing villains to justice? Guilty as charged.

And now, here he was, about to lead his own team into battle in their first major case since he'd taken over. The inner circle, the police staff investigators and CSIs, the uniforms. He looked at each of them in turn, waited for complete silence.

'Angela Halpern. Known from now on as Angie. And Kai Halpern, her son. Angie was a single mum. A widow. Murdered sometime in the last forty-eight hours.'

'COD, guv?' Jan asked, prodding her heavy-framed glasses higher on her nose.

'While we wait for the PM report, it's all conjecture, but it looks as though Angie was throttled, and Kai – well, I don't know,' he said. 'No obvious signs of violence, so poison? Doc Eustace will tell us.'

'What about the scene?' Mick asked.

'The primary scene was a bloodbath. She bled out. And someone – the killer, we assume – wrote the number 666 on the wall in blood.'

'Bloody hell!' Mick said with feeling, running a palm over his shaved skull.

'Satanic murderer hits Salisbury!' one of the police staff investigators called out.

Ford waited until the banter evaporated under his stern gaze. He turned to the left side of the table. 'Jan, I want you to set up a search. The house, obviously – all three flats – then, what, a fifty-metre perimeter?'

She nodded and made a note. 'Should be about right. Anything you want me to look for in particular?'

'There was a lot of blood. Gallons of the stuff. If he got away without leaving some sort of trail, I'd be amazed.'

'Lose your breakfast again, did you, guv?' Mick muttered, just loud enough for Jan to hear.

'Leave it, Mick,' she hissed. 'You know what today is.'

'Joke.'

'Right. So, blood drops, footprints or partials?' Jan asked.

'Exactly. Other than that, the usual,' Ford said, offering her a small smile of gratitude. 'I'd like to recover whatever he used to wound her, too. The murder weapon might be his bare hands, but he must have used some sort of edged or pointed weapon to bleed her out as well.'

'Sir?'

'Yes, Olly.'

'Sorry, sir, but you keep saying "he". Shouldn't we be a bit more open to the idea of a female killer?'

Ford caught Mick Tanner's eye-roll. 'Let's settle on "they" for now. Now, what about motives-slash-lines of enquiry?'

'Robbery gone wrong?' Jan asked.

'Nothing taken. Next?'

'Jealous partner?' This from Mick.

'Husband's deceased, but we'll check for boyfriends. Next?'

'Stalker,' a civilian investigator suggested.

'Possible. Can you look into that, please? Anything else?'

'Work colleague with a grudge?' Olly offered.

'Seems a bit over the top for a professional rivalry, but yes, possible.'

'What if the woman was only collateral damage?' Nat, standing at the back of the room, asked.

'Meaning?'

'We're all talking about Angie. Her ex, her stalker, her colleagues. What if the killer was interested in Kai?'

Ford frowned. *Please don't let it be a child killer.*

'That's an interesting idea, Nat. Let's look at all the nonces in our patch with convictions for violence as well as their usual scumbaggery.'

'Sir?' It was Olly again. 'Aren't we all avoiding the obvious?'

Ford sighed. Bloody graduate fast-trackers. 'Which is?'

'Stranger murder.'

'They're very rare. But then, so are murder scenes like ours. How do you explain the lack of evidence of forced entry or defensive wounds on Angie Halpern's body? Wouldn't she try to fight off a stranger?'

Olly frowned. 'He rings the doorbell and gives her a line. Something to make her trust him. Then he bashes her over the head to subdue her so he can bleed her out.'

'Olly could have a point, boss,' Mick said. 'After all, she's hardly going to let a stalker in, is she?'

'I don't think a woman living on her own would let a stranger into her home just on the strength of a line,' Jan said, making air-quotes around the final word. 'Especially not if her little boy was in the flat with her.'

'Fine,' Mick said. 'Say she knows him, then. Maybe not well. But enough to trust him. He's not a threat, so she lets him in.'

Ford decided it was time to refocus the discussion. 'What about the blood?' he asked the room. 'It's obviously not just a by-product of an attack. Angie and Kai were posed. No violence to the bodies, beyond the obvious. Does blood mean something to our killer? Let me hear your ideas. Word association. Blood.'

'Horror films,' Jools said.

'Menstruation, childbirth,' Jan said, to a groan from Mick Tanner.

'Do we have to?' he complained.

She glared at him. 'You've got a female victim, a mother, posed with her child. You saw the photos. She had her trousers pulled down and Kai's curled into her lap like a foetus. If that doesn't say her gender mattered, you need to think harder.'

'A&E,' Nat said. 'We've all been up there in our careers. Place is awash with it. My youngest cut his hand on a new penknife last year. I took him up there with blood leaking all over my new upholstery.'

'Those LA gangs, Bloods and Crips,' someone added.

Then the flood gates opened.

'The bucket of blood in *Carrie*.'

'Haemophilia.'

'*Rambo First Blood*.'

'*Dracula*.'

'*My Bloody Valentine*.'

Ford held his hands up for quiet. 'Well, well. I didn't realise what a creatively out-there team I had. Well done, everyone. That was illuminating. Not sure where it gets us at the moment, but keep in mind that the blood probably means something to our killer.' He started gathering his papers together. 'Assignments. Jan, you're sorted. Mick, can you take Olly and start looking into Angie's background? Jools, I want you to run a search on the PNC, HOLMES, all the usual databases for murders and/or violent assaults where blood played a role over and above the usual spillage. I want reader/recorders for all the data we pull in.'

Ford hated the alphabet soup of acronyms spawned by modern policing. PNC, the Police National Computer, wasn't too bad. But he reckoned whoever had thought up HOLMES – Home Office Large Major Enquiry System – should be shot.

'Sir?'

Ford bit back a sigh. 'Olly, yes.'

'What about a psychologist? You said we shouldn't focus on the weirdness, but the number painted in blood and everything. I mean, shouldn't we call in a psychologist or a profiler?'

'No. I'm not going to waste money on some minor-league academic out to make a name for themselves. They'll charge a fortune then tell me what my gut does ten times better and for nothing. And it's the easiest thing in the world to dip up some blood and do a little bit of finger painting. If *I'd* just killed my wife' – he swallowed, and continued – 'and I wanted to throw the cops off my scent, I'd give it a go.'

Olly folded his arms across his chest and looked away.

'When's the PM, boss?' Jan asked as people started shuffling papers together and leaving their seats.

'Tomorrow morning. I'll grab a few of you to attend with me. Thanks, everybody.'

The meeting broke up with much chatter as the teams discussed their assignments.

'Do you want me to have a word with Olly?' Jan asked from beside Ford.

'Why?'

'You were a bit sharp with the lad. He's only being keen.'

'He'll be fine. Just needs to learn to walk before he can run. Like we all did.'

She smiled. 'I know, boss. But I could just . . .' She paused. '. . . fill him in on why you're extra-moody today.'

'Because of Lou, you mean?' Ford asked in a low, hard-edged voice. 'Is that what you're driving at?'

She held his gaze. 'I've known you how long, boss?'

'Eight years.'

'Nine. I was here when it happened,' she said. 'Maybe you don't remember, but I took you home a couple of times after you'd had a few too many at the Wyndham Arms. Made sure Sam was staying with your neighbours.'

He frowned. Of course he remembered. 'What's your point, Jan?'

'My point is that you need to forgive yourself.'

His heart flipped. A wave of nausea rolled through him. 'What?'

'It's called survivor guilt. I read a book about it. You weren't to blame, but you feel you were because you lived and Lou – well, Lou died. And you can be a bit hard to be around on the anniversary.'

He forced himself to smile. Felt the muscles and ligaments in his jaws creaking. 'I'm OK. Really. But don't talk to Olly. If I'm the worst boss he ever has, he'll look back on this time with great fondness.'

Jan shrugged. 'You're the guv'nor.'

She left him alone in the meeting room.

Ford checked his watch. Four hours gone out of the magic twenty-four, the so-called 'golden hour'. Nobody knew when inflation had turned one hour into twenty-four. He had a sneaking feeling this one wasn't going to be filed in the 'Solved inside a day' file, where the vast majority of brawl-based homicides and domestics resided.

THREE WEEKS EARLIER

Is there a God? he wonders, smiling, as he squats in the crook of two thick tree branches. *Because if He does exist, He must have a soft spot for me.*

His pleasure stems from his discovery that his chosen victim lives in the middle of nowhere. Some sort of eco-cottage on the edge of a farm. It squats between a bramble-choked copse and a boggy field cut in two by a fast-flowing river.

He is hyper-alert, senses fine-tuned. A crow hops towards a greyish-cream clump in the middle distance he suspects is a dead sheep. Stink from muck-spreading in a field three over drifts on the breeze. The bark is rough against his skin. Then he catches sight of his quarry through the lenses of his binoculars, and everything else fades away.

Marcus will be his first human. But he's not inexperienced. Far from it. The cats will testify to that. And the rabbits, the badger and the lamb he stole from under its mother's nose in the depths of the night. But this is different. This is for the project.

Marcus strolls towards the cottage, swishing at the long grass with a stick. He resembles a tramp, in an old army jumper and greasy-looking jeans. He's tied his long, raggedy blond hair into disgusting tangled lumpy strings. What do they call them? Dreads?

Well, Marcus, my boy, you'll have a lot of dreading to do when you meet me for the first time.

He waits for the tree-hugger to go inside, then climbs down, straightens his jacket and saunters over to the door.

He pastes that dopey smile on to his face, the one that charms the old dears up at the hospital, and he knocks. Three times.

The door opens. Marcus smiles at him. *Stupid, trusting human beings.*

'Hi, Marcus. My name's Harvey. From the food bank. May I come in?'

DAY TWO, 6.30 P.M.

Ford finished updating his policy book and grabbed his car keys. On the way out to the car park, a shout made him turn round. Hannah was hurrying towards him.

'DI Ford, wait!'

He waited for her to reach him.

'Can I speak to you, please?'

'What is it?'

She was twisting the ring around her finger again. 'When DS Cable asked about psychologists in the briefing, you dismissed the idea.'

'Only because it's unnecessary. The young ones always want to go outside for profilers at the merest sniff of something unusual, instead of doing proper coppering.'

'I didn't mention this before, but my PhD is in cognitive neuroscience. I went on to develop expertise in forensic psychology. I specialised in the psychology of lying. That's what I was working on with the FBI.'

'Which is amazing. But I don't see—'

'If you think there's some value in discussing the killer's mental state, you wouldn't need to spend money on an external profiler. I could help you.'

Ford checked his watch. 'I have to get home to my son. Can I offer you a lift? We can speak in the car.'

'Yes, please. I live in Harnham. It's—'

'I know it. We live there, too. Rainhill Road.'

'I've walked that way. Which house is yours?'

'Jump in. I'll show you.'

She cast an appraising eye over the dusty Discovery. 'Your car isn't very smart. I thought all detectives drove classic cars. You know, old Rovers or Saab convertibles.'

He smiled. 'I think you've been watching too much TV.'

A summer shower had created wide puddles on both sides of the narrow road leading to Ford's house, and he took childish delight in running his nearside wheels through as many of them as possible, making Hannah laugh.

'Sam used to love doing that,' he said. 'He'd beg me to take him puddle-hunting after a big rainstorm.'

He turned off the road and parked on a gravel drive encircling a flower bed. Somehow, on the short journey home, he'd invited Hannah to stay for something to eat. She had a way of speaking that he found unsettling, yet fascinating; direct, seemingly unembarrassable and ready to discuss anything and everything under the sun.

'Come on,' he said. 'I'll introduce you to Sam.'

She pointed at an engraved slate rectangle set into the wall beside the front door, half-hidden by honeysuckle. 'Windgather. What's that?'

'It's a crag in the Peak District.'

'Why did you name your house after a crag in the Peak District?'

'My wife and I loved climbing there when we were beginners.'

'OK,' she said.

Inside, his head still full of the honeysuckle's sweet perfume, he led her through to the kitchen, yelling up the stairs as he went. 'Sam. Come down. We've got a visitor.'

Upstairs, a door slammed. Then came a thumping on the stairs, as if a heavy item of furniture had toppled over and tumbled all the way to the bottom. Hannah turned to Ford and raised her eyebrows in a question.

He smiled. 'Wait.'

The door opened. Framed in the rectangle stood a boy, nearing six foot, dressed in skinny jeans and a Metallica T-shirt. His shoulders were narrow, his hips slim, his legs long. His curly hair drooped over dark brown eyes above a prominent nose waiting for the rest of the face to catch up with it.

He looked at Hannah.

'Hello,' she said, extending her hand. 'I'm Hannah.'

Not Dr Fellowes, Ford mused.

Sam said, 'Hi,' as he took her hand and had his pumped up and down three times.

'Hannah's a colleague at work. She's a CSI,' Ford said.

At this, Sam's eyes, projecting biblical levels of boredom just a moment earlier, flashed wide. He pushed hair away from his forehead. 'Like on the TV?'

'Yes,' she said, smiling. 'In fact, I am a senior CSI. I am also the deputy manager of the CSI team, and I have a PhD. I used to teach at the FBI Academy in Quantico, Virginia.'

'That is so cool.'

'What? You never say my job's cool,' Ford protested.

'Yeah, and there's a good reason for that, Dad. It's not.'

'Today I investigated a murder scene,' Hannah said. 'It was very gruesome. The victims were seated in a pool of blood.'

'Whoa! No way. Like, what happened?'

'We don't know yet. But I expect we'll find out. How old are you, Sam?'

'Oh, er, fifteen.'

'And is Sam your nickname?'

'Not really. At school they call me Mondeo. You know, because of—'

'Ford. Your surname. The Ford Mondeo was the best-selling large family car in the UK until 2007. At that point it was over-taken, which is a joke, by the way, by the new-look Vauxhall Vectra.'

'Awesome. Do you, like, know all about cars and everything?'

'I don't know all about everything. But I looked it up on Wikipedia today. Because DI Ford is called Henry at work. After Henry Ford, who founded the Ford Motor Company on June the sixteenth, 1903.'

'Wait, what? Does he make you call him DI Ford at work?'

'He wouldn't tell me his Christian name, so yes, I call him DI Ford.'

Ford held his hands out. 'I said Henry was fine. Or plain Ford. I think *Dr* Fellowes is having some fun at my expense.'

She put her hand flat against her chest. 'Me? No. I would never do that.' Then she winked at Sam.

'Ooh, burn! Dad, she totally owned you!' Sam held up his right hand, palm towards Hannah. 'High five!'

She cocked her head to one side and looked at Sam's upraised palm. Ford noticed a fleeting tightness around her eyes. Then she raised her own right hand and smacked it hard against Sam's, pro-ducing a loud pop in the kitchen. For some reason he couldn't explain to himself, Ford found Sam's shocked expression amusing.

Sam cooked a scratch meal of pasta and pesto with a pile of grated Parmesan. As his son placed heaped bowls in front of the two adults and a third for himself, Ford's eyes prickled and he had to swallow down a lump in his throat. Hannah was sitting where Lou used to. Back when it had been the three of them together.

After taking a few mouthfuls, Hannah looked up at Ford. 'Your wife,' she said. 'Is she travelling on business?'

Ford shook his head. Sighed. Why did it never get any easier? Even after all this time? He caught Sam's eye. Sam looked down at his bowl of pasta. *Poor kid. He doesn't deserve to have this raked over every time someone new comes to the house.*

'She died six years ago,' Ford said quietly, looking at a photo of the two of them taken at Windgather. Lou was smiling, her eyes sparkling in spring sunshine, a loose strand of hair whipping in front of her face.

'How did she die?' Hannah asked, eyebrows raised.

That was interesting. No confused attempt to say something sympathetic.

'It was a climbing accident.'

'Was she not roped on properly? That is one of the five main causes of death for climbers.'

Ford glanced at Sam, who had frozen, a fork laden with green-tinged pasta halfway to his open mouth.

'Something like that,' Ford said, finally.

'I'm sorry she died.'

'Thanks.'

Looking down so a floppy lock of hair covered his eyes, Sam scraped up the last of his food, clanked his spoon and fork into the bowl and left the table, already fishing his phone from a trouser pocket.

Hannah watched him go, then turned back to face Ford. 'If you try to climb Everest, you have a one in sixty-one chance of dying. If you reach the summit, it's one in twenty-seven.'

Something about the way the woman sitting opposite him saw the world made him smile, despite Sam's earlier reaction.

She frowned. 'Did I say something funny? I was just telling you about mortality rates on Everest.'

He shook his head. 'No. It wasn't you. Tell me, what did you make of the crime scene this morning?'

'He's organised. We found very little physical evidence. No DNA. And he didn't mess up her flat. I think he was focused on the blood.'

'And the 666? That's the number of the beast.'

'According to the latest theological research, the number of the beast is 616,' she said. 'But if our killer is following the text of Revelation 13:15, which I suspect he may be, then he could think that.'

'What is its significance for us?' Ford asked.

'I have no idea. It depends on its significance for the killer. If he's sane, it could be a taunt, or an attempt to throw you off the trail,' she said. 'If he's insane, he may believe he is doing the Devil's work. Either way, I would focus on hard evidence and try to find someone who had a reason to kill her. It would be unwise to fixate on the supposedly satanic implications unless and until we have a compelling reason.'

Ford nodded. She'd expressed his own feelings. 'I agree. Too many coppers get an idea in their minds and then they're unwilling to consider alternatives. You can miss vital pieces of evidence that way, ignore leads, even miss suspects sitting right in front of you.'

She nodded. 'If you think in a typical fashion, you arrive at typical conclusions. You seem to be different. Have you done any lateral-thinking courses?'

He smiled. 'No. But my mum used to say I'd never do anything the easy way if there was a different way of doing it. I used to make model aeroplanes but ignore the instructions.'

'And what were your results like?'

'Interesting. Not airworthy, but definitely unusual.'

'Even if you *had* followed the instructions, they still wouldn't have been airworthy.'

'Why not?'

She frowned as if he'd said something stupid. 'Because they were models.'

'Good point. I never thought of that before.'

She looked up at the kitchen clock. 'I should go. I have to feed Uta Frith.'

'Who, or what, is Uta Frith?'

'My cat. I named her for the Emeritus professor of cognitive development at UCL Institute of Cognitive Neuroscience. Uta Frith is my hero.'

Wrongfooted yet again, Ford stood. 'Need a lift home?'

She shook her head. 'No, thanks. I can walk from here. See you at work tomorrow.' A shy smile. 'Henry.'

With Hannah gone, Ford went in search of Sam. He always made a point of asking him how his day had gone, even if it was only met with a grunted 'Fine.' Hannah's arrival had skewed their normal routine.

Sam wasn't in his bedroom. Or the garden, sitting on the old swing and scrolling through his social media. That left only one place. Ford sighed. Sam felt the anniversary of his mother's death just as keenly as Ford. He just dealt with it differently. *Maybe bringing Hannah home wasn't such a great idea.*

Ford walked back to the house and opened a door to the right of the kitchen. It led to the garage. Neon tubes cast an unforgiving glow over the spotless interior. Sam was where Ford had expected to find him, slumped in the red leather driver's seat of a long, low silver E-Type Jaguar, his long fingers caressing the smooth wood of the steering wheel.

Ford remembered the day Lou's parents had presented them with the keys. It was two days before their wedding. Lou's father had made a lot of money in banking and spent a good deal of it building up a small collection of classic sports cars.

'Dad!' Lou had said, a huge grin lighting up her suntanned face. 'You're not serious?'

Her father smiled as he ushered his daughter into the driver's seat, closing the door with a soft click once she'd settled behind the wheel.

'You've always loved her. Mummy and I want you to have her.' He turned to Ford. 'Get in, then. Take her for a spin, and we'll have some champagne when you get back.'

Laughing, the wind blowing her hair about her face, Lou drove fast through the Berkshire countryside. And Ford watched his wife-to-be, astounded that she was soon to be his.

◆ ◆ ◆

Ford ran a finger along the cold, smooth side of the car, its paint unmarked by a single scratch, its chrome reflecting his distorted face so that his eyes drew down into ovals.

'You OK, mate?' he asked, opening the passenger door and sitting beside his son.

Sam was staring straight ahead. His eyes glistened in the neon light. 'Why did she have to ask about Mum?'

Ford laid a hand on his son's shoulder, but Sam shrugged it off, irritably. 'Hannah was interested, that's all. She doesn't seem to have much of a filter.'

'*You think?* Is she, like, on the spectrum, or something?'

'I don't know. Would that matter?'

'Of course not! I said, she's cool. It's just—' Sam heaved a sigh, raising his slender shoulders and letting them slump again.

'What?' Ford asked. He knew, though. Knew what was coming. 'Tell me what happened.'

'I've told you. Lots of times. And I know you've searched for the media reports.'

'Tell me again!' Sam snapped, hammering his palm on the steering wheel's wooden rim.

Avoiding seeing the scene that played out in his nightmares, Ford began his well-rehearsed version of the truth like a witness coached by an exacting brief.

'We were climbing Pen-y-holt. It was a beautiful day. Your mum's eyes really shone in that bright sunshine. We were trying a new route and it was harder than we expected. Mum hurt her leg. It happened in a split second. There was nothing I could do. I went for help, but by the time the coastguard arrived it was too late to save her. She drowned.'

'*Why* couldn't you do anything? Why couldn't you save her, Dad? Tell me the truth for once.'

Ford sighed. 'If I could have, Sam, don't you think I would have?'

Sam's tears were flowing freely now, dripping off the sharp point of his chin on to his lap, creating dark splotches on the denim.

'You're lying,' he said quietly.

'No, I'm not. Why would you say that?'

'You always told me Mum was a great climber. She wouldn't mess up. I know she wouldn't!' Sam's voice cracked on this last word.

Ford's heart turned over at its frail sound. He replaced his hand, and this time Sam left it there.

'When does it stop hurting, Dad?' he said, after a long pause.

'I don't know. Maybe it never stops. Maybe it just dulls a little, each passing day.'

DAY THREE, 10.00 A.M.

The specialist forensic post-mortem suite at Salisbury District Hospital shared a basement with two huge incinerators. They were kept busy day and night burning medical waste, from bandages to body parts. It was agreed that the guys tending 'Vesta' and 'Vulcan' possessed the darkest sense of humour in the hospital.

FPM Room 1 was full this particular morning. Standing behind the stainless-steel table bearing a sheet-covered body was Dr Georgina Eustace, the pathologist, clad in navy scrubs, rubber boots and a hinged visor on a white plastic headband. Flanking her, also in scrubs, were a mortician and a photographer. Ford had brought Mick and Jools. Alec Reid was there. 'Wouldn't miss it for the world, Henry,' he'd said earlier that morning. He'd brought Hannah with him, too.

The mortuary air-extraction system was fighting a losing battle against the smell rising from what had once been Angie Halpern. A sharp tang of disinfectant overlaid the stink.

Eustace handed round a blue glass screw-top jar. 'My signature blend,' she said to Hannah. 'Menthol, camphor, eucalyptus and thymol.'

Once everyone had smeared a little of the waxy paste under their nostrils, Georgina began. Without any ceremony, she drew the dark-blue sheet back and handed it to the mortician. He balled it and tossed it dead-centre into a plastic scrubs bin in the corner.

After removing and examining the clothes and jewellery, and describing their condition for her recorder, Georgina began work on the body.

She took a large-bladed scalpel and cut deep into the skin of the left shoulder, passed beneath the breasts and drew the blade down in a long, single cut to the pubic bone. A second diagonal cut formed the Y-incision that allowed access to the internal organs.

In Ford's mind, a victim – a *named* victim – was the person on his murder wall at Bourne Hill. Their earthly remains, which were by no means always as intact as those in front of him, were just a body. Separating the two like this helped him cope.

'Henry, come and look at this,' Georgina said.

She was using a stainless-steel rod to lift a patch of blood-matted hair from the left side of the skull. As she pulled it away, the hair detached from the scalp, draping over the polished steel like noodles on a chopstick.

He looked down at a crescent-shaped gash through which bone gleamed. The skull appeared intact.

'Doesn't look hard enough to have caused her death,' he said.

'Agreed. If it was textbook blunt-force trauma, I'd expect to see comminuted spiral fractures in the temporal bone and a depressed fracture beneath the wound site.' She spoke to the mortician. 'Pete, could you pass me the tweezers, please.'

Peering at the upper edge of the crescent, she picked free a blood-soaked scrap of tissue. Wordlessly, the mortician proffered a glass dish, into which she tapped it.

Next, she turned her attention to the throat. She used the pointer to prod at the upper end of the windpipe, just before it disappeared beneath the jawline.

'See that? Her hyoid bone's broken.'

'Manual strangulation. Is that what killed her?'

Georgina shook her head. 'I think not. She was exsangui-nated, which required her heart to be still beating. Unless I find any other injuries, here's what I think happened.' Ford noticed Mick and Jools opening their notebooks, which pleased him. 'Her attacker knocked her down with a blow to the head using a weapon with a curved edge. She would have been disorientated, if not knocked out. Then he throttled her into unconsciousness. Finally, he bled her.'

Ford pointed to the blackened puncture wound high on the inside of the right thigh. 'What's that?'

Georgina took a second rod, just a couple of millimetres thick, and probed the wound.

'There we go,' she said, a note of triumph in her voice.

The thin rod slid upwards into the thigh.

'He used a needle,' Ford said.

'More than likely. Something wide-bore. Like a trocar.'

'So cause of death was exsanguination,' Ford said, 'preceded by throttling and a hefty whack with a weapon of some kind.'

'I'll need to complete the PM, but yes, that's what it looks like.'

'What about the boy?' he asked, trying not to visualise the invasive procedures she would have to inflict on his little body.

'I conducted a cursory examination first thing this morning. No BFT. No cuts. No signs of strangulation. You'd think he'd just gone to sleep, except—'

'Except for what?'

'Except for a needle prick on the left side of his neck.'

'Another trocar?' Jools asked.

Georgina shook her head. 'Regular hypodermic. I've sent a blood sample to toxicology.'

'When will you know what it was?'

'I fast-tracked it. Tomorrow?'

'Excellent. Thanks, George.'

They watched the rest of the PM, but Ford's mind was already wandering. Away from the sterile confines of the autopsy suite and on towards the next couple of days. Because whether the killer was sane or not, he was a rat gnawing at Ford's insides. And Ford was starting to suspect he'd have another body on his hands if he didn't move fast.

SPRING, THIRTY YEARS EARLIER

His father towers over him, a rugby ball in one massive hand, his florid face a snarling mask of hatred.

'I'd rather go for a walk, Daddy,' the big man simpers, in cruel mimicry of his young son's voice. ''Course you would. The idea you might, actually, want to do something manly . . . Jesus! You're worthless, aren't you? I can't believe my blood runs in your veins.'

The boy knows what's coming and so he steels himself for the tirade. Maybe he can say something to pacify the ogre in front of him.

'We could go for a walk in the countryside together, if you'd like?'

'What, and bring back some disgusting roadkill like you did last time? I think not. You know, if Luke had lived, if *he'd* been born and *you'd* died in your mother's belly, I bet I'd be out there now, cheering him on at a match, instead of this, this . . . *charade* of fatherhood.'

Without warning, his father backhands him across the face. It's his favourite blow. The chunky gold signet ring catches him on the lower lip, as it has so many times before. A spray of blood jets out and hits the wall.

The taste of his own blood – salty, coppery – is as familiar to him as his morning cereal. He glares up at his father. *One day, Dad.*

'Don't look at me like that, you little poofter!' his father shouts. 'You can go crying to your mummy, but you clean up that mess first,' he adds, jabbing a thick finger at the arc of scarlet spattering the bedroom wallpaper.

Later, when he can hear his father's drunken snores, he retrieves his sketchbook from under his mattress. He opens his box of ninety-six Caran d'Ache coloured pencils – a present from Granny and Grandpa – and frowns. The reds are always so much shorter than the others.

As he colours in the splashes and streams, the spots and the spatters, he thinks of his dead twin.

He turns the pages, looking for a clean sheet. Past a dead rabbit, guts spread out like butterfly wings each side of the torso. A deer, missing its eyes. A man, dismembered, legs where arms should be, arms splayed from the pelvis. Red. Always lots of red. He smiles, turns over the page, and begins a fresh image.

A quiet double knock at the door jerks him out of his reverie. He snaps the sketchbook shut just in time. His mother twists the knob and enters, a shy mouse compared to her roaring lion of a husband.

She purses her lips when she sees his swollen, scabbed lip.

'Did Daddy lose his temper with you again?' she asks, kneeling beside him.

'Yes, Mummy. I wish he was dead.'

'Oh, no, darling! Never say that. Not ever. Daddy is a good man. He does love you.' She pauses. 'In his own way. But losing Luke, it made him so very unhappy. We both have to try to understand him. Poor Daddy.'

Then she encircles him and draws him close. But while he stays inside her protective embrace, all he's thinking is, *When you're gone, I* will *kill him. I promise. Even if it takes the rest of my life. I'll make him watch his own blood leaking away.*

73

DAY THREE, 2.55 P.M.

Ford had been right, Hannah mused. Forensics *was* quiet. Which was just how she liked it. She could manage an hour or so in the noise and hubbub of the CID office. Or outside of work, in a busy pub with a friend. But eventually it all got too much and she needed to find somewhere quiet to recharge her batteries.

Here, though, in her corner of the office, noise-cancelling headphones clamped over her ears, the overhead fluorescent tubes removed in favour of an Anglepoise lamp on her desk, she could focus. And focusing was her superpower.

The pathologist had sent over a sample she'd recovered from the woman's body. Hannah took a scalpel and slit the red tape sealing the transparent plastic evidence bag. Using a pair of slender tweezers with angled tips, she picked the tiny scrap of material from the corner of the bag and mounted it on a slide.

For larger items of physical evidence, like this one, she liked to begin with a hand-magnifier before going to the microscope. Sometimes that was all she needed. And it was a bit like Sherlock Holmes, so obviously that was good.

'Elementary, my dear Ford,' she whispered, as she bent her head to the fat circle of precision-ground glass.

She found herself looking at an irregular corrugated fragment of turquoise paper, tinged red across one half, and measuring, according to a transparent plastic ruler she placed next to it, six millimetres by two.

Using the scalpel tip and the tweezers, she stretched the fragment out flat. The lower half of a set of characters became visible: printed characters, white out of the turquoise. She copied them on to a sheet of paper.

'It's a postcode,' she said, before sketching in the upper halves. 'SE1 9SG.'

She swivelled round to her PC and tapped it into Google. Nothing meaningful. Just a list of sites offering postcode look-ups. She tutted and tweaked her search terms.

Companies in SE1 9SG

She scanned the first page of results and smiled as the underlying turquoise beneath the blood stain fired the connection in her brain. 'Heinz!' she said. 'You hit her with a tin of baked beans.'

She liked the fact that here, in the quiet, ordered calm of Forensics, nobody said mean things when she talked to herself. Everybody did it.

She took a cotton bud, dipped the end in distilled water and lifted a sample from the paper. She put it into a second evidence bag and sealed it, writing, *Halpern, A, Blood sample from PM head wound fragment*, and a computer-generated reference number on the label.

Alec Reid wandered over. 'Find something interesting, Hannah?'

She looked up, pleased that he was standing one metre back from her chair. 'I think she was knocked out with a Heinz baked-bean tin.'

'I dare say Henry would be interested to know what you've discovered.'

She frowned. 'You "dare"? Are you worried, then?'

He smiled. 'It's just my way of saying I think you should go and tell him.'

'OK. Then I will.'

◆ ◆ ◆

Ford looked up from his screen to see Hannah striding across the room towards his door. Whether he'd sensed her or whether it was simply that her distinctive gait sounded different to anyone else's, he didn't have time to consider further. She walked into his office without knocking. He didn't mind in the least, but it showed a certain level of confidence from the new girl.

'I've got two pieces of evidence for you.' She paused. 'Henry.'

She laid the bags before him, like a cat depositing a dead mouse in front of her owner.

He peered at them. 'What have we got?'

'That's a fragment of the label from a tin of Heinz baked beans. That's a sample of the blood it's soaked in: Angie's. We have the weapon used to stun her.'

He smiled up at her. 'That's excellent, Hannah, really good. Listen, I'm a bit short-handed here, everyone's out. Could you get over to the crime scene and see if you can find any tins of Heinz beans? Bring them all back here. Maybe we'll get lucky and find a print.'

Grinning, she nodded, and about-turned.

Ford returned to the question that he wanted answering next. The sex of the killer. Ford's every instinct said the killer was male. The odds on this being a female attacker were tiny. An amelogenin test on a DNA sample would confirm it, but until then he'd content himself with his hunch.

In a notebook he wrote:

Suspect profile
Likely male, or muscular/strong female. (If female, cross-fit/bodybuilder/athlete?)

At some point he would be drawing up a suspect matrix and assigning priority scores. He'd score women low unless they fitted this new criterion.

Later that afternoon, he gathered the team together for a progress meeting. He'd put Olly Cable on victimology – compiling a detailed profile of Angie: her work, hobbies, clubs, where she went grocery shopping, her spending habits, medical history, past relationships . . . the works. It was to him he turned first.

'Olly, tell us about Angie.'

Olly lifted his chin and squared his shoulders. 'We're just starting out, but so far what emerges is a solid, hard-working single mum whom the neighbours all liked. Kept herself to herself, mainly on account of having Kai to look after.'

'Anything stand out?' Ford interrupted, not wanting a straight recitation of something they could all read for themselves.

'The neighbour—'

'The Gregorys?'

'No, the ground-floor flat.' Olly consulted his notebook. 'A Mr Angus Fairford. Freelance IT worker. Said Angie had money worries. We're waiting for her financial records to come in.'

'Maybe she was borrowing off a loan shark,' Mick said. 'Got behind on her payments. He decides to make an example to put the frighteners on his other *clients*. Maybe he goes too far, panics, kills the kid.'

Ford nodded. 'Good. We'll call that a line of enquiry. Check on the local nominals. See if anyone's been throwing their weight around. Maybe even newcomers trying to muscle in.'

'Any boyfriends?' Jan asked. 'Maybe the downstairs neighbours heard rows, stuff being thrown around?'

Olly shook his head. 'I talked to the Gregorys. They said, apart from Kai having the odd paddy, they were so quiet you wouldn't have known they were there.'

Ford surveyed his team. It was early days. Maybe not the golden hour any more, but everyone still had that sharp-eyed, eager look about them. He knew it wouldn't last for ever. Time to broach the subject that was sitting like an uninvited guest in the corner.

'Let's speculate about the idea of a stranger murder,' he said, glancing at Olly, who nodded back. 'He gains entry using subterfuge. Tells her he's from the gas company, or whatever. He's plausible, charming, self-effacing, he makes himself appear unthreatening. And she invites him in. Jools?'

The DC sat up straighter. 'Right. It's a stranger murder. But not like in a fight or a random street attack when the pubs close. I think he chose her. Her specifically – otherwise, why take the risk of going to her flat and encountering potential witnesses inside?'

Ford nodded. It was good thinking, and once again demonstrated Jools's background in the Criminal Investigation Branch of the Military Police. 'Go on.'

'The question we need to answer is, why did the killer choose Angie Halpern? And did he also choose Kai? Or was he just' – she shrugged and pulled a face – 'having fun?'

'Why *did* he choose her, then?' Ford asked the room as a whole.

'She turned him on,' Mick said. 'He's got a thing for petite blondes.'

'No sexual assault, Mick, remember?' Jan said.

Mick thrust his jaw out. 'He could still've had a thing for her type. He just wants to, I don't know, possess them.'

'The scene didn't look like a sexual fantasy to me,' Hannah said.

Ford noticed her blush as the rest of the team looked round. 'Because?' he prompted.

'Although her trousers were pulled down, her breasts and genitals were covered. And not mutilated, as we saw at the post-mortem. No bite marks. No semen or other bodily fluids found at the scene in any of the obvious places. Her underwear drawer, her bed, her body. But—'

'She could still—' Mick interrupted.

'—the main reason I say this is the positioning of Kai. He was sitting in her lap, hands tucked up under his chin, head turned in towards her chest. To me it was a tableau of motherhood. *Caring* motherhood.'

'What are you saying?' Mick asked her, turning fully round in his chair to face her head-on. 'We've got a killer with mummy issues?'

'I'm saying it doesn't look sexual, as I think I said a moment ago.' Hannah, though pink to the tips of her ears, held her ground.

Ford was impressed. 'I'm with Hannah. I don't see sex as the motive. I think it's the blood.'

'You think he's drinking it, boss?'

The questioner was a retired general CID detective sergeant with thirty years under his belt and a new job as a police staff investigator.

Over brief banter about vampires, Ford said, 'I hope to God not.'

'You don't need to hope to God,' Hannah said. 'Ingesting more than a few millilitres of blood produces an emetic reaction.'

'You're saying he'd vomit,' Ford said.

'It's the combination of the iron-rich haemoglobin, the warmth, the salt and the viscosity. It also leads to kidney failure.'

'So any more than that—'

'—would be far too much to keep down. I took a random sampling at twenty spots in the pool. No saliva. And no vomit at the scene.'

Ford ran a palm down from his forehead to his chin. He groaned. 'Great. Not sex. Not robbery. No sign of a stalker-ex. No vampirism. Fine. Let's forget motive for the moment. I want us to be all over her life tomorrow. Interviewing friends, former partners if we can find any, people she worked with up at the hospital, any volunteering she did. I want a suspect pool.' *Before he does it again.*

He gave out actions, listened to reports from each team, then dismissed them with an instruction to remember to eat and to get some sleep when they went home. He saw a long evening at his desk stretching ahead of him. Possibly a night, too. He had to make a call before he resumed working. To his neighbours.

Miles and Eleanor Pitt were good people – and their son and his were best friends. Sam often stayed over with Josh. But he didn't want to have to explain the situation on the phone. Not to a civilian. He texted Miles instead.

Can Sam stay with you guys tonight, pls?

A few minutes later, the reply pinged back.

Of course, mate. Take care.

K. Thanks.

He texted Sam.

Working late. Tea at the Pitts and a bed, too.

Ping.

K

An hour later, his concentration waning, Ford was relieved to see Hannah standing at his open door.

'You're working late.'

He spread his arms out to indicate the mass of papers on his desk. 'It would seem so.'

'I was thinking about Kai Halpern.'

He beckoned her in. 'What about him?'

'The way the killer posed him says that whatever motivated him to kill Angie didn't translate to Kai,' she said.

'Go on.'

'The bludgeoning, the strangling: they say the killer was angry at her. Angry enough to kill her, even though he probably didn't know her.' She pushed a stray strand of hair back behind her ear. 'But he took care to arrange Kai so he looked peaceful and cared for. Protected.'

'Meaning?'

'Meaning, you could be looking for a man who felt unloved as a child. It's no good for profiling,' she added hurriedly. 'But when you arrest a suspect, it could be useful in your interviews.'

Ford nodded. 'Did your parents shout at you? Call you names? That sort of thing?'

'Exactly. Childhood abuse often figures in the psychopathology of murderers.'

Something told him the young woman sitting opposite him was wasted in Forensics. 'That's really interesting thinking. Thank you. Any news on the physical evidence?'

'I'm starting on the fingerprints next. We retrieved a couple from the grocery items on the table. I'll let you know what we get as soon as I possibly can.' Hannah turned to go.

'Wait! I've been thinking about trophies. What do you think about the idea that he took a photo of the scene? It was so carefully staged, he'd feel it was a waste never to see it again, don't you think?'

'That's an interesting idea,' she said. 'We know men tend to be visually orientated, sexually, so although he didn't carry out any sexual activities at the crime scene, he may be using the photo, or photos, as masturbation aids.' And with that, she left.

DAY FOUR, 3.15 A.M.

Matty checked the time. Three fifteen. Perfect. He approached the old woman's bed. He knew her name. June Evans. He knew all their names. He made a point of it. They loved him for it.

June was asleep. Her dementia had worsened since she'd come in for her surgery, and now she didn't know where she was half the time. Which, in some ways, was a blessing. For Matty, anyway.

He looked around the darkened ward. The only nurse on duty, Marisol, was nowhere to be seen. He bent over June and felt under the covers for her left wrist. Found it, as thin as a bird's leg. He could break the fragile bones like that!

The gold bangle was warm, from her blood, he supposed. It was loose around her bones and he had no trouble slipping it off. Just as he pocketed it, she awoke and screamed.

'Help, I'm being murdered!'

Matty's heart jumped into his throat, and he patted her as she sat bolt upright in bed. Around them, her neighbours were waking or turning over in their sleep, asking what was wrong, then, seeing it was June, tutting or sighing and flopping back down again.

'Nobody's trying to murder you, Mrs Evans,' he crooned. 'You had a nightmare, that's all. Look, it's Matty.'

She held a thin arm up, the veins blue under the papery, liver-spotted skin. 'My bracelet. He stole it!' she said, quieter now.

Matty shook his head as he thrust her arm back under the covers. 'You left it at home. You remember? In your jewellery box.'

'Did I?'

'Yes. It's perfectly safe. Now, close your eyes and go back to sleep. Sweet dreams.'

Her eyes closed. 'Night, night, Daddy.'

'Night, night, Junie.'

He met Marisol on his way out.

'Hi, Matty. Everything all right?'

'I was just dropping off some clean bedding. Mrs Evans had a funny turn. I managed to quieten her down before she woke the others.'

Marisol smiled. 'You're a star.' She looked past him at the old lady's bed. 'Poor old dear, doesn't know what day it is any more.'

'I know,' he said. 'Tragic.'

Ford looks down at Lou. She dangles beneath him from a rope. She's screaming the same three words over and over again.

'Don't kill me! Don't kill me! Don't kill me!'

The blood spurts from the trocar protruding from her naked thigh. Who goes mountaineering naked? It's not worth the risk. On the Pembrokeshire coast, the weather can change in an instant.

He looks up. Hannah's at the top of the stack, reaching down to him.

'Take my hand, Henry,' she says. 'You have a seventy per cent chance of living if you do.'

He shakes his head. 'I can't. I have to stay here, with Lou!' he bellows, as the wind whips across the stack, chilling him to the bone.

A gout of blood issues from Lou's thigh. It sways beneath her, trailing all the way to the rocks below. She's caught between the two ropes, the white nylon and the scarlet blood, suspended in time, in the 'now', between 'then' and 'to come' . . .

. . . then: happy family. Mummy, Daddy, Sam.

. . . now: screaming wife, weeping husband.

. . . to come: widower. Motherless boy. Corpse.

The rope parts with a snap. She falls, screaming, 'It's the blood! Follow the blood!'

He wakes, sweating, shouting, 'Lou!', his face wet. His digital alarm clock tells him it's 3.23 a.m.

DAY FOUR, 8.23 A.M.

Five hours later, Ford was drinking coffee while he waited for the team to assemble. His eyes felt as though someone had poured sand into them. Once everyone was seated, or standing, in front of him, he assigned jobs. He asked Jan to search Angie's workplace.

'She must have had a locker. Check that, and anywhere else she could have stored stuff.'

Jan nodded and made a note.

'Everyone else, I want you up at the hospital. I want you to find anyone and everyone who knew Angie. What was she like? Who did she pal around with? Any difficulties with patients, or their relatives? You know the drill.'

'What are you doing, Henry?' Jan asked him.

'I'm up there, too. I want to know more about blood.'

After the nightmare, he hadn't been able to sleep, so he'd gone online and found SDH's Haematology Department and its head of service, Charles Abbott.

As soon as the meeting closed, he called the hospital and found his way to Charles Abbott's secretary.

'He's extremely busy, Inspector. His list is absolutely crammed as it is. Can't this wait? I'm sure we could slot you in later this week.'

'Someone murdered a nurse at your hospital. I am the lead investigator,' he said. 'So I'm afraid it can't wait. If you could slot me in any time this morning, that would be perfect.'

◆ ◆ ◆

At 9.28 a.m. he knocked on Charles Abbott's office door.

'Come!'

That single syllable set his hackles rising.

The broad-shouldered man behind the desk radiated power and confidence. His office was a stage, set for its leading man. The wall behind him groaned under the weight of framed medical diplomas and photographs of their holder in evening dress beside minor royalty, the city's mayor in full regalia and a couple of locally based TV and film actors. A type Ford had met before. And never liked.

Abbott stood and offered his hand, smiling. They shook, briefly, and he gestured to the chair facing him.

'Please, take a seat.'

Despite the heat, Abbott wore a crisp pink shirt and navy tie. An expensive-looking suit jacket swung on a hanger from a wooden coat-rack in a corner. Sunlight streaming in through a large south-facing window gilded his tanned skin. An arrow-straight parting revealed white scalp beneath his short brown hair. Ford caught a whiff of expensive aftershave.

'Thanks for seeing me at such short notice, Dr Abbott,' Ford said.

Abbott's lips compressed into a thin, disapproving line. 'Justine tells me you gave her little choice but to comply,' he said. 'Before we go any further, and forgive me for being pompous, but might you accord me the respect to which my position as a consultant entitles me?'

'I'm sorry?'

'I am a "Mr" as in *Mr* Abbott. Not "Dr". That's for my less successful colleagues and the pill-pusher you visit when you have a sore throat or whatever. I'm sorry to insist, but I worked hard to reach my position, as I'm sure you did.'

Ford smiled. Breathed in, softly, and out again. *'Pompous' doesn't even begin to cover it.*

'My apologies, *Mr* Abbott.'

'Thank you.' Abbott checked his watch, a chunky gold number that Ford suspected was a Rolex. 'Now, please be brief, Inspector. I have patients who depend on me, rounds, and so forth.'

'What can you tell me about blood?'

Abbott frowned. 'That's a rather . . .' he paused, *'unfocused* question. I have spent the last twenty-seven years studying blood in all its many and varied forms, and the diseases that affect it, particularly cancers. I'm afraid you'll have to be a little more specific.'

'I am investigating the murder of a nurse who worked here. You may have read about it on the *Salisbury Journal* website.'

'I'm sorry, I haven't. I take the *Telegraph* for news. Old-fashioned, I know, in this digital age, but there we are,' he said, spreading his hands wide.

Ford forced himself to stay calm. 'She was exsanguinated. Bled out.'

'Yes, yes, I know my Latin.'

'We are working on the assumption that blood is significant to the killer, and I want – I would *like* – to know what blood might mean to him. Or her.'

Abbott's eyebrows shot up. 'What it might *mean*? Oh, for heaven's sake. I thought you were coming here to access my scientific knowledge. Not waste time discussing psychology.'

Ford's initial dislike of the man sitting opposite him had mutated into a deeper feeling: a sense that this alpha male was using his power to intimidate him. Or to hide something.

'Isn't psychology scientific?' Ford asked, clenching and unclenching his fist in his lap.

Abbott snorted. 'I am a medical man, Inspector. I look, rather as I imagine you do, at the evidence. Are these red blood cells sickle-shaped? Is this patient's blood deficient in clotting factors? Why is this patient's haemoglobin level so low? Facts, do you see? Not fancies.'

Ford nodding, feeling as if he were the one being interviewed, and not the other way around.

He decided to try one more time. 'Is there anything you can tell me that might help our investigation? Anything at all?'

Abbott sighed and looked at the ceiling. 'In history, blood has been associated with three principal forces. First, rather obviously, life. Second, the soul. Third, heat – from the Greek *haema*, meaning "hot" or "incandescent",' he said, in a professorial tone. 'If you *force* me to venture into psychology – and, may I add, I feel extremely uncomfortable doing so – I should imagine your killer believed he was somehow releasing his victim's life-force.'

Ford caught Abbott's suppressed shudder as he spoke the last word. What was that? Discomfort at being forced to use psychobabble, or disdain for the murder victim?

Ford nodded, writing up the insight on his mental whiteboard. It wasn't much, but it was better than nothing. Though he would have preferred something less nebulous.

'Thank you. Before I go, I'd like a list of everyone who works in this department, please. From nurses up to consultants.'

Abbott steepled his fingers in front of his face. 'I'm sure you would.'

'Shall I ask your secretary?'

'You can ask her, but I'm afraid she won't be able to help you. Not without a warrant.' Abbott smiled ruefully. 'I'd love to help, Inspector, really I would. But it's these damned privacy regulations. GDPR: ever hear of it?'

'General Data Protection Regulations.'

'Then you see the bind I'm in,' Abbott said.

Ford decided he'd had enough of this supercilious consultant. *My gut never lies to me, Abbott. I don't like you.* 'When I return with a warrant, I will obviously want to interview each person on the list, yourself included, in a more formal setting. I'm thinking Interview Room 1 at Bourne Hill Police Station. The interviews shouldn't take long. No more than an hour each. Of course, as the head of service, yours would take longer.'

'Are you threatening me?' Abbott asked smoothly. 'Because, you should know, I don't take very kindly to intimidation. I am also on rather good terms with the chief constable of Wiltshire. So tread carefully.' He smiled. Wider than before, exposing immaculate and expensive-looking dentistry. 'Just a friendly piece of advice.'

Ford breathed deeply. Observing the man facing him, but listening to his gut. *You're hiding something. That's why you're warning me off. Are you protecting someone?*

'Noted. But as I'm simply trying to solve the murder of one of your colleagues, perhaps you could try to help me. I'm sure the chief constable would appreciate your efforts.'

Abbott sighed. 'Very well, though if HR find out, I'll be for the high jump.' He picked up the phone on his desk. 'Justine? Would you print out a list of Haematology Department staff for Inspector Ford, please. He's just leaving.'

The secretary appeared a few moments later with a single sheet of A4. She dropped it into Ford's lap. The look she gave him would have cut steel.

'Thank you.'

She closed the door behind her with what he felt was rather more force than was needed.

'Have you always been interested in blood?' Ford asked.

'It's my life's work, as I believe I told you before.'

'Of course.'

'Listen, Inspector,' Abbott said, his voice softer now. 'I understand the pressures under which you're working. As a public servant myself, I have the same issues. Too many demands on my time, too little budget. Oversight, watchdogs, patients' rights groups, managers with their infernal targets. All I want to do is practise medicine – heal people – but they have me chained to a PC half the time, filling out forms like a bloody pen-pusher.'

'What's your point?'

'My point is that whilst I sympathise with your professional desire to follow every avenue, however' – he laid a flat palm on his chest – '*unlikely*, you'd be better off pursuing those with a greater chance of leading you to the killer.'

Ford frowned. 'Sorry, you've lost me. What do you mean?'

'If you really want to find your killer, why don't you look somewhere you're more likely to find him?'

Ford stood his ground, and offered Abbott a smile. 'Where would you suggest?'

'Among the lower classes, obviously.'

Ford counted to three before responding. 'Do you have any names or addresses we could investigate?'

Abbott smiled. 'Please don't patronise me. I mean, look at my own ward, for example. There's this dreadful man. A porter, for God's sake. Forever addressing me as if we're colleagues. He's always asking me about my work. Why don't you interview him?'

'Maybe I will. What's his name?'

'Now, there I can't help you. We move in completely different circles, both professionally and' – he shuddered – 'socially.'

Ford shrugged. 'Not much to go on, then.'

'No, wait!' Abbott said. 'One of my junior staff spilled some blood earlier this week. I asked this chap, the porter, to mop it up, and the ward sister found the damned fellow drawing in it, muttering all sorts of language about me as he did it. That's odd, wouldn't you say?'

Ford's pulse kicked up a notch. Abbott was a gold-plated snob with an ego that would overshadow the cathedral, but what would Sandy say? *A hunch is all very well, love, but bring me some bloody evidence.* Maybe this porter could supply it.

'Name?' he pressed.

'He said his name was—' He looked up for a second, then back at Ford. 'Matty!'

Ford looked at the list. At the bottom he found 'Kyte, Matthew, porter'. He underlined the name. 'Thank you, that's very helpful.'

Major Crimes was humming when Ford returned. He announced a meeting for 4.00 p.m.

He checked his emails. Georgina had sent him a copy of her post-mortem reports on Angie and Kai. Ignoring all the other messages, he opened the attachments. He skim-read the report on Angie first and made notes, including the manner, cause and time of death.

Angie Halpern
MOD: homicide.
COD: exsanguination.
TOD: likely between 5.00 p.m. on July 2nd and 5.00 a.m. on the 3rd.
No sexual assault.

No mutilation.

Other injuries: head wound; hyoid bone broken and bruising consistent with manual strangulation; puncture wound extending from inner left thigh into femoral artery consistent with large-bore needle such as trocar.

Toxicology: clean. Trace amounts of ibuprofen and paracetamol, female contraceptive pill.

He repeated the process with Kai's.

Kai Halpern
MOD: homicide
COD: lethal injection.
TOD: likely between 5.00 p.m. on July 2nd and 5.00 a.m. on the 3rd.
No sexual assault.
No mutilation.
Other injuries: puncture wound to left side of neck consistent with hypodermic syringe.
Toxicology: sufficient fentanyl to cause death.

Ford stared at his last note. Fentanyl? Wasn't that a powerful painkiller they gave to cancer patients? That meant the killer had taken it with him. Who had access to fentanyl? Three thoughts flashed through his mind in rapid-fire succession. Junkies. Cancer patients. Medical staff.

◆ ◆ ◆

At four that afternoon, with most of the team assembled and another cup of strong coffee in front of him, Ford asked Olly to kick off.

'I've collated the relevant data from the interviews with hospital staff. Angie Halpern was as close to the stereotypical angel as you could imagine,' Olly said, miming a halo over his own head. 'Nobody had a bad word to say about her. I even talked to a couple of patients. I'm surprised they hadn't put up a statue to her.'

The door banged back on itself. Mick came in, a grin gleaming from the black nest of his moustache and goatee. 'Sorry I'm late, Henry. Just finishing up an interview. One of Angie Halpern's work colleagues is off sick. I went round to his house to talk to him. Quite interesting, actually.'

'Go on,' Ford said, ignoring Olly's frown.

'Earlier this year, one of her patients died. They investigated, and the finger of blame was pointing at Angie. She'd got careless, he said. Administered the wrong medicine.'

'Was she disciplined?'

Mick shook his head. 'They transferred her to a new ward and the hospital authorities covered it up. Nothing dodgy, but they paid off the family and got them to sign an NDA. Apparently, that way they can keep the death off their stats and it doesn't affect their performance data or their ranking in the league tables.'

Various tuts accompanied this last revelation. 'Sounds like the force,' someone said, to general groans of agreement.

'Thing is,' Mick continued, stroking the top of his head, 'the dead woman's son wasn't happy. He said he was, and I quote, "going to get justice for Mum".'

Ford nodded and made a note. 'Good work, Mick. Find out the son's name. He's a person of interest. Have a chat with him and establish his whereabouts for the time of Angie and Kai's deaths, which, people, I have circulated, along with the PM reports. Check your emails. Speaking of administering medicine, and for anyone who hasn't read the PM report on Kai yet, he was killed with an injection of fentanyl. That means we look at local druggies and the medical community. Someone find out if vets use it as well.'

'Also, guv,' Mick said, holding up a finger.

'Yes?'

'I spoke to Christos Fariakis this morning.' Various officers shook their heads at the mention of Salisbury's biggest loan shark. 'He said he hadn't heard a word of anyone in the business doing Angie and Kai. Or anything like it. In his words' – Mick assumed a kebab-shop Greek accent that had eyes rolling – '"Maybe a couple of slaps or a broken bone if it was a bloke, Mr Tanner, but killin' a lady and a kid? Never. I swear before the Virgin."'

Feeling mounting frustration, Ford turned to Hannah and asked her to summarise where Forensics had got to. The blush was less pronounced this time. Maybe she was settling in. She concluded with the news that although she'd been able to lift a couple of partial fingerprints from the Heinz beans tin she'd recovered from the crime scene, there was no match from the IDENT1 database.

'So they have no evidential value until we have a suspect in custody,' she concluded.

'This is all great, but ruling things out isn't ruling them in. We need to break this – soon,' Ford snapped. 'Anyone remember the golden hour? Because I do. It ended a long, long time ago. Every passing hour we don't catch him is an hour closer to when the killer gets away with it.'

After the briefing ended, Ford retreated to his office. He'd barely sat down when Jools knocked and entered, closing the door behind her.

'You all right, guv?'

'Yeah, fine. What do you want, Jools?'

'Don't let it get to you, that's all.'

'It's a big case. My first as a DI. How can I not?'

'You've got a good team. We'll catch him.'

Ford smiled. 'Listen, when I was talking to Charles Abbott this morning, he mentioned a porter, name of Kyte. Said the guy was drawing in a puddle of blood or something. I want you to go and have a chat.'

Jools wrinkled her nose. 'Charming.'

DAY FIVE, 8.15 A.M.

The quartet enjoying eighteen holes together on Saturday morning weren't unusually powerful, by the standards of the others making their way around the sunlit course. The cathedral's canon treasurer. An army colonel. The chief constable. And Charles Abbott. But their influence overlapped in the four critical organisations bound into the fabric of the city.

Abbott swung his driver, smiled at the clean metallic click as the club head made contact, and followed his ball's progress as it flew in a beautiful arc down the centre of the fairway.

'Nice shot, Charles,' the canon treasurer said.

'Thanks, David.'

The men walked on.

Abbott hung back a little and touched the chief constable's left elbow. 'Eamonn, I know you hate talking shop on the course, but one of your chaps barged into my office yesterday and, well' – he sighed – 'he really upset me.'

'Upset you how?'

'Despite my making every effort to help him out, he actually threatened to arrest me and drag me into his police station to be interrogated.'

'Name?'

'A detective inspector, name of Ford,' Abbott said. 'He insinuated I was mixed up in this ghastly murder of one of our nurses and her little boy. Just because I'm the blood expert at the hospital. I mean, it's outrageous!'

The chief constable smiled and patted his friend on the shoulder. 'Leave it with me, Charles. I'll see he's put back in his box.'

DAY SEVEN, 8.35 A.M.

After a precious Sunday off, Jools parked her silver Mondeo in the vast Number 8 car park at SDH. On three sides, it looked out over mile after mile of rolling countryside, a patchwork of greens, golds and yellows smeared here and there with a hazy brushstroke of scarlet poppies. The fourth side faced the collection of red-brick-and-steel buildings comprising the hospital.

She made her way through the labyrinth of corridors, nodding to the odd staff member she recognised, until she came to the main reception.

'Hi,' she said, showing the middle-aged black woman on the desk her police ID. 'I'm looking for one of your porters. What would be the fastest way to track him down, please?'

'What's his name, dear?' asked the receptionist.

'Matthew Kyte. Might be known as Matty?'

The receptionist's eyes lit up, and she beamed at Jools. 'Now there's a true Christian. You know, dear, if I ever find myself in here, God forbid,' she said, crossing herself, 'I hope Matty'll be working my ward. That boy, oh, my stars!'

'Popular, is he?'

'Popular? Did you know, darling, relatives buy *him* flowers when they come to collect their loved ones.'

Jools liked to think that she'd managed to avoid falling into a copper's easy cynicism about people. Although it was many a year since she'd been to church, she did try to follow the old rule: 'Judge not, lest ye be judged.' Maybe not the easiest motto to live up to as a detective, but she tried.

But she found she'd already taken a dislike to Matty Kyte. And she hadn't even met him. *Sounds like a right teacher's pet,* she thought. *I bet he tries to smarm his way into their wills.* Then she admonished herself for this uncharitable thought. *I'm sure he's lovely. Someone has to be.* The cynical side of her character managed to get the last word. *And that goes for people who draw in spilt blood, does it?*

She smiled at the receptionist, noting her name badge. 'Where can I find him, Marjorie?'

'Hold on, let me check our staffing roster.' Marjorie's purple-varnished fingernails clicked over her keyboard. She frowned at her monitor then looked up at Jools. 'Bodenham Ward,' she said. 'Women's cancer.'

Jools thanked her and followed the direction of her pointing finger to a signboard at the T-junction where the lobby narrowed into a corridor heading left and right, away to different parts of the hospital.

Outside the ward, she pressed the buzzer for admittance. When a nurse in sage-green scrubs peered through, Jools flattened her ID against the small square panel of wire-reinforced glass. Smiling, the honey-skinned woman let her in.

'I'm looking for Matty Kyte,' Jools said. 'Reception told me he was working on this ward today.'

'That's right.' She looked round. 'He was here a minute ago.' She called out to one of her colleagues, who was carrying a bedpan away from a curtained-off bed. 'Annie, did you see where Matty went?'

The second nurse came over. She frowned. 'I think he went down to get Mrs Rennie a sandwich from the shop.'

'But she only just had one!'

'Said she didn't like it. Matty volunteered to get her something else. I told him they all take advantage, but he just smiled, like always.'

Jools felt her resentment of the saintly Matty building. 'OK if I wait here for him to come back?' she asked.

'Be our guest,' the first nurse said. 'You can sit at the nurses' station if you like.'

Jools plonked her bag under the small desk and sat on one of the blue-upholstered swivel chairs. A half-eaten box of Cadbury's Dairy Box chocolates lay beside a small pile of women's magazines. She flicked through a much-thumbed copy of *Vogue* while she waited. The ward was hot, and the beeps and hums from the various monitors and machines made her drowsy.

'Excuse me, Officer? Marisol said you wanted to talk to me?'

Jools jerked her head round, realising she'd been half-asleep and lying on a sunlit beach waiting for someone to bring her a mojito. Standing to her right was a smiling man in the midnight-blue uniform of a hospital porter: baggy trousers and long-sleeved tunic.

She stood and extended her hand for him to shake, buying a little time for her brain to wake up. His skin was dry, and the pressure of his grip was firm, but not hard. Nothing like the bone-crushers favoured by a few of her male colleagues at the nick.

'Matty?' she asked.

'That's me! Given name Matthew, but only Mum and Dad call me that.'

She assessed his appearance. He was a white male, around six feet tall, and looked fit, though not muscle-bound. His hair was a middling brown – the kind that witnesses describe as 'average' – short, straight and parted on the left.

He also had dark brown eyes; rather beautiful dark brown eyes, she couldn't help thinking, fringed with thick eyelashes that she, personally, would kill for.

'I'm DC Julie Harper, Wiltshire Police,' she said, holding up her ID. 'Could we find somewhere quiet for a chat?'

His eyes slid sideways. 'It's not my break for ages.'

She pasted a smile on her face. How eager was Matty to help? Really? 'I'm sure your boss would understand if they knew you were helping the police.'

'It's not him I'm worried about, it's my patients.'

Your patients? She leaned closer and was gratified to see him mirror her body language. *Win them round, Jools, before they even realise what you're doing.*

'I'm investigating two murders. A nurse and her young son. You might have read about them,' she added in a conspiratorial whisper.

This close, she could smell his aftershave, a pleasant, woody aroma she always associated with her father.

His hand flew to his mouth, fingers fluttering. The gesture looked stagy to her.

'I did. It's so awful. If it was one of my ladies, I'd have just died.'

His outward appearance was throwing her off. She realised she'd been expecting some poorly educated lump for whom portering was the highest up the ladder he was ever going to get. Yet here was a well-spoken, well-groomed, if slightly camp individual, with movie-star good looks and an apparent passion for going above and beyond to care for the patients on his wards.

'So, is there somewhere we can go for a quiet chat, Matty?' she asked him again.

He looked over at the row of windows facing the fields and hedgerows. 'Sometimes I get a takeaway latte and sit on a wall just down there,' he said. 'I like listening to birdsong.'

Thinking he was just too good to be true, Jools consented, nonetheless. 'Let's go there, then,' she said. 'See if anyone's singing today.'

There! A flicker of a different kind of expression crossed his face. Blink and you'd miss it. Jools did neither.

DAY SEVEN, 8.55 A.M.

They sat on a low red-brick wall on the edge of a sunlit courtyard. Jools opened her mouth to speak, but Matty held a finger up to his lips.

'Sshh!' he whispered. He leaned towards her. 'Close your eyes and just listen.'

This close, she fancied she could feel his body heat, despite the warmth of the sun. The aftershave, which a few minutes ago had aroused only pleasant memories, now smelled overpoweringly male. A flake of dried blood nestled in the crease of his chin.

'You first,' she said.

'OK,' he said.

And he did, just like that. Closed those long-lashed eyelids, let his mouth curve upwards into a smile, inhaled and sighed out a long breath.

Her muscles twitched as they loaded up with adrenaline, ready to defend her with reasonable force at the slightest suggestion he wasn't going to play nice.

As she closed her eyes, she detected, or rather heard for the first time, the wheedling song of skylarks. Then the fluting trills of a blackbird, which imitated a mobile phone ringing at one point. And something else, a distant keening she couldn't place.

She opened her eyes and looked to her right.

Matty was looking straight at her. Still smiling.

'Beautiful, isn't it?' he said.

'Lovely. What's the high-pitched one?'

'The long cries?'

'Yeah, that.'

'Buzzard. Look,' he said, shielding his eyes with his left hand and pointing up with his right.

High above a field of ripe wheat, she picked out a broad-winged bird describing lazy circles.

'People think they're predators,' he said, looking back at her. 'But they're just as happy scavenging. You know, foxes' leavings.' He paused. 'Or roadkill. Something nobody else wants. Something worthless.'

His final sentence sent a cold shiver through her. She wished she'd brought an extendible baton or a can of PAVA spray.

She turned through ninety degrees so she was facing him, taking the opportunity to plant one foot on the tarmac and add a further six inches to the distance between them.

'So, Matty,' she began, 'we've been investigating the murders, as I said upstairs, and—'

He put his hand to his chest, palm inwards, fingers splayed. 'Oh, my God! You don't think *I* had something to do with them, do you?'

'Did you?'

It was a simple counter-question, but she'd found that asking a suspect straight out if they'd done it did, occasionally, work. If they denied it, she got the chance to assess the shape of their denial. Bluster, flat-out lies, aggression, sudden elective muteness: she'd seen them all.

'Did I what?'

'Have something to do with the murders?'

'Did *I* have something to do with the murders?' he repeated, staring at her.

'Yes.'

He paused, then looked out, over the fields.

'No. I did *not*. How could you even *say* that?' he asked, his voice taking on a whiny tone. 'I love people. Ask anyone. Ask my ladies. They'll tell you. They *love* me.'

Bloody hell, Matty! Even if you're not our man, you've definitely got something going on behind that pretty face of yours.

'Sorry, Matty,' she said, modulating her own voice so that it took on a soothing quality. 'Cop humour. We're terrible, worse than medics.'

His shoulders, which had been jacked up under his ears, dropped. He smiled, the outrage passing like a summer storm.

'I know what you mean about doctors. The way they talk about blood. I overheard Mr Abbott talking with another consultant the other day,' he said. 'He had just come from theatre and, oh my God, it was so hilarious. He said, "There was so much ketchup spraying around, I nearly ordered some chips!" That's what they call blood, you know. Ketchup.' He dropped his voice and leaned towards her. 'What do you call it? Cops, I mean?'

'Claret, sometimes,' she answered, mechanically.

'Claret. Funny.'

'Are you interested in blood, then?' she asked, striving to keep her voice light.

He shrugged. 'Kind of, I suppose. There's a lot of stuff goes on in the hospital. Operations, amputations, abortions,' he said, then giggled. 'Blood everywhere.'

Jools was listening with all her attention, but a checklist in neon floated between them. And one after another, boxes were being checked.

Appearance. Tick.
Interest in blood. Tick.
Hospital worker. Tick.

Makes my flesh crawl. Tick.

'There was an accident the other day, wasn't there?' she asked.

'Accident?' he echoed.

'Yes. Mr Abbott said one of the junior doctors dropped a blood bag.'

Matty rolled his eyes. 'Oh, yes. But it wasn't her, it was him. I saw. He dropped it on purpose, to humiliate her. Probably because she's Indian.'

'And poor old you got the mucky job of mopping it up.'

'I don't mind them treating me like shit,' he said, then flushed. 'Sorry, I mean like dirt. But I'm the lowest of the low, aren't I?'

'Is that why you drew in it, Matty? Were you angry with them?'

His eyes flash-bulbed. 'What? I didn't!'

'No? I heard that the ward sister saw you.'

He grinned, but it looked lopsided, forced. 'She was mistaken. I shouldn't say this, but Sister McLaughlin's half-blind. I wasn't drawing. Why would I?'

Jools smiled. 'Don't worry about it, Matty. I'm sure it was an honest mistake.'

She consulted her checklist.

Liar. Tick.

Suddenly, she wanted, very badly, to have him in an interview room. And at least one more officer beside her. With a taser.

'We're having a chat with a few people who might have known the victims,' she said, still doing her best to keep her tone breezy, unthreatening. 'You know, through work. Would you be happy to come into the station for a chat at some point?'

His eyes flicked away from hers, across to the fields and miles of countryside beyond.

'Happy? Of course. Why wouldn't I be?'

Jools agreed a time the following day and walked with Matty back up to the ward. As she was leaving, an older lady caught her eye and beckoned her over. She was sitting up in bed, wrapped in a knitted shawl in soft-looking, medicine-pink wool.

'Are you police, dear?'

'Yes.'

'What were you talking to Matty about?' she asked, fixing Jools with a stare from watery blue eyes, their rims inflamed and crusty.

'Just asking him a few questions. We're looking for help catching this' – she paused, looking for appropriate phrasing –'dreadful man who's killed people in Salisbury.'

'I hope they lock him up and throw away the key when they catch him,' the lady said, feelingly.

Jools smiled. 'Well, there'd have to be a trial first.'

The lady snorted. 'Huh! It's a shame they did away with hanging, that's what my Bert used to say.'

'Mmm,' Jools said, checking her watch. 'Was there something you wanted to tell me?'

'Me, dear?'

'You called me over?'

She tutted. 'Of course, silly me! I'll be forgetting my own name next. Which is Ivy, by the way. Ivy S. Johnson. The S stands for Sheila, if you want to make a note.'

Jools sensed that the old lady was looking for a little excitement. Something to tell the nurses, or her next visitor.

She smiled and pulled out her notebook. 'Ivy S. Johnson,' she repeated, though she scribbled *Call Ford ASAP* on the open page.

'Well, dear, all I was going to say is, you can't possibly believe Matty has anything to do with that horrid business in the town,' she said.

'Why?'

'Couldn't you tell, dear? That man is the sweetest, kindest thing. Why, only yesterday he offered to sit with me because I felt a bit woozy after my injection.'

DAY SEVEN, 9.30 A.M.

With his father's long-ago taunts ringing in his ears – '*You stupid little shit! You can lick that up!*' – he pushes the grubby bell button. He has to wait for two minutes before it crackles with an answer.

'Yeah?'

'Mr Eadon? Paul?'

'Who wants him?'

'My name is Harvey. Harvey Williams. I'm from the Purcell Foundation. May I come in?'

'Why?'

'I think you dropped your rolling tobacco at the food bank. I have it here in my hand.'

The latch buzzes, and he's through. He pats his jacket over the pocket containing his equipment. The hallway stinks, as does the stairwell. Nothing but junkies and alkies. Losers! Pathetic, worthless losers.

He climbs to the fifth floor, not trusting the foul-smelling lift. Turns left out of the stairwell and knocks on the scuffed red front door three from the end of the walkway.

The man who opens the door has red-rimmed eyes and a rash of sores around his mouth. He's thin, but his cheeks are still a reasonable colour. Nice and pink.

'You got my baccy?'

'May I come in? I have something else for you.'

'Knock yourself out,' the man drawls, turning and shuffling back into the gloom.

Grinning, Harvey punches hard into the right side of Eadon's neck. The vagus nerve isn't an easy target, but he's done his research. Eadon goes down.

Harvey drags him into the kitchen, positions him and takes out the cannula with its razor-tipped trocar.

When he's finished, he takes a scummy-looking pan scourer from the dirty sink, dips it in the pool and paints a number on the wall.

With the number behind him, he smiles into his phone's lens and takes a selfie. *Another one for you, Dad.*

At 3.47 p.m. Ford parked on Terry Road in Morland's Field, a run-down area of the city known for high levels of petty crime, from drug-dealing to bike thefts.

Five minutes later, shaking his head, he stood on the threshold of the filthy kitchen.

'Who found him?' he asked Nat.

'Social worker. I've started house-to-house enquiries. All we've got so far is, he was an Olympic-level pain in the arse.'

'Keep on it.'

Looking at the body seated in the pool of blood, the yanked-down jeans, the puncture wound, the number daubed on the wall, Ford knew what he was dealing with. 'Multiple linked offences' be damned. He closed his eyes, ignoring the seasick feeling as his world tilted.

He saw a man. Strong, but non-threatening. Older? In a suit and tie? Well spoken? An authority figure? He opened his eyes as his gut heaved, and reached into his pocket for a bag.

He was back at Bourne Hill by 5.00 p.m. and pulled everyone into a briefing. He turned on the projector and beamed the latest outrage on to the wall.

'Paul Eadon, twenty-eight years old. Lived in Raymond Molyneaux House. Identical MO to Angie Halpern.'

'Any link between him and Angie, guv?' Olly asked.

'That's what we're going to find out. I want you to talk to his social worker. She's happy to give you chapter and verse. See if his and Angie's lives overlapped. Maybe she treated him once.'

'Cause of death?' Jools asked.

'I could see the edge of recent bruises on the back and sides of his neck. Dr Eustace will confirm, but I'm thinking the killer stunned him with a punch then throttled him and stuck him with a needle like before.'

He clicked the mouse to bring up the next image, a bloody 500, dripping down the wall towards a tattered calendar, the current month featuring a picture of a golden retriever.

'He wrote this on the wall,' Ford said, as if they hadn't got the message.

'Shall I run Eadon through the PNC?' Jan asked.

Ford nodded. 'OK, thanks everyone. Hannah, you got a minute?'

He waited for the room to empty, noting the way Mick glared at Hannah.

'What is it?' she asked, holding a sheaf of papers in front of her like a shield.

'It's the same guy, isn't it?'

'I can't be one hundred per cent sure.'

Ford sighed with exasperation. 'Yes, but, on balance?'

'On balance, yes. Identical MO. Identical signature. I would say both murders were carried out by the same individual.'

'Is this a serial killer? On balance,' he added, hurriedly. 'You worked with the FBI. You must have talked to people about them.'

A shadow flitted across her eyes. 'I did. It looks probable. I would expect to find a third body very soon, unless we catch him.'

'"Him?" Not them?'

Hannah shook her head. 'It's a man. I'm certain.'

'I'd be interested to know what else you could come up with about him.'

Her eyes widened, and she smiled. 'You mean you want to profile him? And you want me to help you?'

'Yes. If you're up for the challenge.'

'You said no before. You said . . .' She closed her eyes, frowning. '"It's unnecessary. The young ones always want to go outside for profilers at the merest sniff of something unusual, instead of doing proper coppering."'

Trust you to nail me with my exact words, Hannah. 'Yes, I did. And at the time I meant it. But I think we need to work a bit harder at getting inside his head. It means extra work, and I'm afraid there won't be any overtime authorised.'

She shook her head. 'It's fine. I have more than enough money for me and Uta Frith to live on.'

'Good. Come with me. There's someone I want you to meet.'

◆ ◆ ◆

Sandy looked up from her computer.

'Henry! And you must be the Dr Fellowes I've been hearing so much about,' she said effusively, standing and rounding her desk to shake hands with Hannah. 'Have a seat. You offered our new deputy forensics chief a coffee, Henry?'

'No, boss.'

'Well, go and get her one, then. Poor woman looks parched. How do you take it, Dr Fellowes? Your coffee, I mean?'

'White, no sugar, please,' she said.

Sandy looked at Ford. 'Off you go, then. I'll have my usual, please.'

When Ford returned with the drinks, it was to the sound of the two women laughing. He took it as a good sign. He slid papers aside on the desk before placing the mugs down on the small clearings he created.

'Here you go. White, no sugar, for you, Hannah. Black, two spoons, for the boss. And a peppermint tea for me.'

'I thought you preferred coffee,' Hannah said.

'Just trying not to OD on caffeine.'

Sandy picked up her mug and took a sip. 'Not bad. So, Hannah, how are you finding life at Bourne Hill?'

'I am enjoying it very much. The work is very stimulating and I'm learning people's nicknames. Like Henry and Jools. They work quite well. And yours, of course. The Python.'

Ford winced, hiding the grimace behind his tea mug. People never called Sandy the Python to her face.

'And does *mine* work?' she asked, arching one eyebrow.

'It's hard to say. It doesn't relate to your name. Pythons are snakes, constrictors. They're slender and muscular. You're tall, and more generously proportioned, though still very beautiful. I would call you Juno.'

'And Juno would be?'

'To the Romans, Juno was the queen of the gods. Her associations are the subject of much controversy among scholars, but all agree she embodies vital force, energy and eternal youthfulness.'

Sandy laughed loudly. Ford relaxed. No blood on the carpet today.

'I'll take that, Dr Fellowes. I'll take that. You should come up for a chat more often.'

'You heard we've got another body?' Ford said.

'Someone may have mentioned that little fact to me.'

'Hannah and I think we've got a serial killer, unlikely as that sounds. We need to get ahead of him before this gets nasty. Nastier,' he corrected himself.

'Agreed. What do you want?'

'Press conference later today. Keep the invites to the locals for now. If Sky or whoever gets wind of it from social media, they'll be down here anyway.'

'Done,' she said, making a note with a gold propelling pencil in a small red-leather-covered notebook. 'What else? I said budgets were tighter than a gnat's chuff, if you remember.'

'I do. But we need to get inside his head. Hannah has high-level experience in forensic psychology. I want her to help me work up a suspect profile.'

Sandy looked at Hannah. 'You're going to accompany Henry into the dark recesses of the human psyche? Is that it?'

'I've never heard it put quite so poetically before, but, yes, broadly speaking.'

Sandy nodded, her eyes never leaving Hannah's. 'What are your first impressions?'

'What, tell you now?'

'If you wouldn't mind. We do have a nutjob bleeding the good citizens of Salisbury dry out there.'

Hannah tugged on her plait, then began, in a quiet voice. 'To the untrained eye, the crime scenes may appear horrible, but they are meticulous,' she said. 'The victims were both bled out the same way. The killer removed whatever equipment he used to take their blood.'

Ford observed the way her voice grew stronger as she became involved in explaining her thinking. He liked what he was seeing. 'He was controlled. There is no blood spatter, which indicates he didn't lose control. No evidence of torture. Or of sexual assault. He just did what he had to do and left.'

Sandy nodded. 'Go on.'

'Killers relate to blood in one of three ways. To the first group, it's just a liquid, sloshing around the crime scene after they've stabbed, bludgeoned or shot their victims,' Hannah said. 'It's an inconvenience. Something to be avoided in case it sticks to them or takes a print.'

'And the second group?'

'To them, it's part of the pleasure. Watching it spurt out, spattering the walls, the floor, the designer sofas and expensive art on the walls. They masturbate into it, or defecate in the middle of it, none of which our killer did.'

'Which leaves—'

'The group for whom blood *signifies*. It's part of what they're doing. Even *why* they're doing it. That's what I'm seeing with our killer,' Hannah said. 'He bled both principal victims dry. And he painted numbers with the blood.'

'What about the little boy? What's your thinking, Henry?'

'Honestly? I don't know. Was he part of the ritual? Or just surplus to requirements? But there are a couple of features that I find interesting. Maybe you saw them too?'

'I saw him placed in his mum's arms. I saw his hands folded in prayer. I saw him killed, but he wasn't bled out.'

'Exactly. The killer isn't a nonce. Or not the common-or-garden variety anyway. If he took pictures, I don't think he's getting off on them.'

'No?'

'No. There was nothing sexual about the way he posed the boy,' Ford said. 'It looked reverential to me.'

'Reverential?'

'If it was a painting, it would be called something sickly-sweet like "Asleep at Last". I think Kai was incidental,' Ford said. 'At home with his mum and a witness to her death.'

Sandy nodded. 'Compared to what these men can get up to with kids, I'd say this was unusually merciful,' she said. 'Like he didn't want to inflict pain on him at all. What about the numbers?'

'First six-six-six, then five hundred,' Hannah said. 'Apart from the rather obvious – though incorrect – biblical association for the first one, they could mean all sorts of things.'

'Smart girl, not jumping off at the deep end. What else does the physical evidence tell you?'

'The killer knows the exact location of the femoral artery and how to insert a trocar to drain the blood out,' Hannah said. 'Those two facts tell me he has medical experience. That he chooses to leave us messages in blood also suggests he is confident.'

'Are you about to say the p-word?'

'That depends on which word you have in mind.'

'Psychopath.'

'I think it's too early to comment on whether he suffers from antisocial personality disorder, which is the clinical term used in America's *Diagnostic and Statistical Manual*, by the way.'

'But he could be. A psychopath?'

'Psychopaths are organised, cunning, able to blend in, despite their lack of empathy. They're deceitful. They use people to get what they want. They can come off as arrogant, even hyper-confident. Our killer appears to fit those criteria, yes.'

Ford's mind flew back to his encounter with Abbott. She could have been describing the consultant haematologist from life.

'Does their pathology give them any weak spots?' he asked.

Hannah nodded. 'Psychopaths believe they are omnipotent. It can lead them to make errors. Even quite basic errors.'

'What sort of thing?'

'Their compulsion to kill and their sense of godlike power can make them careless. They may leave physical evidence at the crime scene. Even their own DNA.'

'What about sociopaths?' Ford asked. 'Are they basically the same thing?'

'Sociopaths are far less controlled. When they turn to violence, it is often chaotic, unplanned, brutal. They make very little effort to hide their tracks. If this killer fits into one of these two layperson's terms, it's "psychopath".'

'Shit!' Ford inhaled, closed his eyes, took himself back to the two crime scenes and the glaring images of blood loss and degradation. *It's all about the blood, isn't it?* 'I think he was calm throughout,' he said. 'No practice jabs. Just one puncture wound, straight into the femoral artery. No shaking hands or sweat clouding his vision. Also,' he carried on, leaning forward in his chair, 'most murderers, even if motivated by extreme rage, would find it hard to switch from a brutal, bloody killing of an adult to a precise, drug-induced murder-by-injection of a small child.'

Sandy leaned back in her chair and clasped her hands behind her head. She looked at them in turn. 'Fine. I sanction the two of you working as a profiling team. And while we're on the subject, I've read your file, Hannah. We're a small team down here. Not exactly overburdened with resources, if you know what I mean? It would be a criminal waste, no pun intended, not to make use of your US experience.'

'What do you mean?'

'If Henry wants to involve you in the wider investigation, interviewing suspects, say, and you think you can add value, go ahead. OK with you, Henry?'

'Fine by me, boss.'

Sandy pointed a finger at Ford and Hannah in turn. 'But that's in *addition* to your normal CSI duties, not instead of, understood?'

Hannah nodded. 'Understood, Juno.'

To the sound of the Python's unrestrained laughter, Ford led Hannah out of the office.

DAY EIGHT, 9.15 A.M.

With the help of a social worker and a friendly GP, Ford had Eadon's medical records open in front of him. One phrase leapt out at him:

In-patient, SDH, 15–17/03/18, blood poisoning.

The hospital again. Four people, all connected by this one workplace: Angie Halpern, Charles Abbott, Matty Kyte and now Paul Eadon. His heart beat a little faster as he picked up the phone. While he waited for the hospital records office to answer, he circled the phrase 'blood poisoning'.

He requested information on Eadon's stay – specifically, which ward he was on and who was involved in his treatment and care. The records clerk promised to call him back.

He walked over to Jools, who nodded at him, one hand clamped over the mouthpiece of her desk phone. The call finished, she tapped a couple of keys on her PC.

'There you go, guv. Our Mr Eadon had a record going back to the early noughties. Mainly low-level thievery and public order offences. Nothing I can see linking him to Angie, though.'

His mobile rang. It was the records clerk from the hospital. He noted down the names of doctors and nurses who'd looked after and treated Paul Eadon, underlining two:

Seema Patel (N)
Rajnesh Kumar (N)
Jean Stretton (N)
Becca Gordon (N)
Angela Halpern (N)
Dr Vida Katalammy
Dr Cameron Thorne
Mr Charles Abbott

He rubbed his chin, frowning. A concrete link between both adult victims and Mr Abbott, God's gift to haematology. He added Paul Eadon and doodled a couple of extra words.

Paul Eadon – victim
Seema Patel (N)
Rajnesh Kumar (N)
Jean Stretton (N)
Becca Porter (N)
Angela Halpern (N) – victim
Dr Vida Katalammy
Dr Cameron Thorne
Mr Charles Abbott – blood/cancer (fentanyl?)

He imagined red lines linking the different players. Was someone targeting everyone who'd treated Eadon? Was that it? Did it mean other people on the list were potential targets of the killer? Abbott knew all about blood. His life's work. No motive as yet, but according to Hannah's typology, for the killer, blood *signified*.

His phone rang again. 'No caller ID' message.

Scowling, he answered. 'Ford.'

'Hi. Kerry Battle, Sky News?'

Ford swiped a hand over his face. He knew without having to be told what this meant. Someone had gone social with the news and now it was a matter of hours before the London media and the world's descended on his city.

'Yes, what can I do for you, Kerry?'

'A source tells me you're investigating three rather unusual murders down there. Would you care to comment on that?'

Play hard to get or softly-softly? Try to keep a lid on it and risk alienating the media? Or feed the killer's appetite for notoriety and get press help with public engagement?

No contest. He pulled a face and nodded at Jan, who was miming, 'Coffee?' as she passed his desk. He mouthed, 'Media,' back at her – grimaced as Jan rolled her eyes.

He remembered words of advice on a media training course he'd attended. 'Don't say anything you don't want to see on the front page of the *Daily Mail*. And there's no such thing as off the record.'

'Your source is correct. Five days ago, a woman was murdered, along with her young son. Yesterday, a man was murdered. We believe we are looking at the same killer.'

'My source tells me he's bleeding them dry. Can you confirm that?'

'The adults, yes.'

'Not the little boy?'

'No.'

'How did he die?'

'We're holding that back. To screen out nut— I mean, people who enjoy confessing to crimes they didn't commit.'

'So it's a serial killer.'

'The offences are linked.'

'Which makes it a serial killer, yes? Three victims?'

Ford mouthed a 'thank you' as Jan put a fresh mug of coffee and a home-baked flapjack on his desk.

'Kerry, I need to be straight with you. You can help us get people who might have seen something or know somebody dodgy. But you can also help the killer by feeding his fantasies, which I absolutely want to avoid. Is there a way we can work together?' he asked.

'Meaning?'

'Meaning you get your story and I get help, but we don't get lurid headlines. I'd like to keep it as low-key as possible. We don't want to start a public panic. You know, "Blood-soaked city living in fear of vampire killer."'

'That's a nice headline. You should come and work as a sub-editor for us. The pay's better.'

'I'm sure it is. So, do we have a deal?'

'Let's call it a working arrangement.'

◆ ◆ ◆

At that afternoon's case meeting, the whiteboard was in heavy use. Ford stood to one side as he drew suggestions and links from his team.

'Let's look at people we know of who might have had a reason to kill Angie.'

'I tracked down the son of the woman Angie gave the wrong drugs to, guv,' Olly said. 'William Farrell. Lives in the St Marks area.'

'Background?'

'Working on it.'

'Go and see him. Check if he's got alibis for the murders.'

After a few more minutes of discussion, Ford held up a sheet with the names of the people who'd treated Paul Eadon's blood poisoning.

'Our two adult victims are on this list. Angie nursed Paul. It may be that the others are on a kill list. I want them contacted, discreetly, and offered advice on staying safe.' He held up a warning finger. 'And before anyone asks, we've no money for officers to do guard duty, so if anyone requests it, explain we'll be doing everything in our power to catch the killer up to but stopping short of police protection.'

'I'll assign calls,' Jan said.

'Leave Abbott to me,' Ford said. 'Now, on to the victimology. Superficially, Angie and Paul had zero commonalities. She's a nurse, clean as a whistle, not even a parking ticket.'

'Don't forget that malpractice thing, guv?' Mick called out.

'Noted. Eadon had a string of convictions for petty crime. So dig deeper. The blood-poisoning incident might be something, but don't let's get stuck in a rut.'

◆ ◆ ◆

Ford's phone rang. Sandy.

'Henry, got a minute?'

'What is it, boss? I'm in the middle of something.'

'My office?'

Sighing, he closed the database screen and headed for the Python's lair.

He sat in the chair facing his boss, saw her expression and felt his stomach turn over.

'What is it?' he asked.

She ran her hands through her hair. Sighed. Plucked at the front of her blouse. 'I think you're a bloody good detective, you know that.'

'Yes. What's going on?'

He had a flash of the most unwelcome insight. My God, was she going to take over the case?

'I've just had the chief constable on the phone.'

Shit! Abbott had executed a pre-emptive strike. Normally, men like him rattled their sabres but never swung them.

He tried to ignore his racing pulse and fluttering stomach. 'And?'

'Have you been questioning a Charles Abbott about the murders?'

'Yes. He's a consultant haematologist. I wanted to know about blood.'

Sandy sighed. 'According to the chief con, you behaved in a, and I quote, "threatening and intimidatory manner, without cause or provocation", end quote.'

'That's bollocks! Abbott's hiding something, or he knows something. I just tried pushing a couple of buttons and he went into the standard "I know your big boss" spiel.'

'Trouble is, Henry, he really does. You need to back off. Find out about blood from Google.'

Ford leaned forward, placed his hands on the edge of her desk, glaring at her. 'Back off? There's something off about him, boss. I can feel it!'

Sandy stared him down. 'One, please don't shout at me, Henry, I'm not deaf. Two, what I *am* is your boss and the SIO on this case. So if I say back off, you back off. You've got other leads, lines of enquiry?'

'Yes,' Ford answered, hearing the surliness in his voice and thinking of Sam in one of his strops.

'Then pursue them. If you get evidence that points to Abbott that doesn't come from your famous gut, let me know first. Do not – I repeat, do not – go barging into Abbott's office uninvited again. Understood?'

Ford stood. Barely trusting himself. 'Understood.'

He managed to leave her office without slamming the door, but it was a close call.

He didn't have time to brood for long; Jools told him Matty was due in thirty minutes.

'Let's have a quick chat about how to handle him,' he said.

They decamped to Ford's office to discuss interview strategy. On the way, Ford phoned Hannah and asked her to join them.

'I want to get Hannah's take on this. Did you know she worked with the FBI?'

Jools gave a wry chuckle. 'I think *everyone* knows that. Including the cleaners. She's fairly open about her life, or hadn't you noticed?'

Ford smiled. 'I had.'

◆ ◆ ◆

'We've got half an hour before the interview,' Ford said, once all three were seated round the small table in his office. 'Jools, what're your thoughts?'

'Right from the moment I met him, I felt as though he was toying with me. All innocence and campy hand gestures one minute. Then, I don't know, he just—'

'Said something that brought you up short?'

'Yes! Exactly.'

'Did you ask him any direct questions?' Hannah asked.

Jools consulted her notes. 'A few. Mainly innocuous stuff just to put him at ease. Except for one.'

'What did you ask him?'

'If he had anything to do with the murders.'

'How did he answer?'

'Strangely. First, he repeated my question back to me. Then he sort of looked into the middle distance. Then he denied it. Made quite a fuss about it. As if it was an insult that anyone would dare to think that.'

'When people with nothing to hide get asked straight questions, they tend to answer readily,' Ford said. 'It's the dodgy ones who begin blustering. As if they can't believe what they've just been asked and are frightened of incriminating themselves.'

'The FBI agents I worked with called it GSS, which meant "guilty secret syndrome",' Hannah said.

'Meaning?'

'Suppose you get interviewed by the police about a serial murder. Or a rape,' she said, adopting a more authoritative tone of voice than Ford had heard her employ before. 'You know you're innocent, and you have an alibi as well. But you're also having an affair with your wife's best friend. Or you're fiddling your work expenses.'

'I get it,' Jools said, interrupting and earning a cross expression from Hannah. 'They're not talking about *your* guilt, but that's how you interpret it. So you start dodging the question.'

'It could mean one of two things,' Ford said. 'He could be such a good person, as the staff and patients described, that your questions horrified him, Jools . . .'

'Or?'

'Or he's hiding something.' He turned to Hannah. 'Any advice on handling Matty?'

'You said he was acting camp, Jools?'

'As a row of tents, which is odd, given he's married. To a woman,' she added.

'Then he won't mind being interviewed by you,' Hannah said.

'I know you can have camp-acting straight guys, but what if he *is* gay?' Jools asked.

'Then the presence of a man, especially a good-looking man like Henry' – Hannah glanced at Ford – 'may throw him off balance. Maybe you could be the bad cop, Jools, and Henry could be the good cop.'

'It's a voluntary interview,' Jools said, smiling. 'I don't think we're quite ready to start working him over.'

Hannah blushed. 'Yes. I see that. Sorry. But I meant it. Henry, if you were to flirt with him, it could destabilise him.'

'Yeah, or he could file a complaint for sexual harassment against me,' Ford said. 'And I just *know* how much the Python would love me for that.'

Hannah sighed. 'I *mean*,' she said, 'play the traditional softer role that often goes to the female detective. Be empathetic. Smile.'

'Flutter my eyelashes?'

She frowned. 'I think that would be inappropriate.'

'Boss?' Jools said, winking at Hannah.

'What?'

'You could always undo another button on your shirt.'

She and Hannah burst out laughing, and Ford smiled. It was good that they could still find time for a safety valve, given the case surrounding them.

'All right, enough. I get it,' he said. 'Of course, if he's not our man, he'll start to wonder about our methods.'

'No, he won't, Henry,' Hannah said. 'He'll just ask you out.'

More laughter. Ford closed the meeting and they agreed Hannah would go down to meet Kyte.

◆ ◆ ◆

Paula called Hannah when Matty arrived at Bourne Hill. Feeling a squirming anxiety in the pit of her stomach, despite the medication she took to keep it at bay, she rose from her desk and made her way to the stairs.

He was waiting for her in reception. She could tell it was him because there were no other men in the sunlit space; that, and the fact that Paula had whispered, 'He's very good-looking,' before hanging up.

She hung back for a few seconds, making herself as unobtrusive as possible beside a tall potted plant. She took her time to assess his body language.

He was leaning against a wall, legs crossed at the ankle, arms folded in front of him. That much limb-crossing could be interpreted as defensive. It could just as easily mean he was finding a comfortable way to stand. It was important to see the person as a whole.

He smiled at a couple of female police staff crossing the reception area on their way to the lifts. Hannah noticed the way they smiled back, then leaned their heads closer together and giggled.

I can't read you, she thought. *Which is fine, because it's not my job. It's Henry's. And Jools's.*

She stuck on her best social smile and strode across the reception area.

'Matty?' she said, from six feet out.

'That's me,' he said as he turned, smiling. His face fell as he saw her. 'You're not Julie.'

'No, I'm not. My name is Dr Hannah Fellowes. I'll take you upstairs.'

In the lift, he made no attempt to start a conversation, for which she was grateful. It allowed her to control their interaction. She noticed the forefinger of his right hand twitching against his thigh, beating out a tight little rhythm.

'I was nervous, too, the first time I came here,' she said.

He looked down at her. 'Why did you say that? I'm not nervous.'

'I'm trying to make you feel at ease. Members of the public often get anxious inside a police station.'

He laughed. 'Maybe they should visit more often. Get it out of their systems.'

'Have you?'

'Have I what?'

'Visited more often?'

He pointed up at the row of orange numbers. The '4' had just illuminated. 'Is this us?'

She nodded.

'On with the show!' he said, waggling jazz hands at her.

Ford smiled at the man Jools had just introduced. Clearly fit, and strong enough to lift a dead body. Smart, too, for a hospital porter. Jacket and tie, pressed beige chinos. But then, being invited in 'for a chat', however informally, often had that effect on people.

He was finding it easy to maintain eye contact, which a lot of suspects couldn't, looking anywhere but into the eyes of the cop who'd nicked them.

'Thanks for coming in, Mr Kyte,' he said, still smiling. 'Can we get you something to drink? There's tea, coffee, or a glass of water?'

'Please, call me Matty. Do you have anything herbal?' Matty asked. 'Chamomile? I'm feeling a little, uh, you know . . .'

'There's no need to feel nervous, Matty,' Ford said, 'and I'm sure there's a box of chamomile somewhere. Sometimes I like peppermint myself. Can you sort them, Jools?'

'Okey-dokey,' she said brightly. 'Back in a jiffy.'

The exaggerated matiness and office small talk was part of their strategy: keeping Matty as relaxed as possible as they probed for the truth.

Jools returned after a few minutes with three steaming mugs, setting them on a low table in the centre of an arrangement of three armchairs.

Ford watched as Matty took a cautious sip of the herbal tea, blowing first across its steaming surface. He winced. 'Ouch! Burnt myself!'

Jools pooched out her bottom lip. 'I know just how that feels, did it myself last week. Silly cow!' she finished, smiling sympathetically.

Matty grinned back at her.

'Matty,' Ford said softly, to catch his attention. 'First of all I need you to know that, as this is a voluntary interview, you can leave whenever you like. You are also entitled to legal advice. And you don't have to answer any of our questions, OK?'

Matty nodded, and tried his tea again. 'I'm happy to help, honestly. What with all these awful' – he dropped his voice to a whisper – '*murders*, I think it's the least I can do.'

Ford looked at him. *How shall I present myself to you?* He wasn't as tall as Matty, but he was in good shape, broad through the shoulders and with a flat stomach. People told him his brown eyes turned dark when he was angry and that he clenched his jaw in a way that gave him a mean look, as if he wanted to hurt the person he was interviewing. Which, he reflected, was often true.

Lean back and look relaxed, or forward, hands clasped loosely: interested.

He leaned back and nodded for Jools to begin.

'Did you know Angie Halpern?' she asked.

'Angie Halpern,' Matty repeated, looking at the ceiling. 'No.'

'She was a nurse.'

'Was she one of the victims?'

'That's right.'

'I wish I could help. But I don't know her. Didn't,' he corrected himself.

'We think whoever killed her was interested in blood. You know, a bit like you.'

'Me?' he said, raising his voice. 'I'm not interested in blood.'

'Oh. I thought you told me yesterday you were.'

'No. You're wrong. I said I was interested in all sorts of things. Not blood specifically.'

'And you didn't draw a face in a pool of blood after a doctor dropped it?'

'No! I already told you,' he said, scratching his right cheek then rubbing the tip of his nose. 'That woman's so short-sighted, I'm surprised they let her dish out drugs. She'll end up giving fentanyl to someone in for a minor op and killing them.'

Ford's antennae twitched. *Fentanyl.*

'I checked with Sister McLaughlin,' Jools said. 'She was adamant she saw you. And she seemed perfectly clear-sighted to me,' she finished pleasantly.

'You don't know her like I do,' Matty said. 'She's got it in for me. Just because I'm a porter.'

Ford sat forward. 'Are you married, Matty?' he asked.

Matty stumbled over his reply. 'Er, yes. I am. Five years now. Her name's Jennifer. I call her Jen, though.'

'Nice name. Does she work?'

'She wanted to be a nurse. But they want everyone to be a graduate nowadays.'

'Like the police,' Ford said. 'Soon you won't be able to mend the road without a degree.' He added a spread-hands, 'Whaddya gonna do?' gesture.

'She works in a care home now. For the elderly. She loves it there. The old ladies like her to read to them.'

'A caring soul.'

'She *is*,' Matty said.

Ford smiled. 'This is going to sound a bit official – sorry. Are you able to provide details of your whereabouts on the dates the murders were committed?'

Matty pulled his head down so that his chin tucked in and thin rolls of fat appeared beneath it. 'I can try. When were they?'

Ford handed him a sheet of paper with the times and dates printed out in two rows.

Matty looked up at Ford. 'I'm not sure, but I was probably at home with Jen,' he said. 'We try not to go out much because we're saving up for a deposit on a new house. I could check with her, if you like. She does everything on her calendar. A real one. Paper,' he added.

'Of course. Ask her at home and call me once you've checked on the calendar.' He handed Matty a business card.

Matty slipped the card into a worn leather wallet. 'Was there anything else?' he asked, looking at his watch.

'No, I think that's everything for now. Thank you so much for coming in, Matty, you've been really helpful.'

Ford stood and extended his hand. They shook. Matty's grip was firm but damp.

'Hard work, being a hospital porter, I should imagine,' he said, holding Matty's hand for a fraction longer.

'I manage,' Matty said, with a small smile.

After Matty had left the nick Ford called Jools into his office.

'Well?' he said.

'He's lying. About a lot of things. I checked his last few weeks' shifts. He worked with Angie five times.'

'Maybe he has other reasons for lying. But if his alibi checks out, we're back to square one.'

'What, "I was at home watching telly with the missus"? That old one?'

'People have been known to do that.'

She shook her head, as if denying the reality that ordinary people did, in fact, spend their evenings slumped in front of the flat screen watching soaps or reality TV.

'I want to keep an eye on him,' she said.

'There's no budget for surveillance, you know that.'

'Fair enough. But I want to dig into his background a bit more.'

'Go for it.' *It's not him.*

DAY NINE, 8.35 A.M.

The next morning, Ford arrived to find an email from Georgina.

Subject: Prelim PM findings on P. Eadon

> *Hi Henry,*
> *I know you'll be champing at the bit, so here are my top-line findings on Paul Eadon.*
> *MOD Homicide*
> *COD Exsanguination (trocar inserted into left femoral artery)*
> *TOD Between 9.00 a.m. and 1.00 p.m.*
> *Large bruise on back of neck consistent with a 'rabbit punch'. Clear imprints of knuckles. Eadon was 5'8". Angle of blow indicates attacker to be 5'10" or taller.*
> *Hyoid bone broken. Bruising round throat indicates manual strangulation (non-fatal).*
> *Coarse toxicology fast-tracked. No fentanyl. Presence of alcohol. You'll have my full report by the end of today.*
> *G*

◆ ◆ ◆

The rest of the day passed in a flurry of meetings, briefings and a court appearance on an unrelated case. At 5.00 p.m., Ford made his way to Forensics. He found Hannah squinting at a screen on which two partial fingerprints were displayed.

'What have you got there?' he asked.

'On the left you have a partial latent I lifted from the tin of beans the killer used to stun Angie. On the right, one from Paul Eadon's front door.'

'Any points of comparison?'

'That's what I'm looking for. I've found three, but you know that's insufficient evidence to even think of taking to the CPS.'

'I'm leaving for the day. I need to be in for Sam. Do you want to start work on our profile? I thought, if you didn't mind, we could work at mine.'

She scrubbed at her eyes and smiled up at him, nodding. 'I drove in today, so I'll see you at Windgather.'

'OK. I have a few things to finish up, so don't worry if you get there before me. Sam can always let you in.'

A little later, Ford pulled on to his drive to see Hannah getting out of a shiny black Mini. Correction: a *sparkling* black Mini, with glossy, wet-look tyres.

He pointed at it. 'Nice. New?'

She shook her head. 'I've had it for one year, three months and four days.'

'Wow! Did you just have it valeted?'

'No,' she said, a note of surprise evident in her answer. 'I like to look after it myself.'

Ford turned back and clocked his own car. The Discovery was coated with a fine brown powder. According to the weather forecast that morning, it had been blown all the way to England from the Sahara. Then he saw Hannah's number plate.

'Cool plate for a CSI.'

'It is, isn't it? I bought it at auction and I paid £1,650.73, including VAT and buyer's premium.'

Ford smiled, shaking his head. He didn't think she could help it. In fact, he didn't think she knew she was doing it. But he liked her for it. How lovely to be that unselfconscious.

'Hi, Sam,' Hannah said when they arrived in the kitchen. 'Homework?'

Sam looked up from under his mop of curls. 'Biology. It sucks.'

'I got an A-star in A-level biology and studied human endocrinology as a subsidiary during my BSc. I took a starred first. Maybe I can help?'

Ford watched as his son, sometimes as uncommunicative as a stroppy suspect with a savvy brief, bonded with a virtual stranger over the science of monoclonal antibodies. He smiled, shaking his head and putting the kettle on. His ears pricked as he heard Sam talk about 'cancer treatment' and 'measuring blood hormones'.

There it was again. Blood. Cancer. Fentanyl. Medics. A dead nurse and a dead inpatient at SDH. *Are you the key, Abbott?*

◆ ◆ ◆

Later, after a brief meal, Ford took Hannah up to the spare room he'd kitted out as a home office.

'Have a seat,' he said, indicating a worn leather armchair.

He grabbed an A4 notepad and a sharp pencil from a clay pot on his desk, glazed with 'Daddy' in childish brushstrokes.

'Do you want to start?' he said.

'We're looking for a man. I'm ninety-nine per cent sure. It could be a tall, powerfully built woman, but' – she wrinkled her nose – 'I don't think it is.'

'Agreed. A man fixated by blood.'

She nodded. 'As I said to Detective Superintendent Monroe, I am prepared to say that we are looking for a psychopath.'

'No emotions.'

'That's a common misconception. Psychopaths have what we call shallow affect. It means his emotional responses are very basic. Anger, frustration, lust. When interviewed they will talk about love, but if you probe, all they mean is sex.'

Ford had a flash of insight. 'Have *you* ever interviewed a psychopath? Is that what you were doing in the US?'

Immediately, she dropped her gaze from his. 'I prefer to not talk about that.'

There it was again. That closed-down look in her eyes. A fractional shift in her posture to shield herself.

What is it, Hannah? What happened to you? I sense it was bad, because you're so open about everything else. Wanting to help her but unwilling to probe her well-established defences, Ford decided to leave it. For now.

'Let's talk about the killer. Our killer,' he said instead.

'He has no empathy,' Hannah said flatly. 'He sees other human beings purely as things he can use to gratify his desires.'

'So he won't understand that other people have feelings?'

'He might know it, on an intellectual level. But he won't care. And he won't be able to imagine what those feelings are. Plenty of psychopaths enjoy inflicting pain,' she said. 'So we can assume they at least understand the pain response as some sort of feeling. But he'll feel no remorse.'

'Clever? Below-average IQ?'

'He can talk his way into people's homes. He's forensically aware, as we've not found any DNA so far, and minimal physical evidence. Psychopaths can be very high achievers. Plenty of corporate CEOs score highly on the Hare Psychopathy Checklist.'

'What if I go out on a limb and say I think he's organised and therefore on the clever end of the spectrum?'

She blinked. 'What do you mean, "spectrum"?'

'The scale of how intelligent psychopaths tend to be. You just said—'

'Oh. Yes. Let's say cunning, though,' she said. 'For your information, we tend not to talk about organised versus disorganised killers these days. Many cases have come to light where the perpetrator's levels of control shift over time. But using the term for now, *organised* serial killers often live with a partner,' she said. 'So we won't find a six-foot-tall, shaggy-haired monster driving a grey transit van with a red stripe over the roof. And I think he has some level of medical knowledge.'

Ford picked up on the oddly detailed hypothetical description. Filed it. Moved on.

'Although he could just have got that off the internet,' he said.

'Yes, or by working in a hospital.'

'When you were investigating the scenes, did you get any sense he might have taken a trophy?'

She shook her head. 'Not from the bodies. The trouble is, you can't see what's missing if you don't know what was there before. What philosophers call a known unknown.'

'Fair enough. We'll leave that for now. But if we find something on a suspect or at their property, it'll be fantastic in court,' he said. 'So we have an MO: talk his way inside, bludgeon, throttle and exsanguinate. We have a signature: the numbers.'

'Yes. The numbers.'

'What do you think they mean?'

137

'We've covered 666, although, as I said, it's a misconception that it's the number of the beast. But in any case, I think the biblical angle is too obvious. Too clichéd. As to 500, it could be the Indianapolis 500. You know?'

'The road race.'

She nodded. 'Or cars. The Fiat 500. Or lots in the US made by Ford. Henry Ford!' She grinned. 'The Ford Five Hundred, the Galaxie 500 and the Custom 500, to name just three. It's also a web status code for internal server error.'

'Or "I'm Gonna Be (500 Miles)" by The Proclaimers.'

'Who?'

'The Scottish band. The geeky-looking guys with glasses?' Ford tried a few lines of the song.

Hannah stared at him blankly. 'You're not a very good singer,' she said when he petered out.

'True. Although I play a mean blues guitar.'

'Really? When?'

He shrugged and sighed. 'Whenever I can. Me and a few guys from the station started a band a few years ago. We're called Blues and Twos. There's me on guitar. Alec Reid plays bass and sings. A DS from the drugs squad plays piano and Georgina Eustace's mortician, Pete, plays drums. We've done a couple of gigs up at the Wyndham Arms.'

'That is very cool. Tell me when you're next playing somewhere. I'd like to come. Where's your guitar?'

'D'you want to see it?'

'I'd love to! Yes, please.'

He got to his feet. 'Wait there.'

He returned a minute later with a battered brown leather case. He laid it on the floor, popped the four brass catches and opened the lid. The electric guitar within gleamed in the light, though its cherry-red finish had faded and its surface bore scars, scuffs and chips. In some places, hard use had worn the thin skin of paint through to the bare wood so that the grain was visible.

'What make of guitar is that?' she asked.

'Fender Stratocaster – 1962. Ash body, maple neck, rosewood fingerboard. The colour's Fiesta Red.' He paused. In his mind's eye, he saw the case encircled by a huge silver ribbon. It was his birthday. Lou was laughing as he unwrapped it. 'My wife gave it to me.'

'Can I hold it?' she asked, reaching out both hands.

He hesitated, just for a second, before handing it to her. 'Careful. It's vintage.'

He watched as she settled the guitar on her knee and plucked at the strings.

She wrinkled her nose. 'Yuk!'

Ford laughed. 'Well, of course "yuk". You need to play a chord.'

'Teach me one.'

Ford reached forward and took the tip of her index finger between his own finger and thumb. She flinched at the contact, then relaxed as he placed the tip on one of the strings.

He pointed at her middle and ring fingers.

'Put that one there, and that one, no, not there – there, yes! Now strum it. Gently.'

She drew the pad of her thumb across the strings and smiled as the guitar emitted a soft, musical sound.

'What is it?'

'E major. The start of a million blues songs.'

She handed the guitar back to him. 'Play one for me.'

He noticed his hand trembling and felt a fluttering in the pit of his stomach. Ignoring both, he began a simple blues shuffle, muting the strings with the palm of his right hand. He sang a few lines quietly, then, as she smiled, built up the volume.

When he finished, with a few little flourishes on the top strings, she clapped loudly.

'You're an excellent guitarist. Did you play for your wife when she was alive?'

Ford wiped the neck of the guitar with a soft cloth. He put the guitar back in its case and snapped the catches shut. Something about Hannah made him feel OK talking about things he'd been keeping tamped down ever since . . . *it* happened.

'Sometimes. It's how we met. I was playing in a pub. She came up to me in the break and we got talking.'

'You're still mourning her, aren't you? Even though it's been six years since she died. Many widowers work through the five stages of grief quicker than that.'

'You're very direct, did you know that? Most people try to pretend it never happened. Either that, or they think I should have got over it by now.'

'Why haven't you?'

He hesitated. Should he just tell her? This unusually frank young woman with a forensic brain might understand why he did – why he *had* to do – what he did. And how it had affected him ever since. No. Not worth the risk. Stick to the story.

'When Lou died, it fractured everything. I lost faith in the universe for a while.' *Especially since the universe made me choose between leaving her to drown or making Sam an orphan.*

'I don't think death is fair or unfair. I think it just happens. Your wife died. You didn't. Tomorrow you might get killed in a car crash. Or I might. Or Sam.'

'Are you always this blunt, or are you making a special effort just for me?'

Ford meant it as a joke, but Hannah frowned and her eyes darted towards the door. Her lips parted, as if she was about to speak. Then she clamped them together again. She looked straight at him, and he felt as though he was being evaluated. Tested against

140

some criterion only she knew about. The muscles in her face relaxed again.

'It's my Asperger's,' she said, her face impassive.

Now he understood. The foreigner-in-a-strange-country vibe he picked up at their first meeting. Her precise way with numbers and dates. Her lack of a filter. He felt pleased she trusted him enough to share this part of herself with him.

'Is that why you frowned when I said our killer was on the intelligent end of the spectrum?' he asked gently.

She nodded. 'I thought you were making fun of me.'

'But you hadn't told me then.'

'I thought you could tell. I know some people think I come across as odd.'

He smiled. 'Listen, for a CSI, believe me, you are way down the oddness scale. Have you *met* Alec?'

'Of *course* I've met him! You introduced me to him on my first day, remember?'

'Joke?'

'That's another thing you might notice about me. Word-jokes are hard for me to understand.'

'Sorry. What sort of jokes *do* you like?'

'I like slapstick. Charlie Chaplin. Buster Keaton. Laurel and Hardy.'

'I used to watch them with Sam when he was little. He used to laugh so hard.'

'He's nice. You're lucky.'

Ford nodded. 'He's OK. He misses his mum, though.'

A silence thickened between them. Ford looked out of the window, watching the tremulous leaves of a silver birch flutter in the breeze.

'Let's get back to our killer,' he said.

After another thirty minutes, Ford held up a sheet of paper on which he'd written notes on their tentative assumptions about the murderer.

MO: bludgeon/throttle/bleed
Signature: writes number in blood on wall
Motive: not sex – stealing life-force (Abbott hypothesis)?

Profile
Interested in/fascinated by blood
Male, strong, fit and over 5'10"
Organised/intelligent/in control
Prob lives with partner
Charming – gift of the gab
Lacks empathy
Shallow emotional responses
Some medical experience as well as knowledge
– not necessarily doctor, could be nurse or even aux. staff – porter?
May have been abused as child

Hannah left at 11.00 p.m., turning down Ford's offer to walk her home.

DAY NINE, 11.45 P.M.

He leans back against the soft cushions she's plumped up for the latest procedure. His heart is racing. That's good. It makes the whole process more efficient.

If it was at the hospital, he'd have just rolled up his sleeve. But here, at home, there's no need for modesty. Especially given what's coming afterwards.

So he's hard. And completely naked. She's not, though. She's got her uniform on. The upside-down watch, everything.

'You're going to feel a little prick,' she murmurs before she slides the needle in.

He leers up at her. 'You're going to feel a big one when we're done.'

'Naughty,' she says, grinning as she releases the clamp.

He watches as the polluted blood drains into the plastic measuring jug he bought from the kitchen shop in town. When the blood reaches the topmost mark, she chokes off the flow.

'Be back in a minute,' she says.

He watches her behind as she carries the jug to the sink and tips the blood away, anticipating the rush when she replaces it.

DAY TEN, 9.15 A.M.

Pale's Mead Farm occupied 243 acres on the south-west side of Salisbury, in a fertile V between the Ebble and Avon rivers. As many farming families had done, faced with global competition and predatory supermarket prices, the Pales had diversified from agriculture, in their case into renting out sustainable eco-cabins on their land.

Outside the cabin furthest from the farm's main buildings, Rory Pale's two-year-old border collie Gem was signalling fear with short, sharp barks. Her tail was tucked between her legs. Her ears lay flat against her skull. Body rigid, she turned and crept back to her master, where she lay down, whining softly.

Rory hadn't seen his tenant for a couple of weeks and had made the two-mile trip on a quad bike to check on him. He stroked the dog's silky head, shushing her, trying to ignore the anxiety he felt at Gem's behaviour.

'Quiet now, girl. Quiet now.'

He walked up to the front door. And caught it immediately. The smell of death. He'd come across enough dead badgers, deer and foxes to recognise it. Knowing in his churning gut that he'd be calling the police in a minute or two, he tried the handle.

The door opened.

He tried to call out his tenant's name. 'Mar—'

The '—cus' died in his throat.

He turned and ran for the quad bike, fumbling his phone out of a pocket.

◆ ◆ ◆

'So, Sandy, if you *could* try just a *little* bit harder, the mayor, the City Council and I would all regard it as a sign of your renewed commitment to getting Salisbury back on its feet again. Cheers, now!'

Sandy slammed her phone down. Her heart was thumping against her ribs like a drunk whacking his head against the cage in a Black Maria. Conversations with the police and crime commissioner rated on her list of favourite activities somewhere above being shot at but below having a smear test.

She stood, knocking her chair back into a framed photo of her shaking hands with a minor royal on his visit to the cathedral. The glass smashed.

'Shit!' she yelled.

Feeling that her options were limited to taking some brisk exercise or suffering a heart attack, she left the shards on the carpet and headed down to see Ford.

She found him in the kitchen on the fourth floor, staring at a jar of coffee and a box of peppermint tea bags.

'I'd go for the caffeine, if I were you. You're going to need it,' she said.

He turned. And he frowned. 'You all right? Someone dent your new Merc?'

'Believe me, that would have been preferable.'

'To what?'

'Martin-effing-Peterson, that's what.'

'What's he done now?'

She felt the rage banked up inside her threatening to burst free again. Took a deep breath. Ran her hands through her hair.

'Our dear PCC has just called to, and I quote, "offer some well-meant advice" on this serial case of ours.'

'Let me guess.' Ford mimicked Peterson's snooty accent: '"You see, Sandy, we've managed to put the whole Novichok business behind us, and we can't afford another dent in our reputation as a global tourist destination. Just get it cleared. Soonest, yes?"' He paused before adding the PCC's favourite sign-off. 'Cheers, now!'

'Bugging my office, are we?'

He shrugged and poured boiling water into a chipped mug. 'Informed guesswork.'

'We could do with a bit of that on these murders. How's it going?'

'My office?'

She took a chair at a small round table covered in papers. Ford sat opposite her.

'I've worked up a preliminary profile with Hannah,' he said.

He outlined their working assumptions about the killer. She listened in silence, nodding at things she liked, pursing her lips at some she didn't.

When he'd finished she said, 'Does any of that help us get closer to finding him?'

'I think it does. And I think it's a close match for Abbott. The profile fits him like a glove. The killer's obsessed by blood. Abbott's a haematologist, for God's sake. How much more do we need?'

Sandy sighed. 'I'm assuming you remember our last conversation. So how about evidence? Something we can take to the CPS? There's hundreds of blokes up at SDH who fit that profile, let alone in Salisbury as a whole.'

'I can feel, it, Sandy. Right here,' he added, placing a hand over his belly. 'He's a wrong 'un.'

She shook her head. 'Not good enough. Not by a long chalk. This is the twenty-first century. How's it going to look if I waltz into a press conference and say, "Morning, ladies and gents, well, it's good news. My star DI has solved the case because his tummy told him who did it"?'

Ford bit down to prevent himself saying something he'd regret. 'We're digging into links between the victims,' he said instead. 'Maybe we'll get lucky that way.'

'Keep me posted, OK? If I have to speak to Peterson again before you have someone in custody, I'll have a stroke.'

Ford's phone rang. It was Jools. She sounded rattled.

'We've got another one, guv. Really bad. And really old.'

Ford drove all the way to the cabin in his own car. The Discovery may have lacked the finesse and sparkle of some of his CID colleagues' wheels, but when it came to investigating rural crimes it had them beat. While they waited for a ride in one of the station's Skoda Yeti 4x4s, he was already heading to the scene.

Gagging as he walked up to the front door, he nodded to Hannah, clad, like her colleagues, in a white paper suit and wearing a rebreather.

'You want one?' she asked him, her voice muffled by the mask.

He shook his head, extracting the tobacco tin from a jacket pocket. 'Got my patented stink-busters.'

With the menthol's minty fumes chilling the inside of his forehead and making his eyes water, he entered the cabin.

Standing at the edge of the room, he logged the similarities with the two earlier crime scenes. His stomach was roiling already, as it always did in the presence of death. Ever since Lou. He began fishing in his pocket for a bag. Realised he'd used his last one at Paul Eadon's flat.

Decomp and hot weather had reduced what had once been a human body to a blackish-purple heap through which off-white knobbles protruded here and there. Maggots writhed over it, their noise a loud, liquid hiss. It lay in a vast patch of dried blood the colour of treacle.

Gulping, and sensing he only had a few more seconds, he looked around the rough, lime-plastered walls.

And, as he'd known he would, he saw it.

167

Black smears. Runs and drips. Clots stuck to the bare plaster. Cruder than the first two numbers.

He closed his eyes. Desperate to catch even a fleeting sense of the killer. *Male, female, kid, adult, I don't care. It's not sex. It's power. I hate them. I hate their blood. I hate blood. That's why I let it all out.*

He gulped. Felt the sweat sheening his face. The smell was so bad. Worse than rotting meat and sewage.

Ford felt his gorge rising.

Ran.

Made it to a hedge.

Puked. Spat. Heaved again.

Straightening, he saw Mick walking over.

'You OK, Henry?'

'Tip-top. You?'

Mick smiled maliciously. 'Might be a while before I have Heinz Big Soup for my tea.'

Ford looked away and drew a cleansing lungful of air. 'Priorities. Identify the victim. I want to know if he or she had any connection to the hospital. Especially to the team that treated Paul Eadon.'

Mick nodded. 'Already done. I talked to the farmer. His name's Rory Pale. I went to school with him.'

Ford raised his eyebrows. 'The victim, Mick?'

'Sorry, boss.' He consulted his notebook. 'Marcus Anderson. Alec said he gave his occupation as environmental activist. One of those bloody troublemakers who—'

'He's not going to cause any trouble now, is he?' Ford snapped.

'Sorry, guv.'

'No, I'm sorry, Mick. The City Council's squeezing the mayor, he's squeezing the PCC, Peterson's squeezing the Python and she's squeezing me.'

'Cosy.'

'As a rat's nest. Listen, it's the same killer. And that means we're going to have a media shitstorm breaking over our heads in the next twenty-four hours or so. We'll have a team briefing about that at five this afternoon.'

He saw Jan talking to a team of uniforms. She was a great POLSA. She knew the police search adviser's job better than he did, so when he walked over to her it was to receive information, not give instructions.

'What are you thinking?' he asked her.

She turned a full circle, shading her eyes against the sun as she faced into it. 'No other dwellings in sight. There are more of these cabins in the next field,' she said. 'The one beyond the river. I'm thinking our killer must have driven, parked out of sight, then walked the last bit. Less likely to arouse suspicion from an eco-warrior like Marcus.'

'There's a track over there. I used it myself.'

'Exactly. I've got a couple of guys looking for tyre marks the CSIs can cast. Other than from a Discovery, obviously,' she said, favouring him with a smile.

'Initial perimeter? How big?'

She inhaled deeply, then wrinkled her nose. 'That muck-spreading doesn't half pong. Fifty-metre-diameter circle?'

He nodded. They'd have their work cut out covering even a small area like that, given the overgrown vegetation. He pointed at a towering oak, its lower limbs kissing the ground.

'It's outside your circle, but check that, too, would you? Call it a captain's pick.'

DAY TEN, 11.38 A.M.

Ford returned to Bourne Hill and convened a team briefing. Standing in front of a whiteboard full of crime scene images, including the three blood-daubed numbers, he looked at each of his team in turn before speaking. He saw tiredness, but not despair. They were still in the game and up for the challenge. Whether they'd be looking like this in six months' time, or in a year, he had no idea. He only knew he had to protect them from the flak that was about to hit them from every angle.

'At some point in the next twelve hours or so, we're going to have the ladies and gentlemen of the media descending on us. I want to set a few ground rules. One' – he held up a finger – 'as always, assume you're speaking on the record. Two, if you say it, expect to see it used where the world and his wife can read it. Possibly with your ugly mug next to it.'

'Better keep Mick out the way, then, guv,' Jools said, provoking laughter from the rest of the room.

Ford smiled. Noted that Mick managed a diplomatic 'Fuck you, Jools!' in response.

'Three, nobody is to mention how Kai Halpern was murdered. Nobody. Understand?'

A chorus of 'Yes, guv/boss/Henry.'

'Olly, how are we getting on with the son of the dead woman? Farrell, was it?'

'William, yes, guv. He's a fit lad. A bodybuilder. Says he was at his gym working out when the first two murders were committed.'

'Corroborated?'

'Working on it.'

'Work harder. And as soon as the pathologist gives us a time of death for Marcus Anderson, ask him for that date too.' He gestured to Jan. 'Anything from the searches yet?'

'Sorry, Henry. Nothing so far, but they're still up there, so fingers crossed. You want me to widen the perimeter?'

'Not for now. He used what came to hand to stun Angie, a punch with Paul, and God alone knows with Marcus. It's classic serial-killer MO evolution. He's refining and adapting as he goes.'

'The signature's consistent, though,' Olly said. 'The bleeding out and the numbers.'

Ford turned to the whiteboard and stabbed an index finger at the three images of the bloody numbers.

666 – tap.

500 – tap.

167 – TAP.

'Significance?'

The room fell silent. Someone snapped a pencil. The crack was loud.

'The numbers are in the wrong order,' Hannah said, keeping her gaze fixed on Ford as all heads swivelled round to look at her.

'No, they're not,' Mick said. '666 was Angie, 500 was Paul and 167 was Marcus.'

'That's the order of discovery. Not the order they were killed. I think Marcus had been dead for longer than a week. More likely, over two. Though we'll need a forensic entomologist to confirm it.'

'You're saying it should go, 167, 666, 500?' Ford said.

'Yes, I am.'

Ford rearranged the photos on the whiteboard. 'Anyone?'

'I'm still seeing that 666, guv,' Mick said. 'Look, serials are nutters, right? This one happens to be a satanic nutter. It's not getting us anywhere, is it?'

Ford agreed. The numbers, the signature, the profile: none of them meant anything until they had a suspect. 'What do you suggest, Mick?'

'What about this guy Jools interviewed? What was his name again?'

'Matty Kyte,' Jools said.

'He works at SDH. So did the first victim. And the second vic was treated there, by her.' Ford tapped the name beneath the photo on the whiteboard. 'Angie, I mean,' Mick corrected himself. 'Then we've got Olly's guy. The justice warrior. His alibis are "I was training at the gym". They're all selling each other steroids, so it'll be flimsy. Just sticking together.'

'Right. I want you and Olly to tie those up. Get CCTV of him arriving and leaving for the times and dates of the murders. Or in their café, if they have one. See if they have a check-in system, time-stamped till receipts or swipe-card data.'

'Guv?'

He looked over at Jools. 'What is it?'

'I was looking at the crime scene photos earlier. From Angie's kitchen. Something weird.'

Jools clicked a couple of keys on her laptop and projected an image on to a blank section of wall.

'Go on.'

'These are the groceries on Angie's kitchen table. What do you notice?'

Silence fell as the assembled investigators scrutinised the image in front of them.

Hannah broke the silence. 'They're all different brands.'

'Of course they are,' Mick said. 'She had coffee, pasta, tinned stuff, cereal. Who buys all one brand?'

'No, not that. The store brands, look.' Hannah pointed. 'Tesco, Waitrose, Asda, Sainsbury's.'

'Exactly,' Jools said. 'When most people go shopping, they stay loyal to one store.'

'Not if they're a bit strapped for cash. Then they shop around for offers,' Mick said.

'Maybe. But Waitrose? Not cheapest for anything, is it?'

Ford saw it. 'The food bank.'

Jools smiled and nodded. 'That's what I reckon. I think poor Angie had more month than money, and when things got tight she went off to the Purcell Foundation.'

Ford made a note in his policy book. 'Thanks, Jools, that's another line of enquiry. Can you start digging, please? Anyone there giving her grief, that sort of thing.' He turned to the end of the table housing the sergeants. 'Mick, can you find out if Paul Eadon was a food-bank user?'

Once the meeting was over, Ford walked with Hannah to Forensics.

'I want to see the photos from the other two crime scenes,' he said.

Seated beside each other at her desk, Hannah called up three folders, labelled *Halpern/S1*, *Eadon/S1* and *Anderson/S1*.

'Those are the primary crime scenes,' she said, before double-clicking on the folder labelled *Eadon/S1*.

She scrolled through until she found a set of images detailing the kitchen cabinets. Slowly, she tabbed through until she found an image of a food cupboard.

She pointed. 'Look.'

There they were. The same random assortment of branded packages. Biscuits from Lidl. Tea from Sainsbury's. Tinned stew from Tesco. Pasta from Aldi.

They looked at each other. 'Food bank,' they said in unison.

The results from Anderson's eco-hut kitchen were the same. More in the way of lentils, beans and wholewheat pasta, but a similar variety of store brands.

'I don't think this is about the hospital at all,' Ford said.

Half an hour later he was on his way to meet Leonie Breakspear, the manager of the Purcell Foundation's food bank.

DAY TEN, 12.30 P.M.

The young woman walking towards Ford with a smile and an out-stretched hand had the tanned face and sun-kissed blonde hair of a surfer.

'I'm Leonie. Welcome,' she said as they shook hands.

She showed him to a partitioned corner of the Purcell Foundation warehouse. The space was fitted out with rudimentary office furniture, including a coffee percolator.

She gestured at it. 'Would you like a cup? Or is that just a TV thing? You know, policemen always drinking coffee?'

He smiled. 'No, it's real-life coppers, too. And yes, please.'

She sat beside the desk rather than behind it, so that they were knee to knee.

'How can I help you?' she said, eyes wide, enquiring.

'Have you seen in the news about the murders?'

She nodded. Ford was impressed by her reaction. No immediate stagy look of horror.

'Of course. Those poor people.'

He nodded. 'We think they were all' – he paused, unsure of the correct term – 'customers. Of the food bank.'

'Here?' she said.

'Unless there's another food bank in Salisbury?'

'No, just us. But, how? I mean, why? Who would do such a thing to people who are already so vulnerable?'

Not wanting to explain to her that muggers, killers, stalkers, paedophiles and rapists *preferred* to go after society's most vulnerable members, he stuck to his training and asked his own questions. 'Do you have a list of people who come here?'

'Yes. We ask all new customers to fill out a simple form. We help the ones with literacy problems. But it's confidential. You can see that, surely? To preserve their dignity.'

'Of course. But if they *were* customers, that's a very strong link between them. The killer may be targeting people who use the food bank. Believe me, I have no interest in subjecting any of your customers to intrusive or undignified questioning, and we would keep their identities confidential.' *Unless and until we arrest one. Then all bets are off.*

She looked as if she was in pain, screwing up her face and hunching her shoulders. 'I do understand, really I do. But there are rules. Policies. Procedures.'

Fighting down an urge to shout that he was trying to prevent any more of her customers being bled to death, Ford switched tack. 'Let's leave your customers for now. How about a list of employees? And do you have volunteers?'

She puffed her cheeks out, nodding. 'I suppose that would be all right. Can I email it to you?'

'I'd rather take it away with me.'

Back at Bourne Hill, Ford gathered the team together. He passed a stack of A4 sheets of paper to Olly. 'Take one, pass them on, as they say at police college.'

'Who are they, guv?' Jan asked.

'Purcell Foundation employees and volunteers. Divide them up between you and put a basic personal and lifestyle profile together for each one. Use the PNC, social media, Google, whatever. Everyone on it, please. Back here at three.'

With the team reconvened in the conference room later that afternoon, Ford clapped his hands to still the buzz of conversation. 'These are all persons of interest. I want them interviewed as soon as possible.'

'In pairs?' Mick asked.

'Ideally, yes,' he said. 'But there are a lot of people on that list and we're up against a serial killer who's already accelerating. So, let's map them against our suspect profile and score them. Do the ten with the highest scores in pairs, the rest take one each.'

Half an hour passed in a hubbub of activity as the assembled investigators and CSIs reviewed every person on Ford's list against the basic suspect profile he and Hannah had drawn up. Finally, he had ten names written up on the whiteboard.

Geoff Dowd
Mark Packham
Lance Williams
Philip O'Rourke
Matthew Kyte
James Collins
Lenny Hayes
Jason Torrance
Robert Babey
Jasmin Fortuna

He looked at the fifth name, then at Jools. She was staring at the list, lips pressed together. Focused. Hungry.

'OK. Those are our top ten,' Ford said. 'Nine men and one woman who won a medal in the European Powerlifting Championships.' He looked to his left. 'Jan, can you and Mick sort out the interviews, please? Bring in a couple of PSIs, if you can find any spare in General CID.'

Ford emerged from the briefing room to see Sandy marching down the corridor towards him in full battle dress: cobalt-blue jacket over a white shirt, tailored charcoal trousers, heels that matched the jacket. And a lot more make-up than usual.

'Henry!' she barked. 'Where do you think you're going?'

He pointed to his office. 'Work?'

'Wrong! Well, right. With me. Press conference in the big meeting room in five.'

He sighed. Was there any point protesting? Did anyone win arguments with the Python? *Worth a try.*

'Do you really need me? I've got a ton of paperwork to catch up on.'

She reached out, clapping her hands on his shoulders. He recognised her perfume: Chanel No5. She always wore it for press conferences. Claimed it gave her confidence to stare down the mob.

'Welcome to my world, *DI* Ford.' She gave him a wry smile. 'Of course, if handling the media isn't your thing, I could always bump you back down to DS. I'm sure Mick Tanner would be more than willing to step up to the plate.'

'It's fine, boss. No need to take such a drastic step. You want me to lead?'

'You spoil me,' she said, winking.

He fell into step beside her; they took the stairs.

Sandy stopped dead on one of the half-landings, causing Ford to bump into her. 'Oh, and Henry?'

'What?'

'Smarten yourself up a bit. That suit looks like you slept in it. Can't do much about it now, but run a comb through your hair, at least.'

Although the new building was supposed to be air-conditioned, the system was struggling against the heat generated by thirty journalists and their assorted equipment.

With no great relish, Ford opened proceedings. 'Good afternoon.' He hesitated, startled by the sudden volley of flashes as the stills photographers grabbed their first pictures. 'Three days ago, the body of a man was discovered in a flat in the centre of Salisbury. Today, we discovered the body of a second man on a farm on the southern outskirts of the city. We are treating—'

'Were they bled dry?' a voice rang out.

Frowning, Ford tried again. 'We are treating both deaths as suspicious.'

'Is there a vampire at work in Salisbury?'

General laughter.

'Keep calm, Henry,' Sandy whispered, looking down at her notes.

'At this point I am unable to speculate as to the killer's identity,' he said, fighting the urge to get up and leave. 'The cause of death in both cases was exsanguination, which matches that of Angela Halpern.'

'So it *is* the same killer?' a journalist shouted. 'Is there a serial killer in Salisbury?'

Sandy pressed her leg against Ford's, her signal for him to let her take over.

'There isn't enough evidence at this stage of the investigation to draw such a conclusion,' she said. 'We're asking the public for two things. One, to be vigilant. Think twice before letting a stranger into your home. And two, to inform the police by calling Bourne Hill Police Station, or Crimestoppers, if they see or hear anything suspicious.'

'What, like someone turning into a bat?' the same journalist shouted, prompting more laughter.

Sandy kept a fixed smile plastered on to her face, and waited them out. The room fell silent under her glare.

'If anyone has a *sensible* question, now would be the moment,' she said.

'Do you have any suspects yet?' a young woman with a FREELANCE badge pinned to her top called out. Several of the older male journalists craned their necks to take a better look at her.

'At the moment, we are pursuing several lines of enquiry. We have identified a number of persons of interest, and DI Ford and his team are working flat out to interview them all for elimination purposes.'

'So, that's a no, then?'

Sandy smiled again. 'I have full confidence in DI Ford and his team. They will identify a suspect, and when they do, I can assure you, we will communicate that fact to you.' She stood. 'Thank you all.' Then, under her breath, as the noise levels soared, 'Come on, Henry, let's grab a quick drink at the Wyndham Arms.'

Sitting with their drinks, a large vodka and tonic for her and an orange juice and soda for him, Sandy combed her fingers through her hair.

'Who was that loudmouth making the wisecracks?'

'I couldn't see. To be honest, I haven't done many of these, boss. I'm not sure I'd know him by sight anyway.'

'How about the girl? The one with the tight top the blokes couldn't keep their eyes off. Have you seen her before?'

Ford shook his head. 'I had someone called Kerry Battle on the phone from Sky a couple of days back. Maybe the girl was her stringer.'

Sandy grunted. 'Huh! I'd like to string her up. Impertinent little cow.'

Ford grinned. 'And there was me thinking you looked like butter wouldn't melt.'

'That's the magic power of Chanel for you. Seriously, though, what are your thoughts so far?'

He sipped his drink. 'Despite your nice deflection of that journalist's question, we *do* have a serial killer on our patch,' he said. 'And he's working fast. I mean, Christ, three adults and a kid in, what, a month?'

'I know. He's going to keep on going, isn't he?'

'Until he's caught, or we put too much heat on him and he leaves the area, yes.'

'What do we know about him?'

'Taking the cases as a whole, there are two interesting features. The adult victims were all using the food bank. And I have this feeling there's also a link to the hospital.'

'This isn't about Mr Abbott, again?'

Yes. It is. Ford shook his head. 'Angie Halpern worked there. Paul Eadon was treated for a blood infection up there. And the killer has shown more than a rudimentary knowledge of anatomy and medical procedures for drawing blood.'

'You think it's a doctor?'

'Yeah, or a nurse. Or a care assistant. Or the chief executive, for all I know. Just, they've got some sort of connection. I'm sure of it.'

'I know you're doing your best. So forgive me for what I'm about to say,' said Sandy, looking him straight in the eye. 'But, just try, you know? To catch him before he does another one.'

'That's the plan,' he said.

They finished their drinks and walked back down College Street towards Bourne Hill and their respective offices.

After catching up on witness statements, interview transcripts and reports from the different investigating teams, Ford checked his watch, and swore.

It was 6.15 p.m. He still had a mountain of paperwork to get through, and he'd promised to drive Sam to a friend's house out in the sticks for a paintball party.

He called Miles. 'Any chance you could run Sam out to Broad Chalke? He's due at a party at seven and I'm going to be stuck at work for another couple of hours.'

'Sorry, mate. Eleanor and I are just leaving for a charity do. It's in the opposite direction. I'm really sorry.'

'It's fine. I ask too much of you guys as it is. I'll leave now. Take the work with me.'

◆ ◆ ◆

Fifteen minutes later, stomach clenched with tension from fighting to get through the rush-hour traffic, Ford swerved off Rainhill Road and scrunched to a sliding stop on the gravel. His phone had been pinging incessantly. He looked down, hoping it was Jools with a breakthrough in the case.

Where are you? Lift to Max's, remember?
Where are you? Party starts @ 7
Not cool, Dad
Where are u?
Don't make me late
u knew about this for weeks
WHERE ARE YOU?
WHERE ARE YOU?
WHERE ARE YOU?
WHERE ARE YOU?

Sam was sitting on the front doorstep, staring at his phone. He looked up as Ford peered out at him. His face was dark, those deep-brown eyes black with fury.

'I'm sorry, Sam,' Ford said. 'You ready?'

Wordlessly, Sam got to his feet and climbed into the rear of the Discovery.

The drive took them deep into the countryside, down single-track lanes beneath ivy-throttled trees leaning towards each other like drunks walking home from a country pub.

Ford tried again. 'Sam, I'm sorry I had to keep you waiting. It's the case. It's—'

'—obviously more important than I am.'

'No! Of course not. Nothing in this world is more precious to me than you. You know that.'

'Do I? Oh, thanks for updating me on what I know. Because sometimes I wonder if I even *have* a dad,' Sam said. 'I spend more time with the Pitts than I do with you.'

'That's not true. I'm doing the best I can. But since my promotion, I'm taking on a lot more responsibility. It's going to get better, I promise.'

'"It's going to get better, I promise,"' Sam said in a mocking little voice.

'For Christ's sake, Sam, I've got a mortuary with four dead bodies in it, three bled dry by some psycho with a thing for blood. I'm here, aren't I? Driving you to the paintball party, as agreed. What's the problem?'

'What's the problem?' Sam's voice cracked as he yelled at Ford. 'The problem is you care more about dead people than me!'

Ford slammed his right foot down on the brake pedal. The Discovery lurched to a stop on a patch of grass verge, the anti-lock brake system juddering, a dust cloud swirling past the windscreen.

He spun round in his seat, glaring at Sam, who was red-eyed, on the verge of tears, staring out of the side window.

Ford's pulse was painful in his throat. He felt his own held-back tears threatening to burst their banks beneath his eyeballs. He inhaled and let the breath out gently.

'I miss her, too. I miss her so much it hurts,' he said quietly. 'Every day. And when I look at you, my darling boy, I see her. And that makes it better, and worse, because you look so much like her.' He watched as Sam sniffed and dragged a sleeve across his nose. 'I'm sorry if I've been ignoring you. I'm trying my best, but it's hard bringing you up on my own. You know, the way Gran brought me up on *her* own. It's hard,' he finished, lamely, wishing he could spin back the hands on the clock of his life to ten minutes before he and Lou set off to climb Pen-y-holt for the final time.

'Can we go, please?' Sam asked.

Ford took his foot off the brake and pulled away. He dropped Sam at his friend's house at two minutes to seven.

◆ ◆ ◆

Later that night, as he sipped from a bottle of beer while reading interview transcripts, a pair of texts from Sam arrived:

Staying at Max's.
His dad's bringing a few of us home tomorrow

A second later, a follow up.

Sorry

He tapped out a reply. Equally terse.

Me 2

That was what you did. Ford had learned the hard way. Less is more. Desperate to narrow the gap between them but not knowing how, he took a fresh bottle from the fridge door and climbed the stairs to the spare room. He opened his guitar case, lifted out the red guitar, plugged it in and switched on the amp.

DAY ELEVEN, 9.05 A.M.

The next morning, another of Ford's lines of enquiry collapsed in on itself. Olly knocked on his office door and told him William Farrell's alibi was watertight.

'Like you said, guv. I checked with the gym's CCTV, everything. He's there in glorious technicolour, arriving and leaving when he said he did,' he said. 'Plus, I've got corroboration from the receptionist, a couple of lads working out with him and one of the personal trainers.'

'What about the drugs angle? You think anyone might have been covering for him? He could have arrived then slipped out again.'

'I had a quiet chat with the manager there. He told me they had some trouble with steroids a couple of years back – one of the trainers.' He shrugged. 'They sacked him, and now there's an instant ban for anyone caught with them. I think they're clean.'

'Thanks, Olly, good work.'

Ford looked down at the list in front of him: the staff of the Haematology Department at SDH. He'd had them all interviewed informally, pulling in a couple of PSIs to help with the task. All the males with a high score on his suspect matrix had alibis. The low-scoring males, and the women, he discounted for now. The PSIs' interview notes all came back with different versions of the same story. Basically 'I don't see him/her as a serial killer.'

Sighing, he cradled his cheeks in his palms and stared at the now-useless list. Had his instinct for a wrong 'un deserted him? He'd felt sure Abbott was involved somehow, but he had an alibi and Ford knew he had no evidence to take to Sandy, let alone the CPS. The porter was looking like a dead loss, too, with his own alibi.

He screwed up the list and tossed it into the bin in the corner.

'Follow the evidence, Henry,' he said with a sigh. 'Follow the bloody evidence.'

And he started to reread the files from the beginning.

◆　◆　◆

The conference room at Bourne Hill was packed: Ford's immediate team, plus Hannah, Alec Reid, the PSIs, CID detectives drafted in and a few uniforms, including Nat Hewitt.

The door opened and everyone turned to see who'd arrived after the scheduled start time.

There was a chorus of 'ma'ams' as the latecomer revealed herself to be Sandy, resplendent in a tailored mustard top and black leather skirt.

'How's it going, Henry?' she asked, pulling out a chair and sinking into it with a grateful sigh.

'Good.' *Bad, but that's not what the troops need to hear.*

'OK if I say a few words?'

He nodded.

She pushed back from the table and made her way round the edge to the front, squeezing past a couple of the chairs whose occupants were too slow to pull themselves in. She ran a hand through her hair and took her time looking around the room, building the tension.

Then she released it. 'Serial killers. Don't you just hate the twisted little sods?'

The room erupted in laughter. Ford joined in, grateful for the chance to let off some steam in their own safe space, free of the prying eyes and ears of journalists, police and crime commissioners and all the other people who reckoned they knew better than the cops how to do the job.

Once a semblance of order was restored, apart from a few sniffs as the female officers dabbed at mascara tears, Sandy continued.

'Three's the charm, you all know that. Some of you might have known in your waters you were facing a serial. Well, now it's official,' she said. 'Which means more resources, but also more scrutiny.' She turned to Ford. 'I had the PCC on the phone earlier, bending my ear about the need for a "swift resolution to this distressing case".'

This prompted more smiles.

'And more media, I suppose,' Ford said, scowling.

'Than you could shake a stick at. Just play nice and try to use them as much as they use us.'

'I'll behave. I promise.'

'Which I choose to take at face value,' she said, offering him the faintest of winks. 'One more thing. Three linked homicides makes this a Home Office-specified Cat 1 investigation. You get an operation name.'

'What are we on this time, ma'am?' Jools called out. 'Wild flowers? Birds of prey?'

'Coastal features. You're now the investigative team on Operation Shoreline.'

Olly fought the urge to punch the air. He exited the CCTV program. He saw Ford in his office, frowning as he typed, and hurried over.

'Guv?'

Ford looked up.

'I got a hit on the CCTV at the city end of Wyvern Road. The road's dead most of the time. But at 8.32 p.m. on the night Angie and Kai were murdered a grey VW Polo drove by. Looked like a male at the wheel.'

'Index number?'

Olly shook his head. 'Obscured.'

'Track every grey Polo in Salisbury, then widen it out to the rest of Wiltshire, Dorset and Hampshire. I want to know who was behind the wheel.'

Ford watched the young DC's back as he marched to his desk. *The boy's ambitious, like I was. Am! Jesus, I need to get a result on this. My first big one since becoming a DI. The media will hang me out to dry if it turns into a runner.*

Wanting to banish the negative thoughts, he called Mick. 'How are the food-bank interviews coming?'

'Slow, but good. Nobody stands out yet. Most have alibis. A few don't, but you know the type,' he said. 'They're the library volunteers, the people who plant flowers on verges and roundabouts, the Neighbourhood Watchers, the PTA chairmen. I'm not picking up a vibe from any of them. Same for the others.'

'Keep at it. I'm going mad here with report-writing. Can you send me a couple of names off the list you haven't interviewed yet?'

While he was waiting for Mick's email, Jan stepped into his office. She looked pleased.

'Cat got the cream?' he asked.

'A whole bucket. Look.'

She held out a clear debris pot with a black screw-top lid. He read the label.

Holding it up to the light, he saw a scrap of fabric.

'It was caught on a sharp bit of bark in a fork,' Jan said. 'Your captain's pick. Looks like our man might have been hiding there while he waited for Marcus to appear.'

'Good work, Jan, although it could just have come from a kid playing. Get it to Forensics. Maybe there are some epithelials or hairs attached.'

A few minutes later, an email arrived from Mick. Ford had two people to trace, interview and eliminate – TIE, as the jargon had it: Lenny Hayes and Jasmin Fortuna, both volunteers.

Hayes's phone went straight to voicemail. Ford left a short message requesting an interview. He dialled Fortuna next.

'Hi, this is Jaz.'

'Jasmin Fortuna?'

'Yes. Who's this?'

'I'm Detective Inspector Ford from Wiltshire Police. I'd like to have a chat with you about the Purcell Foundation. Today, if possible.'

'Do I have to come into the police station?'

Ford smiled and injected a lightness into his tone he wasn't feeling. 'Nothing as formal as that. I can come to you, if you like.'

'You can come round now, in that case. I'm doing my nails. Gonna be a while yet. I've only just started.'

Ford parked the Discovery on the street a few doors down from Fortuna's house, a new-build on an estate on the western edge of the city. The developers had mixed styles and sizes of dwelling, giving the impression of a village rather than row after row of identical boxes.

A metallic-pink BMW 3 Series convertible sat on the concrete drive beside the house, its twin-kidney radiator grille facing the road.

He heard a chain rattling, then a lot of metallic clicks and scrapes from the far side of the door. 'Bugger! Hold on. It's my nails.'

The door swung open. Ford tried hard not to stare. The woman facing him was dressed in a silky white T-shirt and leggings that did nothing to disguise her physique. Which, Ford reflected ruefully, was more muscular than his had ever been in his life.

Her pectoral muscles bulged sideways from the T's armholes and pushed her small breasts out towards him. Biceps, triceps – every muscle group looked inflated. Her caramel skin, which shone in the sunlight, emphasised their interlocking angles, curves and planes.

'Mrs Fortuna?'

She cackled. 'Blimey! That's a bit formal. Call me Jaz. My clients do.'

An unworthy thought flickered through Ford's mind. 'Clients?' he repeated, striving to sound neutral.

His efforts failed. 'Not that kind. Naughty boy! Nails,' she deadpanned, waggling the backs of the fingers on her right hand at him. They were tipped with pink-and-white candy-striped talons studded with sparkling gemstones. 'Look,' she added, pointing at the side of the BMW.

He turned.

Flowing pink script read 'Nailz by *Jaz*', with website, email, mobile number, plus social media icons.

'Can I come in?' he asked.

Having accepted the offer of coffee and then being told to 'make one for me too, would you, a latte? It's my nails,' Ford explained why he was there and what he and his team were doing. He gave her the date and time of Angie and Kai Halpern's murders.

'Where were you then, Jaz?'

'Easy! I was in Reading, at a competition. I'm a powerlifter.' She flexed her biceps, kissing each in turn. 'Big guns, tight buns, eh?' She cackled again.

He gave her another date.

She looked upwards. 'Tenth wedding anniversary. Out with my family. Loads of us. We're Filipino. My mum works up at the hospital. Lot of Filipinos up there.'

'One final date, Jaz.'

She listened carefully, then paused before answering. Looked up and to the left, then back at Ford. She shrugged. 'Here, I think, with Dom. He's my husband. I'd have to check, but I'm pretty sure. We only go out at the weekend, and I know I wasn't training or at an event.'

'It's fine. But if you wouldn't mind letting me know once you've double-checked.'

He handed her a card, which she took between the pads of her outstretched finger and thumb.

'Is this about the murders?' she asked, putting the card on a side table.

'Yes. Did you know any of the victims?'

'Remind me of their names again?'

'Angie and Kai Halpern. Paul Eadon. Marcus Anderson.'

'I used to say hi to Angie when she came to the food bank. I met her once, up at the hospital when I was collecting my mum. She was such a caring person – why anyone would want to hurt her, I don't know.'

'How about the other two?'

She wrinkled her nose. 'Paul, I remember. Horrible man. God forgive me for saying this,' she said, crossing herself, ''cause he was poor and using the food bank, but he was trash. You know that, right?'

'I do. But even trashy people have the right to life.'

She rolled her eyes, which were a deep brown and fringed by thick curtains of lashes. 'You sound like Reverend Cox.'

'And he is?'

'Chairman of the trustees. Like, not the ones who work there. They're more like posh people who make sure everyone's doing their best for our clients,' she said. 'There's even a lord. That good-looking one, you know? Lord Bodenham?'

Somewhere in Ford's brain, two unconnected cogs meshed together.

He stood. 'Thanks, Jaz. You've been really helpful.'

She bounced to her feet. 'Is that it, then?'

He smiled. 'That's it.'

'You're not going to slap the cuffs on me?' she said, holding out her hands.

'Not today.'

She pouted. 'Shame. I wouldn't mind getting the third degree off of you.'

Then she winked. Ford felt a blush heating his cheeks.

At the Purcell Foundation's main office on Castle Street, a converted Georgian townhouse, Ford asked the receptionist if Leonie Breakspear was available.

'I'm sorry, she's at a conference in London on food security and sustainability.'

'Is there someone else in a position of authority I can speak to?'

'Rachel's here. I don't think she has any meetings until later.'

'Rachel?'

'Taylor. She's the CEO.'

'Could you let her know I'm here, please?'

The woman in jeans and a polo shirt who welcomed Ford at the top of the narrow flight of stairs was tall, with an athletic physique. Despite her height, she moved gracefully, as if she'd been a dancer. She was in her mid-forties, her dark brown hair cut short, with a low, straight fringe. Her dark eyes sat above a wide, smiling mouth.

'Sorry about the climb. We're listed, so no lift.'

She led him to her office, a room that must have been the master bedroom, with a marble fireplace and triple sash windows that gave out on to a small courtyard garden.

'Are you wondering about my clothes?' she asked, catching him staring at her jeans.

'Sorry. Force of habit. Your receptionist said you were the CEO.'

Smiling, she tapped the embroidered logo on the polo shirt. 'Staff uniform. I was helping out this morning. I save the power suits for the big donors.'

'People like Lord Bodenham?'

'Ben's a good friend. He's very generous. With his time *and* his money.'

'I'm investigating four murders. You've read about them?'

'Yes. Leonie told me they were all customers of ours – the adults, at least,' she said.

'We've been interviewing your staff and volunteers. One mentioned the trustees. Do you have a list of their names and contact details?'

'Surely you researched our website? They're there in plain view.'

'I did. But websites show what organisations want to tell the public. Not necessarily what they want to tell the police.'

She frowned and pursed her lips. 'What are you suggesting? We have nothing to hide.'

He shrugged. 'I'd like to make sure I have a complete list. Perhaps you have new ones you haven't got round to putting on your website.'

Her face relaxed and she smiled a second time. 'I'm sorry. I'm under a lot of pressure as it is, and these murders. . .' She tailed off. 'Those poor people.'

'Which is why I and my team are working hard to try and catch their killer. So, the list?'

'Of course,' she said, nodding and opening a laptop. 'Hold on.'

A laser printer beside her desk hummed. She gave Ford the single warm sheet.

He scanned the list.

Geoff Riley
Paul Wallace
Frances Mackay
Chris Law
Nicola Cronin
Charles Abbott
Revd Julian Cox
David Valentine
Lord Bodenham (President)

'Tell me,' he said, eyes locked on to the sixth name, 'are they actively involved, your trustees, or just names on the letterhead?'

'Oh, very much the former. I encourage them to put in a few hours at the sharp end every month. I have no time for people using us to add some right-on credentials to their CV in the hopes of an MBE.'

'And they do that, do they? Get involved at the sharp end?'

She smiled. 'Some more than others, but yes, they do. They're all very committed to our work.'

Back in his car, Ford sat with the key in his hand. *It's you, Abbott. It has to be. Everywhere I turn, there you are. To hell with the chief con. And Sandy will thank me when I bring you in.*

DAY ELEVEN, 2.00 P.M.

Ford sat at his desk and made a call, trying to ignore the resentment making his lip curl. It was answered after ten rings.

'Hello again, Mr Abbott. DI Ford here. I—'

'I must say, I'm rather surprised to hear your voice interrupting my afternoon,' Abbott said. Ford heard the smile in his voice. 'I thought I'd made my feelings about your behaviour clear.'

'You did. And I must apologise for my manner at our last meeting. I was out of order. I'm sorry.'

'Well, that's better. Apology accepted. We all lose our tempers from time to time. Some more readily than others, but there you are. How may I help you?'

'I wonder whether you'd have time for another chat.'

'If you're after more blood talk, I assume you have the internet. Just Google it. No doubt Wikipedia has more information than you could possibly need or want.'

'No. No more blood talk. I'd like to talk to you about your work for the Purcell Foundation. This afternoon, if possible.'

A theatrical sigh. 'I have rounds from three till four. I can give you fifteen minutes, then I have a meeting with some colleagues.'

'Four it is.'

Abbott's suit jacket was on its hanger, as it had been during their last meeting. Ford discerned the edges of dark patches under the arms of the consultant's pink shirt.

'Tell me about your work at the Purcell Foundation,' Ford said, notebook ready on his knee.

'I'm a trustee.'

'Which means?'

'I oversee the work of the management. It's largely about good governance,' Abbott said. 'Making sure everyone's acting according to the Foundation's ethics policy – the charity laws, yes? A quarterly meeting, the odd fund-raising reception. Tiresome, if I'm being brutally honest, but one has to do one's bit, doesn't one?'

'Oh, one does. One does.'

Abbott's lips tightened and his eyes flashed. A momentary expression, then it was gone. He checked his Rolex, pulling his cuff up to give Ford an eyeful. 'Was there anything else?'

'Yes. What do you do when you volunteer at the food bank?'

'I think I just told you.'

'I'm sorry,' Ford said, smiling. 'I didn't make myself clear. I spoke to Rachel Taylor today and she said the trustees all put in time on the frontline. I think the phrase she used was "We don't want CV-polishers on our board." Something like that, anyway. What do you do when *you're* on the frontline, Mr Abbott?'

Abbott pulled his cuff down again. 'You know, handing out food parcels, helping people carry their bags to their cars. Or the bus stop. The usual.'

'Did you ever help Angie Halpern?'

'I can't remember. I might have done.'

'Paul Eadon?'

Abbott frowned and touched his lower lip. 'Maybe. I'm not sure. There are rather a lot of them.'

'Doesn't say much for our society, does it?'

'I really wouldn't know. Most of them could pay their way if they put in a bit more effort. Look, where are you going with this?'

'How about Marcus Anderson?'

'No, again. I'm sorry.'

Ford shrugged. Onwards. 'I'm trying to build up a picture of the victims and their lives. They're linked by the food bank, so I need to ascertain whether that's how their murderer selected them,' he said. 'Tell me, have you noticed anyone acting suspiciously when you've been volunteering there?'

'Pocketing baked beans meant for the poor, you mean?' Abbott said with a smirk.

Ford waited a few seconds before trusting himself to answer. *Was that a deliberate choice, Abbott? Are you taunting me?* 'Possibly. Or engaging in inappropriate conversations with customers.'

'No. Nothing like that. Nothing.'

Ford gave his 'reassuring the suspect' smile and leaned back in his chair. 'Just a few more questions, and then you can go to your meeting.'

'Thank you. It is rather important.'

For the third time, Ford recited the times and dates of the murders. 'Where were you on each of those dates?'

Abbott's face was neutral. 'I'm afraid I'll have to get back to you on that one.'

'No diary?'

'Of course. I'm sorry. You just flustered me there for a second.'

'It's just routine. So we can eliminate you from our enquiries.'

Abbott checked his phone, swiping, frowning, swiping, frowning.

'Any joy?' Ford asked.

'I was at home each time.'

'With someone, or alone?'

'With my wife.'

'Well, that's you in the clear. Thank you, Mr Abbott. You've been most helpful.'

Abbott smiled, briefly. 'You're just doing your job.'

Ford rose from his chair and turned towards the door, then back to Abbott, over whom he now towered. 'Do you work out?'

'What?'

'You're in good shape for a man of your age. Do you go to the gym?'

'Oh. I see. No, is the answer. I play tennis when I can.'

Ford tutted. 'Best I ever manage is cutting the grass, and even that's behind a motor mower.'

Then he turned on his heel and left. Planning his next moves. Which in his mind involved handcuffs and a lengthy stay at Bourne Hill's custody suite.

DAY ELEVEN, 7.45 P.M.

Just nineteen, Nina Gow was old beyond her years, having spent most of her childhood bouncing around foster families and children's homes, before that glorious, bloody *immense* day when she turned eighteen and sharing the flat with her bestie became a reality, not a dream. OK, so they had no money, beyond the crappy little amount they got each week in benefits. But they had fun. And the food bank meant they didn't starve.

She spat out a curse when her key refused to turn in the cheap lock the landlord insisted was 'perfectly all right for the likes of you'. Then, with a crack, the mechanism admitted defeat.

'Thank God for that, I really need a wee,' she said, slamming the thin door behind her. 'Babe! You in? I got cider.'

She checked her phone on the way up the stairs then put it back in her pocket. She placed the plastic bag of cans on the kitchen counter and walked down the hall to the bathroom, already tugging at the stretchy belt on her jeans.

She opened the door. And she screamed. Her bladder let go. And she didn't notice.

Aimee was standing in the bath, arms above her head, her naked body sagging. Why was her face dark purple? And why were her eyes bulging out like that? And why was her tongue sticking out? And what, what, oh, Holy Mother of God, what was that in the bath? Blood? *No. Not that much, it's impossible.*

Shaking violently, Nina tried to pull her phone out of her jeans pocket, but it wouldn't budge.

She sank to her knees. 'Oh, please, oh, please, come on, come on, come ON!'

Finally, she managed to yank it free, and with a trembling finger tapped out the number she'd only ever associated with trouble for her or Aimee. Or both of them.

◆ ◆ ◆

Ford arrived at the flat on Water Street at 8.45 p.m. The road was cordoned off, with uniformed loggists at both ends. A white CSI van was parked outside and he spotted the pathologist's car double-parked a few doors down. He pushed through the crowd of phones-aloft onlookers, gave his collar number to the PC on duty and ducked under the blue-and-white crime scene tape.

He met Jools outside the house. She was pale, her lips were clamped into a line.

'You OK, Jools?'

'Yes, fine. It's just, you know.'

'Yeah, I do. Never gets easier, but you'll find you get better at coping.'

'Jesus, I hope so.'

'What do we have? Judging from your face, I'd say it's our boy again?'

'Female victim. Exsanguinated. But he's changed his MO.'

Ford felt his pulse quicken. Changes to the MO might mean the killer was escalating. And that might mean he was getting confident. And *that* might mean he'd get careless.

'Changed it how?'

'It looks like he's knocked her out, then dragged her into the bathroom and manhandled her into the bath, and then he's hung her from the open window over the tub. He must have put the plug in. It's all still in there.'

Ford nodded. 'Get a door-to-door going. Say, ten houses in each direction, plus all the flats here. Someone must have seen *something*.'

Jools pointed to a young woman talking to a paramedic. 'She found the body. She shares the flat with her. I tried to talk to her, but she's pretty shaken.'

'Make sure she doesn't leave. I want to talk to her. I'll be down in a while.'

He went inside and climbed the stairs to the second-floor flat, pausing on the landing to don a crime scene suit and bootees.

The bathroom was tiny, less than six feet square. There was only room for a single CSI, and Ford recognised Hannah, crouching by the bath and inspecting spatters on its white plastic sides. He looked at the body, suspended by its wrists from the window. Looked away.

'Hi,' he said, inhaling, then regretting it as his stomach twitched.

'Hi, Henry.'

'This is new.'

'Yes. It's very exciting.'

'Why?'

'He's changed his MO. That means a lack of discipline, and I'm fairly sure *that* means he's losing control.'

'How sure?'

'Eight-seven point nine per cent.'

'Not eighty-eight?'

'Ha! Got you!' Her eyes flashed in the gap between her hood and facemask. 'I can't really calculate my certainty levels to that degree of accuracy.'

He nodded. 'Good one,' he deadpanned. 'And at a crime scene, too. We'll make a detective out of you one day.'

'No, thanks. I'll stick with the dead.'

He looked around, but the number he'd been expecting was absent. Then he saw why. None of the walls had enough free space. The shower attachment blocked one. Another held a mirrored medicine cupboard. The third, toothpaste-whitened glass shelves crammed with cosmetics, shampoos, hairbrushes, boxes of tampons, hair slides, scrunchies, toothbrushes and, tucked behind a plastic unicorn with a rainbow mane, a packet of condoms.

'It's in the bedroom next door,' Hannah said.

Ford entered the pink-curtained room and looked at the bed. Above the headboard, each digit scrawled in four bloody streaks, was a number. *Did you do a finger painting, like Kai's?*

333

Ford closed his eyes. Allowed the nausea to rise, focused on the enveloping sense that he was growing to know the killer.

I enjoyed this one. I enjoyed her a lot. She was a fleshy thing. And I was alone in here. That's why I spent time displaying her like a butcher's shop turkey. I'm going to make a mistake soon. You just have to be smart enough to find me.

Ford opened his eyes and left the bedroom. He felt the nausea fade away. *Is that because I'm close?*

Outside again, he went over to the ambulance. Legs dangling from the tailgate, a skinny young woman – late teens, he guessed – was smoking a roll-up. A paramedic had wrapped her in a blanket and she was clutching it to her chest.

She looked up, eyes red-rimmed, and blew out a lungful of smoke in Ford's direction. 'Don't tell me it'll kill me. I don't care.'

'I won't. Not my place. I'm Ford. What's your name?'

'What sort of a name is that?'

'You can call me Henry, if you'd prefer.'

She shrugged and looked away. 'Don't care, do I?'

He'd met girls like her before. Hard-nosed as a Raymond Chandler gangster's moll on the outside. But scratch the surface and, nine times out of ten, you found a lost little girl. Battling to play the shittiest cards life could deal her, short of dropping her in front of a train.

'So, what do they call you?'

'Nina. Nina Gow.'

'Nina, I'm so sorry you had to be the one to discover your friend like that. Can you tell me her name?'

She took a trembling drag on her roll-up and exhaled. 'Aimee. Cragg.' She burst into tears. 'Who *does* something like that? It's that serial killer, isn't it? *He* did it!'

'Can you tell me what time you found Aimee, Nina? It's important.'

She sniffed. 'Quarter to eight. I know 'cause I checked my phone on the way in.'

'Where had you been?'

'The shops. I got some cider.'

'Which shop?'

'Tommy's Store on Brown Street.'

'I know it. Were you with Aimee before you went to the shops?'

She nodded. 'We were watching YouTube.'

'What time did you go out?'

She shuddered and scrunched herself tighter into the blanket, even though it was a hot evening. 'Must have been about seven.'

'Forty-five minutes to buy cider?'

'I met a couple of mates, OK? We had a chat and a smoke. Look, can I go now?'

Ford made a quick note. It was a very tight window. The killer must have waited for Nina to leave. She was lucky to be alive.

'One more question. Did Aimee ever use the food bank?'

'Sometimes. We both did. Aimee went up there earlier today. Money's tight, you know? It's not our fault. We're not scroungers.'

'I know.' He beckoned a uniformed male PC over, thinking, *Why Aimee, and not Nina?* 'Nina, this is Mark.'

'Yeah, I know 'im, don't I?' Nina said, scowling. 'Bloody nicked me a couple of times, didn't he?'

'Hi, Nina,' Mark said. 'All right?'

'What do you think?'

'I have to go,' Ford said. 'Mark's going to look after you, OK? Make sure you've got somewhere to stay tonight.'

Ford left them to it, signalling an apology to Mark with his eyes. Mark grinned back. Used to it. From cop to babysitter in five seconds flat.

DAY ELEVEN, 9.00 P.M.

A few miles away, he lies back against the cushions. He's naked, like the last time. He's shivering. It's a common side effect of transfusions, and he's not bothered. Why should he be, when he's washing that poison out of his system? He can feel himself growing stronger after each kill. More his own man, and less *his*.

He's told her he's getting the blood from work. And she believes him. Soon he won't need her any more. Then the world had better watch out.

DAY ELEVEN, 9.55 P.M.

At the crime scene, Georgina Eustace stood with her arms folded, staring at the pale corpse hanging from the window. The killer had used a length of plastic clothes line. The ligature had bitten deep into the wrists.

No wound on the inner thigh this time, either. He must have gone for the posterior tibial artery in the ankle.

'Excuse me, ma'am,' a young DC said, coming in from the hallway to stand beside her. 'How do you want to get rid of the blood? Shall I let the plug out? Or is that contravening health and safety rules?'

She shook her head. 'No, it's fine. The sewerage system receives far worse than a few pints of blood, believe me.'

He nodded. 'OK, then. Wish me luck.'

He pushed the sleeve of his Noddy suit up past his elbow and leaned over the bath. He hesitated, then moved his hand downwards, swatting away the flies that rose towards his face.

'Wait!' Georgina shouted.

He jerked his arm back, as if bitten by something beneath the surface. 'What?'

'I saw a plastic swing-bin in the kitchen. Can you fetch it for me, please? Take the bag out first. And a measuring jug. Failing that, a bottle, or something we can use to get the blood out of the bath.'

Thirty minutes later, the bath was empty. The plastic swing-bin was a third full of blood.

Georgina sprayed the body's feet with the shower head. Once they were as white as the rest of the body, she leaned closer, examining first the left, then the right, ankle.

'There you are, my little beauty,' she said.

In the indentation behind the outside of the right ankle bone she discerned a two-millimetre-diameter hole. A hole such as might be made by a trocar.

DAY TWELVE, 9.30 A.M.

Ford stood beside a large whiteboard he'd wheeled in from the incident room. A4 photos of the five victims were stuck along the top edge, Kai Halpern's cheeky smile beside his mum's.

'Thanks for getting here so quickly, everyone,' he said. 'Especially on a Saturday. Let's get started. Yesterday, at 7.45 p.m., a fifth murder victim, a female, was discovered. Not counting Kai Halpern, Aimee Cragg is the fourth in what is a series of linked killings.'

He turned to the whiteboard and scribbled four numbers in red. A bit of showmanship to make them stick in people's minds.

666 – 500 – 167 – 333

'At each of the kill sites, the murderer wrote a number on the wall in the victim's blood.'

'That's the order of discovery, yes?' Sandy asked.

'Yes. But if we redo them in the order he killed them, we get this.' He rubbed them out and rewrote them.

167 – 666 – 500 – 333

'We're working on trying to figure out whether it's a code or some other sort of clue. But it may all be psycho bullshit, to use a technical term. The concrete facts are these.'

He summarised what was known about the victims and their movements, laying emphasis on them being food-bank customers. As he concluded he noticed Hannah was frowning, her lips moving silently.

'What's on your mind, Hannah?'

She came to the front and held her hand out. 'Can I have the marker, please, Henry?'

He handed it to her and stood aside. She scrubbed at the numbers with the eraser, leaving a pinkish smeared oval in their place. Then she wrote the numbers out a third time.

$$167 - 333 - 500 - 666$$

She turned to face the room, and Ford noticed the beginnings of a blush stealing across her neck. *This is hard for you, and yet you're pushing yourself to do it.*

Hannah cleared her throat. 'This is a more logical sequence. Low to high. I don't think they're Bible verses or satanic symbols or record speeds or road races. I think they're an arithmetic progression: a sequence of numbers where the difference between successive term members is a constant.'

'Glad we cleared that up,' Mick said.

'Good,' Hannah said. 'As you can see, DS Tanner, the constant in this sequence is 167.' She frowned. 'Well, 166 or 167, anyway.'

She started scribbling, then turned back and tapped the column of simple equations she'd written.

$$1 \times 167 = 167$$
$$2 \times 167 = 334$$

$$3 \times 167 = 501$$
$$4 \times 167 = 668$$

'That's not the sequence, though, is it?' Mick complained. 'The second, third and fourth numbers are out, by one, one and two.'

Ford saw the solution. 'They're rounded,' he said. 'Hannah, can I have the pen, please?'

She handed it over wordlessly and resumed her seat.

Ford scrawled numbers on the board.

$$167 = 166.66666$$

'Look at all those sixes,' Jan said. 'We're back to the number of the beast. He *is* a religious nutter. That's a fiver you owe me, Mick.'

Ford shook his head. 'No. Hannah's right. It's all about the numbers *as numbers*. Come on, people. What does it mean? Think!'

A heavy silence descended on the assorted investigators. The wall clock ticked the seconds over.

'It's a sixth!' Hannah shouted, making Jools, who was sitting next to her, jump.

'Jesus, Hannah! We're only here!'

'Sorry. But I'm right, aren't I? One divided by six equals one point six, recurring.'

'She is, guv,' Olly said. 'I just checked it on my phone.'

'I didn't need it checking,' Hannah said. 'That's the answer.'

Ford cleared some space on the board and wrote up a new set of numbers.

$$1/6 = .167$$
$$2/6 = .333$$
$$3/6 = .500$$
$$4/6 = .666$$

'Guv?' Olly said, sounding anxious.

'What?'

Olly pointed at the lowest number. 'I think it means there are two more to go before the sequence is complete.'

An indistinct male face shimmered before Ford. Clean-shaven. Respectable. Grinning. Evil. *Catch me if you can.* He fought down a shudder.

◆ ◆ ◆

After the briefing, Sandy hung back. When the room was empty but for her and Ford, she closed the door.

'What is it?' he asked, sensing from her tight expression that she didn't relish what she had to say.

'I trust you, Henry, you know that.'

'Thanks. And yes, I do.'

She heaved a sigh. 'I am getting significant pressure from the chief con, *among others*,' she added, 'to close this case.'

'We're doing our best,' he said, feeling his heart bumping in his chest. 'The whole team is literally spending every waking hour on it.'

'I know. And I'm grateful. But I hear you've been to see Abbott again and more or less accused him of the murders.'

'What? Abbott jerks the chief con's chain, he jerks yours and you—'

'Do *not* finish that sentence, Henry,' she snapped. 'Because – and I'm sorry if you didn't realise this – I *did* get my chain yanked by the chief con. And I can tell you, I didn't enjoy it at all. I'm ordering you to lay off Abbott. I hear Jools likes this Kyte character for it. Go with that. Support her. Manage this case by the book and stop acting like some maverick gunslinger.'

Ford returned her stare, then dropped his eyes. He knew he was being unfair on her. But how could he ignore the one, sure, unique talent he knew he possessed: the ability to sense the presence of a killer?

'Sorry, boss.'

She frowned at him. *Great. More to come.*

'Look, there's no easy to say this,' she said. 'They're pushing me to appoint a more experienced DI, someone qualified as an SIO, to take over from you.'

'What? You're joking?' he said, raising his voice, unable to stop himself.

She shook her head. 'I wish I were. Look, it's not certain. I fought them off. But they want me to come back to them with a recommendation in a week if we're no further forward. I'm sorry.' She held up a hand to forestall his outburst. 'It's the best I could do.'

◆ ◆ ◆

Thirty yards away, in a quiet corner of Major Crimes, Hannah was talking to Jools.

'Can I ask you something?' Hannah said. 'Something to do with Henry?'

Jools nodded. 'Ask away. What? Is he giving you grief over those fingerprints?'

Hannah shook her head. Wishing she didn't need to have this coaching in what everybody else did by instinct. Hoping she'd read Jools right. 'It's not that. He's very patient, despite the immense pressure he's under.'

'Then what?' Jools said. 'You can ask me anything, Hannah.' She laid a gentle hand on Hannah's forearm.

Hannah looked down and was pleased to realise she didn't feel any need to pull away.

'It's quite . . .' She hesitated. Should she stop? *No, Hannah. Now or never.* '. . . personal.'

Jools put her finger to her lips and winked. 'In that case, let's head for the ladies.'

Leaning back on the wall between the hand dryer and the mirrors, Jools smiled at Hannah. 'Well?'

'Do you know if Henry is seeing anyone?' Hannah blurted out, feeling her cheeks heating.

Jools frowned. 'Romantically, you mean?'

'Yes.'

Jools shook her head. 'No. I don't think he's been on a single date since Lou died. Why?'

'I want to ask him out, but I'm worried he'll reject me.'

'Why would he do that?'

'You know, because of my, I mean, that I'm . . .'

'On the spectrum?' Jools asked softly.

'Is it that obvious?'

'It is to anyone who's interested in other people,' Jools said. 'But, to answer your question, no. I don't think he'd reject you because of that. You're attractive, you're obviously super-bright, which I know he likes. But just—'

'What?' Hannah asked, her pulse quickening.

'Just take it in baby steps. He's still mourning her. I know it's been a long time, but he just seems, I don't know, stuck.'

Hannah nodded, smiling. Happier than she'd been since arriving at Bourne Hill. 'Baby steps.'

DAY FOURTEEN, 8.15 A.M.

Striding into the mortuary, Georgina called out a cheery 'Good weekend?' to Pete, who was carrying the swing-bin out from the walk-in fridge. He'd added a small but sufficient amount of anti-coagulant to keep it liquid.

'I want to know how much blood she had in her,' she said. 'It's the first time we've been able to measure it. Would you?'

He set to work with a stainless-steel ladle and a transparent measuring jug. Although eager to begin work, she found something irresistible about the simple dip-and-pour process her assistant was engaged in, and sat watching, finger to her chin. He filled the jug to a marker line, made a note, tipped it away into the sink, then repeated the sequence.

He turned to Georgina. 'Minus the anticoagulant I added, that's two point five litres.'

'I reckon I left about 100ml in the bath, so let's call it two point six in total, which is odd,' she said, furrowing her brow and turning to the sheeted corpse behind her. She lifted a corner and assessed the size of the dead young woman. 'I'd have expected more than that. Let's get Aimee weighed, shall we?'

First, Pete wheeled an identical gurney on to the weighing plat-form set flush into the mortuary floor. He pressed a button to zero the scale, then removed the gurney. Together, they wheeled the body into position.

Georgina made a note of the weight. 'Fifty kilos, or seven stone twelve.'

She took a seat at a desk and launched a spreadsheet, tapping keys and humming as she went.

Pete stood by her left shoulder, watching her work.

'And?' he said, when she leaned back.

'Odd. Exsanguinated, she weighs fifty kilos. Pop quiz: how much of the human body comprises blood?'

'Seven per cent.'

'Yes. So if fifty kilos equals ninety-three per cent of her original body weight, the body and the blood together should weigh roughly fifty-four kilos.'

'Which means there should have been closer to four litres in the bath.'

She pulled a calculator towards her and tapped a few buttons. 'Factor in the higher density of blood compared to water and you get three point six litres.'

'We're missing a litre,' they said together.

'Could it have seeped away?'

Georgina shook her head. 'The plug was in tight.'

'Left in the body?'

She took him over to the gurney and indicated the needle puncture with a gloved finger.

'He suspended her from a window. That's right at the lowest point of her body. He drained her.'

'So he took it.'

'Or drank it. I need to call Ford.'

Ford tried to ignore the squirming anxiety he felt twisting his insides into knots. In his initial euphoria after Sandy had confirmed his promotion, he'd prayed he wouldn't have to wait long for his first major crime investigation.

A murder would have been his first choice. It was a grim truth, but coppers in Major Crimes were never happier than when they had a juicy murder to investigate. It was what they did. What they were *born* to do, some reckoned.

But five? Five! He felt he was drowning in paperwork. Every action – and there were now hundreds – had to be noted, rationalised and duplicated, with top copies to the designated officer and the original for his policy book.

There were tips coming in from the call handlers at all times of the day and night. Some well meant, others the work of cranks and fantasists. Still others were malicious: angry neighbours or envious colleagues, ex-lovers or disaffected spouses. All out to cause mischief, and bugger the waste of police time. And every single, mother-loving one of them had to be followed up, documented and entered into HOLMES.

To top it all, Sandy had told him the PTBs wanted him replaced.

His phone rang. He unwound a crick in his neck and put it on speaker.

'Henry, it's Georgina. I have something odd for you.'

His pulse ticked up a notch. Georgina had a way of underemphasising things she found interesting. 'Odd' promised much. 'What is it?'

'I'll spare you the maths, but your latest victim was missing a litre of blood.'

'Say again?'

'OK, I won't spare you the maths. The human body is seven per cent blood. Aimee Cragg should have been dabbling her feet in three point six litres of her own blood. We recovered two point six.'

'You're certain? None was splashed about or lost in transit?'

'I'll assign your apparent doubt in my professionalism to investigative rigour. No mistake. None lost in transit. She was missing a litre.'

Ford sat back and stared at the ceiling. Saw in his mind's eye a patch of blood like the one that had appeared on the Gregorys' kitchen ceiling.

'Are you drinking it, after all?' he muttered to himself.

'Is who drinking what, after all?'

He straightened. Hannah was standing in the doorway to his office.

'Georgina Eustace just called me. Aimee Cragg was missing a litre of blood. But you said before that he wouldn't be drinking it.'

'I did.'

'We found no vomit at the latest scene?'

'No. Nor at any of the others.'

The others. He had an idea. 'Hannah, is there any way you could estimate the volume of blood found at any of the other scenes?'

She took the seat facing him across the desk. 'Marcus Anderson's was too decomposed and dried out. Angie Halpern was on a vinyl floor, but some of her blood had leaked away through a crack into the floorspace,' she added, looking upwards, as Ford had been doing earlier. 'But Paul Eadon might be easier. His blood was reasonably fresh and contained.'

'Could you try it?'

'Of course. I have a contact in the FBI who wrote the book on blood-spatter analysis,' she said. 'Literally. Because he wrote a book called *Blood Spatter Analysis*.'

'Talk to Georgina, too. She may be able to help.'

Hannah rose from her chair. 'On it. Guv,' she said, smiling nervously. 'Was that OK?' she said immediately. 'I heard one of the DCs call you that.'

'It's fine. Though I like it better when you call me Henry.'

'OK. Henry.'

'Was there something you wanted?'

'What?'

'*You* came to *me*, remember?'

'Yes. Yes, I do remember.'

She was blushing. Which was odd, because he'd only seen that reaction when she was in a stressful situation.

'Is everything OK?'

'Fine! It's fine. I'll start work on the calculations.'

She turned on her heel and was gone. He watched her navigate the open-plan office, noticing how she picked a circuitous route that allowed her to avoid getting too close to other people.

DAY FOURTEEN, 9.30 A.M.

Ford leaned against the doorjamb to his office and scanned the incident room. He saw Jools at her desk and called out, 'Hey, Jools, got a minute?'

She hurried over. 'Guv?'

'I need someone to bounce ideas around with. Got time for a walk?'

'You're saving me from paperwork. What do you think?'

They headed across the city to the Town Path, a raised pedestrian walkway across the water meadows bordering the Cathedral Close. They stopped at a gate into a field inhabited by a couple of hundred sheep. Water-filled channels criss-crossed the tussocky grass.

A man in waders approached the gate from the other end of the path and nodded to Ford as he arrived. He carried a worn iron crank.

'Morning,' he said. He glanced at Ford's ID on its lanyard. 'You detectives, then?'

'That's right,' Ford said.

'You'll be investigating them murders?'

'Right again.' Ford glanced at the crank. 'Changing a wheel?'

The man smiled and pointed into the water meadow. 'Got to raise a sluice gate, haven't I? Cathedral's getting a bit low.'

Ford frowned. 'Low? Sorry, what do you mean?'

'No foundations, are there? Ground's too soggy. So it rests on a six-foot-thick gravel pad filled with water from the meadows. We manage the water level so the gravel doesn't dry out.'

'What would happen if it did?'

The man pointed at the spire. 'That'd come down, for a start,' he said, winking. 'Every morning, the clerk of the works gives me a little tinkle and says what he needs. I might let a little in, or let a little out. Keep it level and everyone's happy.'

The man unlocked the gate and walked into the field. He turned. 'It's not just the cathedral, mind. Whole city's practically afloat. Five rivers run through it, don't they? Like arteries.'

He waved and strode away.

'He took a litre of blood from Aimee Cragg,' Ford said, watching the man ratchet up the sluice gate.

'Shit! Did he drink it?'

Ford shook his head. 'I don't think so. Hannah says you'd vomit if you tried to drink that much.'

She nudged him in the ribs and grinned up at him. 'Oh, Hannah says, does she?'

'And what's that supposed to mean, DC Harper?'

She put a hand, fingers splayed, over her chest, and popped her eyes wide in a show of innocence. The grin widened, though. 'Nothing. No, nothing at all. Absolutely not one thing.'

'Good. As I was saying—'

'—before I so rudely interrupted you, talking about Hannah.'

'The blood, Jools. Please?'

'Did he take a litre from the other victims?'

'Is the right question. Hannah,' he continued, glaring at her, daring her to say anything, 'is working on it. But let's assume he did.'

'If he's not drinking it, is he keeping it? Is *that* his trophy?'

'It looks like it, doesn't it?'

She shuddered. 'I can just see it. A home blood bank with typed labels and him having a wank right in the middle of it.'

'Thanks for that charming image.'

'You're welcome.'

'If Olly's right, he's got two more kills planned. So what I'm wondering is, why six? Why would he want six? Why not seven, or ten, or a hundred?'

'How much blood is there in a body?'

'None, in our cases.'

'No, I mean how much blood does the average human being have?'

'I don't know. We were taught it was eight pints at school.'

Jools wrinkled her nose. 'Surely it depends on the size. I mean, look at us. You're six foot in your socks and what, thirteen stone?'

'Something like that, if I don't hit the beer and curry too hard.'

'I'm five foot six and eight one, ditto. We can't both have the same amount of blood. Never mind some of those people you see lumbering about the market square on a Saturday.'

Ford took her by the shoulders and looked into her eyes. 'Jools, you're a genius.'

'Thanks, guv. Er . . . why?'

'Georgina told me the human body is seven per cent blood, right? That's the formula. So if I'm thirteen stone, I've got seven per cent of that in blood and if you're, sorry—'

'Eight one.'

'—then you've got seven per cent of that.'

'Sorry, guv. You've lost me.'

'He's planning on taking six litres of blood, one from each of his victims, yes?'

'OK.'

'What if that's how much blood he's got? In him, I mean.'

203

Her eyes widened as the import of his words hit her. 'Then we can calculate his weight.'

Ford pulled out his phone and spoke aloud as he tapped numbers into the calculator.

'Six litres equals seven per cent of the killer's body weight.' Tap. 'How much does a litre of blood weigh?'

Jools looked it up on her phone. 'Just under a kilo. Nought point nine four, to be exact.'

'OK, so seven per cent of the killer's body weight equals six times nought point nine four, which equals' – he paused, tapping some more – 'five point seven-six kilos. Help me out, Jools. How do I get from seven per cent to a hundred percent?'

'Divide five point seven-six by seven and multiply by a hundred.'

'Eighty-two point three kilos,' he said.

'Hold on, let's just do a quick online conversion,' she said. 'That comes out to thirteen stone, near enough.'

'So, if our assumption about the six litres is correct, we're looking for a thirteen-stone man.'

'I think we can say more than that.'

'Go on.'

'He's fit, right?' she asked. 'He manhandled Aimee's dead weight over the lip of the tub and supported her while he tied the clothes line round the top of the window.'

'So you're saying it's thirteen stone of mainly muscle, not fat?'

'Which means that he's going to have a strong build. Plus, the pathologist has already given his height as five ten or taller.'

'Like Abbott,' Ford said.

She frowned. 'Who has an alibi. Like Matty Kyte.'

'Who also has one. Bloody hell, Jools, it has to be one of them. I'm sure of it.'

She nodded. 'Then let's find out which one it is and get him in an interview room.'

Back at Bourne Hill, Ford and Jools took the stairs to the fourth floor.

At the door to Major Crimes, he turned to her. 'Can you run all our interview lists against that body type? Deprioritise anyone of the wrong weight or build.'

Jools smiled, nodded and returned to her desk. He liked that about her. No dumbass questions like 'Why?' and 'Can't you get someone else to do it?', like Olly. She just got on with it.

He believed in giving the younger detectives on his team a bigger share of the grunt-work; after all, he'd done it, and you needed to break them in properly. But if they knuckled down to it uncomplainingly, he'd make sure he rewarded them with something juicier to keep them keen and to develop their skills.

He went straight to his desk, and the collated findings from Georgina's post-mortems. All four adult victims had been exsanguinated, which had killed them. Kai Halpern had been given a lethal dose of fentanyl. Ford was just as sad for the little boy as his mother, but had to conclude that from the killer's perspective, Kai was just an obstacle to his getaway. No sexual assault at any of the crime scenes.

I have to stop him.

He picked up his phone and called Abbott, who sighed when Ford introduced himself.

'What now?'

'How much do you weigh, Mr Abbott?'

'I beg your pardon?'

'Your weight, Mr Abbott. What is it?'

'I'm sorry, *how* is this relevant?'

'Please. Your weight?'

Ford waited the consultant out. *Three strikes and you're out. I'll bring you in and stand you on the scales myself.*

He counted to seven before Abbott answered.

'Twelve stone, ten pounds, not that it's any of your business. Is that all, or did you want my inside-leg measurement, too?'

Ford smiled at Jan, who stopped at his open office door and made a T with her two index fingers. Ford nodded and mouthed, 'Thank you.'

'That's all for now. Thank you. You've been a great help.'

◆ ◆ ◆

Later, Ford made his way to Forensics.

Hannah was bent over a microscope. He cleared his throat.

'You can get lozenges for that,' she said, without looking away from the eyepiece.

'I was trying to get your attention.'

Now she did turn away from her kit. 'Joke! I know. People clear their throats for two reasons. One, to loosen phlegm. Two, to make their presence known to somebody without using their name.'

He grinned. Her sense of humour was completely off-kilter, but it still made him smile. 'I'm looking at ways to get under Abbott's skin.'

'And you want me to help?'

'You mentioned you taught at Quantico. The psychology of lying, wasn't it?'

'That's right. There are many aspects of lying, from facial expression to the use of contractions in speech, that we can use to determine levels of truthfulness.'

'Do you think our killer's a good liar?'

'I haven't met him, so I can't answer that. But organised, in-control serial killers are often marked out by high levels of intelligence and/or cunning. The latter demands skills in dissembling, even if the former doesn't.'

'That's a yes, then?'

She frowned. 'I just said that, didn't I?'

'How do you fancy some fieldwork later on?'

'Fieldwork?'

'A chat with the god of haematology himself.'

Her dimples appeared. 'Sounds like my kind of evening.'

Ford returned to Major Crimes and wandered over to Olly's desk. The young DC looked up, as eager as a puppy whose master appears with a ball.

'Yes, guv?'

'Can you work up some background for me on Charles Abbott?'

Olly appeared at Ford's office door two hours later with a sheaf of paper. Ford beckoned him in, and the DC spread out the papers on the desk.

'Looks like a straight arrow. Did his medical training in London, worked up there at a couple of teaching hospitals and transferred down here about five years ago,' he said.

'What are these?' Ford asked, picking up a stapled set of papers.

'He's written loads of articles. The magazines have these weird titles. My favourite one is just called "Blood".'

'What about outside of work?'

Olly riffled through the documents, unearthing a series of montages of colour photos. In each, pairs or small groups of people holding glasses of wine were mugging for the camera.

'I got these from all the local society mags. You know, *Salisbury Life*, *Wiltshire Society*. That's Abbott,' he said, stabbing a long finger at one picture showing the man in a dinner suit and a woman in a short cocktail dress of a startling kingfisher blue with a plunging neckline. 'His wife's a bit tasty, don't you think, guv?'

Ford took in the images of Charles and Lucinda Abbott rubbing shoulders, sometimes literally, with the great and the good of the city. *Quite the local power couple*, he mused.

'Thanks, Olly. Good work.'

Olly beamed. The puppy praised.

DAY FOURTEEN, 6.50 P.M.

Ford and Hannah drove to Britford straight from Bourne Hill. Most of the houses were built of brick that glowed golden in the evening sunlight. They drew up outside a converted barn. Two cartwheels leaned against the black-painted clapboard wall; a stone well and an old horse-drawn plough repainted in scarlet flanked the iron-banded oak front door.

Hannah cocked her head towards the triple garage next to the house. 'Nice car.'

Ford followed her gaze and saw the sleek profile of a metallic-grey Aston Martin resting on the gravel beneath the branches of a hazel tree.

'And look at the other two. A top-end Merc and a Range Rover. That's the thick end of three hundred grand, right there,' he said.

'I wonder if he paid cash for them?'

'You think he's in debt?'

'It's been shown to be a major stressor.'

'Let's go and see how stressed he is by a visit from the cops. I'll do the talking, OK?'

Hannah nodded. Ford scanned the upper windows as they approached the front door, saw something and made a mental note. He leaned on the bell push and took a step back, straightening his tie.

The door swung inwards, revealing the master of the house. Abbott wore a floor-length cotton robe printed with characters in a language Ford fancied might be Thai, or Khmer. Lots of loops, anyway.

Abbott offered a ghost of a smile. 'Well, well. If it isn't Salisbury's answer to Sherlock Holmes,' he said, before glancing at Hannah. 'And I see you've brought Dr Watson with you.'

'May we come in?' Ford said.

Abbott looked over Ford's shoulder, then up and down the street. 'Do I have a choice?' he asked.

'Of course!' Ford said. 'You're not under arrest, Mr Abbott. No need to call your friend the chief constable.' *Though if I decide you're our prime suspect, you'll have a pair of Quik-Cuffs round your wrists faster than you can say 'haemoglobin'.*

'We're in the garden,' Abbott said as he stood aside. 'Lucinda and I, that is.'

He led them through an immense kitchen packed with oiled timber units Ford imagined were advertised as being 'hand-built by craftsmen'. A six-burner range cooker jostled for space with a duck-egg-blue fridge large enough to conceal at least one body, if not two. Ford resisted the urge to open it and see whether it contained a neat row of blood bags.

Ford dismissed the word 'garden' as being wholly inadequate for the vista that opened up as they walked through a set of French doors.

The striped lawn stretched a couple of hundred metres to a river, on which Ford made out the prow of a clinker-built boat nosing out of a smart blue-painted boathouse. He glimpsed a fenced-off tennis court and a single-storey brick building abutting the house, which, he assumed, contained a swimming pool.

Abbott had turned and was watching Ford. 'Twenty metres, heated year-round, costs me a bloody fortune, but you know what they say: "If you've got it, flaunt it!"'

The man was unbelievable, crowing over his wealth as he led Ford and Hannah to a set of expensive-looking wooden garden furniture: low-slung recliners that some people called steamer chairs, their brass hinges glittering. And a matching table, on which a jug of something cold, amber-coloured and garnished with mint leaves stood, condensation beading its lower half.

A long-limbed blonde woman in a high-cut zebra-print swimsuit lay back in one of the steamers, an arm draped over the edge. Ford put her age at late thirties, judging by her skin and muscle tone. She uncurled herself and stood, advancing towards him, one slender arm extended, the wrist jingling with multiple silver bracelets.

'Inspector Ford,' she purred as they shook hands. 'Lucinda Abbott. We meet at last.' She flicked a glance at Hannah. 'And I see you've brought a friend.'

Hannah held out her right hand. Gave Lucinda Abbott the one-two-three treatment. Ford smiled inwardly at the consternation that flickered across Lucinda's face.

She reclined again, bringing one knee up and extending her other leg and folding her arms behind her head, her cornflower-blue eyes holding Ford in a searchlight beam.

'Darling, I think you're making Inspector Ford uncomfortable,' Abbott drawled.

'Relax,' she said. 'I'm sure the inspector has more pressing issues on his mind.' She looked up at Ford again. 'Or were you enjoying the view?'

'Do you own a grey metallic VW Polo?' Ford asked Abbott, ignoring the provocation. He'd met at least one couple before who clearly found this sort of flirting a turn-on.

'What? You saw our vehicles when you parked, did you not?'

Interesting. Avoiding a straight answer to the very first question I ask you. Well, now we're on my territory. My rules.

'I saw *three* vehicles, yes. Do you own any others?'

Abbott's gaze flicked leftwards. 'I do not.'

Ford nodded and pursed his lips, as if impressed by this straightforward answer. 'So, if, purely hypothetically, we were to take a look inside that very impressive garage of yours, we wouldn't find any more cars? A grey metallic VW Polo, for example.'

'No, you would not. Not that you would be able to, as I doubt you have a search warrant.' Abbott folded his arms across his chest as he said this, then looked down and unfolded them.

Ford caught a movement out of the corner of his eye. Lucinda Abbott had swung her legs over the side of the steamer and was sitting up, as if she were a spectator at a tennis match.

'Could we go and have a look?' Ford asked.

'No, we could not,' Abbott said calmly.

'We believe that the murderer drives one,' Ford continued.

'How very fascinating for you.'

Ford changed tack. 'Your alibis for the dates of the murders?'

'What of them?'

'You claimed you were here each time.'

'I didn't *claim* anything,' Abbott said. 'I *told* you where I was, and that was the truth.'

'I'm afraid he's right,' Lucinda Abbott said with a smile. 'Charles was here with me.'

'Just the two of you?'

'Just the two of us.'

'No friends popping round? No unexpected dinner guests?'

She shook her head. 'I don't know what sort of social life *you* lead, but ours is rather dull, I'm afraid. Charles and I were watching television.'

'I don't suppose you remember which programmes were on those days?'

Lucinda grinned, and Ford sensed he had walked into a trap.

212

'How delightfully *old-fashioned* of you. We were binge-watching *Game of Thrones.*' She turned to her husband, who was bestowing on her a frank stare of admiration. 'Weren't we, darling?'

'Yes, darling. Yes, we were.'

'Each time?' Ford asked.

'Each time,' Abbott repeated, that superior smirk back in residence.

'Tell me, I noticed a Megadeth poster in one of your upstairs windows. Are there any other people living here with you?' He paused, unable to resist a quick dig. 'Or are you the heavy-metal fan, Mr Abbott?'

'That would be Gawain.'

'The knight?'

Abbott's lips twitched. 'My son.'

'My lad's into that kind of music, too. He favours Metallica, though,' Ford said, trying to unsettle Abbott with the random change of subject. 'I don't know why, sounds like chainsaws being put through a wood-chipper to me. Now, B.B. King, on the other hand—'

'Have you quite finished?' Abbott burst out.

'I'm sorry, did you have to be somewhere?'

'No. As my wife said, we lead a quiet social life. But I fail to see how my children's tastes in music are relevant to a serial killer investigation.'

Ford frowned. He turned to Hannah. 'Did I mention we were investigating a serial killer?'

She shook her head.

He turned back to Abbott. 'You said children. So more than one?'

'Obviously, children being the plural of child. I would have thought even a police officer could deduce that.'

Ford smiled, pleased to have rattled the consultant at last. 'Quite. So, how many more? One, two?' He looked down at Lucinda Abbott. 'Three? I must say, Mrs Abbott, you've certainly kept your figure.'

She repaid him with a smile that stopped just this side of a leer. He sensed he was in the presence of two operators, not just one.

'One,' she said.

'Name? Age?'

'Scheherazade. Seventeen.'

'Gawain and Scheherazade,' Ford said, face impassive. 'My lad's called Sam.'

'Believe me, Inspector,' Abbott drawled, 'at the school where they board, those names wouldn't earn you a second glance, let alone the mockery you seem bent on delivering.'

Ford shook his head. 'On the contrary,' he said. 'I was going to compliment you. So many kids nowadays sound like their parents just made something up.'

Ford's calculated appeal to the man's rampant snobbery worked. Abbott took the bait.

'Oh, God,' he groaned. 'Yes, it's all Saxona this, Meadow that, Kai the other.'

Ford had only intended to soften Abbott up, but the last name to leave the man's lips had his heart racing.

'You do know that was Angie Halpern's son's name, don't you?'

'What? Oh, yes, so it was. Forgive my lapse of taste, Inspector. Long day, and all that. Was there anything else?'

'Scheherazade. You said she was seventeen?'

'Yes.' Abbott drew out the single syllable in a sing-song tone. 'Because she is.'

'Does she drive?'

'What?'

'It's a simple question. Does she drive?'

'Well, she *can* drive, if that's what you mean. She passed her test this March.'

'And, as proud and wealthy parents, did you celebrate by buying her a car?'

Abbott glared at Ford, his jaw jutting. And then he spoke. 'I have gone out of my way to be helpful to you and your investigation. I shift meetings. I cut rounds short. I answer all your questions,' he said, his voice shaking. 'And now you come to my house and, once again, have the temerity to treat me like some common criminal.'

'Not at all. I—'

Abbott held up his hand, palm out. 'I think, Inspector, that if you have any further questions for me, or for my family' – he looked down at his wife, then back at Ford – 'you should arrest me. At which point I will first introduce you to one of the most expensive lawyers in the south of England, and then have him grease the slope down which you will hurtle all the way to directing traffic on market days. Are we clear?'

'I look forward to it,' Ford said, leaving Abbott to puzzle out the ambiguity: whether he eagerly anticipated the arrest, or the new job in a high-vis vest.

DAY FOURTEEN, 8.30 P.M.

'Do you fancy a quick drink?' Ford asked Hannah when they were sitting beside each other in his Discovery after the interview with Abbott.

'Yes. That would be nice.'

He drove to a riverside pub and ordered a pint of lime and soda for him and a glass of Sauvignon blanc for Hannah. The last rays of the setting sun cast a warm glow over the garden. They took a picnic bench beneath an old gnarled apple tree at the far end. A pair of ducks waddled through the benches before sliding into the water. Ford watched as they paddled furiously against the current without getting anywhere. He knew the feeling.

'Cheers,' he said, as they clinked glasses.

'Cheers.'

The lime and soda at least had the virtue of being cold, though as Ford surveyed the other early-evening drinkers, he reflected he'd much rather have been sinking a pint of Wadworth 6X.

'The Abbotts thought they were being clever with their alibi,' Hannah said.

That had been Ford's conclusion, too, but he wanted her take on this apparent power couple. 'Meaning?'

'Meaning that by claiming they were binge-watching, there was no need to check they'd got the transmission times right,' she said. 'Shows get cancelled or postponed, and that's your alibi sunk.'

'They lied about their social life, too. According to them, they spend their lives at home doing jigsaws, when Olly's research showed them at all these swanky parties and launches.'

She nodded. 'I think there's a very good chance Abbott was lying when you asked him about the car.'

'And you say that because . . . ?'

'The January 2002 issue of the *Canadian Journal of Behavioural Science* carried an article written by a member of the RCMP's Organized Crime Investigation Division and a forensic linguist. They analysed the speech patterns of suspects found to be lying.'

'What did they discover?'

'When lying, people have to maintain two parallel narratives in their heads—'

'The truth and the fiction.'

'Yes. That effort calls for additional care in speech as they strive not to incriminate themselves, and people tend to drop the use of contractions. They might say "I did not" rather than "I didn't", for example.'

'Is that what Abbott was doing?'

She nodded. 'On four occasions he used uncontracted verbs, which gave his answers a stilted feel you may have picked up on.'

'What were they?'

Hannah looked up into the branches of the apple tree as she recited. 'He said, "did you not?" for "didn't you?", "I do not" for "I don't", "you would not" for "you wouldn't" and "you would be able" for "you'd be able".'

'That could just be his way of speaking. He is rather pompous, in case you hadn't noticed,' Ford said, grinning.

Hannah tossed her head back and laughed loudly, drawing a few smiling glances from the occupants of the other benches. 'Yes, I *did* notice! But, actually, he uses a lot of contractions. He said "isn't", "you've" and "we're" in the first thirty-five seconds.'

'That's very interesting. Did you notice I didn't ask Mrs Abbott whether *she* owned a grey Polo?'

'No, I didn't.'

He smiled. 'That was my way of relaxing him a little, letting him think he'd won that one. I'll get Olly to check. Or he may have registered one in the name of his daughter. Who has a name to live up to, by the way.'

Hannah nodded. 'Poor thing. I wonder what her classmates are called.'

'Artemis?'

She shook her head. 'Desdemona?'

Ford grinned. 'How about Petronella?'

'No. I've got it,' she said, smiling back at him. 'Madagascar!'

'Zanzibar!'

'Casablanca!'

Their laughter erupted wildly.

When it subsided, Hannah nodded to her left at a young couple. 'Do you suppose they're on a date?' she whispered.

He shrugged as he took in the fact they were both engrossed in their phones. 'Could be. You see that more and more these days.'

'If *we* were on a date, I—' She hesitated, then smiled shyly, blushing. 'I wouldn't mind.'

That caught Ford by surprise. He covered by taking a swig from his lime and soda, promptly choking and coughing a spray of it into the air.

'No?' he croaked out.

'No. Do you want to know why?'

'Why?'

'You're very clever, which I like a lot. You do really well at juggling a senior detective's role with single parenthood. And' – her blush deepened and spread down to her neck – 'you're very sexy. Especially your eyes, which are the same colour as conkers. And I like this, too,' she said, stretching out a finger and prodding the scar on his chin.

Ford put his drink down. Of all the possible outcomes from his trip to see the Abbotts, he hadn't foreseen fending off romantic overtures from the new deputy chief CSI. Hannah was attractive. And he found her intelligence and directness a relief rather than offputting. But . . .

'Listen, Hannah. I like you, too,' he added, trying to read her emotions, and failing. 'But I'm not ready for another relationship.'

She frowned as he spoke, looking directly at him with those piercing blue eyes. 'According to a University of Indiana sociologist called George Cale, the average widower remarries two and a half years after his wife dies,' she said. 'You've been in mourning for over six, which is unusual.'

'What do you want me to say, Hannah? Maybe I'm at the far end of that particular spectrum?'

She frowned. 'So it's not because you don't fancy me?'

He had to smile. She was so direct even gentle sarcasm flew miles over her head. And as questions went, it was a killer. A Tier-3 trained interviewer's question. Answer 'no' and it implied he did fancy her. Answer 'yes' and it painted him as a weapons-grade shit.

'It's all still a bit raw,' he said, dodging the bullet. 'Lou, I mean. Sam and I, we're coping, but it's hard, you know?'

She took a sip of her wine, then finished the glass in a few convulsive swallows. 'He's lucky to have you as a dad. You know that, right?'

Ford felt relief wash through him as he congratulated himself on deflecting the conversation to a safer path. 'We rub along, I suppose. I'm just as lucky to have him as a son. He likes you, by the way,' he said. 'I can see it in the way he is around you. Normally, he becomes monosyllabic when other adults are around. Not rude, but not exactly forthcoming, either.'

'Is it hard, bringing him up on your own?'

Always straight to the point, Hannah. 'It has its moments. But we have some good friends in our road who've been there for him – well, us really – since Lou died.'

'Are you still grieving? Is that why you don't want this to be a date with me?'

He took the lifeline she'd thrown him. 'Yeah. I guess I am.'

The truth was, he didn't know *what* he felt. He'd had friends who'd lost a spouse, to cancer, or once a fatal traffic accident – a FATACC. They'd mourned, sunk into depression, but risen again, like Lazarus, still bearing the scars of their grief but able to move on, find new partners and, on one joyous occasion, marry in a country churchyard amid clouds of rose petals and the laughter of grown-up children.

'Then let's just forget I mentioned it,' she said. 'For now. Can I have another drink, please?'

DAY FIFTEEN, 1.15 P.M.

Ford had spent the morning reading thousands of documents, looking for something – anything – in the reports, actions and tip-offs that might provide a lead. Yes, Abbott looked iffy, but there was no hard evidence against him. Sandy had made her feelings pretty clear on the subject. Ford wanted to prove Abbott was the killer, but he had to hold on to the investigation in order to do that.

He focused on the latest murder. Two young women – girls, really – living together. Both food-bank users. But he chose Aimee, not Nina. Why? Aimee was a big girl; Nina was skinny. Was that it? But then, Angie was somewhere between them physically, and Paul Eadon and Marcus Anderson weren't even the right gender. He gave up.

After a snatched lunch – a ham sandwich and a takeaway coffee from a nearby café – he was back at his desk. His personal mobile rang. He glanced at the screen. The caller ID read: *School.* His pulse jacked up.

Please let him be OK. Not at A&E with a concussion. No gushing blood from a fall through a window. Please, God, let Sam be safe.

'Mr Ford, this is Marion Anthony. We met at the last parents' evening. I'm head of Middle School?'

'Yes, I remember. What is it, Mrs Anthony? Is Sam all right?'

He heard her inhale. Prayed harder for his son to be fine.

'Sam has been . . . That is to say' – the words tumbled out in a rush – 'I have suspended Sam for a day. He was involved in a fight.'

'What? Sam would never get into a fight. He's a good boy. He knows the rules.'

'Normally, yes, I agree, Sam is a good boy. But not today. He was caught fighting another boy from Year Ten. In point of fact, he was the aggressor. Could you come and collect him, please? The suspension is effective immediately.'

'Collect him?'

'It's school policy.'

'He's fifteen. He can walk home.'

'I'm afraid the rules are quite clear. Where a boy has been suspended he must be collected, in person, by a parent or carer,' she said primly. 'We must have the boy discharged from our duty of care. We are, as you know, in *loco parentis*. That means—'

'I know what it means, but I'm in the middle of a complex murder investigation. You may have read about it. Or seen it: we're national news.'

'I have seen it, and you, Mr Ford. But the rules are there for a reason. If we make an exception for one parent, pretty soon every parent would be demanding one.'

'Look, I understand the rules. I am a policeman, after all,' he said, striving to inject a jocular tone into his voice. 'But surely, just this once, you could bend them. Just a little?'

She sniffed. 'I'm afraid that won't be possible. He'll be waiting in reception.'

I bet you wouldn't be such a stickler if your family member was lying dead in a lake of their own blood, he wanted to shout.

'I can't get away from the office right now,' were the words that escaped his lips. 'I'll' – his thoughts raced, then crossed the finishing line – 'I'll send someone for him.'

◆ ◆ ◆

Ford pushed through the swing doors into Forensics. Hannah was at her desk, staring at a split-screen fingerprint image on her monitor. She looked round as Ford approached. Smiled. He was relieved after his attempted gentle brush-off the previous evening.

'Hi, Henry,' she said.

'Hi. Listen, I need to ask you a massive favour.'

Her forehead creased and she swung round on her swivel chair to face him. 'What favour?'

He sighed. 'Sam's in trouble at school. They've suspended him for fighting. Could you go and pick him up, then run him home for me? I know it's not your job and I have absolutely no right to ask you, but he likes you, and . . .' He stopped, aware he was on the point of gabbling.

Hannah was already on her feet. 'It's Chequers, isn't it?'

'Yes.'

She nodded. 'On my way, guv,' she said, and winked.

He watched her go, wondering if he was doing the right thing. He knew how Sam would see it: *Dad's too busy to come and get me, yet again.* His son's words came back to him – 'You care more about dead people than me.' Was it true? Because the one dead person he'd *never* stop loving was his wife, Sam's mother.

◆ ◆ ◆

'Sam, you in, mate?' Ford called out as he closed the front door behind him, after making a huge effort to leave Bourne Hill before six. He'd left the nick with a briefcase stuffed with reading matter and a force-issued laptop with the Operation Shoreline HOLMES account downloaded on to its hard drive.

The house was silent. No distant thud from Sam's wireless speaker upstairs. Though that meant nothing: Sam had some new earbuds. Ford took the stairs two at a time and knocked on his son's bedroom door. No response. Wary of just barging in, Ford held up his fist to knock again, then stayed his hand. He placed his lips close to the bare wooden panelling.

'Sam, you in there?' he said softly.

No response.

Fearing a volley of abuse, yet needing to know his son was in, and OK, Ford twisted the doorknob and peered in. A heady mixture of Lynx body spray and teenage fug wafted out. But the room was empty.

He completed a circuit of the downstairs rooms. All empty. *The garage, then.*

Sam was sitting in his usual spot behind the steering wheel. The earbuds were in place, his eyes were closed and his mop of curls was nodding in time to the beat of whatever band he currently favoured.

He turned round as Ford sat beside him. His eyes looked puffy, and the left one sat in the centre of a yellowish bruise that had spread down on to his cheek.

He plucked the buds from his ears. 'All right?'

'Long day, sorry,' Ford said. 'You want to tell me what happened?'

'A fight happened.'

'I heard. Who with?'

'You don't know him.'

Ford's stomach clenched. 'Who, mate? Never mind if I know him or not.'

'Oscar Welling.'

'OK, and what were you and Oscar Welling fighting about?'

'It doesn't matter.'

Ford twisted round on the worn leather seat. He reached out and brushed the backs of his fingers across Sam's undamaged cheek. Sam pulled away.

'Yes. It does matter,' Ford said. 'Why, Sam? You never get into trouble.'

'I just did, didn't I?'

Ford wanted so much just to cuddle his son, like he used to. But now that he was as tall as his dad, Sam had changed. Ford felt their days of cuddles were vanishing.

He tried a different tack. 'I care about you, mate. If you've been fighting, I need to know why.'

'Fine!' Sam shouted, the single word echoing in the hard-surfaced cube. 'Mr Super-cool Detective. If you must know, we were fighting about you!'

Sam's chin was quivering.

'Me? Why?'

'Welling said his dad reckoned if you were up to the job, you'd have caught the killer by now,' Sam said, as tears rolled over his lower lids. 'He said you must be a really shit detective not to catch someone leaving a trail of blood over half of Salisbury.'

'So you hit him?'

'No. I didn't.'

'But I thought you said—'

'Not then. I just told him at least my dad did something interesting for a living instead of moving numbers around on a screen.'

'So why the fight, Sam? Come on, buddy, I'm trying here.'

'Welling's dad said if you'd been a better husband, you'd have saved your wife from drowning,' Sam blurted, before wiping his nose on the back of his hand. '*Then* I hit him. Happy now?'

Ford felt his love for his teenage son surge through him. Sam knew Ford didn't need anyone fighting his battles. But his mother? No, that would have been a step too far.

'I'll write to the head. Explain. See if we can't—'

'No, Dad! Don't you get it? I *was* fighting. I *deserved* to get punished. Please don't wade in and try to get me off because it was all about Mum. Just let it go, OK?'

Ford laid a hand on Sam's left knee. He was pleased when Sam let it rest there. And he fantasised about taking Oscar Welling and his father to a remote piece of woodland and beating the crap out of the pair of them.

DAY SIXTEEN, 11.00 A.M.

He pulls on jeans and a jacket. Slips the ID badge over his head. Frowns. What he did at Aimee's place was a mistake. Those stupid plods won't catch him, but even so, it won't hurt to up his game a little.

He dons three items purchased from a vintage shop in town: plain-lensed glasses, black wig and matching moustache. The overall effect is surprisingly realistic, and under the straw hat – well, his own mother wouldn't know him. If there *are* any witnesses to his arriving at Lisa's, they'll be seeing a phantom.

He winks at Harvey.

Harvey winks back.

DAY SIXTEEN, 11.45 A.M.

Lisa Moore repeated her mantra as she unpacked the tins and packages from her battered shopping bag: 'It's just temporary.'

Somewhere along the line, things had got out of control. A few debts that piled one on top of the other like Jenga blocks. An abusive ex who stole five hundred quid – her entire savings – from her. A zero-hours job with too much zero and not enough hours. And she'd ended up using the food bank.

While she waited for a salaried job in the police force to come up, she was volunteering as an unpaid police community support officer and topping up her weekly shop at the Purcell Foundation.

At least she'd been able to give something back. They'd organised a blood drive earlier in the month and she'd been glad to donate. Anything to pay it forward. Or back, she supposed, given she was in receipt of their charity.

The doorbell rang.

She broke off from unpacking and went to the front door. When she opened it, she smiled. 'Hi. Can I help you?'

The unassuming-looking guy standing on her doorstep returned the smile, though there was something unreadable in his expression. The primitive part of her brain, the part that would once have ordered her to run at the first whiff of a predator, was screaming. But she ignored it. Had she not, things might have turned out differently over the next five minutes.

'Hi, Lisa,' he said. 'My name is Harvey. From the Purcell Foundation?' He looked embarrassed behind those old-fashioned glasses.

He seemed vaguely familiar, but she didn't want to seem rude by saying she couldn't remember him. She felt a sudden rush of shame and stared at her feet.

'Harvey, yes. Did you want something?'

'It's a bit delicate . . .'

'Oh,' she said, wondering if they were going to cut her adrift. Maybe there was a limit on how many times you were allowed visit the food bank, and she'd overdone it.

'Could I come in, please? I'd prefer not to discuss it on the street. You know, where people might overhear us.'

She nodded, fighting down an urge to explain, to plead for a little more time. Just until the permanent post came up and she was back on her feet again. She turned and led him down the hallway, intending to offer him a cup of tea.

He closed the door behind him. She heard the click. Then a scuffling as his shoes slid over the worn flooring in the hall. Now she did listen to her hind-brain. Her old training kicked in, hard.

He grunted as he hit her. A vicious blow to the back of the head that would have knocked her cold had it connected properly. But she was already spinning round to face him and the blow glanced off the side of her skull, dizzying her but leaving her fully conscious.

'You're worthless,' he murmured as he stepped back, preparing to strike again.

The fist came up and over a second time.

It passed over her head as she crouched. Then she drove her own, hard, into his solar plexus. He doubled over, with a groan, and she danced back a step, intending to kick him in the head and put him down.

But he thrust forwards, grabbing her shoulders and slamming her back into the wall, walloping her head into a door frame.

He reared up in front of her, hands outstretched, going for her throat. She grabbed his forearms, digging her nails in, spread them wide and stepped forward. She jerked her right knee up into his balls. With a howl, he turned, scrabbled at the door handle and escaped into the sunlit street.

Panting, she slammed the door and with shaking fingers slotted the security chain home.

'What the hell?' she shouted to her empty flat.

She fled to the bathroom and retched into the toilet bowl, bringing up a thin steam of yellow bile. She straightened, flushed, and was about to grab a flannel when she looked at her hands. Her fingernails were bloody and clogged.

She went to the kitchen and separated two clear sandwich bags from a roll she kept in a drawer. She placed one over her right hand and secured it with an elastic band. She repeated the process with her left hand. Then she grabbed her keys and left the flat, heading towards Bourne Hill.

◆ ◆ ◆

'Guv?' Jools called from across the incident room.

Ford turned away from the whiteboard.

'What is it?'

'It's the front desk. There's a female down there says she was just attacked and she thinks it's our guy. She wants to talk to you.'

'Tell her I'm on my way,' Ford said, grabbing a notepad and a pen and sprinting for the stairs.

He arrived on the ground floor in under a minute to see a young woman with reddish hair pulled back into a ponytail chatting to the receptionist. She had a smear of blood on her face, although she was smiling and didn't seem to be in any pain. Her hands were jammed into the pockets of a pair of pale grey jogging bottoms.

He hurried over. 'I'm Inspector Ford,' he said to the woman, trying to bring his breathing under control. 'You were just attacked, yes?'

'In my flat, yeah.'

'What's your name?'

'Lisa Moore.'

He smiled. 'OK, Lisa, I'd like you to come with me, please.'

He ushered her into the lift and hit the button for the fourth floor. As the lift ascended, he had a chance to take a look at someone who just might have escaped the killer's clutches. She was wearing a racerback gym top that revealed tanned, muscular arms. Not quite the 'guns' displayed by Jasmin Fortuna, but the woman worked out.

Physically, she bore no resemblance to Angie Halpern. Nothing in her facial features or colouring, either. But then, the target was killing men *and* women, so if he had a preferred type it had nothing to do with looks.

'Did you come straight here?' he asked.

'Yes. I fought him off and then got here as fast as I could.'

'That was incredibly brave of you.'

'Thanks. I hope I hurt the bastard.'

'Good for you.'

The doors opened. He motioned for her to leave the lift car ahead of him. 'Let's get you along to see the police surgeon. She can check you over.'

In the doctor's office, having been seated on the examination couch, legs swinging over the edge, Lisa pulled her hands from her pockets.

'I scratched him,' she said simply, holding her bagged hands up for Ford and the doctor to see.

Ford shook his head with admiration. 'You fought him off *and* collected his DNA. We should get you a job in the nick.'

To his surprise, she laughed.

'What's so funny?' he asked.

'That's the plan. I'm a PCSO at the moment. I'm on the waiting list for a proper job to come up.'

'Right. We'll get you looked over by Dr Perry and then we'll go along to the incident room. And I'll have a word later with my guv'nor. See if we can't fast-track you in the system.'

'Wow! Thank you. You'd do that for me?'

'What can I say? I'm a sucker for women who fight back.'

Dr Perry was fifty years old, a small-boned woman known for her collection of rainbow-hued Dr. Marten's boots.

'Did he hit you, Lisa?' she asked, shining a pen torch into Lisa's eyes and moving the beam from side to side.

'Back of the head. A glancing blow. I heard him coming for me and was already turning into it.'

'Most commendable. Any other strikes?'

'He pushed me back into the wall. I caught the back of my head on a doorjamb.'

'Let's have a little look, shall we?' Perry said, manoeuvring Lisa's head round and peering at the back of it. 'No lacerations.'

She probed a little with her fingertips, and Lisa yelped.

'You'll have a nice goose egg there for a few days, but other than that, you're fine. If it hurts, just take the normal dose of paracetamol, and you can double up with ibuprofen if you need to,' Perry said, switching off her torch. 'When you're back at home, if you feel at all woozy, or sleepy, get yourself to A&E. Say I sent you – it may help you get triaged faster.'

The examination over, Ford took Lisa to Forensics office.

'Tell me, Lisa, do you have any links to the hospital?' he asked her as they walked.

She shook her head. 'Never been up there.'

Then he asked her the question that might unlock the case. He knew it could embarrass her, but he needed to know.

'How about the food bank?'

She winced. 'Money's a bit tight, so . . .'

He smiled. 'Listen, I'm not here to judge you.'

'Thanks. People do, you know,' she said, feelingly. 'In fact, the bastard said he was from there. Can you believe it?'

Oh, Ford could believe it.

He pushed through the doors into Forensics. Hannah was nowhere in sight, but Alec was peering at a colleague's screen.

'Alec, got a minute?' Ford said.

'Of course, dear boy,' Alec said, smiling. 'Hello, who do we have here?'

'Lisa Moore. Pleased to meet you.'

'Lisa just fought off an attacker who I'm ninety-nine per cent sure is our boy,' Ford said.

Alec glanced down at Lisa's hands. His smile widened and his eyes twinkled. 'And you preserved the evidence, smart girl. Come with me, Lisa.'

Alec sat Lisa at a desk, then hurried away and returned with debris pots and a fingernail scraper. He widened the elastic bands and placed them in a pencil pot.

'Waste not, want not,' he said, with a wink for Lisa.

He removed the bags and took her right hand in his own.

'Be gentle with me,' she said, grinning.

Ford marvelled at her resilience. Having just fought off a murderous assailant, she was bantering with the chief CSI. *Yes, you'd make a* great *copper.*

Exercising his usual care and keeping up a muttered commentary, Alec ran the slim tip of the scraper under each of Lisa's fingernails. When he'd finished, he held the lidded pot up to the light.

'*Lots* to be going on with,' he pronounced. 'We'll fast-track these.'

'What does that mean these days?' Ford asked.

'It all depends on their workload. Anywhere from twenty-four to forty-eight hours. At the moment, "fast" means forty-eight. Which *is* fast, by the way, Henry, before you unleash a tirade.' He turned back to Lisa. 'Now, let's get your face cleaned up as well.'

He swabbed a sample stick across the blood smear on her forehead, bagged and labelled it and then fetched a bowl of water and a cloth. With infinite care, he dabbed, wiped and blotted until, with a flourish of the now pink washcloth, he said, 'Much better! You don't look like an extra from a horror film any more.'

With Lisa patched up, Ford took her back to Major Crimes and a seat in his office.

'Can I get you anything?' he asked. 'Tea, coffee, a medicinal brandy? A bar of chocolate?'

'I'll pass on the choccy, but a tea would be lovely. Milk, no sugar, please.'

When two mugs of tea were placed on the circular table between them, Ford opened his notebook.

'First of all,' he said, 'how on earth did you come off best in a fight with a possible serial killer?'

By way of answer, Lisa twisted round in her chair and pulled the straps of her top to one side, revealing a tattoo of a bugle suspended from a crown with the word RIFLES beneath it.

'Regimental judo champion,' she said. 'I left the army two years ago. I kept up my training, plus a ton of cross-fit. I heard him coming and all my instincts kicked in.'

'Impressive stuff. And now for the sixty-four-thousand-dollar question. Could you describe him?'

She took a quick sip of tea. 'I'm really not sure. It all happened so fast.'

Ford nodded. 'Let's start with an easy one, to get you going. How old would you say he was?'

She shrugged. 'Late thirties? It was hard to tell. He had one of those young faces.'

'That's good. What else can you remember?'

'OK, he was a white male, about six foot . . .'

'Good, keep going,' Ford said encouragingly. 'Build?'

'Quite muscular. Not a bodybuilder but, you know, in good shape.'

'How about his face?'

Lisa started to speak, but then her face crumpled; tears welled over her lower lids and ran down her cheeks. She swiped at them angrily. 'Bastard!'

'It's OK,' Ford said. 'You're in shock. It does funny things to the memory. Let's start with something simple. Do you remember anything about his eyes?'

'He was wearing glasses. Thick frames.'

'What about eye *colour*?'

'Brown? Maybe? I'm sorry, I can't remember.'

'That's fine. Don't worry. You're doing really well.'

In this way, Ford prompting without leading, Lisa answering, he built a description of her assailant.

Male
IC1

35–45
5'11"–6'0"
Medium/ athletic build/ broad-shouldered
Eyes: unknown/ thick-framed glasses
Black moustache
Clean-shaven
Dress: dark jacket, jeans
Accent: general southern English

'Thanks, Lisa,' Ford said when she'd finished. 'That's really helpful.'

The trouble was, the description, give or take a black moustache, fitted hundreds of men in Salisbury. Including Matty Kyte. And Charles Abbott.

He called Jools. 'Can you bring photos of Matty and Abbott to Forensics, please?'

When they showed Lisa the two pictures, one from the SDH website, the other from the PNC, she studied both but then shook her head. She pointed to Matty's vacant, staring face.

'It *could* be him. He looks a bit more like him than that other one. I'm sorry, but I'm still not really sure.'

'Thanks,' Ford said. 'And don't worry about not making the ID. Your fight-or-flight reflex kicked in hard, which probably saved your life. But that amount of adrenaline also does funny things to memory. One last thing. Did he say anything to you while he was attacking you? Anything sexual, for example?'

She wrinkled her nose and shook her head. 'Not sexual, no.' Then her eyes popped wide. 'He called me worthless. Bastard,' she added, feelingly.

Ford nodded his agreement. 'I'm going to get one of my detectives to take a formal statement from you. Can you stay here till it's done, or do you want to go home and have them take it there?'

She shrugged. 'Here's fine. I can get the feel of the place. You know, for when I'm working here.'

He smiled, amazed yet again at her coolness. But then, he reflected, infantry regiments weren't exactly places for shrinking violets.

DAY SIXTEEN, 2.10 P.M.

The pain in his balls is bad enough, a dull ache that's spread up into his belly. It makes walking upright hard: he has to stumble, bent at the waist, to the front door and let himself inside.

But it's the pain in his head that's worse. A searing, blinding rage. How *dare* she! She should have gone down like the others, his to bleed and dispose of like the piece of trash she is.

He hears his father's voice again, the relentless insults and demeaning remarks throughout his childhood: 'You're a worthless piece of shit! You killed your brother before he was even born. Catch it! CATCH IT! Oh, you dumb little twerp, it's a *rugby ball*, not an atomic bomb, it won't hurt you!'

Grinding his teeth so hard he can hear them scrape together, he goes looking for her. Finds her in the sitting room with one of those, those, *bloody* magazines! She turns and smiles up at him.

He rolls his sleeve up and holds the injured arm out for her to see.

'Look,' he says. 'I've got a blood injury.'

'Oh, baby,' she says. 'How?'

He gives her the answer he has dreamt up in the car. 'One of the patients had a fit.'

She fetches a first-aid kit and frees the flap with a rasp of Velcro. She selects a fresh tube of Savlon and twists the cap off. She squeezes a pea-sized blob of the ointment on to the tip of her index finger and smooths it on to the first of the scratches. He watches each movement. She's good enough to be a real nurse.

She repeats the process until each of the nasty little wounds is smeared with the antiseptic. She takes her time circling the pad of her little finger over each scratch.

One of the cuts has started weeping. Holding her husband's gaze, she bends her head to his arm and touches the tip of her tongue to it, licking away the pink cream.

'Does that feel better, baby?' she asks, keeping her head down, cradling his forearm against her cheek.

'A little.'

'Do you want to play doctors and nurses later?'

He grunts. 'You'd like that, would you?'

She lowers her head further. Unzips him. 'I like what you like,' she mumbles.

He drags her head away by the hair, making her yelp. The frustration is overwhelming. He's missed out on the fifth litre and now his whole plan is ruined.

The slap isn't hard. Not really. Not compared to the blow he *feels* like delivering. But his wedding ring catches her lip and splits it, and at the sight of the blood he screams in anger and frustration. 'Bitch!'

'But, sweetheart,' she says, lisping as her lip swells, 'why—'

He grabs her face, squeezing his fingertips deep into the flesh of her cheeks so her bleeding mouth pooches out in a way he finds comical.

'Shut up! Do you hear me? Shut. The hell. Up!' He stares into her face. 'I couldn't get any blood today. They . . . They were doing a stock check.'

She croaks out an answer, but it's inaudible because of the hard grip he has on her jaw. He releases her.

'What did you say?'

'Can't you just get some more?'

He slaps her again. Harder this time. Her head swings to the left with the force of it. If she knew where the blood was really coming from, she wouldn't ask such a stupid question.

He raises his hand again and enjoys the way the movement makes her flinch. *Maybe when this is all over I'll get rid of her. Find someone younger.*

He changes his mind about hitting her. Instead he reaches over and sticks his hand inside her blouse. Finds her left nipple and pinches it hard. She moans with the pain, but there's something else below that, something animalistic. He feels his erection growing.

'Take your clothes off,' he says hoarsely.

After they finish, he gets dressed and goes into town. He buys some loose buckshot from Berret & Sartain, the gunsmiths in the city centre. He spends an hour in his workshop sewing a rectangle of leather cut from an old jacket into a tube, and filling it with the shot. He smacks the finished sap into his palm.

◆ ◆ ◆

Later, working his way down a bottle of vodka, he pulls up Tasha Young's Facebook page. He shakes his head as he peruses her photos.

'If you only knew who you were allowing into your life, Miss Young, you'd change your security settings like *that*,' he says, snapping his fingers.

She'd put her whole life out there for anybody to see. Relationship status: single. Favourite movie: *Sleepless in Seattle.* She'd provide her blood group if the Yanks put a field in the form for it. *Stupid cow! Stupid, worthless cow!*

Next time I see you at the food bank, I'll be sure to be at my most helpful. Seems the least I can do, given what I've got planned for you.

He spins round in his executive computer chair, bought online and delivered by some immigrant from Eastern Europe. Consults his chart with the victims' food-bank membership cards he took neatly taped beneath their names. The first four photos have been crossed through with a black marker. But it's all wrong, isn't it? Because Lisa Moore didn't donate.

~~Marcus Anderson~~	~~#1~~	~~.167~~
~~Aimee Cragg~~	~~#2~~	~~.333~~
~~Paul Eadon~~	~~#3~~	~~.500~~
~~Angie Halpern~~	~~#4~~	~~.666~~
Lisa Moore	#5	.833
Tasha Young	#6	1.00

He'd killed them when he could. That was down to circumstances. What mattered – what *really* mattered – was the order in which he'd *used* their blood. Alphabetical, just like dear old Dad would have liked.

But now Moore had ruined everything. Too late to stop, though, when he was so close to purifying himself. So close to that tantalising goal: purging himself of *his* blood for ever.

You've no other option, then, have you? Track Young and, when she next comes in, it'll have to be a 'buy one, get one free' deal at the food bank.

The thought makes him laugh. He swivels round and looks up at the photos. Smiles with satisfaction. *Soon, Pops, very soon.*

DAY SEVENTEEN, 10.45 A.M.

Jools hurried into Ford's office. He looked up from his screen, grateful for a break from the growing number of documents he needed to read.

'Guv, you're going to want to see this.'

Curious, and with a flicker of excitement igniting in his gut, he followed the ambitious young DC out of his office and across the incident room to her desk. She dropped into her chair and jiggled her mouse to wake up her screen.

'What have you got?' he asked.

'It was when I took Lisa Moore's statement yesterday,' Jools said with a grin. 'She said she'd been to the food bank that same morning.'

'Don't keep me in suspense, Jools.'

'I got to thinking. What if he's picking them on the day they go there? I don't know, watching and waiting. Like a hunter.'

'Plausible. How does this help us?'

She jabbed a finger at the screen where she'd typed the list of adult victims, plus dates.

'I checked with the Purcell Foundation. They keep records of who comes in and what they buy – I mean, take. But they give them a sort of pretend credit card to scan. It's about preserving their dignity.'

'You did well to get that out of the food bank. You didn't get any of that GDPR crap, then?'

'I explained to the manager, Leonie Breakspear, that legally, dead people don't have rights. To property, or privacy.'

Ford nodded. 'Smart. You know your law.'

Jools's grin widened. 'Thanks, guv. But there's more. First of all, Angie and Paul visited the food bank on the days they were murdered,' she said, indicating the table of dates and names. 'It was harder with Marcus, on account of the wider time-frame, but it looks good.'

'Excellent. We can cross-check with the food bank to see who was working on those days.'

'Already asked. Leonie said she'd get back to me later today.'

'Jools, this is great. We'll have a much narrower pool of persons of interest, and I hope to God our Mr Abbott is on it.'

She frowned. 'You still like him for it, don't you?'

He thought of the profile he and Hannah had drafted. 'In the absence of anyone else, yes, I do. And we need to think about getting a DNA sample from him for cross-reference when the samples come back from Lisa's fingernails. Anything else?'

She shook her head.

'Briefing at noon. Keep on it till then. And check whether any of our victims had their card on them.'

◆ ◆ ◆

The conference room was packed, once more. Just as Ford was about to speak, the door banged back on itself, making everyone jump. Sandy stood in the doorway, her face unreadable. Ford saw a face behind her and scowled reflexively.

'Morning, all,' she said, in a jovial tone that Ford recognised as her fake-jolly voice. 'We have a guest for this meeting. Someone make space for our police and crime commissioner.'

Peterson squeezed past Sandra and took the chair pulled out for him by Mick Tanner.

'Don't mind me, everyone,' he called out. 'Just here in an over-watch capacity. Pretend I'm not here.'

Ford bit back the obvious comment he saw written on the faces of the investigators in the room. He began by running through the leads they had, the forensics and the progress of each of the lines of enquiry.

'Excuse me, DI Ford?'

Ford turned to face Peterson. 'Yes, Martin. You have a question?'

'This is your first murder investigation as a DI, isn't it?'

'Yes,' he answered, cautiously. 'Although I ran plenty as a DS.'

'But they were Cat Cs, for the most part, I think I'm right in saying. Straightforward domestic killings, and the odd brawl-gone-wrong between drunken squaddies?'

Ford knew where Peterson was going, and didn't like it. 'Sorry, Martin. Not following you.'

Peterson looked round the room, his smile as out of place as a giggle at a funeral. 'This is a complex serial-killer investigation. I'm just wondering whether you've made any *real* progress. I've seen a name double-underlined on your board out there.' He gestured at the wall separating them from the incident room. 'Abbott. Is he your prime suspect?'

Sensing Peterson would love to get his hands on the crucial line of enquiry – *and leak it, too, you bastard* – Ford downplayed its significance. 'He's a person of interest.'

'As I said, a suspect.'

Ford failed to stifle his sigh. 'Someone tell Martin why *Mr* Abbott isn't a suspect, please.'

Hannah beat all the assembled detectives and PSIs to the punch. 'A person identified as a suspect must be arrested as soon as is practicable. Although it gives us extra tools in terms of surveillance, search and interview, it also sets the PACE clock ticking.'

Her eagerness surprised Ford, but then he realised: she enjoyed proving points with logic.

Peterson folded his arms and glared at her.

'Jools, take us through what you found this morning,' Ford said.

'It looks like he's targeting food-bank users on the days they visit. Also, I have a list of who was working-slash-volunteering there on the dates the murders took place. Can I?' She looked at Ford and gestured to the whiteboard.

'Go for it,' he said, pleased to see how people were shifting in their chairs and whispering to each other. He felt the energy level lifting: good news when the golden hour was a distant memory and optimism was flagging.

At the front of the room, and with an uncapped blue marker in hand, Jools addressed the assembled investigators with a confidence that belied her years. 'Here are our four adult victims.' She wrote *Marcus, Angie, Paul, Aimee* in a line across the whiteboard. 'And the dates they were murdered.' The dates followed. 'And here are the only four people who were present on each of those dates.'

Centred below the victims' names, she wrote,

Charles Abbott
Robert Babey
Matthew Kyte
Jason Torrance

The murmuring as she'd been writing intensified.

'Wait a moment!' Peterson's voice, strident, cut through the hubbub.

'Yes?' Ford said, not even bothering to mask his irritation.

'I didn't realise that by "Abbott", you meant *Charles* Abbott.'

'OK. And?'

'Charles Abbott, the consultant haematologist?'

'Yes. What's your point?'

'You can't possibly be serious? I play *golf* with him, for God's sake! And he doesn't *work* at the food bank. He's a *trustee*.'

Ford opened his mouth. Caught a warning look from Sandy, plus a fractional shake of her head. Shut it again.

'Martin,' she said, in a smooth, calm voice. 'Two things. One, as DI Ford said just now when you asked, Charles Abbott is *not* a suspect.' She paused and looked round the room, lingering on Ford. 'Two, sad though it might seem to someone in a purely *over-watch* role, as opposed to frontline officers like my team here, even golf-playing charity trustees are not above either suspicion or the law.'

Peterson folded his arms as Sandy spoke, and looked at the ceiling. He was not so much listening, Ford saw, as waiting for his chance to interject.

'That's all very well, Detective Superintendent Monroe,' he said when she paused for breath, 'but I will say this: tread very carefully. Charles Abbott is a man on the move, with some very powerful friends.'

◆ ◆ ◆

After the meeting, Ford went to see Jools. 'That was great police-work, Jools, really. Can we eliminate any of the four based on their physical characteristics?'

'On it, guv. By the way, none of our adult victims had their Purcell Foundation cards on them. He must have taken them.'

'Trying to hide his tracks,' Ford said. 'Clever.'

She came to see him an hour later, the smile broader than ever. 'Babey's six-seven, and Torrance is my height.'

'Leaving Matthew Kyte and Charles-bloody-Abbott,' he said. 'And *he* won't come in unless we arrest him, I'm sure of it.'

'Kyte's already agreed to come in for another interview. You want to sit in?'

Ford paused, thinking. *It's not him. Abbott's the wrong 'un, I'm sure of it. But let's make certain and have this Kyte in so we can eliminate him.* 'Can you work up a profile on Kyte for me?'

She nodded and returned to her desk, tapping keys as she settled herself before her screen.

Ford made himself a coffee and took it back to his office. Something was bugging him, and he needed caffeine and peace and quiet to let it percolate through his brain.

He pulled an A4 pad towards him and started jotting down thoughts.

It's all about the food bank.
Link: victims all customers/users.
Murdered on same day as visit to FB. Significant?
Matthew Kyte?
Angie hit with tin of baked beans. Deliberate choice? Emphasise her poverty?

As he scribbled down the final word, Lisa Moore's statement came back to him.

'You called her worthless,' he said to his empty office. 'Is that what this is about? Do you feel superior to them? Are they worthless because they're poor?'

◆ ◆ ◆

Hannah sat at her desk, reading through the till receipts issued by the food bank to its customers and marking off items with a freshly sharpened pencil. Her monitor displayed photographs taken at each of the crime scenes.

Beginning with Angie Halpern's receipt, she cross-checked each item from the food bank against the hi-res images in front of her. Reaching the end of the list of groceries, she frowned, then began again. After her second pass, she muttered to herself.

'Where's the Tesco pasta?'

She made a note, then proceeded to the crime scene photos from Paul Eadon's drab, badly furnished kitchen. With a dawning sense that she was on to something, she raced through the images, her eyes flicking from the till receipts up to the crime scene photos.

'Waitrose ketchup.'

Another note, another small smile that crept across her lips.

She moved on to the images relating to Aimee Cragg. She studied the crime scene photos for longer this time, searching for the discrepancy. She found it.

'Sainsbury's teabags.'

The photos from the Marcus Anderson crime scene were next, and last. Ignoring the black pools and spatters, she focused on the shots of the kitchen cupboards. It was hard to tell, but by enlarging sections of the images and flipping back and forth between different shots, she found it.

'Lidl crackers.'

She found Jools in Major Crimes. Everyone else was out.

'He's taking items of shopping.'

Jools looked up from her screen. 'What?'

'The killer. He's taken one item from each victim's most recent shop.'

'Are you sure?'

'Hundred per cent. Not a joke, by the way.' She flapped a sheet of paper at Jools.

'What's this?'

'I've diagrammed it. The crime scenes and the missing food items. Pasta, ketchup, teabags and crackers.'

She watched Jools study her analysis, realised she was holding her breath and let it out in a hiss.

Jools looked up at her. 'What about the missing litre of blood?'

'I've been thinking about that,' Hannah said. 'We know for a fact he took a litre out of Aimee Cragg's bath. And as far as Georgina and I were able to calculate, it looks as though he did the same with Paul Eadon.'

'Right, and you said he couldn't be drinking it.'

'Not right there, no. But he could be taking it away and using it some other way.'

'Such as?'

'Painting with it. Cooking with it. Using it in a sexual way. For example—'

Jools held up a hand. 'I get it. For the sake of argument, let's assume the groceries are the trophies and the blood fits into his MO differently. Then what?'

'Find the trophies, find the killer,' Hannah said, with a note of triumph. 'Unlike items of underwear, jewellery or body parts, you could stash groceries in plain sight and even an experienced investigator might miss them.'

Jools was nodding, making notes. 'Can you make a list of the missing items and circulate them? I'll tell everyone to find a way to take a quick look in each TIE subject's kitchen,' she said. 'We're getting close, Hannah. *Really* close. I'm taking this to Ford.'

DAY SEVENTEEN, 2.13 P.M.

Ford took Hannah's deduction, combined it with his gut feeling about Abbott, and went to see Sandy. As she spoke, he monitored her face for a hint – even a ghost of a hint – as to how she would react to his request. She gave him nothing. Lips as straight as a ruler, eyes neither narrowed nor wide. Relaxed facial muscles. *Remind me never to play poker with you, Sandy.*

'. . . so I want a search warrant for his house and vehicles,' he finished.

Sandy paused before answering. She scratched the side of her nose. *Was that a tell, guv?*

'It's all circumstantial,' she said, finally. 'Every last bit of it. A professional interest in blood? A sketchy alibi? No magistrate'll sign a warrant based on that.'

'Yes, they will!'

Sandy shook her head. 'I can't authorise it, Henry. It's not worth the aggro.'

'Look! You told me the ACC wants to kick me off the case unless I close it. I bring you credible evidence to arrest Abbott and now you're stonewalling me. Why?'

'You heard what Peterson said. Abbott's got connections.'

Ford reared back in his chair. 'What? This isn't some sort of Hollywood mafia movie!' he said, raising his voice, unable to stop himself. 'I don't *care* if Abbott plays golf with Peterson. Hell, I don't care if he plays hunt the salami with the mayor's wife. I like him for it.'

Sandy smiled. 'I know you do. But are you sure it's not just because he's rubbed you up the wrong way somehow? I know what these consultants are like.'

'Yes, I'm sure,' he replied, forcing himself to breathe deeply and avoid shouting at his boss a second time. 'There's just something off about him. One minute he's all helpfulness, then he's cold and haughty, then evasive. He's lying, I can tell.'

'Then prove it. Bring me one single piece of evidence linking him to any of the murders and we'll go to the magistrate together. You can even do the talking! And while we're on the subject of search warrants, why not Kyte as well?'

'It's not him. I know it.'

'How?'

'I just do. I'm lead investigator and I set the investigative priorities, and I say, with limited resources, we focus our energies on Abbott.'

'Are you absolutely sure you want to play it like that, Henry?'

Ford caught the warning tone in her voice and relented. 'I'll have a team go and see Matty. Pull the old "Can I use your loo?" trick.'

'Do that. But no warrant on Abbott for now.'

He knew he wasn't going to get a better offer. He'd argued with his boss, and his mentor, many times in the past and all that had happened was that she'd wrapped a coil or two around him and started to squeeze.

Ford stopped at Jools's desk on the way through the incident room. 'How's your profile on Matty Kyte going?'

She looked up and smiled, brushed a stray strand of hair away from her eyes. 'Got the basics and some background. His volunteering, and his day job, we know about. He's been assigned to Bodenham Ward for the last six months. They have all the cancer patients.'

'Personal?'

'Married for eight years to Jennifer Elizabeth Kyte. She works in a care home out on the London Road. No kids.'

'Record?'

'Nope.'

'Crap! Anything else?'

'I've saved the best till last,' she said.

'Meaning?'

'Guess what car his wife drives?'

Ford's pulse bumped up a few notches. 'Please tell me it's a grey VW Polo?'

'All right then, guv,' she said, and cleared her throat. 'It's a grey VW Polo.'

'Have you cross-checked with Olly yet?'

Jools shook her head. 'Nuh-uh.'

'Do that next. In fact, once you've done that, I want you and Olly to go and see him at home. One of you distract him while the other has a quick look round, yes? And if you get the chance to snag something with his DNA on it, take it, OK?'

'OK. How about you, guv?'

'I'm going to try to find a way to shake something loose about Abbott.'

◆ ◆ ◆

He hands Tasha the carrier bag with her groceries in it. Takes in her wide-set eyes and freckle-bridged nose.

'There you go,' he says, with a smile.

'Thanks,' she says, gaze lowered, not making eye contact.

'Listen,' he says, 'would you like a lift home? I'm finishing my shift here and my car's parked round the back.'

Now she does look up. 'Oh no, I couldn't. I'll get the bus, it's no problem.'

'Oh, I know it's not a problem, but I'd like to. Really,' he says, turning up the wattage on his smile. 'Save you struggling with your bags if you have to go upstairs. Come on,' he adds, 'we can go now. Where do you live?'

She's powerless. He knows it. She'd feel ungrateful if she refused him again. He's just packed her bloody free food, for God's sake.

'Morley Road. Do you know it?'

'Know it? You won't believe this, but I grew up on Morley Road,' he says, hand flat against his chest.

'No way,' she says, smiling now.

Well, technically, she's right. It's a lie. But now she's relieved to be on safe ground, he can see that. 'Actually, yes, way!' He accompanies her out of the front door and leads her to the side road where he's left the car. 'Come on, I'm parked over there,' he says, pointing.

The car is just a few yards away. He's walking a half-step behind her. Looking over at her neck. The carotid pulses at him through her translucent skin. He's not done one there, not yet. Maybe Tasha can be the trailblazer. He'll have to be careful. It'll be like pushing a needle into a firehose.

His stomach is fizzing.

She's talkative now. Gabby. He wishes she'd shut up. He pictures the moment when he hits her. He's brought something for the job this time. After Moore fought back, he's decided he needs to be more careful. The slim, saggy cosh he made now lies snug in the small of his back, tucked inside his waistband.

They're at the car now. He's opening the boot.

'Nice car!' she says appreciatively.

'Tasha!' a woman's voice calls out.

He looks round. An older woman is hurrying across the road towards them. Tasha has turned away from him. He's losing her. *No!*

'Hi, Lesley,' she says.

'I was just going to grab a coffee and a cake before work. You got time?' the woman says. 'My treat.'

'I was just about to run Tasha home,' he says, trying to keep his voice light.

Tasha turns back to him. 'I think I'll just grab a coffee with my friend. Lesley, this is . . .' She frowns. 'Sorry, I don't even know your name. How rude!'

He grimaces. 'It's Harvey. Harvey Williams.'

The woman steps in and shakes his hand. 'Pleased to meet you, Harvey.'

Inside, he's screaming obscenities. He pictures her dying in a welter of her own blood. Arcs of crimson spraying into a cloudless sky. Like rainbows.

He watches the two women walk away with the shopping bags, heads bent towards each other. Almost weeping with frustration, he gets into the car and after a long time staring at their retreating forms, starts the engine.

DAY EIGHTEEN, 9.05 A.M.

Charles Abbott stood talking with a colleague in the centre of the ward.

'Has that bloody policeman been poking his nose in your business, too?' Abbott asked his colleague.

'What, *Detective Inspector* Ford?'

'Yes.'

'As a matter of fact, he has. One of his team has, anyway. I told her what I could, and I gave her a list of my team's contact details, for which, incidentally, I have already been reprimanded by the chief operating officer.'

'Bad luck. But at least she only asked you for help. For some reason, the bloody man's got it in for me.'

'What did you tell him?'

'About as little as I thought I could get away with.'

'Good for you, Charles. Bloody plods marching in here, thinking they own the place. Don't they know it's men like us who are doing the real hard work? We save lives, for God's sake.'

Abbott nodded his agreement as a porter approached, pushing a bedding-laden trolley.

''Scuse me, gents,' he said cheerily. 'Hello, Mr Abbott.'

Abbott glanced at the man bent over the push-rail of the trolley, hairy wrists protruding from his uniform's shirt-cuffs.

'Good morning, er, Matt, isn't it?'

'Matty, that's right,' the porter answered with a smile before continuing to the end of the ward.

'Fraternising with the lower orders?' Abbott's colleague asked, grinning slyly. 'You'll be signing people's leaving cards next.'

Abbott snorted, and had opened his mouth to answer when a scream shattered the quiet.

They whirled around, just in time to see an overweight woman slowly collapsing to the ground. The screamer was an elderly lady in the nearest bed. Before anyone else could react, Abbott rushed over to the stricken woman. In a fluid move he scooped her up, arms under her knees and shoulders, and laid her on her bed before standing back as nurses rushed to take over.

'Impressive work there, Charles,' his colleague said. 'Be careful now. They'll start a rumour you care about your patients!'

Abbott smiled back. 'Bet you a tenner she's dead of a coronary within the year.'

DAY EIGHTEEN, 9.30 A.M.

Ford shook his head, furious. 'Thanks, Jools. Tell Olly he's buying the first round tonight, for the whole team.'

Grim-faced, Jools nodded and left.

Apparently, Olly had blown the plan to snoop around Matty's place, informing Jools it didn't 'sit well with my personal and professional ethics'. He'd asked to search quite openly, and Matty had refused point-blank to let them in.

His phone rang. The Python.

◆ ◆ ◆

Sandy looked across her desk at Ford. Her stomach was a ball of iron and her pulse hammered in her chest. A call ten minutes earlier from Martin Peterson was the proximate cause of her spiking blood pressure. But behind it was the mounting sense that Operation Shoreline was destined to be a runner, maybe months or years from resolution. She'd seen good detectives brought low – sometimes to the point of suicide – when large, long-running cases fizzled out. She didn't want it for Ford. And she definitely didn't want it for herself.

'Surely you're making a *little* progress towards arresting someone, Sandy?' Peterson had said, in that infuriating manner of his – a pretence at concern only just masking his contempt.

And now here was Ford, glaring at her, demanding to know why he couldn't arrest Charles Abbott. Her chest felt tight, like she'd fastened her bra on the wrong hooks.

'We need to do something, Sandy,' he said. 'He's the best lead we have.'

'He's got an alibi,' she said, rubbing her left bicep and wondering if she were about to have a heart attack right in front of her new DI.

No! She wouldn't suffer the indignity of it. The sheer bloody *indignity*. She'd worked like a Trojan to get the D/Supt nameplate on her office door. And no PCC or over-eager DI was going to catapult her from her hard-earned space into a bed at the hospital.

'Provided by his wife, for God's sake!' Ford was saying. 'Look at him, Sandy. A blood expert. He's arrogant, clever, disdainful, manipulative, charming. He's a basic fit for Lisa Moore's description.'

Sandy's eyes widened. 'A basic fit? Your report said her attacker had dark hair and a moustache, plus glasses. You showed her photos and she said it wasn't Abbott, but it might have been Matty Kyte.'

'Come on, Sandy. Please trust me. What more do you want?'

'For a start, a bit more than your prejudice against a toffee-nosed doctor. How about some hard evidence? One piece, Henry. One! A fingerprint. A DNA trace. A fibre that places him at one of the crime scenes. How're the forensics coming along?'

'Slow. Could be faster if you gave me more money.'

Sandy sighed, closing her eyes and massaging her temples. Thought of spreadsheets. Contingency funds. Recruitment. Equipment. She opened them again. 'Come back in an hour with the amount you need. I'll see what I can do.'

He jumped to his feet. 'I'll be back here in forty-five minutes.'

'No promi—' she shouted at his retreating back, but the final syllable was cut off as the door closed behind him.

Maybe an arrest was off the cards, for now. But that didn't mean Ford couldn't keep investigating Abbott. And now they had the DNA analysis from the blood taken from under Lisa Ford's fingernails, this could be the key.

He'd asked himself whether his conviction about the man was triggered more by resentment of his abrasive manner than a copper's feel for a 'wrong 'un'. Answering himself truthfully was hard, but the circumstantial evidence was strong. And plenty of killers had gone down with no more than that.

He called the hospital. The receptionist put him through to Abbott's secretary, and she informed him that 'Mr Abbott isn't working today.'

'All right for some,' Ford said, aiming for a jokey tone.

'Mr Abbott does a lot of charity work. I'm sure he's at home catching up on his voluntary work as a trustee at the Purcell Foundation,' she said.

'Was he working the day before yesterday?'

'Yes.'

Ford cursed inwardly. 'At SDH?' he said.

'In the afternoon, yes. In the morning he was at Revelstoke Hall Hospital in the New Forest, where he sees his private patients.'

'From what time in the afternoon?'

'I'll have to check. Hold, please.'

Classical music filled the earpiece. Ford winced and held the receiver away from his ear, then hurriedly brought it back as the music cut out again.

'Here we are,' the secretary said. 'He saw his first patient here at two forty-five.'

◆ ◆ ◆

Ford rang the bell. He was nervous and wiped his palms on his suit trousers. He'd discarded Sandy's loyalty and protection to pursue a hunch. *If I'm wrong on this, she'll hang me out to dry. She'll have to.*

Abbott answered his front door wearing a pair of khaki shorts, scuffed brown leather boat shoes and, incongruously, a long-sleeved dress shirt with the collar open. His shoes and shins were flecked with green. Ford caught the sappy smell of fresh-cut grass.

Abbott rolled his eyes. 'Back so soon?' he said, crossing his arms over his chest. 'People will start to talk.'

'May I come in, Mr Abbott?'

'Why?'

'For a chat.'

'I'm in the middle of mowing the lawn.'

'Push-along or ride-on?'

Abbott frowned. 'Ride-on. Why?'

'No reason.' He took a half-step closer to Abbott. 'It won't take long.'

Abbott groaned. 'Oh, very well.'

Pausing at the sink to drink off a tumbler of water from the tap, Abbott held a second, empty, glass out towards Ford. 'You want one? It's awfully hot out there, isn't it?'

'No, thanks.'

Abbott shrugged and gestured for Ford to take a seat at the kitchen table. Then he sat facing him, spread his hands out in front of him on the gleaming oak surface and lifted his chin.

'Well?'

Ford noticed a dark spot on the inside of Abbott's left shirt sleeve, about halfway between wrist and elbow. Filed it. 'He attacked another food bank customer the day before yesterday.'

'Attacked? Not murdered?'

Ford shook his head, scrutinising Abbott's face for a twitch, a flicker of the gaze, anything that might betray his inner landscape: innocent, guilty, sane, psychopathic. Saw nothing.

'He picked the wrong victim. She's ex-army. Gave the bastard a hiding.'

'Good for her,' Abbott said with a smile.

'She got a good look at him, too.'

'Did she identify him? That would be a good lead, I'd imagine.'

'She said he looked like you, Mr Abbott.' Ford kept his face straight as he delivered the lie.

'Really? What – average height, average build, brown hair, brown eyes? That sort of thing?'

Ford felt his gut twitch: an unpleasant sensation as if he'd swallowed something alive. 'A bit more than that. And here's the thing. The attack took place in the morning.'

Abbott smiled a lazy smile. 'I sense you're building up to something.'

'Where were you on Wednesday morning at eleven forty-five?'

'Why do I get the feeling you already think you know the answer?'

'At SDH?'

'No,' Abbott said, drawing out the word with the falling/rising inflection of someone explaining something simple to an idiot. 'I was at Revelstoke Hall Hospital.'

'Can anyone confirm that?'

'I doubt it. I was working in my office on a paper for the *British Journal of Haematology*. It's a very prestigious journal.'

'How about hospital CCTV?'

'They have it, of course. But not on the consultants' corridor,' he added.

Ford made a mental note to check the footage. He pointed at the spot on Abbott's shirt sleeve. 'Cut yourself?'

Abbott rotated his forearm outwards and looked down. 'Brambles. Bloody things are taking over down by the riverbank.'

'We have a few in our garden, too,' Ford said. 'Want me to take a look? I'm a trained first-aider.'

'Oh, for God's sake! It's a scratch, not a knife wound.'

Ford held out his hand. 'Please.'

Shaking his head in evident disbelief, Abbott unbuttoned his cuff and took his time folding it back on itself. He extended his arm, the tender skin on the inside surface uppermost. A series of ragged scratches extended for a span of about four inches, beaded with dark-red clots like the inky pearls of blackberries.

'As I said,' Abbott drawled, 'I'm fairly sure I'll survive this . . . *insult.*'

Evidence. Sandy had asked for it. And now it was staring Ford in the face.

All he needed was a single epithelial cell from Lisa Moore in one of the scratches, or Abbott's DNA in the tissue retrieved from under her fingernails, and he had his man down cold.

'I'd like you to come into Bourne Hill Station, Mr Abbott,' he said in as calm a voice as he could manage, wondering if he was staring into the emotionless eyes of a serial killer. Heart racing. Stomach churning.

'Why? Do you have a new first-aid kit you want to try out?'

'Because there are aspects of this case that lead me to believe you may' – he paused –'know something about the murders.' *Like the fact that you committed them.* 'And I'd like you to provide a DNA sample.'

'What aspects?'

'It would be a voluntary interview. No need for lawyers. Or cells,' Ford added.

Abbott's left eye twitched. 'You'd like that, wouldn't you?'

'Like what?'

'To get me into an interrogation room without my lawyer present.'

'Firstly, we call them interview suites' – Abbott barked out a short, mirthless laugh – 'and secondly, if it would make you feel more comfortable to bring a legal representative, that would be fine with me.'

It was a gamble. Any half-decent lawyer would advise his client to say nothing. Ford wiped the sweat from his forehead. Felt his mouth fill with saliva.

'You know what?' Abbott said, getting to his feet. 'What I *feel* like is finishing my lawn. It's very, very big and I'm only a quarter done.'

Ford stayed sitting. He looked up at his quarry. *One more push.* 'I really would like you to come in. If for no other reason than to exclude you from our investigation. A DNA sample would take care of everything.'

Abbott sneered. 'And, as I think *I* just said, I really want to continue mowing my lawn. After which I intend to open a very expensive bottle of Sancerre and enjoy a glass or two looking over the fields. So if there's nothing else . . .'

'I could always arrest you.'

'I doubt that. I already gave you my alibi. I think you're over-stepping your authority.'

Ford took his second gamble. 'Your alibi for Wednesday looks shaky in the absence of CCTV or witnesses, and courts assign minimal weight to spousal alibis. Without anything stronger than your wife's word that you were binge-watching *Orange Is the New Black*—'

'*Game of Thrones.*'

'—on the dates of the other murders, there's enough circumstantial evidence to place you under arrest right now.' Ford stood. 'What's it to be?'

Finally, he saw a crack in Abbott's disdainful facade. His eyes flicked upwards. 'You can't.'

'I can.'

Ford watched him. Waited for him to make a decision. Ignored the tickle as sweat ran down his ribs from his armpits.

Abbott slumped in the chair. 'I wasn't at Revelstoke Hall, and I wasn't watching *Game of* bloody *Thrones* with Lucinda either,' he muttered.

Ford made a show of cupping his hand behind his right ear. 'Say again? I didn't catch that.'

'I wasn't here,' Abbott said, louder this time. His eyes flicked left. 'Or at Revelstoke Hall.'

Ford tensed. Was Abbott about to run? He looked fit, and he claimed to play tennis. If he went for the French doors, Ford would have to negotiate the kitchen table to give chase.

'Then where were you?'

'Christ, man, isn't that enough? I've admitted I lied. Would a serial killer do that?'

'I don't know. I've never met one before.'

'Look,' Abbott said, leaning forward and clasping his hands together. He dropped his voice. 'We're men of the world, aren't we?'

'Are we?'

'I mean, you're experienced in the way things are in the real world. You've seen it all, I should imagine.'

'I've seen all sorts of things. Some of the most recent will live with me for ever.'

'Exactly. Look, if I explain to you here, in confidence, what's been going on, man to man, you need to respect that and keep it to yourself.'

'What is it you want to tell me, Mr Abbott?' *And if you say you killed them, I'm going to knock you down. Pre-emptive force in exigent circumstances.*

'I was with an escort,' Abbott blurted.

'An escort?'

'Yes, man, you know. A call girl. A prostitute. A tart!'

'On each of the dates I gave you, when you claimed you were either here watching the telly with your wife or working at Revelstoke Hall?'

Abbott swiped a hand across his brow. He looked relieved, even essaying a small smile. 'Yes!'

'Why did you lie before?'

'Why do you think? I have a reputation to preserve. I hardly think being known for associating with prostitutes gets one invited to the better parties.'

'Name?'

'What?'

'Her *name*. This escort. What is it?'

'Oh. Yes, of course. But, as I said, you'll keep this under your hat?'

'I think we'd better just have it.'

Abbott hesitated. He sighed and spoke the name on the out-breath. 'Zoe.'

'Last name?'

'She said it was Denys, but, you know . . .' He smirked. 'It could be a *nom d'amour.*'

'And Mrs Abbott will confirm this, will she? That you weren't here after all?'

'Of course she will. We have' – he paused – 'an understanding. I'll go and get her.'

Abbott stood and turned towards the door.

Ford was round the table in a second. He placed a restraining hand on Abbott's right shoulder, aware, even in this moment of heightened stress, that technically, he'd just used force and might be asked to complete a form at the nick if Abbott complained.

'No. If she's upstairs, shout.'

'She's not. She's in the garden. Down by the river, I think.'

'Does she have her phone with her?'

Abbott returned to his chair and fished out his own phone. 'I think so. Never goes anywhere without it.'

'Call her, then. Ask her to join us.'

Five minutes later, Ford sat facing both Abbotts. Ford marvelled at Lucinda Abbott's ability to come in from a garden in rural Wiltshire looking as though she had been on a beach in the south of France. Today, she wore a bronze bikini, over which she'd tied a gauzy, dark-blue sarong. A gold pendant lay against her breastbone. The translucent sarong heightened rather than diminished the impact of her figure. Her bee-stung lips, frosted in heavy pink gloss, curved upwards just a little as she caught him staring.

He cleared his throat. 'Mrs Abbott, your husband has just told me that he was not, in fact, here with you watching *Game of Thrones* on the dates I have previously mentioned, as you and he have claimed.'

Her lips parted.

Ford held up a hand. 'Would it surprise you to know he now claims he was in the company of a sex worker named Zoe Denys?'

She smiled. 'Not at all.'

DAY EIGHTEEN, 2.05 P.M.

Ford managed to avoid letting his mouth drop open. She'd blind-sided him.

'My husband had been working rather hard recently, Inspector,' she said with a confiding smile. She took Abbott's hand in her own, enfolding it so that her long turquoise nails rested on his knuckles. 'He's been under enormous stress. From time to time, poor Charles feels the need to let off a little additional steam. With Zoe. It's not ideal, but tell me, what marriage is?'

'So, you're confirming that when you provided your husband with an alibi, that was a lie.'

'I was trying to protect his *reputation*,' she said indignantly. 'As a loyal wife.'

Ford had had enough of being given the runaround by this would-be local power couple.

'And how do you think his reputation will look – and yours – if I decide to charge you both with obstruction and wasting police time?'

Her mouth dropped open. 'You wouldn't!'

'Try me.'

'Look, Inspector,' Abbott said. 'There's no need for that.'

Ford looked at Abbott, who was all smiles now, his features once more arranged in that infuriatingly smug expression that had been winding Ford up since their very first encounter. He didn't need the aggravation of booking them both, but he did want information.

'I need contact details for Zoe Denys, now.'

'I'm afraid I can't help you,' Abbott said, the corners of his mouth drooping in a parody of sadness.

'This is your alibi we're talking about here.'

'I know. And I wish I could help you. But I can't.'

'You must contact her when you want to see her? What's her phone number? Or do you use email?'

'I place a classified ad in the *Telegraph*. In the Announcements section. You know, 'Mr X is getting married to Miss Y,' that sort of thing. She calls me and we fix up a meeting.'

'So you have her number in your phone.'

Abbott shook his head. 'She calls me via the hospital switch-board at Revelstoke Hall. Untraceable, you see. She values her privacy just as much as her clients value theirs.'

'So, what you're telling me is that you are replacing your old alibis – that you were here watching TV with your wife, or working – with a new one: that you were having sex with an untraceable prostitute in a hotel.'

'Shamefully, yes. I'm not proud of myself.'

'Which hotels do you use?'

'It varies. Usually country-house places, boutique spots on the coast.'

'I'll need you to give me a list, and the names under which you registered.'

'I'll try to remember and get a list to you.'

'Try hard. I'll give you twenty-four hours. We'll contact the hotels to ask for their registration files and CCTV. If we don't find you there, you'll be seeing me again.' Ford stood. 'Thank you for your time, Mr and Mrs Abbott.'

Abbott stayed seated, but his wife stood and smiled, ushering Ford out of the kitchen and down the wide hallway to the front door, where she paused.

'I'm so sorry you had a wasted trip. Poor Charles. I think he might be having some sort of breakdown. I'll be calling our doctor as soon as you've gone.'

◆　◆　◆

Once the detective's car had disappeared round the bend at the end of the main road through the village, Lucinda stormed back into the living room, where her husband was sipping from a large cut-glass tumbler of whisky.

'That went well,' she said, hands on hips.

He smiled up at her. 'He was on the point of arresting me, darling. I had to come clean about Zoe. He wasn't buying our binge-watching story so I decided he should have the truth.' He spread his hands. 'A bit of police station gossip about my little peccadilloes will be infinitely preferable to me being hauled down to the police station in handcuffs. And we don't want them discovering that I've been pinching blood from work for our little games, do we?'

She stared down at him a moment longer. He was right, damn him. Charles was always right.

DAY TWENTY-ONE, 8.30 A.M.

Ford waited for everyone to fill the meeting room. He checked his watch. No excuses to be late first thing on a Monday morning. Sandy had ordered him to take the weekend off. He'd intended to spend time with Sam, but Sam had spent most of the two days 'hanging out with my friends, like I usually do'. Still, it had allowed Ford to catch up with paperwork, and to think about Abbott.

Jools had urged him to keep an open mind when he'd called her on Sunday morning. 'I know you have this feeling for murderers, guv. But the evidence isn't anywhere near strong enough. You've got to go by the numbers. It's how the majority of cases are solved.'

'Yes, Jools. It *is* how the majority are solved. But the majority of victims know their killers. Ours were killed by a stranger. By a psychopathic stranger. That calls for a different approach.'

'Fine, but you should know, people on the team are starting to question your fixation with Abbott.'

'And by "people", you mean Mick, right?'

'I've heard others, too.'

'Just as long as they remember I'm the lead investigator. I'll deal with the backstabbing.'

'It's not backstabbing, guv! They just want a result.'

'And they'll get one, Jools. They will.'

He shook his head to dispel the memory. Everyone had arrived, and he was eager to get the meeting underway. He surveyed the room, assessing, as far as he was able, the state of mind of each member of his team. Mick looked fed up, doodling on his pad. Jan, ever diligent, sat with her pen poised over her notepad. Jools and Olly sat next to each other on his right: any closer and they'd be sitting on his lap.

Hannah sat at the far end of the table. Her eyes never left his. She smiled when he swept his gaze over her. Sandy had begun attending the morning meetings. She commanded the left side of the table, flanked by Alec Reid and a couple of other DSs, drafted in to help cover the multiplying bases of Operation Shoreline.

'Charles Abbott told me he lied about his original alibis.' A murmur of excitement built in the room. Ford patted the air. 'But before you suggest I rush round there with my iron bracelets, he came up with another one.'

'What is it, guv?' Olly asked.

'Who. One Zoe Denys. A high-class prostitute, apparently. Same basic story, though,' Ford said, frowning. 'Jools, I need you to keep on top of this one. Abbott's supposed to be sending me a list of hotels he and this Denys woman used. As soon as I get it I want you to start follow-up with the hotels.'

'Sure, guv.'

'How about the DNA from Lisa Moore's fingernail scrapings, Alec?' Ford asked.

'It came back on Friday. When you arrest him or he volunteers for a DNA swab, we'll be able to compare the two,' he said.

'If the new alibi checks out, Abbott's in the clear, then,' Sandy said. 'Who else are you looking at?'

'The only other person of interest is this hospital porter, Matty Kyte.'

'Go on.'

'He's strong. I felt his grip. And he's a good fit for the killer size-wise. He's connected to all four victims by the food bank.'

'Any tortured animals in his garden shed? Vampire films in his DVD collection? Serial killer books in his bedroom?' she asked.

'We interviewed him at SDH and here, but that's a really good point,' Ford said.

'What about his alibi?'

'He confirmed it earlier today. It's the same as Abbott's first one. At home with the missus.'

'DNA?'

'He hasn't got a record. We'll work on securing a sample from him.' He flicked a look at Olly, who blushed.

Questions followed about Lisa Moore's tentative ID of Matty, trophies, alibis and other LOEs. Ford rebuffed them all.

'I've met both men. I've looked into their eyes. I've profiled the killer and I've assessed them both against it. Matty's a bit of a weirdo, but Abbott's a wrong 'un. I can feel it.'

'In your gut,' Mick deadpanned, winking slyly at Jan.

Ignoring this minor act of treachery, Ford continued. 'We'll run checks on Matty, but Abbott is still our focus. Is that clear?'

A chorus of mumbled, 'yes, guvs' greeted his sharp question.

'Why don't you leave Abbott alone for now and go and see this Kyte character at home?' Sandy suggested. 'Maybe get a read on the wife, if she's all he has.'

'Sure. I'll go. Hannah, come with me, yes?'

'OK.'

After closing the meeting, Ford headed back to his office. On the way he tapped Jools on the shoulder. 'Got a minute?'

She nodded and rose to follow him.

'What do *you* think of Matty Kyte?' he asked her.

'You *know* what I think. He's too good to be true.'

'To me he just comes across as a people-pleaser.'

'Maybe. But what about the blood drawing he denied doing? That's creepy, don't you think?'

'Creepy, yes. Evidence he's a serial killer? I don't know, Jools. I think you're reaching. Maybe Matty was just acting out.' *Like Sam does. No, because Sam's a teenager and he had a good reason. What's Matty's excuse?* 'He had to clear up the mess when Abbott dropped that blood bag.'

Her eyes popped wide. '*Me reaching?* What about *you*, guv? You hate Abbott because he's educated, rich and posh. I've seen you with guys like him before. Yes, he's a smug arsehole. But where's the evidence he's anything more?'

Ford fought down a sudden desire to tell her how he knew. *Why* he knew. *Takes a killer to know a killer, Jools . . . ?* No, never. Then his last words jumped back out at him. He closed his eyes, picturing the moment when Abbott dropped the bag. He visualised it. Capped off, a heat-sealed edge, that weird silky finish to the plastic. Labelled with blood type and quantity and some kind of best-before date. The dark liquid within.

He opened his eyes. Smiling. Feeling jumpy.

Jools was frowning at him. 'Where did you go, guv?'

'Remember in the water meadows when we calculated the killer's blood volume at six litres?'

'What about it?'

'That old boy with the iron crank. He said the five rivers are like arteries. He said something like, "I let a little in, let a little out."'

'What's your point?'

'What if he's using the blood for transfusions?'

'Into who?'

'Himself, Jools! Think about it,' he said, counting off points on his fingers. 'He murders people, and takes a litre of their blood. He transfuses himself with their blood.'

'And he needs six victims—'

'—to harvest six litres.'

'Why?' Jools asked.

'What?'

'Why would he do that? Transfuse himself with other people's blood?'

Ford held his hands wide. 'How should I know? He's a bloody serial killer! Why do they do anything?'

'Trophies?' Jools asked.

'I thought we agreed the missing food-bank items were the trophies.'

'What if the till receipts were wrong? It's hardly a state-of-the-art system they're running there.'

Ford shook his head. 'Angie was murdered the same afternoon she visited the food bank. All her shopping was there on the table. I reread the pathologist's report this morning,' he added. 'No recently digested food in either Angie or Kai's stomach, so they hadn't had an early tea.'

'We need to talk to Matty,' Jools said at last.

'Yes, but in the meantime, get Charles Abbott's medical records. Maybe he's got some rare blood disorder. Haemophilia or something. Maybe that's why he went into haematology.'

Once Jools had left, Ford started planning his next move. He realised he had only the haziest notion of how blood transfusions were carried out. And who better to ask than the man he'd been on the point of arresting the previous evening? He called Abbott.

'What now, Inspector? If it's the list of hotels, I said I'd get it to you, and I will, but I also have a department to run. A great many people are depending on me for life-saving treatment. You'll just have to be patient, I'm afraid.'

'I understand that, but I have further questions for you. Please remember, you are being interviewed in connection with five murders and one attempted murder.'

Abbott sighed. 'Very well. I suppose it can't wait until later?'

'Not really.'

'Fine. Come and see me now.'

Before leaving for the hospital, Ford pulled up the medical records of the adult victims and checked their blood types. All were A-positive. He called Lisa Moore and discovered her blood type was the same.

Ford reached the hospital twelve minutes later. Four minutes after that, he was outside Abbott's office. He squared his shoulders and knocked on the door.

'Come!' The voice was loud, confident.

Abbott smiled at Ford and waved him to a chair.

'Thank you for seeing me again, Mr Abbott.' *Especially as half my team seem to think I'm barking up the wrong tree.*

'No thanks needed,' Abbott said. 'As we seem to be seeing so much of each other, perhaps you should call me Charles.'

'I wasn't sure you'd see it that way.'

'Really? Because of your campaign of harassment, threats, prying and intimidation, you mean?'

Ford replied in kind, hardening his voice. 'My questions were legitimate ones. If I caused you any embarrassment, I'm sorry, but you've not been straight with me.' A beat. 'Charles.'

Abbott's eyebrows shot up. 'Embarrassment? No, it wasn't that,' he said. 'But for some strange reason, I resent your accusation that I'm a murderer – a *serial* murderer, come to that – in my own home. In front of my wife.'

'You said you'd be happy to answer my questions.'

'I know. I lied.'

'I beg your pardon?'

275

'I lied. I just wanted you up here to give you a piece of my mind,' Abbott said.

It wasn't the first threat of this nature thrown Ford's way, and he supposed it wouldn't be the last.

He decided to get his retaliation in first. 'Yes, you *did* lie. When you fabricated an alibi,' he said, matching Abbott's tone. 'And as I said before, that makes you and Mrs Abbott guilty of the twin criminal offences of obstruction and wasting police time. The second offence carries a maximum sentence of six months' imprisonment.'

'What the devil do you mean?'

'I mean, *Charles*, either you get off your high horse right now or I will arrest you here in your elegantly furnished office, handcuff you and march you out to my car past the disbelieving gazes of your patients and colleagues, charge you and have you in a cell at Bourne Hill nick without your belt or shoelaces inside the hour. I will also issue a press release naming you as a suspect in custody.'

The colour left Abbott's face, just as it had done in his house. Only this time it didn't return. The arrogance left him, too.

He slumped back in his chair. 'What do you want?' he asked in a quiet voice.

'A quick seminar on blood transfusions.'

Abbott sighed. 'What do you want to know?'

'Who can have what type of blood in a transfusion?'

Abbott adopted a scholarly tone, as if addressing a classroom full of medical students. He clasped his hands on the desk. 'Your ABO blood type can be A, B, AB or O. Clear?'

'Clear.'

'Your Rhesus type can be positive, indicating the presence of the Rhesus, or D, antigen, or negative, indicating its absence. Clear?'

'As mud.'

A frown from Abbott. 'Thus, one's blood may be, for example, A-positive, indicating the presence of A and D antigens. Or O-negative, indicating neither A nor B nor D antigens.'

'If you know the blood type of the donor, is it possible to narrow down the blood type of the recipient?'

'That's a very good question,' Abbott said with a smile. 'And the answer is, it depends. For example, a recipient with AB-positive blood can accept donations of any other blood type. We call them the universal recipient. And an O-negative donor can donate to any other blood type, making them the universal donor.'

'Are there tighter pairings?'

'I'll get you a chart that shows all the possibles,' Abbott said, pressing a button on the old-fashioned intercom on his desk, and asked his secretary to print off a 'blood-comp' chart.

Ford's pulse had kicked up a notch. The theory was looking stronger by the second. 'What blood type are *you*?' Ford asked.

'O-positive.'

'Which means you can accept?'

'O-negative or O-positive.'

'I'd like to check that, Charles.' *And your DNA.*

'I'm sure you would, Inspector,' Abbot said smoothly. 'Have you a warrant?'

'If you've nothing to hide, why would you need me to get a warrant?'

'Perhaps the small matter of my rights? Even such a lowly figure as a consultant haematologist enjoys protection from police intrusion into his private life.'

'You could give me a blood sample right now.'

Abbott laughed. 'You're right! Why, I'll just grab a scalpel and open a vein for you. Got anything to catch the blood in? You could—' He stopped the sarcastic outburst and fixed Ford with a smile. 'Actually, you know what? I'm sick and tired of your pursuing me like a common criminal. Come on, we'll go down to my consulting room now. I'll even let you watch.'

◆ ◆ ◆

Ford watched, mesmerised, as Abbott fastened a black Velcro strap around his upper arm, then swabbed the inside of his elbow with an alcohol-soaked wad of cotton wool. Why had he agreed? And then the answer presented itself. *Because he knows he's innocent! Shit!*

Abbott slid in the hypodermic, then withdrew the plunger with his thumbnail. Dark blood flowed into the syringe. He picked up a transparent plastic tube, squirted in the blood and snapped the green plastic cap shut.

'Hand me a label, would you, Ford?' he said, jerking his chin in the direction of a cupboard on the other side of his office. 'There's a roll of them in that box beside the golf trophy.'

Ford fetched one, which Abbott then wrote on before peeling off the shiny yellow backing paper and smoothing it on to the small plastic cylinder of blood.

'There! Happy now?' he said, handing it to Ford. 'I dare say you'll want to send it off to a DNA lab, too,' he added, smirking.

'Thank you,' Ford said, fighting down the black cloud of depression forming in his head. 'Tell me, how easy would it be to do a blood transfusion at home?'

Abbott paused, stroking the side of his nose. 'At home? Well, it would be unorthodox, but then I don't suppose serial killers are exactly what you would call *conventional* people, are they?'

'Not as a rule, no.'

'You'd need a sterile environment. There's a very real risk of infection,' he said. 'As to the equipment, rather simple, to be honest. A tube fitted with a delivery needle and a bag. A stand would make life easier, but you could suspend it from a hat-rack, or even a light fitting.'

'What level of expertise would you need?'

'Not very high. You have to be able to find a vein and insert the needle. After that, it's just plumbing, really.'

'Could a hospital porter do it?'

Abbott nodded. 'Or a healthcare assistant,' he added breezily. He frowned. 'Just a minute. A porter? I told you to talk to that dreadful man. Are you following that up? It's him, isn't it?'

Ford stood and offered his hand. 'Thank you. You've been a great help. I'll collect the blood chart on my way out.'

'Wait!' Abbott shouted as Ford reached the door. 'He organised a blood drive.'

'Who did?'

'Kyte! The porter! He badgered me into it one day when we happened to be working together in the warehouse at the Purcell Foundation. Said it would give "his" customers a sense of dignity.'

Ford made a note. Pieces clicked into place like the tumblers on a cell-door lock. *Maybe my gut has been lying to me. Maybe I've just got a weak stomach, like Mick thinks.*

'What else?'

'Don't you see?' Abbott was out from behind his desk. 'We had to blood-type each donor for the labels. Kyte assisted me. He knew – knows – their blood groups, Ford. He knows!'

Ford bestowed a huge smile on the secretary as she handed him the sheet of A4 paper with the grid of letters, symbols, ticks and crosses. She blushed, which made him smile harder.

As he strolled back to his car, whistling 'St James Infirmary Blues', he checked the blood comp chart. If the blood transfusion hypothesis was correct, then the killer had to have A-positive or AB-positive blood to accept donations from his adult victims. And

Abbott had just cheerfully given him a blood sample of what he claimed was his O-positive blood. His good mood evaporated.

Back at Bourne Hill, he took the blood sample to Alec.

'Abbott just drew this from his arm. I watched him do it. He said he's O-positive, but I want to know for sure. Can you test it?'

'Of course, dear chap. Couple of minutes short enough for you?' Alec said, winking.

'It's acceptable, I suppose.'

Alec's eyebrows shot up. 'Acceptable? It's a bloody miracle!'

Ford waited while Alec ran the blood through a handheld gizmo. He felt a leaden sense of his most promising line of enquiry collapsing before his eyes. And he'd been so sure. Maybe Jools, Mick and Sandy were right after all.

What Alec said next confirmed it. 'It's O-positive.'

Ford's black mood darkened further. Abbott wasn't transfusing himself. And he'd even said that Ford should get the blood DNA-profiled. A guilty man simply wouldn't do that.

'Bugger! Thanks, Alec. Look, just to be doubly sure, can you send it off to the DNA lab for me? Fast-track. We'll compare the profile against the results from Lisa and then we'll know one way or another.'

DAY TWENTY-ONE, 1.19 P.M.

Jools punched the air, freezing the frame on the video playback on her monitor.

'Guv!' she yelled at Ford, as she saw him leaving Major Crime.

He turned and came back to her desk. 'What is it, Jools?'

'We've got him! One of the Traffic guys was on Castle Street when Angie and Kai were murdered. He just called me. This is from his ANPR camera. Look.' She pointed at the screen.

In a grainy but still clear shot was the front end of a VW Polo, with the index number visible.

'Whose is it?'

'It's registered to Matty Kyte's missus, but it's him behind the wheel, look.'

And there he was, in all his glory.

'Great work, Jools.'

She smiled and added a copy of the image to the file. 'What about that list of hotels from Abbott?'

'Leave that for now. His blood's the wrong group. I've sent it off for a DNA profile, but it's looking very unlikely that it's him.'

'Oh, shit, sorry, guv. I know you liked him for it.'

'It's fine. Matty Kyte's now our prime suspect. Listen, don't take this the wrong way, but I'm going to see him tonight and I want Hannah there. She's got experience with psychopaths that none of us has.'

Jools smiled. 'No problem. As long as we get him, I'll be happy.'

'Do me a favour, though. Chase up Abbott's medical records.'

'Because?'

'Humour me.'

◆ ◆ ◆

Hannah watched as Ford crossed Forensics to her desk. Her stomach turned over with anticipation.

'Hi, Henry, what's up?'

'I'm going to pay a call on Matty Kyte, the Boy Scout hospital porter who just happened to organise a blood drive at the food bank. I want you along.'

'Now?'

'No, this evening. I want to catch him at home, get a feel for his domestic set-up and meet his wife.'

'Shouldn't you be taking Jools?'

'I need your expertise. She's OK with it, and a female presence might distract him, make him careless. Plus, after Olly's little ethics fit, I want to look for trophies.' He smiled at her. Her stomach coiled for another flip, then settled. 'Come to mine for six. We'll head over together in my car.'

Back at her desk, Hannah stared at her screen until it faded to black. In its polished surface she could see herself. She was smiling. Was it an attractive smile? She ran one of her plaits through her fingers. She had always enjoyed their knobbly smoothness. Would he?

'Stop it, Hannah!' she said aloud.

'Stop what?' one of the other CSIs asked her.

'Nothing. It doesn't matter.'

Yes, it does matter. It matters a lot.

DAY TWENTY-ONE, 7.00 P.M.

The Kytes lived in a Victorian terraced house on the Devizes Road on the north side of the city. One of thousands in Salisbury, hundreds of thousands in Wiltshire and, for all Ford knew, millions in the country as a whole.

Would the media dub it a 'house of horror' if Kyte were proved to be the killer? Probably, though that was what Ford always found so depressing when he arrested a suspect: the utterly ordinary outward appearance of their lives. They kept koi carp and shoplifted. Built elaborate model railway layouts in their lofts and drove while drunk. Supported football teams and beat their wives. They liked roast beef, avoided lamb, kicked innocent strangers to death behind rough pubs. Ran pub-quiz teams then embezzled money from their employers. Volunteered as Scout leaders and Salvation Army second trumpets and sexually abused children in their care.

Ford rang the bell. An electronic rendition of the chimes of Big Ben sounded distantly. Beside him, Hannah cleared her throat. He caught a movement as she brought a hand up to her hair.

'Nervous?'

'A little.'

'Let me do the talking. You just observe. Smile at him if he looks at you for reassurance.'

A pink shape swam into view behind the moulded foliage of the front-door glass. The door opened. A woman stood there, late twenties or early thirties, five-two, solid build and wearing striking make-up: bright blue eyeshadow, blusher shading her cheeks, wet-look bubblegum-pink lipstick. Thick black hair in an unflattering short style that made her face seem squarer than it was.

'Yes?' she said, her narrowed eyes switching from Ford to Hannah and back again, her mouth pinched, suspicious. 'We're not religious, you know. If you're Jehovah's Witnesses, you can save yourselves time and bugger off.'

Ford smiled. His best black suit did give him a missionary air. 'Jennifer Kyte?'

'That's me. Who are you?'

He held out his ID. 'Detective Inspector Ford. Wiltshire Police. This is my colleague, Dr Hannah Fellows.'

Scowling, she scrutinised his ID. 'We've already had the police round. What do you want?'

'Could we come in, please?'

She folded her arms. 'Why? I've got nothing to say more than what I did before.'

'We'd like to talk to you and your husband, Mrs Kyte. It would be much easier if we could do it inside.'

'I'm sure it would. For you. But he's not here, is he?'

'Where is Matty?'

She frowned. 'His name's Matthew.'

'Where is Matthew? Do you know when he'll be back?'

'He's running an errand for one of his patients. Taking her cat to the vet's. It needs to be put to sleep and the old biddy's too upset to take it herself. Matthew volunteered.' She folded her muscular arms across her chest. 'He's like that. Kind.' She gave the final word such force it sounded more like a challenge to the cops than a description of her husband.

'Could we come in and wait? We do have a few questions for you, as well, if you don't mind.'

In his occasional informal training sessions with new detectives, Ford called it TRAP: 'The Relentless Application of Politeness' – the refusal to be ruffled or antagonised by people making life difficult. They could be hardened gangsters with an expensive lawyer sitting beside them, or snaggle-toothed meth-heads causing problems in one of the city's many parks. Either way, he'd found over the years that rolling with the punches and coming back to ask yet another softly spoken, well-mannered question produced more results than tough talk, bluster or threats.

'Well?' Jennifer was asking. 'Are you coming in or not?'

He realised she'd stood aside and was, if not inviting, then *allowing* them into her home.

They followed her into a sitting room, furnished with a fabric-covered sofa – pink cabbage roses on a yellow background, polished wooden inserts topping the armrests – two matching armchairs and a large flat-screen TV.

A large painting of a Native American warrior holding a pony by a rope bridle dominated the wall facing the TV. Beneath it, an authentic-looking tomahawk decorated with feathers and red and yellow thongs rested on a low bookshelf.

To the left of the painting, a rectangular smoked-glass mirror in a black frame reflected Ford and Hannah back to him as they took the sofa. He shot her a brief smile.

Jennifer Kyte dropped into one of the armchairs and leaned back, elbows cocked, forearms on the shiny wooden armrests. She made no move to speak.

'Mrs Kyte,' Ford began, 'did Matthew ask you to confirm where he was on the dates we gave him?'

'Yes, he did. And you must be mad if you think it was him. Matthew wouldn't hurt a fly. Ask anyone.'

'He told us he was here with you, watching television.'

'That's because he was,' she said.

'Every time?'

'What do you mean?'

'On one of the dates we specified, your car – you do drive a grey Polo, don't you?'

Her eyes flickered to a spot above his head. 'What's that got to do with anything?'

'You do drive one, though – a car of that make, model and colour?'

'Yes. Needs a new clutch. Matty' – the word caught in her throat – 'I mean, Matthew, that's what he says.'

Ford rolled his eyes and tutted. 'Not cheap, are they, clutches? I had mine go on my old Land Rover. Cost me a fortune.'

'We'll be fine. We've got savings.'

'Yes,' Ford said with an encouraging smile, parking the Polo for now. 'Matthew told me. You're saving up for a deposit. This place is rented, is it?'

'None of your business.'

'I just thought, if you were saving . . .' He let the end of the sentence hang.

'It's mine. My aunt left it me. We want to invest in a second property, if you must know. Somewhere with loads of students.'

What had Abbott said about the skills you'd need to do a home blood transfusion? 'Nurses make good tenants, I've heard.'

She pursed her lips. 'That what you think, is it? Bloody tarts, most of them. Out half the night boozing or shagging junior doctors.'

'Not got a good opinion of them?'

'Huh!' she snorted. 'They look down on the likes of me because we haven't got the right qualifications. But I'm just as good as them.'

'What job do you do, Jen?'

If she noticed the switch from the formal 'Mrs Kyte' to the informal use of her Christian name, she didn't show it. 'I'm a care assistant. At Martin's Croft on the London Road. Just the elderly. No disableds or nothing. Couldn't stand that.'

'The nurses there don't rate you?'

'We don't have nurses up there, do we? Well, one, Meg, but she's all right.'

'Then, who—'

'Up at the hospital, of course! Sometimes we have to go up there if one of our residents has a fall or whatever,' she said. 'God, the dirty looks they give us. Like it was us what pushed them down the fucking stairs.' She paused. ''Scuse my French.'

Beside him, Ford caught a sudden stiffening in Hannah's posture at Jen's blurted expletive.

An insight snagged in his brain. 'Did you ever train to be a nurse?'

She folded her arms across her chest again. Classic defensive posture. Ford didn't need an FBI-grade criminal psychologist sitting beside him to know that.

'Started, didn't I?'

'Started?'

Her voice became a whine. 'I did all right in the first year. I was brilliant on the practicals, but the essays were just too hard.' The complaining tone intensified. 'I mean, why do I need to be able to write an essay? Changing shitty nightdresses or pus-soaked dressings, well, it don't exactly call for Albert-bloody-Einstein, does it?'

Was she aware of the aggression in her voice? He didn't think so. It sounded like her natural register. 'So you' – *don't say 'dropped out'* – 'changed direction?'

'Went into caring, didn't I? It's basically the same job. Of course, you don't get the same pay.'

'Lucky you've got some money put by for the clutch on the Polo.'

She frowned and her mouth opened and closed.

Ford continued, 'The thing is, Jen, you remember you told us you and Matthew were here watching television on each of the dates when the murders were committed?'

'It's true!'

Panicky. Too quick. Time to change up a gear with a small white lie.

'Your car was photographed by an automatic number-plate-recognition camera in a police car on Castle Street, just after the time when Angie and Kai Halpern were murdered. What do you have to say to that?'

Ford became aware of several sounds as he waited. Hannah's breathing. The one-tick-per-second of a quartz wall clock to the right of the painting. Cars driving by outside. A key in the front door.

'Babes! It's me. Get your knickers off, I'm feeling randy!'

Matty Kyte's voice was rough, animal – far from the mild and humble tone the charity volunteer and hospital porter used on the job.

Jen's face reddened so that her cheeks matched her blusher. 'I'm in the lounge. The police are here,' she shouted.

The door swung open. Matty stood there in his blue porter's uniform, the long-sleeved tunic dark with sweat at the armpits.

'Inspector Ford!' he said with a broad smile, the cheery voice back. He saw Hannah and walked over to her towards her, hand extended. 'Hello again, Hannah.'

She took his hand and pumped it three times. 'Hi.'

'Sorry about that,' he said, with a guilty smile, like a larcenous schoolboy caught by a shopkeeper with a handful of gobstoppers. 'Just our little joke when I come home from work, isn't it, darling?'

'Yeah,' she said, watching him as he lowered himself into the empty armchair. 'He didn't mean it. It's just his little joke.'

'So, how can I help you?' Matty asked, spreading his hands wide. As he did so, his right cuff rode up over his wrist. Ford's gaze zeroed in on the inch or so extra of exposed skin. And the little scab revealed beneath the dark cotton stitching.

'We were just trying to sort out a little – what shall I call it? – puzzle with what you told us before, Matty.'

Matty raised his eyebrows. Then he frowned. Then he put an index finger under the point of his chin. 'Puzzle?' he said, finally.

'Yeah. About your car.'

'The Polo?'

'With the dodgy clutch, yeah.'

'What about it? It hasn't been stolen, has it? God, that would solve a whole bunch of problems, wouldn't it, Jen?'

He laughed and won an answering chuckle from his wife.

'Wouldn't need to get it fixed then, would we?' she said.

'Car theft tends not to come to Major Crimes,' Ford said, with a smile of his own.

'What then?' Matty asked.

'I was just explaining to Jen before you arrived. It was captured on camera near Angie Halpern's flat, just after she and her son were murdered. So . . .'

Now came the interesting bit. He hadn't told them whether the ANPR camera had caught the face of the driver. Matty could say anything: a friend borrowed it. Joyriders took it, then brought it back. But only if *he* knew what the *police* knew about the driver's identity.

'. . . who was driving it, Matty, you or Jen?'

Ford waited for Matty to answer. He looked around the room. One of the books on the lowest shelf was much larger than the others. Among the cheap thrillers and crime novels, this had a tatty-looking tan cloth binding. The title on the spine was picked out in gold-tooled lettering.

HARVEY'S

DE MOTU

CORDIS

The title was Latin, obviously, which Ford's inner-city comprehensive had not felt appropriate for inclusion on its syllabus. But something about the author's name tugged at his brain.

It was Lisa Moore's witness statement. 'He said his name was Harvey.' A pretty uncommon first name. And here it was on Matty Kyte's bookshelf.

He realised Matty still hadn't answered his question. 'Matty, who was driving the Polo?' he asked again, dropping some gravel into his voice.

'It was me,' Matty said.

Ford stared at him. Was this it? Was he just going to admit to being their killer? 'Go on.'

'I just, it must've slipped my mind,' he said. 'You see, I'm watching telly with Jen that night. But she's pregnant, you see, and she gets this craving for gherkins. Well, I hate them, so we never have them in the house and I says' – he turned to Jen – 'didn't I, babes? I says, "I'll pop out to get some and you tell me what happens while I'm gone."'

Ford turned to Jen, all smiles. 'Congratulations! You must be thrilled.'

'Yeah. It's like, the dream, isn't it?'

'How far along are you?'

Her eyes flicked to Matty then back at Ford. 'Two months. Give or take.'

'I remember when *my* wife was pregnant. She had to have frankfurters. And strawberry ice cream. Together. But you crave gherkins.'

'Yeah.'

'So, just to be clear, for my notes, you were watching telly, then you, Jen, got the old cravings . . .' She nodded. 'And you, Matty, took the Polo and went out to get some gherkins?'

'Yes.'

'What time would that have been?'

'I don't know, about eight twenty? Maybe a bit earlier? Look, I'm so sorry I forgot. Will I get into trouble? It was an honest mistake and I did not, one hundred per cent, mean to mislead the police. Obviously. I mean, you're trying to catch a serial killer, aren't you?'

Ford smiled again, though the effort was beginning to cost him. His cheek muscles felt as if cramp was just one more smile away.

'These things happen, Matty,' he said. 'You'd be surprised how often members of the public forget where they were or what they were doing when a crime was committed. Half the time they can't even describe the face of the person who attacked them, even if it was in their own homes, in broad daylight.'

Matty smiled back. 'Must make your job difficult.'

Ford cleared his throat. Rubbed his neck and winced. 'I don't suppose we could have a cup of tea, could we, Matty? I've been in meetings all day, and I'm parched.'

'Of course,' he said, his posture softening. 'Put the kettle on, Jen.'

◆　◆　◆

Hannah waited for one minute and thirty seconds, timing her exit by the sweep hand of the wall clock. As the thin red wand passed the six, she got to her feet.

'I'll go and give Jen a hand with the tea,' she said, smiling.

The kitchen was cluttered. Every surface held a gadget of some kind: a blender, a food processor, a coffee machine, a toasted-sandwich maker – all in matching shades of red.

'You a detective, too?' Jen asked her, spooning tea into a large dark-brown teapot.

'I'm a crime scene investigator.'

'What, like off the telly? The ones with the white onesies on?'

Hannah smiled. She couldn't tell if the woman was mocking her nor not. 'They're Tyvek.'

'Tie-what?'

'Vek. It's a breathable fabric.'

'Right.'

'What can I do to help?' Hannah asked.

Jen jerked her chin at a row of eye-level cabinets. 'You could get four mugs down.'

Hannah smiled and reached for the first pair of doors and opened them wide.

'Not that one, that one!' Jen said crossly, pointing to the neighbouring pair.

Hannah was about to close the doors when something caught her eye. On its own, the packet of Tesco penne didn't signify anything. After all, lots of people bought pasta from Tesco. But then she looked at the other packets. Every single tub, tin, box, jar and bag she could see bore a Sainsbury's logo.

Her heart thumped in her chest. Mechanically, she closed the doors and moved along to the next cupboard. She retrieved four mugs and set them down on the countertop by Jen's left elbow. As she did so, she noticed a polished stainless-steel cylinder pushed back into a corner.

A layperson might have assumed it was a high-end professional pressure cooker. The black plastic handle and gleaming finish contributed to that impression. But the presence of a large gauge set into the lid and six heavy-duty wing nuts to clamp it shut as the pressure built revealed its true purpose.

Why did the Kytes have an autoclave in their kitchen? They were used for sterilising hospital equipment.

She looked at Jen.

Jen was staring back at her. That over-lipsticked mouth set in a grim line.

'Let's take the boys their tea,' she said, picking up two mugs.

Hannah followed her back into the sitting room. Ford turned round as she came into the room, and she strove for a signal she could give him without alerting Matty. *Nicknames! He knows I like to get them right.*

'Here's your tea, Fiesta.'

Matty grinned. 'Fiesta, did you call him?'

'It's his nickname,' she said, sitting with her own mug of tea. 'You know, like Ford Fiesta.'

'Sounds more like a jazz mag to me,' Matty said.

'Unfortunately, I had no say in the matter,' Ford said, smiling at Hannah and nodding, just slightly.

Arrest him! Hannah wanted to shriek. *And her! They've got an autoclave! And a trophy!*

She looked at Jen, who was scowling. She looked at the wall opposite and its black shelving unit. One shelf held a number of glittery gold and silver statues of men throwing darts, mounted on wooden plinths.

'Look at those, Fiesta,' she said, pointing. 'He's got a collection of trophies.'

She kept her gaze locked on to Ford's, hoping, praying that the penny would drop. Ford smiled. He shifted to the front edge of the sofa cushion so that his heels were under his knees and his torso was tilted forwards.

'Very impressive,' Ford said, standing and reaching under the back of his jacket for the Quik-Cuffs.

'What's going on?' Matty said, starting to rise.

Ford began reciting the formal arrest script, ready to put Kyte on the ground if he showed even a flicker of an intention to run or fight.

'Matthew Kyte, I am arresting you on suspicion of—'

'You can't!' Jen shouted, standing. 'Don't you touch him!'

As Matty opened his mouth to speak Hannah saw Jen dive to her left. When she straightened, her right fist was gripping the polished wooden haft of the ornamental tomahawk.

Shrieking, she swung the vicious-looking weapon at Ford's head.

Hannah screamed a warning. 'Henry! Look out!'

Ford turned towards Hannah. In that moment, the tomahawk glanced off his left elbow. He yelled out in pain. Staggering back, he tripped over the edge of a rug and slammed against the side of the sofa. Grunting as the wood-topped armrest drove the breath from his lungs, he rolled away as Jen drew the weapon back and delivered a second blow. Half a second slower and she'd have split his skull. As it was, the edge buried itself in the wooden armrest. He leapt for her, striking his balled fist into her right shoulder, aiming to paralyse the arm and get her to drop the tomahawk.

'Leave her alone, you bastard!' Matty shouted.

Ford heard rather than saw Matty launch himself towards him, arms outstretched. Hannah dropped to her knees and punched Matty hard between the legs. Matty emitted a high-pitched scream and toppled sideways, clutching his groin.

'I've got him, Henry!' Hannah yelled.

Taking it on trust, Ford shoved his right palm against Jen's cheek, forcing her head over sideways. She'd dropped the tomahawk, but her long nails were clawing towards his eyes. Keeping his face out of range, he dug his knuckle into a spot behind her jaw known as the mandibular angle pressure point. She squealed with pain as he bore down on the bundle of nerves that ran behind the bone.

'Stay down, Jen!' he shouted.

Whimpering, she complied. As Ford pulled her arms behind her and slapped the Quik-Cuffs on her wrists, he had enough time to witness an extraordinary sight.

Hannah had folded Matty's right arm up behind his back in a classic law-enforcement hold. She straddled his prone form, panting and muttering something under her breath, then pulled a thin belt free from her trousers and tied Matty's wrists behind him, jerking the leather tight against the buckle.

Ford pushed Jen down against the carpet. 'Stay there,' he barked. 'You OK, Hannah?'

'I'm fine, thanks, Henry,' she said, grunting with the exertion.

Ford formally arrested the Kytes for murder then pulled out his radio and called it in.

◆ ◆ ◆

Back at the station, while Matty and Jenny Kyte were being booked in by the custody sergeant, Ford turned to Hannah.

'Those were some impressive moves you pulled,' he said, massaging his bruised arm.

'I learned from a former marine at Quantico on a weekend self-defence course,' she said.

Ford smiled, storing away another small fact about Hannah's past. Wondering what it meant. 'I'm glad you studied it so thoroughly. You saved my life back there. I thought Jen was going to scalp me.'

She blushed. 'You'd have done the same for me.'

'Yep. But not with as much style.'

She pointed at his arm. 'How is it? It looked like she really walloped you.'

Ford rubbed the spot where Jen Kyte had smacked him with the tomahawk. It was sore and he suspected he'd have the mother and father of all bruises to show Sam at some point. But thanks to Hannah's warning shout, the blade hadn't inflicted anything more permanent.

'It's OK. That came out of nowhere, though, didn't it?'

'Yes. I'm sorry I didn't spot the signs.'

'Hey, this isn't on you. I don't think there *were* any signs.' Seeing Hannah was struggling with her emotions, he searched for a way to lighten the mood. 'I tell you what, that woman has some severe anger-management issues.'

Hannah smiled, but the expression seemed to cost her. 'I need to go home now, Henry. That was all very overwhelming. I need some peace and quiet. I'll see you tomorrow.'

'OK, Hannah. Get some rest. And thanks again. I'm going to go home too, for an hour or so, while Kyte's brief gets here.'

With Hannah gone, Ford went back to rubbing his injured arm. *Half a second later and I'd have been invalided out of the force. Shit! I was the one at fault, not Hannah.* Lou's voice echoed inside his head, sending the hairs prickling on the back of his neck. *Yes, you should have seen it coming.*

◆ ◆ ◆

Ford knocked on Sam's door.

'Hello?'

'It's me. Can I come in?'

'Yeah.'

Sam was sitting on his bed, leaning back against a pillow. Earbuds dangled round his neck. The shelves and drawers of the IKEA furniture were all shut, squared off and newly free of the stickers that he'd applied as a kid. Not a T-shirt or pair of pants on the floor, not a chocolate-bar wrapper or empty crisp packet in evidence.

Ford nodded appreciatively. 'Smart,' he said, sitting on the swivel chair by the matching desk.

'I tidied it.'

'No shizzle!'

'Did you want something, Dad? Only I've got homework to do.'

'Is that what you're listening to on your phone?'

'Funny. It's a politics podcast.'

'Sorry. I need to ask you something.'

'What?'

'You do Latin, right?'

'Yeah. Don't know why they make us, though. It's a dead language. It's no use for getting a job or anything.'

'Uh-urrh! Incorrect! What does *de motu cordis* mean?'

'What?'

'*De motu cordis*.'

'Ever hear of Google Translate?'

'Yes. But I wanted to ask you. If you must know, I wanted an excuse to chat to you. It's been a long day.'

Sam smiled. 'You wanna hug?' he said, holding his arms out.

'Actually, yes, please. That would be great,' Ford said, kneeling beside Sam's bed and allowing his son to wrap his arms around his shoulders. They stayed like that for a few seconds, then Sam pulled back.

'OK. Weird now. What was that bit of Latin again?'

'*De motu cordis*.'

'*De* means "of", or "about". *Motu* means "motion". *Cordis* is easy. It's "heart". So *de motu cordis* means "of the motion of the heart".'

'Next question – who was William Harvey?'

'He discovered the circulation of the blood.'

'OK, thanks, Sam.'

'Wait! What the hell?'

'Tell you later.'

'You're going?'

Ford felt it again. That tug. Between being there for Sam and being there for the victims. 'I'm sorry. I have to.'

Sam shot a hard-eyed look at Ford. 'Go on then. Just remember to tell your big boss I did the translation.'

DAY TWENTY-ONE, 8.45 P.M.

Back in Major Crimes with a mug of coffee and a Mars Bar for energy, Ford was immediately surrounded by his team. Everyone was smiling. People came up to slap him on the back.

Ford patted the air for silence. 'We have Matty and Jen Kyte in custody. That means the PACE clock is ticking. I want a team over to their place right now to start searching. Jan, can you organise that, please?'

'Yes, guv. What are we looking for?'

'Evidence of blood transfusions. Needles, big ones. They're called trocars. Blood bags, tubes – you've seen the A&E programmes on the telly.'

'What about the trophies, boss?' Olly asked.

'Get the contents of their food cupboards,' Ford said.

'Who's going to do the interviews, guv?' Jools asked.

'You and I'll take Matty.' He turned to Mick. 'You and Olly take Jen. I think she's the one doing the transfusions. They're a team. And they're in it up to their necks.'

Everyone dispersed. Olly stopped at the door and came back to Ford. 'One thing more, guv. I traced Scheherazade Abbott's Polo. No joy, I'm afraid. It's been at her school all this term.'

Ford and Jools entered Interview Room 4 at Bourne Hill Police Station at 9.00 p.m. Refreshed by a cup of strong coffee and eager to get at their man, Ford paused at the door.

'Softly softly, catchee monkey, OK?'

Jools nodded.

Ford had his pick of interview rooms, and others were far more welcoming. But No. 4 was his favourite when interviewing murder suspects. Somehow it had retained the smell of fear-sweat, despite the nightly attentions of the cleaners. Windowless, its light came from a single unshaded bulb dangling from a foot of grimy flex in the centre of the ceiling.

Sitting on the far side of the table were Matty Kyte and one of the duty solicitors drawn from the South Wiltshire pool. The solicitor, Gillian Kenney, had a careworn but kind face, and short, dull auburn hair. In her forties, she was dressed in a simple black suit and a snowy-white blouse.

Ford had met her professionally and socially on a few occasions and liked her. She was there to do a job and he knew she'd do it to the best of her abilities and with her client's best interests at heart. She always used a yellow legal pad in the American style, and she wrote her notes with a green lacquer fountain pen with a gold nib.

She nodded to him. No smile, but there was a professional's regard in her eyes.

Kyte smiled at Ford. His own clothes having been removed for examination, he was dressed in pale-blue sweats and athletic socks turned grey from much washing.

'This is all a mistake,' he said, as soon as Ford sat down.

Kenney laid a hand on his left forearm. 'Don't say anything yet, Matty.'

Ford reached over and switched on the interview recorder. Other forces used digital kit nowadays, he knew, but Wiltshire was either too slow or too cheap to issue it, so they were stuck with ribbons of magnetic tape.

The bleep finally ended.

After the formal noting of the time and date of the interview, the Home Office-prescribed caution and the names of all participants, Ford began.

'You interested in blood, Matty?'

Matty shrugged.

'Could you answer out loud, please, for the recorder?'

'Not especially. Why?'

'I think you are. You were seen drawing a face in it, as we all agree. And you've got a book on your shelf among the thrillers called *De Motu Cordis* by William Harvey. He's the man who discovered the circulation of the blood.'

'Oh, yeah. That one. It's not mine.'

'No? Whose is it?'

'It belongs to Jen.'

'Why does she have an old book like that, Matty?'

'It was her auntie's. The one who left her the house? It's rare,' Matty said with – what? – a hint of pride? 'I said we should sell it on eBay. You know, to put towards our deposit. But Jen says it's an heirloom and we should keep it.'

'Why did you kill them, Matty?'

Matty shook his head, smiling. 'I didn't kill anyone, Mr Ford.'

'Why did you write numbers on the wall in their blood?'

Matty frowned. 'I didn't! It wasn't me.'

Ford watched Kenney's pen dancing across the ruled sheets of her notepad. Matty's eyes flicked left, right, up, down, unable to settle on a single point of focus in the room. He crossed then uncrossed his arms. Touched the back of his head.

'The adult victims were all food-bank users.'

'Yes, you told me that, Mr Ford.'

'They were murdered on, or shortly after, the last time they visited the food bank.'

'Not by me.'

'And in each case, the murderer took a grocery item with him.'

'Is that why your assistant talked about my darts trophies?'

'She's not my assistant, Matty. She's our senior crime scene investigator. Tell me what you know about trophies.'

Matty smirked. 'Sorry. She didn't say much, so I just assumed, you know, she was your junior. She's quite attractive, isn't she?'

'Trophies, Matty?'

'Serial killers take them, don't they? On the TV, the FBI guy always says how they take their victims' ears, or their knickers or whatever,' said Matty. 'I watch a lot of TV. On account of Jen and me saving. Is Jen all right? I don't know what came over her. I think she was just in shock when you arrested me.'

'She's fine, Matty. Two of my officers are talking to her right now. Among other things, they're asking her why she attacked me with a tomahawk. Do you know what this serial killer took?'

'No. I don't.'

'Tesco penne. Waitrose tomato ketchup. Sainsbury's teabags – English breakfast. Garlic and salt crackers from Lidl.'

'Couldn't make much of a meal out of that lot, could you?' Matty said with another infuriating smile.

'My colleague saw Tesco penne in your kitchen cupboard, Matty. Do you want to tell us how it got there?'

Matty shrugged. 'I don't know. Jen does the shopping.'

'Bit odd to have one thing from Tesco when everything else comes from Sainsbury's, isn't it?'

'She cuts out coupons. Maybe they were on offer.'

'Why have you got an autoclave in your kitchen, Matty?'

'What?'

'An autoclave. It's that thing in the corner that looks like a pressure cooker.'

'I thought it *was* a pressure cooker.'

'It's an autoclave. They use them in hospitals for sterilising surgical instruments.'

'Oh, yes! Now you come to mention it, I've seen them at work.'

'Why is it there, Matty?'

Matty's eyes flicked left, then right. 'I don't know. Jen does all the cooking. Maybe she got it off eBay for pot roasts, or from the care home. She buys cheap cuts because we're saving—'

'—for a deposit. Yes, you told me,' Ford interrupted, losing patience.

'Exactly!' Matty agreed with a grin.

'You seem to have established merely that my client's wife buys her groceries from different supermarkets and uses an autoclave as a pressure cooker,' Kenney said. 'It's unusual, but hardly incriminating. Do you have any more substantive questions for my client?'

Ford nodded, acknowledging that his interest in the contents of the Kytes' kitchen might be considered less than relevant. 'You've already admitted you lied about your alibi, Matty. We can place you at the scene of Angie and Kai Halpern's murders. Did you kill them?'

'No! I already told you, Mr Ford. It wasn't me!'

'How about Marcus Anderson? How about Aimee Cragg? How about Paul Eadon? Did you murder them and drain their blood out?'

'No! Why won't you believe me? All I do is try to help people.'

'And you didn't attack Lisa Moore?'

'Who?'

'Lisa Moore. She's an ex-soldier who gave her attacker a good hiding. That wasn't you?'

'No.'

Ford took a breath. Stared at Matty, who offered a nervous smile in return.

'How did you get the scratch on the inside of your forearm, Matty?'

Matty turned his wrist over and pulled up his cuff. He blushed. 'Jen did them. We were' – he looked down and lowered his voice – 'you know, role playing. In the bedroom. A bit of fun, that's all. Nothing dodgy, like.'

'Sorry, Matty, you'll have to speak up for the recorder. Are you saying your wife dug her fingernails into your arms during sex so hard she broke the skin?'

'Yeah.'

'No. You attacked Lisa Moore, and when she fought you off she got your blood and skin under her fingernails, Matty. She saved it. Clever woman bagged her hands. We sent the samples off to a DNA lab. We took a sample of *your* DNA in the custody suite. What will you tell me when it comes back a match?'

Kenney leaned over and spoke behind her hand to Matty.

'No comment.'

'If you confess now, Matty, make a clean breast, it will look better in court.'

'No comment.'

Ford smiled. 'Interview suspended at' – he checked his watch – '9.14 p.m.'

He stabbed a finger at the tape controls and the recorder switched off with a clack. He got to his feet and left the room, Jools following.

'Let's get a coffee,' he said.

While they waited for the kettle to boil, Ford hissed out a breath. 'Until we get the DNA match, all we've got is a lot of high-quality circumstantial evidence, Jools. But that's it,' he said. 'No forensics, no witnesses—'

306

'What about Lisa Moore? She said it could have been Matty.'

'A defence lawyer would shred that in seconds. We need to put him inside one of the victims' homes. When we go back in, I want you to take over. Get him to talk about the blood drive. I'm sure that's how he selected his victims. He needed to match their blood groups to his so he could use their blood as a transfusion. If I want to jump in, I'll lean forward.'

Jools nodded, stirring the two coffees and adding milk.

The recorder restarted and the formalities dealt with, Jools smiled at Matty as Ford leaned back in his chair.

'Not many people are as public-spirited as you, Matty, are they?' she asked. 'I mean, you volunteer at the food bank, and from what I hear, you go above and beyond your duties at the hospital.'

'I do my best.'

Jools nodded. 'I'm amazed. With your job and your volunteering and Jen, you still found time to organise the blood drive.'

'Mr Abbott organised it. I just helped him out.'

Ford made a note.

'Did you give blood yourself?' Jools asked.

He shook his head. 'I wanted to, but I was on antibiotics.'

Ford made another note.

'You know we could check that with your GP, Matty,' Jools said. 'There's no point lying about it.'

'I thought the medical records were confidential?'

'They were. Right up to the point when you and your wife attacked me and Dr Fellowes,' Ford said.

'What's your blood group, Matty?' Jools asked, speaking fast.

'My blood group?'

'Yes. You know, A, B, O, all that. Which one are you?'

'B-positive,' he said, smiling. 'It's my motto!'

'Not A-positive?'

'My client has answered your question, Detective Constable. You need to move on.'

'Of course. It'll show up on your DNA profile, Matty,' said Jools. 'You know that, right?'

He nodded.

Ford leaned forward. 'We believe the killer is conducting blood transfusions. Taking a litre from each of his victims and putting it into his own veins. How much do you know about blood transfusions, Matty?'

'Nothing. At work, I sometimes have to fetch units from the blood bank, but that's all.'

'I didn't know anything, either. Not until recently, anyway,' Ford said. 'But I had a chat with Mr Abbott.'

'The haematology consultant.'

'Exactly. And he told me all about blood-group compatibility. You see, all the adult victims had the same blood group: A-positive. That means their blood would be compatible with yours. So you *could* be our killer and you *could* be transfusing their blood into yours.'

The lie about compatibility was a trap. According to Abbott's blood comp chart, someone with B-positive blood couldn't accept A-positive blood. Ford wanted to hear what Matty would say.

Matty's brow furrowed for a split second and his lips parted with a wet click. Then he clamped them into a thin line and his forehead smoothed out again.

'Something wrong, Matty?' Ford asked.

'You've got it all wrong,' he said, smiling.

'Sorry, Matty, you've lost me. How?'

Kenney laid a hand on Matty's forearm, but he shook it off.

'My blood *isn't* compatible with theirs. I can only have donations of O or B blood.'

'How do you know?'

'What?'

'How do you know you can only have O or B blood? You said you didn't know anything about blood transfusions.'

'They told me at the blood drive.'

'But you didn't donate. You were on antibiotics, remember.'

'I was chatting to one of the staff. She told me.'

'What was her name?'

Matty smiled. 'Sorry, I can't remember. She was pretty, though. I do remember that.'

Ford was certain Matty was lying, just giving random answers, sure he wasn't going to get caught out in a big enough lie to matter.

'What are you hiding, Matty?'

'Nothing! Nothing,' he repeated. 'Why would you say that?'

'Because I don't believe you're telling me the truth. I think you murdered five people, and attempted to murder a sixth. And unless you give me something to explain your, frankly, erratic behaviour during the two times we've spoken, I will see you charged with those crimes.'

Matty looked at Kenney, then back at Ford. The clock ticked. The tape spools hissed. He dropped his gaze for a moment, then locked on to Ford, his lower lip quivering. He swallowed, Adam's apple jumping in his pallid throat.

'I'm afraid I've been a bit of a naughty boy, Mr Ford,' he said, finally.

This was it. The moment the case ended.

Ford leaned forward, heart pounding. 'What have you done, Matty?' he asked quietly.

DAY TWENTY-ONE, 10.03 P.M.

A tear ran down Matty's left cheek. 'I've been taking stuff from the hospital. Laptops, stationery, bed linen. Sometimes even from the patients. And I've been selling it on eBay. For our deposit.'

Ford jerked his head back. 'What?'

'I'm a thief, Mr Ford. We're so far from our target, me and Jen, what with our wages not being much, even together,' he said. 'And she wants it so badly.' He sniffed and wiped his nose with the back of his hand. 'She said if I could just get hold of a few hundred extra quid a month, we'd be, you know, closer.'

Ford's mind was racing. He desperately wanted not to believe Matty, but saw that it could explain everything: his evasiveness, his wife's hostility. *Bloody Guilty Secret Syndrome!*

'I don't believe this,' Ford said, unable to resist the pull of his earlier conviction that he had his man. 'You're not seriously trying to tell me that, faced with life in prison as a serial killer, your best line is "I've been nicking stuff from work"?'

'I can prove it!' Matty said. 'Our back bedroom's full of it. It's why I didn't want that Detective Cable poking around the house. Check my eBay account. You'll see what I've sold. Ask up at the hospital. Procurement have a record of all thefts from the hospital.'

And then he burst into tears, sobbing loudly and wiping his nose on his sleeve.

'I'd like to suggest we break here, Inspector,' Kenney said. 'You have my client's explanation for his behaviour, which, as it's the admission of guilt in another crime, I think you can take seriously. It's late and he's entitled to sleep.'

Ford stared at her, then at Matty.

'Interview suspended.'

◆　◆　◆

Pulling off the road into his drive, Ford realised he had no memory of the drive home. The traffic guys had told him about it once. You were on a familiar route, your mind drifted to other, more interesting topics and then WHAM! – you'd rear-ended a mum driving her brood to school, or hit a pedestrian too busy on their phone to look before crossing the road.

He'd been so sure he had his man. Under pressure from the PTBs, he'd followed the evidence like a proper detective. They'd identified Kyte as a psychopath masquerading as a goody-two-shoes: keeping under the radar as a shy, mild-mannered doormat, running errands, soaking up abuse from the consultants at the hospital while all the time conducting a twisted murder spree.

He'd wait for the DNA profile to come back the following day, but in his heart, he knew Matty was innocent. And not just because of a 'not guilty' verdict. He *really* hadn't done it, in a black-and-white, God-sees-you-and-He-knows-you're-innocent way.

He cursed himself for ignoring his gut and focusing on Matty when he should have been pursuing Abbott. So what if other people thought it was him. Jools could go by the numbers if she wanted, but he was the lead investigator. *He* was the DI. Not her, not Mick. *Him.*

He stabbed his front door key into the lock and went inside.

'Sam, you up?' he called.

'In the kitchen!' Sam shouted back.

Slinging his suit jacket over the newel post and dumping his briefcase by the hall table, Ford wandered into the kitchen and pulled a bottle of beer from the fridge.

Sam was assembling thick slices of bread, ham, cheese and sliced tomatoes into a sandwich. He squashed the snack down before trapping it in a hinged cage and slotting it into the toaster. He turned.

'You look like your dog died.'

'I don't have a dog. As I think you know.'

'Yeah, but if you did, and it died, that's what you'd look like.'

It was an old routine. They'd use it whenever one of them was looking down in the mouth.

Ford took a pull on the beer. 'The case just went sideways. No,' he said, wiping his lips, 'sideways would have been good. It went backwards. At speed.'

'What happened?'

'The guy I arrested—'

'The porter?'

'Looks like he didn't do it.'

'Clever brief?'

'Nope. He's just confessed to being a common or garden thief.'

'Bummer.'

'Megabummer.'

'Hyperbummer.'

'Bummerpocalypse.'

Sam touched his lower lip. 'You've never talked to me about a case before. Not like this one. You know, the Latin, and now this porter guy.'

'I wanted to protect you. It's pretty horrible stuff I have to deal with.'

'I'm fifteen, Dad. I've seen all kinds of stuff on the internet. Plus, it's cool that you asked, you know? I could be, like, your asset.'

Ford grinned. 'My *asset*?'

Now Sam was grinning, too. 'You always say I'm smart. Let me help. Not with, like, confidential stuff, but tricky stuff. Puzzles, weirdness. You could bounce ideas off me.'

Ford frowned, looked up at the ceiling, then back at his son. 'Hmm. Maybe I could use, you know, an asset,' he said, making air quotes and relieved to see Sam's grin widen. 'But you know the code, OK?'

Sam nodded. 'Not a word to anyone. On pain of death.'

'Worse, on pain of no Wi-Fi. Deal?'

Sam held out his fist for Ford to bump. 'Deal. So what are you going to do now?'

'Me? I'm going to eat something, then I'm going to have another beer, then I'm going to listen to the Allman Brothers' *At Fillmore East*, very loud through headphones, then I'm going to get some sleep, then I'm going to have to review the whole case right from the start and see if I missed anything,' he said.

Sam smiled, then pulled the toasted sandwich out of its cage. He pointed at it. 'Want half?'

'Yeah. That would be great.'

Son and father sat facing each other at the kitchen table, munching on the sandwich.

'I'm going round to Josh's tomorrow after school. So if you have to work in the evening, you know, that's OK.'

Ford nodded, realising his son knew more about the way his job worked than he gave him credit for. 'Thanks. But as soon as we clear this one, you and I are going out for a drive in the Jag. Anywhere you like. A road trip, yeah?'

'Cool. So.' Sam took a bite of his half of the sandwich, chewed vigorously, then spoke through a cheekful. 'What about that other guy? The consultant up at the hospital. What happened to him?'

'It's weird. I was so sure it was him. Still am, really. But his blood group's wrong.'

'Wrong?'

'We think the killer's transfusing himself with a litre of blood from each victim.'

Sam pulled a face. 'Gross.'

'Yeah, gross just about covers it.'

'So, what, the doctor guy has the wrong blood group or something?'

'He's O-positive. The killer has to be A-positive or AB-positive.'

'Oh yeah!' Sam said, his eyes wide. 'We did that in biology. Right before the monoclonal antibodies that Hannah helped me with. You have to have compatible blood groups or your antibodies destroy the new blood cells.'

'Exactly. And Mr Charles-bloody-Abbott doesn't have the right blood type.'

'So, you, like, checked him out or whatever?'

'Yes. He took his own blood right in front of me. Alec tested it. It's not a fit for the killer.'

'Maybe he switched it or something.'

Ford shook his head. 'I was right there, mate.'

'Yeah, but what if, right, he *knew* you'd ask for it and he pre-pared a trick? It's like that magic book I was obsessed with when I was a kid, remember? You use – what's it called? – misdirection. You keep up your patter and you do something to distract the audi-ence, then when they're looking at the beautiful girl or the dove or whatever, you pull the switcheroo.'

Ford thought back to the scene in Abbott's consulting room. Closed his eyes and ran the movie back and forth. A line of dialogue floated free. 'Hand me a label, would you, Ford?'

Ford snapped his eyes open.

'Sam, you're a bloody genius! I love you!'

He seized Sam by the shoulders and kissed him hard on the forehead.

DAY TWENTY-ONE, 11.55 P.M.

Chrissie Norton was nearing the end of her late shift at Revelstoke Hall Hospital. She enjoyed cleaning, and the chance it gave her to have a little poke around in the doctors' offices. She liked reading patients' notes if any had been left up on a screen, but that was rare.

Cupboards were fun, too. Never knew what you might find. Boxes of chocolates were her favourites. Popping a caramel into her mouth, she'd assuage her guilt with the thought that nobody'd miss one or two.

Humming to herself, she unlocked the door to the last office on her corridor. The brass name plate, which she would polish to a beautiful sheen after cleaning the room itself, bore the name Charles Abbott.

So handsome. And those eyelashes. Like a girl's!

He was a careful one, Charles Abbott was. Never left his computer switched on, let alone with the patient database open on the screen. Kept his cupboards locked, too, stingy bugger! Still, he was a charmer, that was for sure, and she quite liked the way his eyes roved over her body on the rare occasions their paths crossed.

Reflexively, she hooked a finger around the slender aluminium handle of the first cupboard along the back wall and gave it a tug.

No harm in trying, is there? Her heart fluttered as the door swung open. *He must be getting careless.* She squatted down and peered inside. And she frowned.

'Now, why would a nice wealthy gentleman like you be shopping in these places?' she said aloud as she took in the odd assortment of groceries arranged on the shelf.

Then the door opened behind her, making her jump. She turned to see Charles Abbott framed in the doorway. He didn't look cross. That was a good thing.

'It's Christine, isn't it?' he asked her, smiling, and locking the door behind him. 'What do they call you? Chris? Chrissie?'

She got to her feet, smoothing her hands over her smock. 'Chrissie. I, I'm so sorry, Mr Abbott. I didn't mean to pry. I was just dusting the cupboard and the door opened.'

'Of course,' he said, still smiling, and taking a step towards her. 'Silly of me, really. Forgetting to lock it, I mean. I've been under a degree of pressure recently.'

Her heart fluttering in her chest like a caged bird, Chrissie backed away from him until the windowsill jabbed her just over her kidneys.

'Please,' she said. 'Don't report me. I'll lose my job.'

'Don't worry,' he said, in a low, reassuring voice she always associated with doctors. *Must teach it them at medical college.* 'I'm not going to report you. But I do need to tell you something. Something personal. Would that be OK?'

'You can tell me anything. I won't breathe a word,' she shot back, anxious to please now he'd offered her a lifeline.

He crooked a finger. 'Come here, then.'

She closed the distance between them. 'What is it, Mr Abbott? What do you want to tell me?'

'Let me whisper it,' he murmured.

He leaned closer and she turned so he could place his lips against her ear. She became aware of his aftershave, a lovely spicy smell. Gently, he cradled the back of her head.

'What?' she whispered back.

'You've discovered my little secret.'

'Secret?'

'My trophy cabinet.'

She frowned. What was he on about? She wanted to step back, but his fingertips were pressed against her scalp, clamping her head against his chest. He was very strong.

'The food, you mean?'

'Yes. You see, Chrissie, I took them from each of my victims. And now you know about them, don't you?'

The hairs on the back of her neck prickled. *You're him. Off the news.*

'I won't tell a soul. I promise,' she whispered, feeling her pulse bumping in her throat.

She tried to pull away, but his grip had tightened.

'I'm sure you think that's true, Chrissie. But we both know you'd weaken. You might let it slip to one of your friends. Or the police will start interviewing people here and you'll just *have* to be honest, won't you?'

Fear was making her knees tremble and she thought she might wet herself. 'Please, Mr Abbott. Please don't hurt me. You could move them. Throw them in the hospital bins out the back.'

'But, Chrissie, you'd still *know*, wouldn't you? Best we just nip this little problem in the bud, yes?'

Oh, God, had he just bitten her? The sharp sting took her breath away. Then it blossomed into searing, burning agony. She clutched her neck and felt the wetness surging out between her fingers. She felt cold. Icy.

He was grinning at her. He was holding a shiny silver knife . . .

. . . a whatchamacallit scalpy is that right no it's a scalper no a sca— . . . sc— . . . sss— . . .

She sank to her knees, and as her hand fell away from her neck and the world darkened, she had just enough time to see the jets of blood splashing against the wall. They sounded like the sea in her ears.

◆ ◆ ◆

Driving away from the hospital two hours later, skin tingling from a thirty-minute scalding shower after the clean-up, Abbott felt so serene he wanted to close his eyes and drive by intuition alone. He resisted the temptation. Tomorrow would be his biggest test yet.

He glanced in the Aston's rear-view mirror. The incinerator's orange glow underlit the plume of smoke issuing from the chimney.

DAY TWENTY-TWO, 9.00 A.M.

Ford woke early and called Jools.

'Morning, guv.'

'Morning. I want you to finish interviewing Matty without me. When his DNA sample comes back, my guess is it won't be a match. And on that basis, I want you to de-arrest him for murder and rearrest him for assault and theft. Jen, too.'

'Got it. And guv?'

'What?'

'I've got some good news for you. Looks like your gut was right, after all.'

'Go on.'

'I got Abbott's medical records. His blood group *isn't* O-positive. It's A-positive.'

Ford smiled. He felt a surge of triumph replacing the black mood that had engulfed him the previous day.

'Thanks, Jools. You're a star.'

◆　◆　◆

Ford called Alec on the drive in to work. 'Has the DNA lab sent back the report on the blood sample Abbott provided?'

'Yes. Just now, as a matter of fact. But it's not a match to the scrapings I took from Lisa Moore. I'm sorry, Henry.'

'I'm not. He switched the blood.'

'How?'

'No time to explain.'

No sooner had he ended the call than his phone rang.

'What is it, Olly?'

'I found a complaint a neighbour made against Abbott's dad back in 1981. The dad was swearing at Charles, turning the air blue, according to the neighbour. She dictated the dad's exact words, guv. Listen.'

As Olly read out the torrent of invective the father had spewed into his son's ears, Ford's gut clenched. This was it: the clue to Abbott's psychology he needed.

At Bourne Hill, he started planning the arrest. And he thought back to his conversations with the Abbotts. There were plenty of examples of married couples sliding into depravity together. Now that he was going to arrest Abbott for murder, he could try to upgrade the charge against Lucinda from obstruction to accessory to murder.

Jools came in and handed him a folder. 'Abbott's medical records. They make interesting reading. I pulled out the juicy bits.'

Ford took the folder and read the single sheet Jools had stapled to the inside of the folder. He nodded. 'Thanks, Jools. How's your interview with Matty doing?'

She grinned. 'Slam-dunk.'

Ford called the hospital and discovered Abbott was taking a day off.

Abbott opened the door in a pair of chinos and a pistachio-green linen shirt, open at the neck. Seeing Ford on his doorstep appeared not to faze him. He smiled. Ford caught a whiff of alcohol on his breath.

'Detective Inspector! What a pleasant—'

Then he looked over Ford's shoulder. Where two of the biggest uniformed officers Ford had managed to find stood side by side. Gary and Mark were each well over six foot and members of the same rugby club.

Beyond them, a police car stood idling on the road, its blue lights flashing, casting their cobalt glow over Ford's Discovery and a white prisoner transport van.

Abbott's face betrayed no emotion as Ford spoke. 'Charles Abbott, I am arresting you on suspicion that you murdered Angie and Kai Halpern, Paul Eadon, Marcus Anderson and Aimee Cragg, and that you attempted to murder Lisa Moore.' He paused, sensing the two big PCs beside him squaring themselves. 'We have compelling evidence linking you to these crimes. You do not have to say anything, but it may harm your defence if you do not mention when questioned something which you later rely on in court. Anything you do say may be given in evidence. Do you understand what I have just told you?'

Abbott pursed his lips. 'I understand your *words*, but what I *fail* to understand is what the devil you're playing at? I thought we'd concluded I wasn't your man?'

'Cuff him, please, Mark,' Ford said, standing to one side.

'Wait!' Abbott barked, in such a commanding tone that Mark stopped with his hand midway to his cuffs. 'I think you're risking your career over a simple misunderstanding, Inspector,' Abbott said, quieter now. 'You know I have influential friends. Are you sure you want me to make a formal complaint against you?'

'One hundred per cent. The cuffs, Mark.'

Mark had Abbott in the cuffs in seconds and, unable to resist, the consultant was frog-marched to the van, where, with a little gentle encouragement from Gary, he climbed up on to the step and made his way into the internal cage.

The van roared away, its diesel engine loud in the sleepy village.

Ford beckoned the two PCs over. 'Inside, with me.'

They nodded grimly. On the drive over they'd agreed the arrest of the wife might prove trickier than that of the husband.

'Mrs Abbott?' Ford called out, reaching the kitchen. 'Police!'

'Upstairs, sir?' Mark asked.

'Go on. Gary, check the downstairs. Shout if you find her.'

Their booted feet heavy on the wooden floorboards and the stairs, the two burly officers left Ford in the kitchen. He looked through the French doors.

Lucinda Abbott lay on a steamer chair, topless, her eyes shaded by oversized round sunglasses. Ford strode across the lawn, conscious of the Quik-Cuffs rubbing the skin in the small of his back and the patch of sweat between his shoulder blades.

Seeing him, she stood and pulled a coral sundress over her head. He was struck, again, by her beauty. She stood, one hip cocked, as a swimsuit model might.

'What brings you to our humble abode, Inspector?' she asked.

Ford approached to within two feet of her. Swallowed. 'Lucinda Abbott, I am arresting you on suspicion of being an accessory to murder . . .'

As he recited the arrest script, Lucinda Abbott's mouth dropped open. Halfway through the caution, her knees gave way and she collapsed on to the chair.

'What on earth are you talking about?' she asked, looking up at him with panicked eyes. 'There must be a mistake. Where's Charles?'

'Your husband is under arrest. At the moment he's in a prisoner transit vehicle, being taken to Bourne Hill Police Station, where he will be formally charged with murder.'

She shook her head, tears forming in the corners of her eyes. 'No. No! This is all wrong. Charles isn't a murderer. Nor am I. He was with Zoe Denys. He told me. He told *you*.'

'I'm afraid I don't believe that. We have no evidence that she even exists. Stand up, please. You need to come with me.'

She stretched up a hand; he pulled her gently but firmly to her feet and completed the arrest script.

'Is this about the blood?' she whispered.

'Why do you ask?'

'He told me he was taking it from the hospital. It was, I don't know, past its use-by date or something. I know it's weird, what we were doing, but it's not illegal. It was just a fetish of his. Nothing serious.'

'Turn around, please,' he said.

'Why?'

'I'm going to handcuff you and then escort you to a police car.'

'That's not necessary, surely?' she protested.

Ford slapped the Quik-Cuffs against her wrists, locking them one above the other. Now she did struggle a little.

'That hurts!' she squealed. 'You've pinched a nerve.'

'Keep still, then. Let's go.'

'I can't. Not like this. All those policemen looking at me. It's not decent.'

'Fine. Come inside and we'll get you a coat or something.'

Once they reached the kitchen, he let her go and she turned to face him. She recovered a little of her previous poise. 'If you can just take these handcuffs off, I'll just pop upstairs to my dressing room and find something more' – she paused – '*appropriate* to wear to your police station.'

Ford smiled. 'I have a better idea,' he said. 'Gary!' he shouted.

The PC arrived in the kitchen doorway, filling it. His eyes strayed over Lucinda Abbott's body before he returned his gaze to Ford. 'Sir?'

'Go and find something to cover Mrs Abbott, please.'

'Sir.'

Ford remained at the house after the convoy had left Britford for the custody suite at Bourne Hill. His heart was racing, but he felt elated rather than nervous. He'd got him, this time. He was sure of it. The media would have to eat their words.

Never mind the false start with Matty Kyte. He'd assaulted Hannah and he'd admitted to nicking stuff from the hospital, so Ford was certain he could spin the story so that Matty came off a villain, even if not of the psychopathic variety. As for the wife, Ford sensed he knew who had the whip-hand in *that* marriage.

He put some bootees on, pulled nitrile gloves over his hands and went upstairs, his Tyvek-shod feet sinking into the thickest-pile carpet he'd ever walked on.

The upstairs hallway reeked of vanilla. He pushed open the first door he came to: a bathroom, dominated by a free-standing claw-footed bath standing in the centre of polished wooden boards. He located the source of the smell. On the windowsill a small glass jar held a few inches of an amber liquid, from which protruded a dozen or so slender sticks.

He opened the medicine cabinet, but it held nothing of interest. Just a few unopened packets and tubes of what he took to be guest toiletries. *Must have an en suite.*

A single door at the end of the hallway beckoned him. He opened it and stepped into the master bedroom.

He gasped. 'Bloody hell!'

The room was vast: at least thirty feet by fifty, with a pitched ceiling supported by exposed oak beams. One end contained a sofa and armchair in matching silver-and-purple brocade fabric. A vast widescreen TV was suspended from the wall. Currently, it was displaying an image of a lake surrounded by lush tropical forest.

A four-poster bed dominated the other end of the room. A *huge* four-poster bed, he realised as he got closer – three pillow-widths across and at least seven feet from head to foot.

He pulled open the top drawer of the night-stand. It contained nothing suspicious beyond a novel Ford himself had given up on the previous year on holiday with Sam. He tried the next drawer down. A rat's nest of cables, chargers, earbuds and a couple of out-dated iPhones.

He tugged at the third drawer, which rattled but didn't open. He frowned and looked closer. On the side facing the bed, a chromed cylinder protruded by a half-inch. His pulse kicked up a beat or three. *You locked it!*

Not wanting to wait for CSIs or fiddle with lock picks, he decided to break it open. But first, a little bit of necessary arse-covering for his policy book. He fished out his force-issued mobile and launched the voice recorder. 'Having spent vital minutes searching for the key, I decided to break into the drawer, as I believed it might contain evidence vital to the case.'

He went back downstairs, fetched a screwdriver from his murder bag and ran back to the bedroom. He bent to the drawer, inserted the flat blade between it and its upstairs neighbour and pushed down. The flimsy lock cracked out of its housing and the drawer flew open.

And there it was. The evidence he needed.

'I knew it!' he shouted. 'I've got you.'

His background nausea subsiding, he placed the items on the bed. The trocars, the tubes and clamps, the blood bags, the vial of fentanyl and a pack of unused hypodermics, a leather sap and a Purcell Foundation ID on a lanyard, printed with Abbott's photo and the name Harvey Williams.

As he surveyed his haul, he pulled out his phone and called Jan.

'I want you to set up a search at Abbott's house.'

DAY TWENTY-TWO,
10.45 A.M.

Just as Matty Kyte had done before him, Charles Abbott sat across the metal-topped table from Ford in Interview Room 4. The pungent aroma of disinfectant and fear-sweat had the man wrinkling his nose. The light bulb above their heads emitted an intermittent hum. Ford had screwed it into the socket himself.

Abbott's solicitor had arrived thirty minutes earlier, striding into Major Crimes and bestowing a look of world-weary contempt on the police officers around him. He was tall and cadaverously thin, with steel-grey hair cropped close to his skull.

After introducing himself – 'Jacob Rowbotham, of Rowbotham, Plummer, Minghella' – and demanding to be taken to his client 'at once', Olly had taken him to Abbott.

Ford had assigned Jools and Mick to interview Lucinda Abbott. For his own interview with Charles Abbott, he'd asked Hannah to join him.

After everybody had identified themselves for the recording, Ford began.

'You almost pulled it off, Charles.'

'I'm not hearing a question,' Abbott said.

'You killed those people.'

'No. I did not kill those people.'

'Would you like to hear a story?'

'Inspector Ford,' Rowbotham said gravely. 'My client is a respected member of this community as well as a very busy, and talented, medical man. If you arrested him, you must imagine that you have good grounds. Let's hear them, rather than engaging in childish games.'

Abbott glanced sideways. 'It's fine, Jacob. Really.' He turned back to face Ford. 'Please continue. I love a good yarn.'

'For some reason, one day this summer, you decided being a consultant haematologist and playing God up at SDH and that private place in the New Forest wasn't doing it for you any more,' Ford said. 'The respect, the money, the kowtowing: they just got stale. You needed something more exciting. Something to impress the little people.'

Abbott smiled. 'I'm gripped already.'

'You gave yourself a whole new lease of life by transfusing yourself with the blood of strangers,' Ford said. 'You selected your victims from the food bank, organised a blood drive to check their blood groups were compatible with yours, then you murdered them. How am I doing so far?'

Abbott spread his hands. 'It's all utter fabrication, but your imagination – well, I take my hat off to you. Is there more?'

'You lied about your alibis, and when the so-called truth came out, that threw me. I thought I had you on the back foot, so I ignored your second lie. And that was the big one, wasn't it?'

'Second lie? I don't follow.'

'The bait and switch over your blood sample. You told me you were O-positive. In fact, you're A-positive.'

Abbott smiled and shook his head. 'O-positive is what I said, and O-positive is what I am.'

Ford changed tack. 'You attacked Lisa Moore in her home. She fought you off and scratched your arms.'

'Brambles, as I told you.'

'When we booked you in, was the cheek swab conducted professionally, would you say, Charles?'

'It was conducted adequately.'

'How will you feel when we identify your DNA in the samples we took from under Lisa Moore's fingernails?'

Rowbotham leaned over and muttered behind his hand. Abbott's eyes never left Ford's as he listened.

'No comment.'

'And when we match the scrap of fabric we found near Marcus Anderson's place to one of the garments we've taken from your house?'

'No comment.'

'If you're innocent, Charles, now would be an excellent time to explain how I found a fake Purcell Foundation ID in your bedroom cabinet in the name of Harvey Williams.'

'No comment.'

'What were the trocars and blood bags for?'

'No comment.'

Ford was ready with another question when Hannah leaned over and whispered in his ear. Ford nodded, and leaned back. *This should be interesting.*

'Mr Abbott, what does the sequence .167, .333, .500, .666, .833, 1.000 tell you?' she asked.

He yawned, covering his mouth with a fist. 'Tell me?'

'Do you recognise it? It's very simple. Even a child could solve it.'

'Then you'd be well placed to enlighten me.'

'It's sixths, isn't it? Approximately.'

'If you say so.'

'I do. Do you know how many litres of blood are present in the average human body?'

'It varies.'

'On average, though. That means—'

'Yes, I know what "average" means, thank you. Six.'

'Correct again. Two for two, as the Americans say. I taught there.'

'Clever girl,' Abbott replied.

'Would you like to know where?'

'Surprise me.'

'Quantico. That's the FBI Academy. Though it's also a Marine Corps base.'

'Bravo. Do we have a Clarice Starling in our midst?'

'Does that make you Hannibal Lecter?'

'What do you think?'

'Well, I know you're not eating people, so I would have to say no,' Hannah said. 'I taught FBI agents how to spot if a suspect is lying. I think you're lying, Mr Abbott.'

'I'm not lying,' Abbott said in a neutral voice. 'Next question.'

Ford nudged Hannah's knee with his own and took over. 'Do you consider yourself a good person, Charles?'

'Yes. I save lives. I am a trustee at the food bank. I even volunteer to pack their shopping away for them.'

'A worthy person?'

'Worthy?'

'Yes.'

'Where does your sense of self-worth come from, do you think?'

Abbott looked at the ceiling, then back at Ford. 'My mother said if you could help someone and you didn't, you weren't being the best person you could be. It was important to show your worth as a human being. I suppose I got it from her.'

Something in that answer sparked a connection in Ford's brain. The word 'worth'. What was it? Then he remembered: Lisa Moore said her attacker had called her worthless. Worth/worthless. Interesting. He made a note.

'That's nice. "Said"?'

'Pardon?'

'You said' – he made a show of consulting his notes – '"My mother *said*, if you could help someone". Not *says*. Is she not with us any more?'

Abbott folded his arms across his chest. It was the first sign of defensiveness Ford had seen from him.

'Charles?' he prompted.

Abbott shook his head. 'She's dead. She died.'

'I'm sorry for your loss. When did she die?'

'Beginning of last year. May tenth.'

'That must have been a stressful time, what with your job and your work as a trustee. So many people depending on you.'

Abbott smiled. 'I managed. I had to. She would have wanted me to.'

'What do you think about the people who were murdered?' Ford asked.

'I'm sorry,' Rowbotham said before Abbott could answer. 'I fail to see what relevance that has.'

Abbott laid a hand on Rowbotham's forearm. 'It's fine, Jacob, really. The inspector has his job to do.' He faced Ford again. 'To be honest, I think far too much is made about food banks. Calling those people customers, for one thing.'

'What would you call them?'

'Simply, what they are. They are society's dregs. They should pull themselves up by their bootstraps. I mean, this isn't the thirties, after all. I see no obvious signs of a Great Depression. They're too lazy, stupid or short-sighted to figure out a way to earn money for food.'

'Angie was a nurse. At your own hospital. Was *she* lazy? Stupid? Short-sighted?'

'Plenty of nurses manage on their salaries, so yes, I imagine she was.'

A feeling of sickness grew, suddenly, in Ford's stomach. He swallowed hard. 'I think you killed them, Charles. I think you killed them because, in your eyes, they were worthless. What I can't figure out is why you were transfusing yourself with their blood.'

'I have absolutely no idea what you're talking about,' Abbott drawled, inspecting his manicured fingernails.

'But I'm right, aren't I?'

'No. You are wrong. I was not doing that for the simple reason that I did not kill those people.'

There it was again. That stilted speech pattern Hannah had talked about: 'was not', 'did not'. Abbott was lying.

'Do you have a single scrap of evidence linking my client directly to these crimes of which you are baselessly accusing him?' Rowbotham asked, shuffling his papers together. 'I suspect you don't, in which case I demand you release him.'

'We have a great deal of evidence. As I've already said. Blood transfusion paraphernalia in his bedroom. During our search we also found a chart listing his victims, alongside the numbers he daubed on their walls.'

'My client has instructed me to say that the medical items were simply research tools he kept at home. The rest proves nothing. I could drive my Bentley through the holes in your case.'

Ford ignored the solicitor – yes, there were holes, and a halfway-decent defence barrister could make hay with them, but they were closing fast, and the DNA results would seal them for ever. In the meantime, he wanted a confession. He stared into Abbott's eyes. Felt his stomach churn. It was like staring into the depths of a well. He saw no humanity there, just his own reflection.

'Worthless. It's a horrible thing to call your own son, isn't it?'

'I wouldn't know. I never call Gawain that.'

Ford changed tack – all part of the interview strategy. 'We did a little digging into your background, Charles. When you were six, you were admitted to A&E at SDH with a fractured wrist,' he said, tapping the folder that contained Abbott's medical notes.

'The doctor you spoke to breached the General Medical Council's code of patient confidentiality,' Rowbotham interjected. 'Anything you gained will be inadmissible in court.'

'No, Mr Rowbotham. I'm afraid you're wrong in law,' Ford said, enjoying seeing the lawyer's face redden. 'We requested voluntary disclosure of Charles's health records under Section 29 of the Data Protection Act 1998, citing an overriding public interest.' He turned back to Abbott. 'Your mother claimed you'd fallen out of a tree, but the doctor who set it added a note saying, and I quote, "bruising consistent with twisting". Who did that, Charles? Your dad? Did he beat you?'

Abbott shook his head, a languid movement as if easing off a tense muscle. 'He did not.'

'I also found a complaint made to the police by one of your neighbours in 1981. She heard your father yelling at you in the back garden, thought he might be beating you. She made a note of the words.' Ford shook his head. 'Terrible stuff to say to a little kid.'

'If it was the old biddy with the cats, I'd take her complaint with a large mouthful of salt,' Abbott said. 'She was probably on antidepressants. They can make you say all sorts of funny things.'

'You can't remember him calling you worthless, Charles? Over and over and over again, how stupid and worthless you were? Is that what drove you to kill?'

'You should give up policework and move to Hollywood,' Abbott said. 'You'd make a fortune with ideas like that.'

'Did your mother think you were worthless, Charles?'

'Not at all. She said I should always remember I was a special person.'

'But not your father?'

'What?'

'Simple question. Does your father think you're worth something?'

Abbott brushed the backs of his fingers under his eye. 'Yes. He would never say anything else. He has never said I was not worth something.'

'No? He's never called you, I don't know, a worthless little shit? No good for anything? A useless waste of sp—'

'You're badgering my client, Inspector,' Rowbotham interrupted, frowning.

But Ford wasn't paying attention to the lawyer. He was looking at Abbott. Glaring at him.

'My son's fifteen,' Ford said, switching to a conversational tone of voice. 'In that respect, we're similar, you and me. I love him so much. And I always tell him that. Whenever I can. He's worth the world to me. I can't imagine the effect on him if I yelled at him the way your dad yelled at you. Can you, Charles? You know, "I can't believe you share my blood. You're worthless. Useless. A worthless piece of shit who should never have been born."'

'Detective Inspector!' Rowbotham roared.

'Did your dad ever give you a hug, Charles?' Ford asked in a quiet voice.

Abbott said nothing. Ford knew he had to keep going. There was a lot of circumstantial evidence, plenty more than he needed to hold Abbott. But he wanted something that would send him away for life. A confession was a prize worth chasing.

'Amusing as this little piece of play-acting is,' Abbot said finally, 'I feel we've reached the end of the road. You have nothing but some rather' – he stretched out the pause to several seconds – '*baroque* ideas about my childhood that sound like they've come from a correspondence course in pop psychology. I want to go home.'

'One more question, Charles,' Ford said. 'Why won't you give me your phone password?'

'You applied for an order to compel me to give it to you, did you not?'

'We did. But if you've nothing to hide, why not help us out?' Ford brought out a sealed evidence bag. 'For the tape, I am showing the suspect evidence item JL/SHORELINE/EF9114/76/3. A Samsung smartphone the suspect was carrying when arrested. Can you confirm this is your phone, Charles?'

Abbott leaned forward and peered at the phone through the evidence bag. 'It is, yes.'

'What's the password?'

'I'm afraid I can't remember. It must be the shock of being wrongfully arrested.'

Ford heard Hannah clear her throat, and turned to her as she spoke.

'You have a personalised number plate,' she said to Abbott. Her face was impassive.

'How very observant of you,' Abbott said with a smile. 'I *said* you were a clever girl. Didn't I, Jacob?'

The lawyer smiled, nodded.

'I do, too,' Hannah continued. 'Mine's SC13NCE. Science.'

Ford looked back at Abbott, content to let Hannah work whatever FBI-level voodoo she had in mind.

'How very original.'

'Yours is A88OTT. Abbott.'

Abbott ignored Hannah and focused his gaze on Ford. A small muscle had started to twitch beneath his right eye. 'Are all your colleagues as brilliant as this one? Or is she' – he paused, looking straight at Hannah – 'an aberration?'

'They're the same, aren't they, our plates?' Hannah asked.

'Are they?' The muscle was firing twice a second. 'I don't see it.'

'Mine is the thing I worship. Science. Yours is, too. You're a vain man,' she said. 'Clever, competent, superficially charming, yes. But also egotistical and arrogant. There's only one human being who matters in your world, isn't there? Yourself.'

'Bravo!' Abbott said, clapping lightly, three times. 'Did you complete the same mail-order psychology course as the inspector?'

'I think we're done here,' Rowbotham said, rising. 'I demand you let my client go.'

Ford recognised the lawyer's action for the desperation it was. He looked him in the eye. And what he saw there gave him renewed optimism. Rowbotham knew Abbott was headed for a cell.

'I think we're *almost* done,' Ford said. 'Please, Mr Rowbotham, stay in your seat, just for a few more minutes. Go on, Hannah.'

She picked up the evidence bag and peeled away the red tape. She slid the Samsung into her palm. Ford noted with satisfaction that Abbott's eyes were glued to his phone. He was breathing more heavily, though he was doing a decent job of hiding it. And the eye muscle was flickering like an insect hatching beneath the surface.

Hannah prodded the locked screen into life. She looked at Abbott. 'It's asking for the password.'

'As I said, I can't remember.' Flicker, flicker, flicker.

'Don't worry. I think I can work it out.'

Hannah tapped the screen, speaking aloud as she did so. 'A, 8, 8.' She looked across at Abbott – flicker, flicker, flickflick-flickflick. 'O, T, T.' Hannah placed the unlocked phone in Ford's hand. 'Try Photos,' she said.

The four most recent images he found in the folder would, Ford knew, put Abbott away for life. In each of them, Abbott grinned into the camera beside a huge, bloody number. In the first, the body of Angie Halpern cradling her dead son could be seen at the foot of the frame, surrounded by her own blood.

He turned the screen towards Abbott. Then angled it towards the lawyer, whose face paled.

'*Now* we're done,' Ford said. 'Anything to say, Charles?'

Abbott didn't speak. Ford counted. Reached twenty-one.

Finally, Abbott smiled. It was a sly expression, delivered with lowered eyes that stared at Ford from beneath those long, thick brown lashes. He broke the silence in the room.

'You asked me if I could imagine what it's like to be told you're worthless,' Abbott said.

'Charles, please,' Rowbotham hissed, still pale.

'Be quiet, please, Jacob. I'll need you later, but not right now, thank you.'

'Charles, is there something you want to tell me?' Ford asked.

DAY TWENTY-TWO, 4.02 P.M.

Abbott leaned back in his chair and folded his arms behind his head. The sleeves of his grey sweatshirt rode up to reveal the scratches on the insides of his wrists.

'I'm rather afraid you've discovered my secret,' he said. 'The kid was incidental to my plan. Call it collateral damage. But the rest? Sure. I killed them.'

'You're admitting to the murders of Angie and Kai Halpern, Paul Eadon, Marcus Anderson and Aimee Cragg, and to the attempted murder of Lisa Moore?'

'I think I just said that, didn't I?'

'Why, Charles? Why them?'

Abbott sighed. 'He used to beat me. I suspect he also beat my mother, but she always denied it. Once, he drew blood and made me lick it up. I can still taste it.'

'Your father,' Ford said.

'My father. Nicholas Ralph Augustus Abbott. Stalwart of the rugby club, the local Conservative association, the Masons, and a sadistic bully who made my childhood hell.'

'He called you worthless? That's what set you off on a killing spree?'

'Oh, the trigger, you mean?' Abbott rolled his eyes. 'I think I've always been – what shall we say, predisposed? – to a lack of empathy. Maybe even possessing certain not entirely attractive traits as far as harming small animals goes,' he said, with a small frown. 'But there was always a chance I might have continued in my more or less blameless life, rising through the ranks of my chosen profession. If not for one thing.'

'And that was?'

'My mother died. It was this May, not last. We were always close. She worried about me. My father couldn't stand it. He thought she'd turned me into a homosexual, though his preferred epithet was "poofter". Very retro.'

'How did she die?'

'The official cause of death was suicide. She washed thirty sleeping pills down with a bottle of vodka. But I know what really killed her. He *drove* her to it. He said it was a lifetime's grief for birthing me that did it. "You killed your brother in your mother's barren womb, and now you've killed her, too, you worthless little shit!",' Abbott growled. 'But it wasn't. It was him. He controlled every aspect of her life.'

'What did he mean? *How* did you kill your unborn brother?'

'They wanted children for ages but they couldn't conceive. Nick sprang for IVF. Three cycles it took and, finally, when my mother was forty-three, it worked. Twins. It's surprisingly common, did you know that? Roughly forty-six per cent of IVF conceptions are multiples, mostly twins.'

'I had heard, yes.'

'Well, the pregnancy was fine until, one day, Mother went for a scan and they gave her the old "We have some sad news, Mrs Abbott" speech.'

Ford felt he knew what was coming. Kept quiet while Abbott was happy to talk.

'One of the babies had died in the womb. *In utero*, as one might say. A boy. I came out alive and kicking three months later. My brother didn't kick so much.'

'That must have been hard for her,' Ford said.

Abbott shrugged. 'I wouldn't know. Other people's emotions aren't my strong point, as you may have noticed. Anyway, from that day on, dear old Nick had it in for me.'

'Why? It was sad, obviously, but he had a son, didn't he? Someone he could love?'

Abbott ran a hand over his hair. 'You'd think, wouldn't you? But it turned out I was the wrong kind of son. Useless at kicking a ball, or catching it. More interested in solo nature rambles than joining his bloody rugby club. He despised me. And he made sure I knew it.'

'So you decided to kill six people and transfuse their blood into yourself. What, to wash his out of you?'

'Give the man a big round of applause, folks!' Abbott said in a cod-American accent, before resuming in his own voice. 'In one. He said he couldn't believe his blood ran in my veins. Well, now it doesn't.'

'Why kill for it? You're a haematologist. Surely you could just have stolen it from the hospital?'

Abbott snorted. 'That's where I told Lucinda it came from. She believed me, as well.'

'She did the transfusions, didn't she?'

'I told her it was a sex thing. She's very' – he paused – '*accommodating* in that area.'

'So why *not* steal them?'

'For one thing, the security and tracking at the blood bank are state of the art. Every single bag has an RFID chip on it. You know what one of those is?'

'Some sort of radio signal device?'

'I won't bore you with the technical details, but, yes, broadly speaking.'

'And for another thing?'

Abbott grinned. 'It wouldn't be as much fun, would it?'

Ford took a moment before carrying on. Until this moment he had never heard another human being admit he killed people because it was fun. He'd read about them. About their incapacity to feel empathy, remorse, or any normal human emotion beyond the most basic. And now he was talking to one of these creatures. He composed himself before answering.

'Why the numbers, Charles?'

Abbott smiled. 'Being an accountant at the time, he was rather obsessed by numbers. Before he dies, I want him to know how completely and utterly wrong he was about me.'

'How will he know?'

'He's enjoying a little slideshow I put together using those photos,' Abbott said, gesturing at the phone.

Ford felt anxiety bloom. 'Where is he?'

'Safe and sound. Don't worry about him.'

Ford made a mental note to come back to Nick Abbott, who he felt was anything but safe, and very far from sound.

'Tell me about the trophies.'

'Oh, that. I wanted to distract you. Too obvious?'

'Not at all. Given that when we find them, they'll help convict you, I'm glad you took them.'

Abbott frowned. 'Ah,' he said, with a note of finality. 'On that subject, I'm afraid they're gone.'

'Gone?' *But we still have you on tape admitting to taking them.*

'Yes. I burned them last night.'

'Where, Charles? Where did you burn them?'

'Revelstoke Hall. In the incinerator. I had to, you see. A cleaner discovered them in my office. I forgot to lock my cupboard door.

Silly, really. Stress, I suppose,' he said, looking pained. 'It wasn't her fault. But I couldn't risk her blurting it out to one of her friends or posting something on social media.'

Ford felt a fresh wave of nausea wash over him. 'What did you do to her, Charles?'

Abbott frowned. 'I killed her, of course! Took me ages to clean up after myself. If you're quick, I suppose you might find some bones in the incinerator,' he said. 'The soft tissue's all flying about up there somewhere,' he finished, looking up at the low ceiling.

Ford made a note: *Contact RHH, suspend use of incinerator. Check for bones. Missing cleaner?*

Forcing himself to remain calm, when what he felt like doing was launching himself across the table and punching the smug expression off Abbott's face, Ford resumed his predetermined line of questioning. 'The trophies were for our benefit, I understand that. Very clever of you, Charles. But it was always about the blood, wasn't it?'

'It was.'

'You were transfusing your father's blood out and your victims' blood in. That's right, isn't it? You wanted to rid yourself of him.'

'In one.'

'Why did you pick people with A-positive blood? Why not use O-negative – the universal donor?'

Abbott smiled. 'Oh, I looked at both, Inspector, believe me. But the ones I selected just had a more pathetic aspect to them.'

Ford fought down his revulsion.

'You're two litres short.'

'True. But soon I'll have more blood in my veins than he has in his.'

A sense of foreboding grew from nothing to a dark grey cloud in Ford's mind. 'Because?'

Abbott smiled his sly smile. 'Can't you guess?'

343

'Was he going to be your final victim?'

'Was?' he said, pausing. 'I'm afraid you've got the wrong tense. *Is* would be more accurate. I said he's nice and safe. I hooked him up to an IV line to keep him hydrated. Oh, and a second line in the median cephalic vein in his right arm. I put a tap on it. Took a few experiments to get the drip-rate correct. He's bleeding to death. Very slowly. I injected him with low-molecular-weight heparin to make sure it doesn't clot. I *had* intended to complete my six transfusions and then open the tap wide.'

'Where is he, Charles?'

'I beg your pardon?'

'Where is he? Let us save him. You're sick. I think you know that. You'll end up in a secure hospital rather than prison, with the help of Mr Rowbotham here and a clever barrister. But this is premeditated. This is revenge. No jury will ever believe you killed your father out of a helpless compulsion.'

Abbott pulled his mouth to one side and tipped his head by ten degrees. 'No? I'm not so sure. I'll have them weeping at my tale of childhood abuse before they've had their first coffee break,' he said, grinning. 'And don't count on a guilty plea, either. I have a very strong suspicion – no pun intended – that my barrister will be entering a plea of not guilty by reason of insanity.' He leaned forward, slowly. 'He's very good. I dare say he spends more on a weekend's shooting than you earn in a year.' Then Abbott winked, before leaning back and folding his arms.

Ford ignored the provocation. 'You're going to go down for a long time, Charles. Tell me where he is and it will look good to the judge,' he said. 'That you cooperated.'

Abbott placed a fingertip to his chin and stared at the ceiling for a few seconds. 'I think not. I've achieved what I set out to do. I'm free of him. Nothing else matters.' He frowned. 'You said earlier

344

we were similar because we both have sons. But I wonder, are we alike in other ways?'

'What do you mean?'

'*I* can move on. But what about you, Inspector?'

'What about me?'

'Can *you* move on?'

'Once you're locked up, yes, of course I can.'

Abbott smiled. 'That's not what I meant. Can you move on after Louisa?'

Ford had to fight down an urge to vomit. 'What?'

'I researched you on the internet. It wasn't hard. "Detective's wife dies in tragic accident", the *Salisbury Journal* had it. Everything's digital these days.'

'That's none of your damn business.'

'Isn't it? I wonder, did you have a hand in Louisa's death? Did you sabotage her harness? What was it? Did you get tired of her constant nagging about doing night feeds?' Abbott's grin widened. 'Did the old sex life peter out after the baby came along? Or were you fucking someone else?' He looked at Hannah. 'I wonder, do Dr Watson's charms extend beyond the intellectual to the physical?'

'Interview terminated,' Ford said, stabbing the STOP button on the tape machine.

He stood up and left, Abbott's final yelled taunt ringing in his ears.

'Maybe we're not so different, you and me, Ford. Death enjoys our company!'

◆　◆　◆

In the corridor, Ford turned to Hannah.

'Nice job on the password.'

'Thank you. I noticed his number plate when we called on him,' she said. 'In an ordinary person, a personal plate means very little. But in a psychopathic personality it's a visible symbol of their narcissism. I thought he'd probably like to use it as often as possible.'

He smiled. 'Come on. Let's get the troops together.'

She shook her head. 'I need to get over to his house in Britford. I'll see you later.'

Having assembled the team in the briefing room, Ford clapped his hands to restore order.

'Charles Abbott just confessed to the killings. All five, plus the attempted murder of Lisa Moore. He also told us he killed a cleaner at Revelstoke Hall Hospital, so I need them contacted. He's been charged and remanded in custody.' The murmurs that had stilled rose again. 'Which is a result you can all be proud of. But we're not done yet.'

'What is it, guv?' Jools asked.

'He's got his old man locked up somewhere, bleeding to death, and he won't tell us where.'

'We should check Abbott's house ourselves,' Jools said. 'You said it was a big place and the CSIs are all working inside at the moment.'

'Yes. I'll take a team over there myself. I saw lots of outbuildings in the garden. Even a boathouse. You're with me.'

'Yes, guv.'

'Mick, see if Abbott has a second property. His sort usually have a cottage in the country, don't they? Or down on the coast. Dorset? Cornwall?'

'On it, boss.'

'Olly, can you check out the father's place, please? Nicholas Abbott, middle names Ralph Augustus. He's probably the only

346

man in the country with that particular moniker, so he should be easy enough to find.'

Olly nodded, making a brief note. 'Yes, guv.'

'The rest of you, keep digging into Abbott's background. I want everything on him that exists anywhere. Our systems, Home Office, GMC, any disciplinaries for sexual touching, inappropriate behaviour. Any juvenile criminal record, school expulsions, animal cruelty, yes?'

A chorus of 'yes, guvs' filled the air.

'Thanks, all. Let's find Nick Abbott before it's too late.'

The heat plaguing the country for the previous month and a half had intensified. The station car park felt like a furnace as Ford climbed in beside Jools in her sporty A3 hatchback. The black leather upholstery seared his skin though his sweat-dampened shirt. He switched on the air conditioning as Jools powered out towards Britford.

'Olly, Mick, call me the moment you find anything, OK?' he said into his radio.

'Yes, guv,' 'Yes, boss,' their answers crackled back to him.

Jools flipped a switch on the dash and blue flickers reflected back to them from the shiny paintwork of the Honda Jazz in front on the congested ring road. She tapped the steering wheel and a siren sounded, a series of stuttering whoops that had the Civic swerving right, the Astra on its left mirroring the manoeuvre to give them space to nose through.

Two and a half minutes later, she slid to a stop in Britford's main street, right outside the Abbotts' house.

'Nice driving, Jools,' Ford said as he exited the car.

'Thanks, guv.'

Inside the house, Ford stopped to think. *Where would I keep a man I intended to bleed to death? Scullery? Utility room? Basement?*

'Take the inside, Jools,' he said. 'When the others get here, you direct them.'

'Guv.'

Ford ran through the kitchen and out through the French doors, grabbing a set of keys off a hook by the back door.

He could see a large garden shed, one window obscured somehow. An octagonal brick-and-glass summerhouse. The boathouse down on the riverbank.

He ran to the summerhouse. It was empty. The shed next. The door was padlocked. He looked at the keys in his hand. There were over a dozen, all Yales, Chubbs or Ingersoll, typical of high-end residential locks.

He didn't have time to try them all so he reared back and kicked out at the door over the hasp. The wood, dry but thin, splintered. He kicked again, smashing the metalwork off the door. He wrenched it open and went inside.

The body was prone beneath a tarpaulin.

'Shit!'

He leaned over and pulled back the tarp.

'Nick!' he shouted.

Then he stopped.

'Oh, for Chrissake.'

He stood up and kicked the torso.

Abbott had stored a full-size medical training dummy in his shed. The insides of both thighs were marked with dotted lines and crosses in blue marker pen.

Ford turned and left. He ran down to the boathouse, but it was a simple shelter, walled on two sides but open at the front and back, containing just a rowing boat, empty save a pair of oars.

He scraped a hand over his mouth and chin. He walked back the way he'd come, only to meet Jools halfway down the lawn.

'Any sign, guv?' she asked.

'No. They're all empty.'

'Us the same. We've been all over the house. No basement, but Trev's gone up into the loft. The place is clean.'

Ford checked his personal and work mobiles. Nothing from Mick or Olly. 'Bugger it! I was sure he'd have him somewhere he owned or controlled.'

They walked back to the house and found Hannah taking samples from the kitchen.

'Any luck?' she asked, switching off an alternative light source.

Ford shook his head. 'The dad's not here.'

She pointed at the bunch of keys. 'Any of those look like they'd fit a lock-up or an industrial unit's padlock?'

'Don't think so. They all look like car or house keys to me.'

'Can I have a look?'

Ford handed the keys over. He and Jools watched as Hannah examined them in turn. She stopped at a silver key with a thick plastic grip.

'This is a Squire. Squire make heavy-duty padlocks.' She handed it to Ford.

'OK, listen up, everyone!' he shouted, then waited until the searchers had gathered in front of him in the kitchen. 'I think Nick Abbott is somewhere on the premises, but he's behind a door padlocked with a Squire padlock. Is there a cellar we've missed? A door behind a curtain or something? Check now, please.'

He called Mick. 'Where are you?'

'On the M5. Abbott's got a little cottage outside Padstow. I'm on my way there now.'

'OK, good work. Listen. When you get there, look for a door secured with a bloody great Squire padlock.'

'Sorry, boss, you broke up there. Say again?'

'A padlock, Mick. Look for a door with a big padlock. A Squire. I think that's where he's holding him.'

Ford ended the call and hit Olly's speed-dial number. 'Anything?'

'Yes, guv. I'm at seven Sarum Avenue, out Pitton way. Nicholas Abbott's place. Heavy security at the front. Window bars and a monster front door. No rear access. I'm waiting for an MOE team. Gary tried to kick the door in and broke his toe.'

'I think he's behind a padlocked door. Jools and I'll meet you there. Mick's too far away.'

Thanks to Jools's spirited use of all the A3's engine, transmission and steering had to offer, she skidded to a stop outside Nicholas Abbott's house just nine minutes after leaving Britford. Infuriatingly for Ford, as he scanned the houses on the even-numbered side of the street, all hid behind high fences or had wide extensions to the edge of the property line.

Ford leapt out. The roadway was choked with police cars. As he ran up the path, the MOE team's Skoda Yeti pulled up and a uniformed sergeant emerged.

'Hi, Danny,' Ford said. 'Get your kit ready, but I've got some keys here. Let me try them first.'

The sergeant nodded and started briefing his team.

With Olly and Jools watching over his shoulder, Ford tried each of the keys, bar the Squire, in the front door. One after another they either failed to penetrate more than a millimetre or wouldn't turn at all when they did slide home.

Ford called over to the MOE sergeant. 'All yours, Danny.' Then, to Olly and Jools, 'We need to get round the back somehow. You two split up and see if there's a lane or an alleyway we can get through.'

'What about you, guv?' Jools asked.

'Old school. I'm going to ask the neighbours,' he said, smiling with humour he didn't feel.

Both next-door neighbours were either out or well into their morning naps. Ford moved to the next house on the left and leaned on the bell. Almost immediately, he heard frenzied barking from inside. Through the frosted glass in the window beside the front door, he saw a smallish dog leaping up and down.

A woman's voice silenced it. 'Walter, quiet! Quiet!'

The door opened. No chain, Ford had time to notice.

'Yes?' the woman asked. She was in her mid-sixties and had striking silver hair tied back with a leopard-print hairband. An air of a schoolteacher about that enquiring gaze.

'Police, madam,' he said, holding up his ID. 'I need to gain access' – *Oh, Ford, ditch the cop-speak!* – 'I mean, get into number seven.'

'Oh, you mean Nick's?'

'Yes. Have you got rear access? A garden. A gate, even?'

She smiled. Looked down at the terrier, whose nose was poking round her calf to sniff at Ford. 'Of course! Follow me. How exciting!'

Ford followed her along a narrow hall hung with watercolour landscapes, through a large farmhouse kitchen and out into an immaculate garden filled with flowers.

'The gate's at the end. No lock. Just latch it after you. Is he all right? Nick, I mean? Only I haven't seen him for a while. He's a very private man, hates prying, as he calls it. But you know, good neighbours, and so forth.'

'I'll latch the gate,' Ford called out, running down the garden.

The row of houses backed on to a small wooded area, mainly sycamores and ash with a few holly and yew trees sprinkled amongst them. Ford pulled open the gate, swung it shut behind him and found himself on a narrow gravelled track.

He ran towards the rear of Nick Abbott's house and found his way barred by a tall wooden gate secured with a Yale lock. Beside the gate was a lockbox, closed with a four-wheel combination lock.

Swearing, Ford hoisted himself on to the top of the gate and dropped down on the other side, ripping his suit jacket on a protruding nail.

Here was his third suburban back garden of the day. More roses. Another pond, overgrown with water lilies and arching sword-leaved irises. And a shed to his left.

He pulled the unpadlocked door open and looked inside. The six-by-eight-foot space was immaculate. Everything stowed tidily. No Nick Abbott.

The kitchen door was open, and as Ford walked up to the house, Jools came out, accompanied by a couple of uniforms. She stood on the deck, raised above the sloping lawn by four feet or so.

'Nothing, guv,' she called. 'He's not here. You?'

Ford shook his head.

Then he glanced at the deck and noticed a dark space in the centre of the wooden facings. He ran up the long lawn, pointing.

'What's in the gap, Jools?'

Jools jumped down and turned to look at the gap.

'Bloody hell!' she shouted. 'There are steps. And a door.'

Ford reached the short set of steps. At the bottom, a four-foot square of concrete lay before a sturdy-looking black-painted door. The timbers were banded with metal of some kind and the whole thing had an air of a medieval fortress.

Hanging from a hammer-finished blue-steel hasp bolted to the wood was a chunky navy-blue padlock. The brand was visible in the gloom.

SQUIRE

The key slotted home with a series of soft clicks. Ford gave it a firm twist and the chromed shackle popped open. He pulled it free of the hasp and opened the door.

A stench of excrement, urine and putrefying blood assailed his nostrils.

He reeled back, gagging, as flies swarmed out of the dark. Turning to look for a light switch, he cried out involuntarily. Charles Abbott was leering at him beside a bloody 167 on the wall of Marcus Anderson's eco-hut. The oversized selfie was projected on to the cellar wall. As Ford watched, transfixed, it faded to be replaced with another, Abbott beside a bloody 333. And another: 500. And, finally, 666.

Holding his breath, he felt around on the inside of the door frame. Nothing on the right. But on the left, a switch.

The cellar flooded with light.

Bound by rope to a kitchen chair occupying the centre of a spreading pool of blackened blood sat an old man. His head, silver-haired, lolled on his bare chest. To his left stood a tall chrome metal stand from which hung a bag half-full of a clear liquid.

A thin tube descended from the bag into a needle emerging from his left elbow. From his right, a sinuous tube, plum-red, snaked to the ground. Halfway down, a plastic tap and clear cylinder interrupted the thin bore.

Ford observed, horrified, as a plum-red bead formed at the upper end of the cylinder, swelled, and dripped down.

He stepped into the centre of the pool of blood and closed off the tap. He withdrew the needle from the old man's right elbow and called over his shoulder.

'Jools, get in here. Put pressure on that and then hold his arm up high.'

Jools squeezed in beside him, muttering, 'Nice,' as she jerked her chin at the cycling images on the wall.

Ford jammed two fingers into the soft place beneath the man's jaw. Waited, eyes closed, searching by feel for a sign of life.

There! Faint, but present: a tremor. A weak, fluttering pulse as Nick's overstressed heart fought to pump the decreasing volume of blood around the body.

Ford reached for his phone and called for an ambulance.

DAY TWENTY-TWO,
7.59 P.M.

A stone's throw from Bourne Hill nick, the Wyndham Arms was packed with police officers, CSIs and police staff.

In a corner, a band was warming up, chords and drumrolls adding to the din of conversation, laughter and good-natured banter. The guitarist, a battered red Fender Stratocaster slung from his shoulder, stepped forward and took the mic.

'Ladies and gentlemen, colleagues, friends, and' – he winked at a fifteen-year-old boy who had his mother's smile – 'Sam.' A cheer. 'We did it. All of us here. I want to thank you for the long hours you put in, for keeping after him and giving up time with your families and friends. For not being downhearted, even if we had knockbacks. For staying calm despite the shit being heaped on your heads by the media and the PCC.' He paused as a huge cheer went up. 'Thank you all for making my first case as DI a success.'

'Hope your playing's better than your speeches, Henry!' Mick yelled out, to a burst of laughter and calls of 'Can it, Mick!'

Ford smiled. 'Let's find out, shall we?'

He stepped back, allowing Alec Reid to reclaim the mic. As the opening notes of BB King's 'How Blue Can You Get?' filled the pub, Ford looked over at Hannah. She turned to face him and smiled, then mouthed something. Taking his hand off the strings, he cupped a hand behind his ear. She said it again, and this time he caught it.

'You're very good!'

High on adrenaline and not a few beers, he smiled back, feeling his blood speeding through his veins.

De motu cordis.

The motion of the heart.

ACKNOWLEDGMENTS

I want to thank *you* for buying this book. I hope you enjoyed it. As an author is only part of the team of people who make a book the best it can be, this is my chance to thank the people on *my* team.

For being my first readers, Sarah Hunt, Jo Maslen and Katherine Wildman.

For sharing their knowledge and experience of The Job, former and current police officers Andy Booth, Ross Coombs, Jen Gibbons, Neil Lancaster, Sean Memory, Trevor Morgan, Olly Royston, Chris Saunby, Ty Tapper, Sarah Warner and Sam Yeo.

For helping me stay reasonably close to medical reality as I devise gruesome ways of killing people, Martin Cook, Melissa Davies, Arvind Nagra and Katie Peace.

For their advice on climbing, Coel Hellier and Norrie Tate.

For sharing their insights into autistic spectrum disorder, Amanda J. Harrington and Dr Hazel Harrison.

For lending Hannah's cat her name, Uta Frith, Emeritus Professor of Cognitive Development at UCL Institute of Cognitive Neuroscience.

For her advice on strategies for detecting lies, Professor Dawn Archer, Research and Knowledge Exchange Coordinator for Languages, Information and Communications, Manchester Metropolitan University.

For their patience, professionalism and friendship, the fabulous publishing team at Thomas & Mercer: Jack Butler, Sarah Day, Laura Deacon, Gill Harvey, Russel McLean and Jane Snelgrove.

And for being a daily inspiration and source of love and laughter, and making it all worthwhile, my family, Jo, Rory and Jacob.

The responsibility for any and all mistakes in this book remains mine. I assure you, they were unintentional.

Andy Maslen, Salisbury, 2020

ABOUT THE AUTHOR

Photo © 2020 Kin Ho http://kinho.com/

Andy Maslen was born in Nottingham, England. After leaving university with a degree in psychology, he worked in business for thirty years as a copywriter. In his spare time, he plays blues guitar. He lives in Wiltshire.